SPEAKING IN B[illegible]

As a forensic anthropol[illegible] province of Quebec, Canada, Kathy Reichs has often said that she works *with* the dead, but *for* the living.

Forensics are an integral part of her world, with cases constantly coming in to her lab. And yet her chosen profession is, she says, like any other job. However, though you may get used to what's happening around you, and to the sounds and smells and sights of death, this doesn't mean you become immune to it.

Each of her books is based loosely on the cases she's worked on, or an experience she's had. She believes that her stories remain fresh because they originate from her being enmeshed and engaged in forensic work on a regular basis.

Kathy Reichs is one of only eighty-two forensic anthropologists ever certified by the American Board of Forensic Anthropology. She served on the Board of Directors and as Vice President of both the American Academy of Forensic Sciences and the American Board of Forensic Anthropology, and is currently a member of the National Police Services Advisory Council in Canada. She is a Professor in the Department at the University of North Carolina–Charlotte. She is a native of Chicago, where she received her PhD at Northwestern. She now divides her time between Charlotte, NC, and Montreal, Quebec.

kathyreichs.com
facebook.com/kathyreichsbooks
@kathyreichs

Praise for Kathy Reichs

"I love Kathy Reichs—always scary, always suspenseful, and I always learn something"
Lee Child

"Reichs' real-life expertise gives her novels an authenticity that most other crime novelists would kill for"
Daily Express

"Reichs is the queen of pathology thrillers"
Independent

"Nobody does forensic thrillers like Kathy Reichs. She's the real deal"
David Baldacci

"Reichs has proved that she is now up there with the best"
Marcel Berlins, *The Times*

"Completely engrossing … drags the reader into a different world where dialogue is tense, dead men tell the best tales and the ice will freeze the bones. Read this and you'll know why the word 'thriller' was invented"
Frances Fyfield

"The forensic detail is harrowing, the pace relentless and the prose assured. Kathy Reichs just gets better and better and is now the Alpha female of the genre"
Irish Independent

"A long way from your standard forensic thriller: all the excitement you crave, indefatigably expert. But conscience-generated and compassionate too"
Literary Review

"A brilliant novel ... fascinating science and dead-on psychological portrayals, not to mention a whirlwind of a plot ... a must-read"
Jeffery Deaver

"Tempe Brennan ... is smart, resourceful and likeable ... an investigator to follow"
Daily Telegraph

"Inevitably compared to Patricia Cornwell, Reichs is actually in a different league. Tempe Brennan is already ... a much more rounded character that Cornwell's heroine Scarpetta: more human, less driven and much better company during the time it takes her to untangle these complex crimes"
Sunday Times

"Kathy Reichs is some kind of writer! Deep in Patricia Cornwell territory, she outdoes the queen of slice 'em and dice 'em fiction ... Terrific"
Independent on Sunday

"Reichs is in real life a highly experienced forensic anthropologist. But her leading character, Temperance Brennan, is a fictional creation and a tough and gutsy heroine she makes"
Scotland on Sunday

"[Kathy Reichs'] novels keep a tight grip on the plot, move along at a ferocious pace and manage to frighten and intrigue the reader in equal measure"
Irish Independent

"Tough, exciting stuff ... you are in for a good, chilling time"
Daily Express

"Reichs gets better with every book, her heroine, forensic anthropologist Temperance Brennan, more feisty ... Gritty detail, chilling atmosphere, engrossing plot"
Woman & Home

"Reichs ... expertly directs a busy plot that moves with electrical force in the final quarter. She capitalises on the morbid, yet captivating aspects of the forensic trenchwork, yet never lets it overwhelm her story. But it is Reichs' ongoing development of Tempe, a woman ... with a mature understanding of human nature, and a self-deprecating sense of humour that truly lifts the book above many of its peers"
Publishers Weekly

Also by Kathy Reichs

Déjà Dead
Death du Jour
Deadly Décisions
Fatal Voyage
Grave Secrets
Bare Bones
Monday Mourning
Cross Bones
Break No Bones
Bones to Ashes
Devil Bones
206 Bones
Spider Bones (published as *Mortal Remains* in hardback in the UK)
Flash and Bones
Bones Are Forever
Bones of the Lost
Bones Never Lie

Bones in Her Pocket (eBook original)
Swamp Bones (eBook original)
Bones on Ice (eBook original)

The Virals Series
with Brendan Reichs

Virals
Seizure
Code
Exposure
Terminal
Trace Evidence
Swipe (eBook original)
Shift (eBook original)
Shock (eBook original)

Kathy
REICHS

SPEAKING IN BONES

arrow books

1 3 5 7 9 10 8 6 4 2

Arrow Books
20 Vauxhall Bridge Road
London SW1V 2SA

Arrow Books is part of the Penguin Random House group of companies
whose addresses can be found at global.penguinrandomhouse.com

Penguin Random House UK

First published in Great Britain by William Heinemann in 2015

(First published in the United States of America by
Penguin Random House in 2015)

www.randomhouse.co.uk

A CIP catalogue record for this book
is available from the British Library

ISBN 9780099558095
ISBN 9780099558125 (Export)

Typeset in Palatino (11/15pt) by SX Composing DTP, Rayleigh, Essex
Printed and bound in Great Britain by Clays Ltd, St Ives plc

MIX
Paper from responsible sources
FSC® C018179

Penguin Random House is committed to a sustainable future
for our business, our readers and our planet. This book is made
from Forest Stewardship Council® Certified paper

For
Cooper Eldridge Mixon,
born July 14, 2014

1

"I'm unbound now. My wrists and ankles burn from the straps. My ribs are bruised and there's a lump behind my ear. I don't remember hitting my head. I'm lying very still because my whole body aches. Like I've been in a wreck. Like the time I crashed my bike. Why doesn't my family save me? Is no one missing me? I have only my family. No friends. It was just too hard. I'm all alone. So alone. How long have I been here? Where is here? The whole world is slipping away. Everything. Everyone. Am I awake or asleep? Am I dreaming or is this real? Is it day or night?

"When they return they will hurt me again. Why? Why is this happening to me? I can't hear a sound. No. That's not true. I can hear my heart beating. Blood working inside my ears. I taste something bitter. Probably vomit stuck in my teeth. I smell cement. My own sweat. My dirty hair. I hate when my hair isn't washed. I'm gonna open my eyes now. Got one. The other's crusted shut. Can't see much. It's all blurry, like I'm looking up from way down underwater.

"I hate the waiting. That's when the pictures take over my brain. Not sure if they're memories or hallucinations. I see him. Always in black, his face crazy red and beaded with sweat. I avoid his eyes. Keep looking at his shoes. Shiny shoes. The candle flame's a little yellow worm dancing on the leather. He stands over me, all big and nasty. Thrusts his horrid, smelly face close to mine. I feel his icky breath on my skin. He gets mad and yanks me by the hair. His veins go all bulgy. He screams and his words sound like they're coming from another planet. Or like I've left my body and I'm listening from far away. I see his hand coming at me, clutching the thing so tight it quivers. I know I'm shaking but I'm numb. Or am I dead?

"No! Not now! Don't let it happen now!

"My hands are going all cold and tingly. I shouldn't be talking about him. I shouldn't have said he was horrid.

"Yes. They're coming.

"Why is this happening to me? What did I do? I've always tried to be good. Tried to do what Mama said. Don't let them kill me! Mama, please don't let them kill me!

"My mind is going all fuzzy. I have to stop talking."

Silence, then the click-creak of a door opening. Closing.

Footsteps, unhurried, firm on the floor.

"Take your place."

"No!"
"Don't resist me."
"Leave me alone!"
The cadence of frantic breathing.
The thunk of a blow.
"Please don't kill me."
"Do as I say."
Sobbing.
Sound as if dragging.
Moaning. Rhythmic.
"Are you in my hands?"
"Filthy bitch!" Louder, deeper.
A soft rasp.
The *tic* of metal snapping into place.
"You will die, slut!"
"Will you answer me now?"
"Whore!"
The drumming of agitated fingers. Scratching.
"Give me what I need!"
Pfff! The violent hurling of spit.
"You will not answer?"
Moaning.
"This has only begun."
Click-creak. The furious slam of a door.
Absolute stillness. Soft sobbing.
"Please don't kill me.
"Please don't kill me.
"Please.
"Kill me."

2

The woman's knuckles bulged pale under skin that was cracked and chapped. Using one knobby finger, she depressed a button on the object in the Ziploc.

The room went still.

I sat motionless, the hairs on my neck lifted like grass in a breeze.

The woman's eyes stayed hard on mine. They were green flecked with yellow, and made me think of a cat. A cat that could bide, then pounce with deadly accuracy.

I let the silence stretch. Partly to calm my own nerves. Mostly to encourage the woman to explain the purpose of her visit. I had flight reservations in just a few hours. So much to do before heading to the airport. To Montreal and Ryan. I didn't need this. But I had to know the meaning of the terrible sounds I'd just heard.

The woman remained angled forward in her chair. Tense. Expectant. She was tall, at least six feet, and wore boots, jeans, and a denim shirt with the cuffs rolled up her lower arms. Her hair was dyed the color of the clay at Roland Garros. She'd yanked it into a bun high on her head.

My eyes broke free from the cat-gaze and drifted to the wall at the woman's back. To a framed certificate declaring Temperance Brennan a diplomate of the American Board of Forensic Anthropology. D-ABFA. The exam had been a bitch.

I was alone with my visitor in the 120 square feet allocated to the Mecklenburg County Medical Examiner's consulting forensic anthropologist. I'd left the door open. Not sure why. Usually I close it. Something about the woman made me uneasy.

Familiar workplace sounds drifted in from the corridor. A ringing phone. A cooler door whooshing open then clicking shut. A rubber-wheeled gurney rolling toward an autopsy suite.

"I'm sorry." I was pleased that my voice sounded calm. "The receptionist provided your name but I've misplaced my note."

"Strike. Hazel Strike."

That caused a little ping in my brain. What?

"Folks call me Lucky."

I said nothing.

"But I never rely on luck. I work hard at what I do." Though I guessed Strike's age at somewhere north of sixty, her voice was still twentysomething strong. The accent suggested she was probably local.

"And what is it you do, Ms. Strike?"

"Mrs. My husband passed six years back."

"I'm sorry."

"He knew the risk, chose to smoke." Slight lift of one shoulder. "You pay the price."

"What is it you do?" I repeated, wanting to draw Strike back on point.

"Send the dead home."

"I'm afraid I don't understand."

"I match bodies to people gone missing."

"That is the task of law enforcement in conjunction with coroners and medical examiners," I said.

"And you pros nail it every time."

I bit back another priggish response. Strike had a point. Stats I'd read put the number of missing persons in the United States at around 90,000 at any given time, the number of unidentified remains from the past fifty years at more than 40,000. The last count I saw placed the North Carolina UID total at 115.

"How can I help you, Mrs. Strike?"

"Lucky."

"Lucky."

Strike placed the Ziploc beside a bright yellow case file on my blotter. In it was a gray plastic rectangle, roughly one inch wide, two inches long, and a half inch thick. A metal ring at one end suggested dual functions as a recorder and a key chain. A loop of faded denim suggested the device had once hung from the waistband of a pair of jeans.

"Impressive little gizmo," Strike said. "Voice activated. Two-gigabyte internal flash memory. Sells for less than a hundred bucks."

The yellow folder called to me. Accusingly. Two months earlier a man had died in his recliner, TV remote clutched in one hand. The previous weekend his mummified corpse had been found by a very unhappy landlord. I needed to wrap this up and get back to my analysis. Then home to packing and the delivery of my cat to the neighbor.

But those voices. My pulse was still struggling to return to normal. I waited.

"The recording lasts almost twenty-three minutes. But the five you heard is plenty to get the drift." Strike gave a tight shake of her head. Which reangled the bun to an off-center tilt. "Scares the patootie out of you, don't it?"

"The audio is disturbing." An understatement.

"Ya think?"

"Perhaps you should play it for the police."

"I'm playing it for you, Doc."

"I believe I heard three voices?" Curiosity was overcoming my reticence to engage. And apprehension.

"That's my take. Two men and the girl."

"What was happening?"

"Don't know."

"Who was speaking?"

"Only got a theory on one."

"And that is?"

"Can we back up a bit?"

I brushed my eyes past my watch. Not as discreetly as I thought.

"Unless you're not 'tasked' with sticking names on the dead." Strike hooked sarcastic finger quotes around the term I'd used moments earlier.

I leaned back and assumed my listening face.

"What do you know about websleuthing?"

So that was it. I vowed to keep my tone patient, but my answers short.

"Websleuths are amateurs competing online to solve cold cases." Wannabe forensic scientists and cops. Overzealous viewers of *NCIS*, *Cold Case*, *CSI*, and *Bones*. I didn't add that.

Strike's brows drew together over her nose. They were dark and looked wrong with the pale skin and fake carrot hair. She studied me a very long time before responding.

"Most people die, they get a funeral, a wake, a memorial service. There are eulogies, an obit in the paper. Some get holy cards showing their faces with angels or saints or whatnot. You're really hot stuff, maybe there's a school or a bridge named in your honor. That's what's supposed to happen. That's how we deal with death. By recognizing a person's achievements in life.

"But what happens when someone just disappears? Poof." Strike curled then exploded her fingers. "A man leaves for work and vanishes? A woman boards a bus and never gets off?"

I started to speak but Strike rolled on.

"And what happens when a body turns up lacking ID? On a roadside, in a pond, bundled in a carpet and stashed in a shed?"

"As I've stated, that is the job of police and medical examiners. At this facility we do everything possible to ensure that all human remains are identified, no matter the circumstances or their condition."

"That might be true here. But you know as well as I do it's a crapshoot elsewhere. A corpse might luck out, be examined for scars, piercings, tattoos, old trauma, get printed and sampled for DNA. A decomp or a skeleton might end up with an expert like you, have its teeth charted, its sex, age, race, and height entered into a database. Another jurisdiction, similar remains might get a quick once-over then storage in a freezer, maybe a back room or basement. A nameless body might be held a few weeks, maybe a few days, then cremated or buried in a potter's field."

"Mrs. Strike—"

"Lost. Murdered. Dumped. Unclaimed. This country's overflowing with the forgotten dead. And somewhere someone's wondering about each and every one of those souls."

"And websleuthing is a way to solve the problem."

"Darn right." Strike shoved her sleeves hard up her arms, as though the cuffs had suddenly grown too tight on her flesh.

"I see."

"Do you? Have you ever visited a websleuthing site?"

"No."

"You know what goes on in those forums?"

Recognizing the question as rhetorical, I offered no response.

"UIDs are tagged with cute little nicknames. Princess Doe. The Lady of the Dunes. Tent Girl. Little Miss Panasoffkee. Baby Hope."

The ping exploded into a full-firing synapse.

"You identified Old Bernie," I said.

Old Bernie was a partial skeleton found by hikers in 1974 behind a shelter on the Neusiok Trail in the Croatan National Forest. The remains were sent to the Office of the Chief Medical Examiner, in those days located in Chapel Hill, and were determined to be those of an elderly black male. A New Bern detective assigned to the case had no luck in establishing ID.

For years the skeleton remained in a box in an OCME storeroom. Somewhere along the way it came to be known as Old Bernie, named for New Bern, the town closest to the point of the old man's discovery.

Articles ran at the time Old Bernie turned up—in Raleigh, Charlotte, New Bern, and surrounding towns. The case was featured again, with the photo of a facial reconstruction, in the New Bern *Sun Journal* on March 24, 2004, the thirtieth anniversary of the gentleman's discovery. No one ever came forward to claim the bones.

In 2007, a technician at the OCME mentioned the case to me. I agreed to take a look.

I concurred that the remains were those of an edentulous African American who had died between the ages of sixty-five and eighty. But I took issue with one of my predecessor's key findings and suggested the victim's nickname be changed from Bernie to Bernice. The pelvic features were clearly those of a female.

I took samples for possible DNA testing, then Old Bernie went back to her cardboard carton in Chapel Hill. The following year, the National Missing and Unidentified Persons System, NamUs, came online. NamUs, a database for unidentified remains, in cop lingo UIDs, and missing persons, in cop lingo MPs, is free and available to everyone. I entered case descriptors into the section for UIDs. Soon amateur websleuths were swarming like flies.

"Yep," Strike said. "That was me."

"How did you do it?"

"Pure doggedness."

"That's vague."

"I scanned a billion pictures on NamUs and other sites listing MPs. Made a lot of calls, asking about old ladies missing their teeth. Came up blank on both fronts. Then I went offline, pulled up stories in local papers, talked to cops in New Bern and Craven County, the park rangers at Croatan, that kind of thing. Nothing.

"On a hunch I started phoning old folks' homes. Found a facility in Havelock had a patient disappear in 1972. Charity Dillard. The administrator reported Dillard missing, but no one really made much effort. The home is close to a boat ramp, so they figured Dillard fell into the lake and drowned. When Old Bernie turned up two years later, no one paid attention because the skeleton was supposed to be that of a man. End of story."

"Until you made the link." I'd heard about the ID through the state ME grapevine.

"Dillard had one living grandson, out in L.A. He provided a swab. Your bone samples yielded DNA. Case closed."

"Where is Dillard now?"

"Kid popped for a headstone. Even flew east for the burial."

"Nice job."

"It wasn't right, her gathering dust in a box." Again the shoulder shrug.

I now knew why Strike was sitting in my office.

"You've come about unidentified remains," I said.

"Yes, ma'am."

I angled two palms in a "go on" gesture.

"Cora Teague. Eighteen-year-old white female. Disappeared up in Avery County three and a half years back."

"Was Teague reported missing?"

"Not officially."

"What does that mean?"

"No one filed an MP report. I found her on a websleuthing site. The family believes she took off on her own."

"You've spoken to the family?"

"I have."

"Is that a common part of websleuthing?"

"Something's happened to this kid and no one's doing dink."

"Have you contacted the local authorities?"

"Eighteen makes her adult. She can come and go as she likes. Blah. Blah. Blah."

"That's true."

Strike jerked a thumb at the Ziploc. "That sound like someone doing as she likes?"

"You think Cora Teague is the girl on that recording?"

Strike gave a slow nod of her head.

"Why bring this to me?"

"I believe you've got parts of Teague stashed here."

3

"I should ask a detective to join us."

"No." Realizing the sharpness of her tone, Strike added, "Not yet."

"Okay." For now. "Tell me about Teague."

"If you'll bear with me, I'll share what I know."

Strike did that shoulder thing again. Not a shrug, more like a slo-mo twitch. Or an unconscious attempt to readjust her spine.

"Cora was born in '93, the fourth of five kids. The father, John Teague, owns a combo convenience store–gas station–hardware–bait shop. The mother, Fatima, is a stay-at-home housewife. She sometimes works the cash register at the store.

"The older brother, Owen Lee, and the two older sisters, Marie and Veronica, are married. He sold real estate, badly, until the bottom fell out, then started a dog-training business. The sisters both live out of state. Not sure about Eli. He's the youngest. Guess he'd be about nineteen. Owen Lee and the parents live within miles of each other up in Avery County."

The Blue Ridge Mountains. Unbidden, an image of Mama flashed and was gone.

I nodded to indicate I was listening.

"According to a posting on CLUES.net, about three and a half years back Cora mysteriously vanished."

"CLUES.net?"

"Citizens Looking Under Every Stone. The site permits anyone to post about a missing person. It's like NamUs, only privately hosted."

"You found a listing on CLUES for Cora Teague." I wanted to be sure I was getting this straight.

"Yes."

"Who posted it?"

"There it gets tricky." Strike planted an elbow on each thigh and let her hands dangle between her knees. "CLUES allows users complete anonymity."

"Is that standard for websleuthing sites?"

"No. But the guy who runs CLUES thinks folks will be more likely to come forward with information if they're not required to identify themselves."

"So a user doesn't have to provide a name to post an MP or to participate in a forum discussion."

"Correct. And those listed as missing don't have to have gone through official channels."

"Meaning a police report is not required." This was sounding flaky.

"You've got it. So not every MP has an investigating

agency attached. When that's the case, the site operator acts as a clearinghouse for tips."

"So any wingnut on the planet can enter any rubbish he or she wants."

"It's not quite that loose." Defensive.

"But you have no idea who listed Teague."

"Do you want to hear this?"

"Go on."

"Since Cora Teague was never officially reported as missing, her case got zero media coverage. And no attention on the site. I figured if she had turned up dead somewhere, and she was in some database of unidentified remains, no one was working to match her up. She was all mine."

"Your challenge."

"Yep."

"And you like a challenge." I was starting to get a really bad vibe.

"Something wrong with that?"

"So what happened?"

"According to the posting, Teague dropped off the radar midsummer of 2011."

"Her LSA?" I used the acronym for last seen alive.

"Avery County. That's about as much as anyone knows."

"Did Teague have an Internet presence?"

"None that I could find. No Facebook, Twitter. No email addresses. No use of Buzznet, Blogster, Foursquare, LinkedIn. No iTunes—"

"Cellphone?"

"No."

An eighteen-year-old kid with no cellphone? That sounded odd. "You spoke to the family. What do they say?"

"They believe she ran off with her boyfriend."

"That's often the case."

"I talked to a few folks up that way. The picture I got doesn't track with that theory."

"How so?"

"Teague was a loner. Not the dating type. And I found not one single solitary person ever heard of or laid eyes on a boyfriend. No BFF. No neighbor. No bus driver. No coach."

"Just the family."

"Just them."

"Who is he?"

"They don't know. Or don't say."

"So she kept the relationship secret. Kids do that."

"Hard to pull it off in the sticks. And Teague moved in a very small circle. Family. Home. Church."

"Perhaps she met the boy at school."

Strike shook her head. "No way, according to those I contacted."

"Was Teague a good student?"

"Not really. She attended a Catholic school for the lower and middle grades. Managed to graduate from Avery County High. No one there remembers much about her. She was on no sports team, participated in no extracurricular activities. The woman I spoke with, a guidance counselor I think, said she was dropped off and picked up daily by a sibling or parent."

"Wait. You called the school?"

"Claimed I was helping the family."

Jesus. This woman was something.

"One odd twist." Strike continued, oblivious to my disapproval. "Teague's not pictured in the yearbook."

"There could be any number of reasons for that. She'd had a bad hair day and hated the shot. She was out sick when photos were taken."

"Maybe. The guidance counselor said Teague's record indicates chronic absenteeism."

"Any history of problems with alcohol or drugs?"

"Nope."

"Any juvie record?"

"I don't know. After graduation, she took a job as a nanny. Lasted a few months, then got sent packing."

"Why?"

"Health issues."

"What sort of health issues?"

"No one would say."

"Where did Teague go?"

"Home."

I waited for Strike to continue. She didn't.

"Let me get this straight. Cora Teague hasn't been seen in over three and a half years."

"That's right."

"But an MP report was never filed with the police."

"Correct."

"The family believes she left on her own."

"They do."

"But you think that's unlikely."

"Me and whoever posted her name on CLUES."

I nodded, acknowledging she had a point.

"You suspect Cora Teague's voice is on that recording." Indicating the Ziploc.

"I do."

"You think she was killed and dumped. And that part of her body was recovered and sent to this lab."

"I'm suggesting you consider the possibility."

"What makes you think Teague is at this facility?"

"About a year and a half ago, you made an entry on NamUs detailing a partial torso found in Burke County. Burke is right down the road from Avery. The time line fits. The geography fits. The descriptors fit." Strike straightened and spread her arms wide. "Call me crazy, but I think it's worth a look-see."

A specimen cart rattled by in the hall. A door opened, releasing the whine of an autopsy saw cutting through bone. Closed abruptly, truncating the sound.

In my head I heard the wretched little voice on the tape.

Please don't kill me.

Please.

Kill me.

As before, I felt a chill crawl up my spine.

"How did this come into your possession?" Gesturing at the key chain recorder.

Strike leaned back into her chair.

"As I said, I kept scanning sites listing UIDs, hoping a set of remains might link to Cora Teague. Nothing ever did. Then I got sidetracked by personal matters. Had to let it go for a while."

Strike paused, perhaps pondering the unnamed matters that had temporarily halted her search.

"Last week, I got back to sleuthing. When I spotted your entry on NamUs it was like harps burst into tune. You know. Like on TV."

I didn't. But I nodded.

"Your entry included information on where the torso was found, so I decided what the heck? It's not a long drive. Why not go up and poke around?"

"You went to Burke County? Seriously?"

"I did. Once I got there, it seemed obvious there was only one place a person in a hurry would off-load a body from that overlook. I walked a pattern downhill from the spot. For hours, turned up nothing but bugs. I was about to quit when I spotted a key chain wedged in the roots of a big old tree. Figured the thing was probably there by happenstance. But, being safe, I brought it home."

Strike's mouth squashed up to one side, and she went silent.

"You discovered the recording function and played the audio," I suggested.

"Yeah." Tight.

"And then?"

"And then I called you."

A very long silence stretched between us. I broke it, using carefully chosen words.

"Mrs. Strike, I'm impressed with your enthusiasm. And with your commitment to the goal of returning nameless victims to their families. But—"

"You can't discuss the specifics of a case."

"That's correct."

"About what I expected." Strike took a quick breath and set her jaw. Preparing to argue? Or to accept rejection?

"But I promise you," I said, "I will look into the situation."

"Yeah." Strike gave a humorless sniff of a laugh. "Don't let the door smack your arse on the way out."

Strike snatched up the Ziploc and pushed to her feet.

I rose. "If you leave the key chain, I will ask someone at the crime lab to evaluate the audio."

Strike repeated the mirthless snort. She really had it down. "I don't think so." Dropping the Ziploc into her pack.

I extended a hand. "I will call you. One way or another."

Strike nodded. Shook. "I'd appreciate that. And your discretion."

I must have looked confused.

"Until an ID is confirmed, no sense getting the media in a twist."

"I never grant interviews." Unless ordered to do so by those higher up the chain of command. I didn't say that.

"I apologize. Didn't need saying. It's just, I prefer doing what's best for the family."

"Of course."

I walked Strike down the hall and watched her disappear into the lobby, all the while debating if and how to share her tale with my boss, Mecklenburg County's chief medical examiner. I knew the look Tim Larabee would give me. And the questions he'd ask.

Back at my desk, I rolled Strike's visit around in my head. Considered possibilities.

Strike was a mental case. A con artist. A shrewd detective lacking a badge.

I started with door number three. Strike was a well-meaning though somewhat overzealous websleuth. She'd found the recorder just as she'd claimed. Problems. How had the police failed to spot the thing when they recovered the torso? How had it survived out in the elements for so long?

Say the girl on the audio actually was Cora Teague. Say Strike was correct, Teague is dead and I have her remains in storage. Had the key chain been hers? Had Teague recorded her thoughts while held in some sort of brutal captivity? Had she been murdered?

I moved to an alternate explanation. Strike fabricated

the whole story. Faked the audio. Problem. The scam would be quickly discovered and Strike revealed as a fraud. Why do it? Because she's nuts? Because she craves media attention? Doors one and two.

Or maybe Teague was the scammer and Strike her gullible victim. Perhaps Teague and two male companions staged the interchange on the recording, and somehow led Strike to the key chain. Teague had been in the wind for three and a half years. Perhaps she wanted to stay there. Problem. The tape sounded eerily real. The anguish in that voice would have the opposite effect on anyone who listened.

Or maybe Teague was working in league with Strike. Same question. Why? What did they hope to accomplish?

In my line of work, I encounter a range of human motivations as broad as the South China Sea. I'm pretty good at spotting deception. At assessing character. Looking back on that encounter, I'm forced to admit, I hadn't a clue what to think of Hazel "Lucky" Strike.

4

I stared at the bright yellow file on my blotter. Larabee would be anxious for word on the mummified corpse.

I was still staring when my iPhone beeped an incoming message. The flight reminder triggered an unexpected wave of uneasiness.

Decision.

Deep breath, then I dialed. As my call winged north, I pictured Ryan and chose words to structure my argument.

Andrew Ryan, *lieutenant-détective*, Service des enquêtes sur les crimes contre la personne, Sûreté du Québec. Translation: Ryan works homicide for the Quebec Provincial Police. I am forensic anthropologist for the Bureau du coroner in La Belle Province. For years we have investigated murders together.

For a period, Ryan and I were also a couple. We both chose to end it. Then he chose to drop off the map.

Recently, he'd chosen to return from exile and propose marriage. Months down the road, my mind was still too boggled to deal.

I pictured Ryan's face. No longer young, but the crags and furrows in all the right places. The sandy hair and electric blue eyes. Eyes that would now show disappointment.

I grinned, despite my apprehension over the upcoming conversation. Ryan had that effect on me. I really did miss him.

Ryan answered, sounding cheerful as a balloon on a string. "Madame. I have reserved a prime table for two at Milos. And organized a full range of postprandial activities. Also for two."

"Ryan—"

"'Postprandial' means after supper. Said activities will take place in the privacy of my home."

"I hate to do this, but I have to cancel."

Ryan said nothing.

"A case has come up. Two, actually. I'm sorry."

"Well, there's some things a man just can't run away from." In a bad John Wayne imitation.

"*Stagecoach*." I guessed the film. It was a game we played. "Do you want to hear about the cases?"

"Perhaps later. When can you reschedule?"

"As soon as I've finished."

A beat, then, "Tempe, deep down I fear that quote really nails it."

"What does that mean?"

"Are you sure you're bailing on this visit because of work obligations?"

"Of course it's because of work." Was it? My throat felt tight and my eyes burned. "Talk tonight?"

"Sure."

The line went dead.

I sat a moment, feeling lonely and confused. Half decided to call Ryan back to say that I'd changed my mind. Instead I dialed US Airways.

As I spoke to the agent, my eyes fell on the yellow folder. On the chair Hazel Strike had occupied.

Again, I imagined the terrified girl on the recording.

I'd bumped Ryan. Recliner Man could also wait.

But before discussing Strike with the boss, I'd check the facts. I remembered little about the case. Only that I'd done the analysis as a special request since the MCME doesn't normally investigate deaths occurring in Burke County. Couldn't recall the reason I'd been tagged for this one.

Thanks to Strike, I knew the remains had turned up approximately eighteen months earlier. And that I'd entered them into the NamUs database.

Logging on to my computer, I used the key words "Burke County" and a limiter for dates. It took just moments. The decedent had been registered at our facility as ME13-229. I pulled my report and scanned the contents.

ME13-229 arrived on August 25, 2013. The remains had been found by a hunter. By his dog, Mort, to be fair. I remembered chuckling at the irony of the name. Inappropriate, but I had.

Mort had made his macabre discovery twenty miles north of Morganton, off NC Highway 181. The bones lay downslope from an overlook, scattered over fifty square meters and covered in leaves and debris. Apparently, old Mort possessed one hell of a nose.

The investigating officer was a Burke County sheriff's deputy named Opal Ferris. It was coming back now. I recalled my surprise that Ferris had been canny enough to spot something suggesting the remains were human. That she'd bothered to walk the site to collect more. That she'd delivered Mort's booty to the local ME.

I read the section of my report titled "Postmortem Condition."

Little soft tissue had remained, the work of scavengers and nature's inevitable march. The small amount present consisted of leathery bits of ligament, enough to keep two segments of spinal column articulated. The rest had survived as isolated elements. My skeletal inventory listed eighteen partial ribs, fifteen complete and three fragmentary vertebrae, two partial clavicles, fragments of right and left scapula blades, and one fragment of sternum.

In the section titled "Age at Death" I'd entered a range of seventeen to twenty-four years. My estimate was based on the youthful appearance of the three sternal rib extremities, the ends where the ribs attach via cartilage to the breastbone. And on recent fusion of the growth cap on the medial end of the right clavicle. The left clavicle had been too damaged for observation.

Using measurements taken from the hunks of intact spine, I'd calculated height as somewhere between sixty and seventy-two inches, a range so broad it was virtually useless.

Based on bone quality, and on the presence and amount of desiccated soft tissue, I'd estimated PMI, postmortem interval, at a minimum of three months to a maximum of two years.

I'd been unable to determine gender or ancestry.

That was it.

I left the MCME system, went to the Internet, and typed in www.NamUs.gov. After entering my credentials, I chose the Unidentified Persons Database, and provided the number assigned to the Burke County torso. The section marked "Case Information" included the date and location of the find, and the date of the file's creation. No modifications had been made since the time of the latter. The individual's status remained "unidentified." I was listed as both the local contact and the case manager. Fair enough. That's how Strike had found me.

I moved through the pages of the report.

I'd had nothing to enter with regard to weight, facial or body hair, eye or hair color. Nothing on amputations, deformities, scars, tattoos, or piercings. No evidence of medical implants or missing organs.

Zilch on clothing, footwear, jewelry, eyewear, or documents. No DNA. No fingerprints. No dentals.

Small wonder the bones still lay on a shelf in my closet. ME229-13 consisted of a headless, limbless, skeletonized partial torso.

Shoving away from my desk, I walked down the corridor to a small room whose walls were lined floor to ceiling with metal shelving. Each shelf was filled with cardboard boxes. Each box was labeled with a case number in bold black marker.

ME229-13 was straight ahead on the door-facing wall, two shelves down from the top. I reached up, slid the box free, and carried it to the "stinky room," a small autopsy suite with special ventilation to accommodate the more odoriferous dead. The decomps. The floaters. My kind of case.

Placing the box on the autopsy table, I pulled latex gloves and a plastic apron from an undercounter drawer, donned them, and lifted the lid. As expected, the contents of the box consisted of a handful of bones. Except for the ten thoracic vertebrae I'd boiled to clean away soft tissue, all were stained a deep mahogany brown.

One by one, I removed and arranged the bones in anatomical position. When I'd finished, a jigsaw-puzzle rib cage lay on the stainless steel. Gaps left by missing parts looked like pieces not yet plugged in.

Over the next hour, I examined every bone and bone fragment under an illuminated magnifier lens. I saw postmortem trauma—gnawed edges and conical punctures left by the teeth of scavenging animals. A few of the punctures had pale yellow spongy bone deep inside. The absence of staining told me this damage could be credited to Mort.

I saw no evidence of antemortem trauma. No healed or healing broken ribs. No joint remodeling resulting from the dislocation of a clavicle or vertebra.

I saw no evidence of perimortem trauma. No unhealed fractures due to blunt force attack or rapid deceleration impact injury. No bullet entrances or exits. No sharp-instrument nicks or gashes. Nothing to suggest violence at the time of death.

I saw no evidence of illness or abnormality. No porosity, thickening, irregularity, or lesion hinting at malnutrition, infectious disease, or metabolic disorder.

Discouraged, I straightened and rolled my shoulders. As before, I was clueless as to ME229-13's gender, race, state of health, or manner of death.

The clock now said 2:37 P.M. Larabee was expecting a briefing on the man with the remote.

So what *did* I know that could shed light on Hazel Strike's theory?

I looked back at the jigsaw-puzzle torso.

Bone size was average, consistent with that of a large female or a small male. Estimated age at death, seventeen to twenty-four, was consistent with Cora Teague's age. Height, sixty to seventy-two inches, was consistent with half of North America.

Consistent with. The darling phrase of forensic experts. Not a match, not an exclusion. I made a note to ask about Cora Teague's height.

Again, I considered. Was Strike a charlatan or a nutcase? Or had she stumbled onto something truly evil?

I saw nothing on the bones to suggest foul play. Except that they had lain miles from anywhere, downslope from a two-lane blacktop.

How had ME229-13 ended up in such a remote spot? Had the victim wandered from the highway? Fallen from the overlook? Jumped?

Or did the explanation involve far more sinister events? Had the body been tossed from the overlook? Dumped from a car in the middle of the night?

In my mind I heard the trembling little voice on the tape. Again felt the chill.

Using a small autopsy saw, I cut a plug from the mid-shaft of the less damaged clavicle, sealed it in a small plastic vial, and marked the lid with the MCME case number, date, and my initials. I wasn't optimistic the bone would yield DNA, but at least we'd have a sample for testing.

Should Strike's theory have legs. Should a member of the Teague family provide a comparison sample. Should Larabee agree to foot the bill for analysis.

Aspects of Strike's story didn't track. Deputy Ferris had walked the site, found other bones, yet she hadn't spotted the key chain? And Hazel Strike had?

Above me, the fluorescents hummed softly. My

neck and shoulders were knotted, and a headache was tuning up at the base of my skull.

Enough.

After returning ME229-13 to storage, I walked back to my office. Passing the other autopsy rooms, I heard not a single rattle or whine. The pathologists had finished cutting Y's for the day.

I still keep hard copy on all my cases. Antediluvian, but there you have it. I went straight to my file cabinet and pulled the neon yellow folder with ME229-13 handwritten on the tab. It felt very slim.

I sat at my desk and opened the file. Clipped to the inside front cover was the small brown packet I sought.

Slowly, I worked through Opal Ferris's "crime scene" pics. As in 2013, I was impressed with the deputy's grasp of the need for documentation. And unimpressed with her photographic skills.

The first three-by-five captured the overlook, though most detail was fried because the camera had been pointed into the sun. Ditto for the next two. The third showed a flat area with a wooden handrail and a steep drop-off beyond. Forest in the distance. The next several shots panned across trees, mostly pine, and dense mountain laurel, presumably the area of Mort's find.

The final series were close-ups of bones in situ: a cluster of ribs dappled by shadow, a segment of spinal column half buried in soil, an isolated vertebra protruding from the ground at the base of a pine.

Each image contained a small plastic evidence marker, but no scale or directional arrow. Some were sharp, others blurred due to inadequate lighting or instability of the camera. And it was obvious that Ferris had done a bit of cleaning and arranging before taking some shots.

The last picture featured the right clavicle full-frame, the squiggly fusion line in sharp focus. I stared at the telltale indicator of youth. When last seen, Cora Teague was eighteen years old. Did the bone belong to her? If not Teague, whose kid had ended up dead on that mountain?

Time to talk to Opal Ferris. Then I belonged to Recliner Man.

After checking the number in my file, I dialed. The phone was answered on the first ring.

"Burke County Sheriff's Department. Is your situation an emergency?" The voice was female, the words robotic.

"No. I'd like—"

"Hold, please."

I held.

"Okay, ma'am, may I have your name?"

"Dr. Temperance Brennan."

"What is the reason for your call?"

"I'd like to speak to Deputy Opal Ferris."

"Can you describe the nature of your business?"

"Human remains found off Highway 181."

"Hold, please."

I held. After a full minute, I switched to speaker and set down the handset.

"Okay. When were these remains found?"

"August of 2013." More clipped than I intended. But my head hurt. And I was finding the grilling annoying as hell.

"Can you tell me anything else?"

"No." Sharp.

A slight hesitation. Then, "Hold, please."

I held. Longer than either of the previous times.

I was finger-drumming the blotter with one hand, rubbing circles on my right temple with the other, when something clicked on the other end of the line. Then the same voice came through the phone's little square holes.

"Deputy Ferris is unavailable. Would you like to provide contact information?"

I gave her both the MCME main line and my mobile number. And pointed out that the former was a medical examiner facility. Brusquely.

The woman wished me a good day and was gone.

I jabbed the disconnect button. A pointless attempt at maintaining control.

The world beyond my door had grown quiet. The death investigators were either out bagging bodies or doing "paperwork" in their cubicles. The pathologists had retreated to their offices or departed for other tasks.

My eyes dropped to the file on my blotter. Shifted to my watch. 3:55 P.M.

I wanted to go home, share dinner with my cat, Birdie, spend time chatting with Ryan. Appeasing?

I pictured Larabee's face. The slow, concerned-but-unconcerned look I'd get for snubbing the mummy.

"Fine."

I scooped up the folder, intending to return to the stinky room. I was swiveling my chair when my iPhone rang. Thinking it might be Opal Ferris, I picked up.

It wasn't.

The call kicked the headache into overdrive.

5

"It's Allan." The voice was Carolina with an undertone of the Bronx.

Crap. Crap. Crap.

"Hey, Allan." With an enthusiasm I reserve for slugs in my garden.

"I'm sure you know why I'm calling."

"I'm working on it." Untrue. I hated the thought of "it." Had been avoiding "it" for months.

"Today is March thirtieth."

"Yes."

"I'm sure you know what that means."

My upper and lower molars reached for each other. That was twice. Allan Fink used the phrase repeatedly in each conversation.

"I'm sure I do." Perky as Tinker Bell's toes.

"This is serious."

"Lighten up, Allan. We have more than two weeks until the filing deadline."

"Tempe." Faux patient sigh. "I need those materials to calculate the total owed."

"I'll get everything to you by Friday."

"Tomorrow."

"I'm really slammed at the lab."

"I'm a tax accountant. This is my slammy season."

"I understand."

"I've been asking since November."

"I'll do my best."

"You are not my only client."

In my head I added, "I'm sure you know." He'd reminded me at least a zillion times.

"Charity donations, business and travel expenses, 1099s for any honoraria or fees I was paid. Anything else?"

Censorious pause, then, "I will resend the list of items I'm lacking."

"I know I saved the receipts." Somewhere.

"That would be good."

"Is it really so important?"

"The IRS tends to believe that it is."

"I make less than a circus chimp."

"What *do* performing primates earn these days?"

"Peanuts."

"Must irritate the elephants." Allan hung up.

It was past eight by the time I finished. As I rolled Recliner Man back to the cooler, the MCME hummed with that exaggerated quiet unique to buildings abandoned after an all-day buzz.

Based on skeletal and dental indicators, the mummified remains were those of the elderly tenant in question. I found nothing on his bones or X-rays to suggest foul play. The old gent had kicked while OD'ing on *The Sopranos* or soaps.

Though Larabee might be annoyed with the tardiness of my preliminary report, he'd be pleased with the content. The rest was now his show.

Outside, the air was warm and very damp, the horizon fading from ginger to gray. Serpentine clouds stretched sinewy dark above the telephone wires lining both sides of Queens Road.

Allan's call had me edgy and cross. The last thing I wanted was to spend the night digging for old restaurant receipts and boarding passes. Every year I vow to be more organized. Every year I fail. Recognizing that the problem was self-created only irritated me further.

I made one stop for takeout sushi and arrived home as dusk was yielding the last of its sway. The manor house looked like a hulking black bunker in the deepening twilight, the magnolias and live oaks like giant sentinels guarding the lawn.

I took the circle drive past Sharon Hall and the coach house to the smallest structure on the grounds. Two stories, five rooms and a bath. The annex, original purpose forever lost to history.

Expecting to be home long before dark, I'd left no lights burning. Every window stared darkly opaque. Though I couldn't see his furry white face, I knew that through one pane a very hungry cat tracked my approach.

I gathered the sushi, got out, and crossed my patio to the back door. As I jiggled the proper key forward on the overburdened ring, I could hear cars starting up across the way at Myers Park Baptist Church. A dog barking. A siren wailing far off in the distance.

"Hey, Bird." I thumbed a switch and placed the bag on the counter. Birdie worked figure eights around my ankles. "Sorry, big guy. You must be starving."

Birdie sat and regarded me with disapproval. I think. Then, catching a whiff of raw tuna, he forgot his grievance and hopped onto the counter.

I filled his bowl, certain he'd ignore the crunchy pellets and focus instead on cadging from me. Then I got a plate and a Diet Coke and settled at the table. Birdie jumped onto the chair beside mine.

"So." Placing a sliver of hamachi in front of him. "Tell me about your day."

Birdie scooped the offering with one delicately curled paw, sniffed, then downed it. No comment on his diurnal activities.

"Mine did not go exactly as planned."

While eating California roll, I described my encounters with Lucky Strike and Recliner Man. Cats don't care if you talk with your mouth full. A character trait I much admire.

"Got a call from Allan Fink." I shared my feelings on filing deadlines.

Bird listened, eyes following my chopsticks as I dipped and downed two amago. I gave him an ebi and ate the rice. He did the paw thing and wolfed the shrimp in one gulp.

Admission. Above all others, one issue was making me churlish. Andrew Ryan's startling proposal.

"What do you think? Should I marry the guy?"

Bird looked at me but offered no input.

"I agree. Later. You up for digging through boxes?"

Same nonresponse.

I climbed the stairs, took a quick shower, and changed into a tee and pajama pants. Then I headed for the attic at the end of the hall.

Here's my three-step filing system. Which would never be disclosed to Allan Fink. Got a receipt, canceled check, or document that might later be needed? Toss it in a box, date the box, shove the box into the attic at the end of the year.

I found the carton quickly, between a stack of obsolete textbooks and two tennis rackets I would never restring. I hauled it to the dining room, slightly uneasy at its lack of poundage.

Seated at the table, I lifted the lid. I needn't have worried. The thing was crammed with more paper than a pulp mill generates in a decade. Inwardly groaning, I started unfolding, deciphering, and sorting into piles. Taxi. Hotel. Humane Society. Animals Asia. Trash.

As my eyes struggled to make out faded credit card numbers and cash register print, my mind veered back to Lucky Strike. To the recording. The girl had seemed terrified, the men horrendously cruel. The voices rang in my head, sharp and jagged as broken glass.

Had the girl on the audio really been Cora Teague? If not Teague, then who? Who had ended up below that Burke County overlook?

I should have confiscated the recorder. Sure, I'd asked and Strike had refused. But I could have been more persuasive if I'd used my wits. Why hadn't I?

Why hadn't Opal Ferris returned my call?

Round and round. Guilt. Irritation. Agitation over the prospect of vows.

After an hour, I'd made maybe a two-inch dent in the mountain of paper. And my headache was back with bells. Screw it.

Shifting to the study, I booted my Mac and googled the term "websleuth." I was astounded at the number of links that came up. Articles. Videos. Sites with names like Websleuths. Official Cold Case Investigations. Justice Quest.

I clicked through page after page, intrigued. At one point Birdie joined me and curled on the desk. His steady purring provided a tranquil backdrop to the staccato clicking of the keys.

There was a similarity from one site to the next. Chat rooms. Forums. Discussion threads following particular cases or lines of inquiry. Unsolved homicides and missing persons seemed to attract the most attention.

The rules varied. Some sites required "verification" of persons claiming to be professionals and having inside information—doctors, journalists, cops, et cetera. Others did not. Some prohibited "inviting"—a request from one poster to another for private contact. Others allowed it.

I scanned an article about Websleuths.com, learned that the site was started in the 1990s as an online forum for discussion of the JonBenét Ramsey murder. That it took credit for uncovering a vital clue in the Casey Anthony case, and for helping solve the murder of Abraham Shakespeare, a Florida laborer killed after a lottery win of $30 million. According to one comment I read, the hosts claimed 67,000 registered members, and up to 30,000 daily hits. No telling if those numbers were true.

I provided the information needed to join and chose a thread at random. The discussion concerned a twenty-nine-year-old hairdresser missing from Lincoln, Nebraska. The MP, Sarah McCall, had left her place of employment the previous January intending to have drinks with friends. Her car was found two days later in a rest area on Interstate 80. No purse. No keys. No sign of McCall.

The number of people tracking the case was truly astonishing. As was the amount of intel they claimed to have gathered. Over the course of two months, websleuthers had found McCall's Facebook page and online videos, and figured out her various Twitter handles, including @singleandfree, @silverlining, and @curlupanddye. An IT specialist named candotekkie had retrieved thousands of deleted Twitter posts. Other websleuths had waded through the content to sort what was relevant from what was not.

And these guys were thorough. A Websleuths.com member named R.I.P. had mailed a copy of McCall's missing-person poster to every women's shelter, hospital, and medical examiner facility in Nebraska. Unfortunately, Sarah McCall had yet to be found.

As I made myself tea, I couldn't help but think how McCall had unknowingly helped in her own investigation. The woman was a prodigious user of social media. The polar opposite of Cora Teague.

Returning to the keyboard, I linked over to CLUES.net. The site was less user friendly than Websleuths.com, the mark of a creator less skilled in the use of web design templates. But Strike was right. No info was required to become a member.

It took some trawling, but I finally located a forum on Cora Teague. Compared to the other cases I'd perused, there were very few threads and only a handful of participants, most of whom had quickly dropped out.

The first thread was initiated on August 22, 2011,

by someone calling him- or herself OMG. The post stated that Cora Teague was missing and in danger due to poor health, and claimed a lack of interest on the part of family and local law enforcement. She or he described Teague as a white female, five feet six inches tall, of slender build, with green eyes and long blond hair.

OMG stated she or he had last seen Teague on July 14, 2011, outside the Teague family home in Avery County, North Carolina. Teague was wearing a long-sleeved blue tee, jeans, a lightweight white jacket, and leather boots. OMG did not describe the circumstances of that sighting, and no detail came out in the brief interchanges that followed.

A websleuth using the name luckyloo joined the thread on February 24, 2012. By that time no one had posted a comment for over six months. I guessed luckyloo was Hazel Strike.

There was some uptick in posting following Strike's appearance, but eventually the thread was down to two participants. OMG was not one of them. In January 2013, following a two-month silence, Strike asked to meet with OMG. The request was not answered. OMG had long since dropped off the radar.

By nature, I am stubborn. I can't step back from a problem that I can't solve.

Sipping my now tepid Earl Grey, I thought about what I'd just read. About Strike's theory.

About the audio.

I wondered what had made Cora Teague tick. What shadowy illness had driven her back to her parents' home.

I wondered about the identity of OMG. Oh my God? I wondered the reason OMG believed Teague had come to harm.

And, for the hundredth time, I wondered if Teague was alive or dead.

Cora Teague was a mystery I was now burning to crack.

I shifted to NamUs.gov and called up the case file I'd created on the Burke County torso. After entering a description of the key chain recorder and denim belt loop, I logged off and headed up to bed.

Unaware of the deadly spiral I'd kicked into motion.

6

The bedside clock said 11:48. I'd decided it was too late to call Ryan when my iPhone blasted "Girl on Fire." Note to self. Change ringtone.

I checked caller ID, clicked on, and slid under the covers.

"Hey."

"Hey what?" Ryan's standard response.

"It's the south," I said, smiling. "It's our way of greeting."

"How was your day?"

"You sound like me trying to engage my cat."

Ryan laughed. He'd recovered from his disappointment over my canceled trip and was in a pretty good mood. "How is the Birddog?"

"Peeved that dinner wasn't served until nine."

"Why so late?"

"Do you want to hear about these cases now?"

"We could talk specials at Costco."

I pictured Ryan in his condo overlooking a dark and forbidding St. Lawrence River. He'd be on the sofa, legs extended, ankles crossed on the coffee table. Ryan never phones from bed. To him, bed means only two things. And he is skilled at both.

First, when Ryan's head hits the pillow, he is instantly asleep. Second. Thoughts of the second sparked a tiny flip somewhere south of my stomach.

"One case involves a mummified old man. Straightforward ID. The second case started with an odd visitor." I told Ryan about Lucky Strike. Cora Teague. The remains labeled ME229-13. The recording. "The voices were unnerving."

"How so?"

"The girl sounded absolutely petrified. Then the men arrived and began harassing her." Recalling the scene again sent a ripple of cold up my spine. "I don't know. Maybe the whole thing is a hoax."

"For what purpose?"

"That's what I can't figure out."

"Who is this Strike?"

"A websleuth."

"I know you'll explain that."

"They're amateur detectives who work the Internet trying to solve unsolved cases."

"God help us."

"Many seem quite competent. And incredibly dedicated."

Silence.

"Can you at least make an attempt at being open-minded?" I asked.

Ryan made a noise I took to mean yes.

"Some work cold case homicides. Some try to match MPs with unidentified remains. They were the ones who interested me."

"Understandably."

I told him about the sites, the forums, the discussion threads. "Some people spend hours looking at images created from decomps and skeletons. Then they comb through antemortem pics of MPs, looking for matches."

"And we know how accurate most facial reproductions are."

Ryan had a point. In my brief cruise through a number of online repositories I'd seen the usual array of artsy color portraits, crude pencil drawings, cartoonlike sketches, wig-topped clay busts with scarecrow features, and unnaturally symmetrical computer graphics. From experience, I knew most were painfully inexact. Some sites contained actual morgue photos, the faces grotesque and distorted in death.

"Others start with UID reports, which include unique identifiers—an odd scar, a distinctive tattoo, an unusual fracture, an implant, an artificial body part. Then they search MP sites for individuals possessing similar traits." Ignoring Ryan's comment. "Still others start with persons reported missing from an area in which remains have been found, then work outward to the county, to the state—"

"To the future, to the horizon."

"Shall we trade Jedi jokes or do you want to hear this?"

"I love how your voice goes all sexy when you're peeved."

"I visited a site devoted to a murdered teen nicknamed Princess Doe. Her body was discovered in Blairstown, New Jersey, in 1982, her face bludgeoned beyond recognition. Close to a hundred potential matches were listed, Ryan, all young women loosely fitting the kid's description, all reported missing after 1975."

He tried to comment. I kept talking.

"And there are dozens like Princess Doe. Scores. Caledonia Jane Doe. Tent Girl. The Lady of the Dunes. Jane Arroyo Grande Doe."

"Sounds like a lot of man-hours."

"And women."

"Noted."

"UIDs are a big problem, Ryan. Both in the U.S. and Canada."

"Like earwigs."

"Are you trying to annoy me?"

"I love how your voice goes all—"

"The National Institute of Justice estimates there are tens of thousands of unidentified bodies lying around in morgues or buried in anonymous graves in potters' fields in this country." Jesus. I sounded like Strike.

"I thought that was the point of NCIC."

Ryan referred to the National Crime Information Center, a mongo computer complex in Clarksburg, West Virginia, containing info on all things criminal. Stolen guns, cars, boats. Counterfeit bonds, pilfered checks. Fingerprints. Names of terrorists, gang members, violent felons. And, as of the past few years, unidentified remains and certain categories of missing persons.

"You know as well as I do that NCIC doesn't get the job done. Hell, until 1999 it wasn't even mandatory for state and local agencies to register their missing or unidentified. As recently as 2007 the National Institute of Justice estimated that only fifteen percent of all UIDs had been input." While online, I'd spent some time querying this topic. "A 2009 National Research Council committee reported that eighty percent of the coroners and MEs surveyed responded either 'rarely' or 'never' concerning their use of NCIC to match their UIDs to MPs."

"Why such a poor turnout?"

"For starters, the database is only open to law enforcement."

"You can't have every bimbo with a missing uncle accessing the system."

"True. But another problem comes from the fact that case entry is incredibly labor intensive. The full protocol is over thirty pages long. You think cops sit down with family members and go over every box that needs checking?"

Ryan said nothing.

"Often what happens is a cop sends in the basics—gender, one of the big three for race, broad ranges for age and height. Maybe date of discovery. The profile is so vague the program spits back hundreds of possible matches. How likely is it the guy's going to plow through all that information?"

"Or gal."

"Noted."

"Cops are overextended these days." Ryan sounded a touch defensive.

"And then there's the problem of incompatibility in reporting. What if dentals on a UID are entered using one charting system, and dentals on an MP are entered using a different system? Though both cases might be in the database, one will never link to the other."

"You're saying NCIC is ineffective and under-utilized."

"For a stolen car or passport, it's terrific. To link remains to an MP, not so much. But things are improving."

"So websleuths go at the problem using sites accessible to the general public."

"Yes."

"Some of which welcome any dolt wanting to post his hat size."

I ignored that. "A few websleuths have had reasonable success."

"Like ol' Truth-or-Dare Strike."

"Lucky."

"What?"

"She goes by Lucky."

"If Strike actually contacted the kid's family and school, that's hardly within the definition you just gave."

"It's called offlining."

"If Strike's telling the truth, she offlined her ass right onto a potential crime scene."

"Look. The torso may or may not be Cora Teague." My voice was light-years from sexy. Ryan's attitude was starting to piss me off. "But Strike has generated a lead."

"Or conned you into wasting time and energy."

"Following up on tips is part of my job."

"Strike's got nads, I'll give her that."

"Perhaps we should talk about something else."

"No, no, no."

"Nice use of trilogy."

There was a long silence amplified by irritation on my end, skepticism on his.

"How's Daisy?"

Ryan's peace offering was not where I wanted to go.

Katherine Daessee Lee Brennan. Daisy. My crazy-as-a-sock puppet mother.

When I was eight, my father died in a car wreck, my baby brother in a pediatric ICU after losing a heartbreaking battle involving white cells. I was relocated from Chicago to North Carolina, and lived the rest of my childhood migrating between the family beach house at Pawleys Island and my grandmother's cupcake Victorian in Charlotte.

After spending decades ferrying her daughter through a ceaseless series of mental crises, Gran finally clocked out at age ninety-six. In the end, I think Mama's craziness just wore her out.

Shortly after Gran's death, my mother disappeared without apology or explanation. Four years later, my sister, Harry, and I learned she was living in Paris with a caregiver named Cécile Gosselin, whom she called Goose.

When I was thirty-five, Mama returned to the States with Goose. Since then they'd shifted between the Pawleys Island property and a sprawling condo on Manhattan's Upper East Side. The arrangement worked well for me. Holiday visits. Emails and texts. Brief chats on the phone.

Then, without warning, Mama pirouetted back into my life shortly before Ryan's own reappearance. With her Louis Vuitton luggage, Hermès scarves, and Chanel No. 5, she'd checked into the only facility ever to meet her extraordinarily high standards. Also traveling in the entourage was an untamed malignancy that would eventually kill her.

"Mama's still terrorizing the staff at Heatherhill Farm," I said.

"Goose remains bivouacked at the B and B down the road?"

"Yes. The woman is a saint."

"Daisy's probably promised to bequeath her the family fortune."

"Mama's estate planning centers on bouncing the very last check she writes. I don't know. It's hard to figure Goose. The woman rarely speaks."

"We French are enigmatic."

"But you produce good cheese."

"And wine."

"And wine."

"Daisy would make a daunting websleuth."

"Don't you dare broach the subject to her." Ryan was right. My mother's skill at mining the Web is unsurpassed. But there's a downside. When she's in a manic phase, a mild curiosity can become an all-consuming obsession for Mama.

"Roger that. Any news on Katy?"

Another topic that kept me constantly anxious. Two years earlier my daughter had enlisted in the army and been sent to Afghanistan. She'd survived her tour, come home, and, to my horror, volunteered to return. She was now in the first month of her second deployment.

"Happy and healthy." Or was at the time of our last Skype call.

"Good."

There was a very long pause. I braced, knowing what was coming.

"I get why you had to cancel your trip to Montreal. But have you given any thought to my pitch?" Ryan's tone was carefully neutral.

Pitch?

"Yes." I ran a hand through my hair. Inhaled. Exhaled.

"And?"

"It's hard, Ryan. With Mama."

"Yes."

"And Katy."

"Katy will be fine."

"Yes."

"I love you."

I knew I should reply in kind. Instead, I fought a wild urge to disconnect.

"I'll take no news as good news."

I shrugged. Stupid. Ryan couldn't see me.

"Here's my suggestion." He changed topics again. "Shoot that recording over to your audio geeks."

"I don't have it."

"Why not?" Still neutral. No one does it like Ryan.

"Strike refused to leave it with me." Alone in the dark, I felt myself blush with humiliation at my own ineptness. "I phoned the Burke County sheriff's deputy who recovered the bones."

"What did she say?"

"I'm waiting for a callback."

"It might be wise to have the audio analyzed." Ryan stated the obvious.

"I'll call Strike in the morning."

That turned out to be a bad idea.

7

That night I attended a Mad Hatter's party of the macabre.

I was seated at a table stretching as far as I could see in both directions. White linen cloth and napkins. Silver spoons and candlesticks. Porcelain tea service.

Ryan was across from me, wearing a bow tie, tux, and red wool tuque. Beside him was a woman who barely came up to his shoulder. Her hair was a foggy nimbus haloing her head, her features a shadowy landscape lacking in detail or definition. The woman's body ended at the bottom of a rib cage rippling below a cut-off long-sleeved blue tee.

Behind Ryan and the woman, a huge arched window framed a neon sunset. Garish yellows, oranges, and reds, heaped layer upon layer, supported an ominous black disk floating just above the horizon.

I knew that was wrong. That the sun should be

light. I tried to tell Ryan. He kept talking to the woman at his side.

Far down the table to my left, Mama and Larabee were engaged in heated discussion. Larabee was in bloodstained scrubs. Mama had on the black Chanel suit she'd bought for Daddy's funeral but never worn.

At the far right, Hazel Strike sat alone in jeans and boots, backpack beside her on the snowy linen. The fiery twilight made her topknot look like brassy meringue.

Everyone was holding a tiny china cup. Ryan's fingers looked huge on the scrolly little handle.

Mama and Larabee grew louder, but I couldn't make out their words. Recognizing a dangerous note in my mother's tone, I tried to stand, but found I was glued to my chair.

Drizzle began falling. No one seemed to notice but me.

I looked at Ryan.

"Will you melt?" he asked.

I tried to answer. My lips wouldn't form words.

"Will you let Cora Teague melt?" Flat.

Still my mouth wouldn't work.

"Melt." Larabee, Mama, and Strike chorused in unison. The word reverberated, as though bouncing off the walls of an enormous chamber. I looked around. All three were staring at me.

"Will you let *me* melt?" Sharp-edged, no echo.

I refocused on Ryan. His eyes were angry blue flames.

"Do I disappear into the black hole?"

Before I could answer, Ryan swirled backward and vanished into the menacing death-disk sun. The woman's fog-hair swirled, sucked upward by Ryan's sudden departure. Her face, now revealed, was devoid of flesh, the empty orbits pointed at me in beseeching accusation. A beat, then the woman swooped a path identical to Ryan's.

Frightened, I whipped my gaze left. Mama and Larabee were gone.

Right. Strike was on her feet, curling knobby fingers inward, telling me to join her.

I turned away. Tried to peer into the wormhole that had swallowed Ryan and the woman. Saw nothing but tomb-like black.

"Ryan!" I screamed.

I awoke, heart racing, skin slick with sweat.

Wildly disoriented, I took a moment to figure out where I was.

The clock said 2:47 A.M.

Birdie was up on all fours, back arched, undoubtedly annoyed that I'd interrupted his sleep. I stroked his head, and he settled at my knee.

I closed my eyes.

Inhale.

Exhale.

Calm.

I repeated the mantra again and again. Of course sleep didn't come. My mind was obsessed with deconstructing the dream. Which typically does not require Freud. Remarkably uncreative, my subconscious simply reworks its recent intake.

The tux and formal table setting represented Ryan's desire for a wedding, the tuque his Canadian roots and love of Quebec. His disappearance into the black hole needed no explanation.

The woman beside Ryan was Cora Teague. Ditto for her pleading look and sudden exit into oblivion.

Strike was present, playing herself. She wanted me to look for Teague. Larabee, at the opposite end of the table, would probably be opposed, given what little we knew about Strike or the remains labeled ME229-13.

And Daisy? Easy one. Mama was constantly in my thoughts of late.

The Chanel suit and bloody scrubs? Anyone's guess.

At my last time check, the orange digits glowed 5:54. The alarm buzzed at 7:00.

I was at the MCME by eight, spent two hours pounding coffee and composing a final report on the mummified corpse, an elderly gentleman by the name of Burgess Chamblin. When finished, I pulled the file on ME229-13, walked down the hall, and knocked on Larabee's door.

"Yo."

I entered and stood in the middle of the room,

unsure whether to proceed or to drop the whole thing. My mind shot dual flashbacks. The face in the dream. The audio.

Larabee was writing at his desk, still wearing civvies. "How's it going?"

"All roses and sunshine."

"Good." Still scribbling. Half listening.

"You saw my prelim on the man in the recliner?"

"I did." Larabee dotted an i. Maybe a j. Slid a handful of photos into a folder and closed it. "Thanks for hopping right on it."

"I've finished the final."

He glanced up. "That's great. Thanks." When I didn't leave, "Something on your mind?"

"If you have a minute."

"Grab a seat."

I dragged a chair forward and sat.

Larabee leaned back and laced long, bony fingers on his chest. Which looked scrawny and concave under his white polo, the result of an overzealous thirty-year commitment to long-distance running.

"Such a crock. No one checks on Grandpa for almost two years, suddenly the kids are on fire to bury the old man."

"Money involved?"

"Not really." Larabee's forehead, permanently lined from hours spent pounding the pavement, furrowed more deeply. "What's up?"

"I want you to hear me out on this," I began.

"Don't I always?"

I made a face, then continued. "A woman came to see me yesterday. Hazel Strike. Strike believes one of our UIDs is a girl named Cora Teague." I tapped the folder in my lap.

"That's terrific. Follow up."

"It's not so simple."

"Go on."

"The remains consist of a handful of bones found in Burke County in 2013."

"Why did the case come here?"

"I'm not sure."

"Can you score DNA?"

"That may be problematical on two levels. First, the bone is badly degraded. Acid soil, animal scavenging—"

"Second?"

"The family may be unwilling to provide comparison samples."

"Why?"

"They don't believe the kid's dead."

Larabee's brows rose, crimping the furrows.

"They think she took off on her own."

"So what makes this Strike think our UID is Teague?"

I explained my entry of ME229-13's identifiers into the NamUs database, then briefed him on websleuthing. On Strike's visit to Burke County and the disturbing audio. As I spoke, Larabee's expression morphed from interest to scorn.

"You're kidding?"

I wagged my head no.

"Fine. Play me this Blair Witch moment."

"Strike refused to leave the recorder with me."

"Jesus, Tempe."

"What was I supposed to do, rip it from her hand?"

Larabee's phone rang. He ignored it.

"What do you propose?" he asked.

"Perhaps I should go up there. Maybe take Joe, run a cadaver dog through the woods below the overlook." Joe Hawkins is a death investigator who's been with the MCME since the Eisenhower years. If any bone remained on that mountain, Joe Hawkins would find it. Or the canine would.

Larabee gave the idea some thought. Then, "You say the remains were already badly damaged when they arrived in 2013. What are the odds more could have survived?"

"It's possible."

"Likely?"

I shrugged.

"Who worked the recovery?"

"A Burke County deputy sheriff."

"Have you talked to him?"

"Her. Opal Ferris. She was unavailable. I left a message."

"Did the NOK file an MP report?" Larabee used the shorthand for next of kin.

I shook my head.

"Who put Teague up on this CLUES site?"

"There's no way to know. All posters are allowed to remain anonymous."

Larabee's face executed something between a grimace and a scowl. Held the expression several seconds. Then he said what I'd expected.

"I can't commit funds or personnel to something this thin. Phone back up to Burke County. Talk to Ferris. See where that goes."

I nodded. Got to my feet and returned to my office.

This time Opal Ferris took my call.

I introduced myself. Ferris remembered me. And the bones. And her trek around the mountain with Mort. She asked if new info had surfaced.

For what seemed the hundredth time I went through the recent time line, focusing on developments unknown to Ferris. Websleuthing. Strike's NamUs epiphany and visit to Burke County. Cora Teague. The audio.

Ferris listened. I think. There seemed to be a lot going on in the background.

"This key chain thingy was just lying in the dirt?" Ferris's voice was raspy, maybe from smoking, maybe from vocal cords working on a node.

"So Strike claims."

"And the family thinks the kid's run off with some local fella?"

"I'm unsure of his place of residence."

"But the bottom line is she's not been reported missing."

"Except on CLUES."

"Which any pig nut can access."

I said nothing.

"Teague have a cellphone?"

"No."

"Any Internet presence?"

"Not according to Strike."

"Uh-huh. I'm sorry, Doc. But it don't sound like you've got squat. A few bones in Burke, someone who may or may not be missing in Avery. That someone being eighteen and free to stay gone if she chooses."

It was hard to argue with that.

"Can you make a couple of calls?" I asked. "See if the mother or one of the sisters is willing to provide a DNA sample?"

I waited. Quite a while. When I was sure Ferris was about to blow me off, she said, "I'll get back to you."

Ferris didn't. But an Avery County deputy sheriff named Zeb Ramsey did. At four that afternoon, as I was pulling into my drive.

The mother and both sisters had refused to allow themselves to be swabbed. Though none of them had heard from Cora since 2011, all believed she was alive and doing just fine.

Deputy Ramsey sounded about as fired up about the situation as Ferris had been. Disconnected before I could pose a single question about the Teague family.

First Ryan, now Larabee, Ferris, and Ramsey. The

enthusiasm level was sending streaks of tension straight up my back.

I tossed my mobile onto the dash and gave it the finger. In answer, it rang. I snatched it up, thinking Ramsey was calling back.

"Brennan."

"Sounds like you're having a real bad day."

"I'm off duty, Ms. Strike."

"Mrs."

I sighed, considered whether to beg off or simply disconnect.

"I won't chew your ear, just wanted to invite you so's everything's on the up and up. I aim to take another pass at that overlook tomorrow."

"You're returning to Burke County?"

"Yep."

"You shouldn't do that."

"I don't, who will?"

"I appreciate what you've done. But it's time to hand the investigation off to professionals."

"Yeah? They kicked free any leads?"

So far no one I'd contacted gave a rat's ass. I kept that to myself.

"Well, I have." Strike allowed a lengthy silence, perhaps to show who was in charge. "Remember the youngest Teague kid? The one I didn't know what become of?"

"Eli."

"Little Eli died shortly after his twelfth birthday."

"Died how?"

"I don't know. I can't get access to medical files."

"Children die. It could mean nothing."

"Or it could mean something."

"How did you learn about his death?"

"I have my ways."

"When are you going?"

"Plan to be there by eight A.M."

I thought of the reaming I'd get from Larabee. And of the damage Strike might do should additional evidence or remains still lie on that mountain.

Digging a small spiral from my purse. "Give me directions."

Strike did. I jotted them.

"Do nothing until I arrive," I said. "And bring the recording."

"Never hurts to say please."

The line went dead.

I sat a moment, iPhone warm in my hand. Was Strike onto something? Had one of Teague's parents harmed Eli? Had one of them killed Cora then tossed her body from the overlook?

Or was I being drawn into a lunacy that existed only in the mind of Hazel Strike?

I didn't want to go to that mountain.

But something told me that not going would be a big, big mistake.

I made a decision.

Thumbed a button on my mobile and waited.

8

In the Blue Ridge Mountains of North Carolina, on the border between Burke and Caldwell counties, a hunk of igneous and metamorphic rock buckles up from the lush greenery of the Pisgah National Forest. As summits go, the buckle isn't all that impressive, 2,600 feet high and a mile and a half long. But the wee peak has inspired Cherokee myths, folk legends, scientific studies, websites, YouTube footage, a modest tourist industry, and at least one popular song. It appears on every list of haunted sites in North America. All because of oddball lights.

For centuries, mysterious illuminations have been observed above and on Brown Mountain. According to eyewitness accounts, the small fiery orbs appear, rise to a fair height, then vanish below the ridgeline. Hundreds have reported seeing the lights, including locals, visitors, and those who have traveled to North Carolina for just that purpose.

Theories abound. The reflection of fires at moonshine stills. Swamp gas. Lantern-bearing Cherokee widows searching for the souls of husbands lost in battle.

The "ghost lights" have merited two investigations by the United States Geological Survey, the first in 1913, another in 1922. Official reports attributed the phenomenon to locomotives, cars, and occasional brush fires. Many folks don't buy it. Especially the Cherokee.

As I followed my scribbled directions, which were barely legible, I had no idea I was heading to an overlook specifically constructed for viewing Brown Mountain. Nor was I well informed on the marvelous lights. I learned all of that after arriving, reading a sign, and doing a quick Google query while waiting for the rest of the team.

In the predawn hours, traffic was negligible, so I took the scenic route. I-40 to Morganton, then NC 181 north toward Jonas Ridge and Pineola. As I got on the two-lane, there was enough light to enjoy the view. The foothills and mountainsides were still glazed with frost, giving the landscape an ethereal, sugarcoated appearance. As the sun sent out its first tentative feelers, I watched the gaps between elevations ooze from black to gray to pinkish yellow.

Knowing the turnoff was easy to miss, Strike had provided GPS coordinates. The woman was thorough, I had to give her that. And right. I never saw it coming.

Ninety minutes after leaving Charlotte, my

iPhone beeped to let me know that I'd arrived at my destination. I braked, cut from the blacktop, and pulled to a stop in a paved parking area. Mine was the only vehicle present.

After killing the engine, I lowered a window. The air smelled strongly of pine and chilled vegetation, faintly of petroleum caught in gravel scattering the shoulder of the road.

Absolute silence reigned in the woods around me. Not a single bird twittered or cawed a welcome or warning. No small creature rustled the undergrowth hurrying home from a night of hunting or setting out for a breakfast stalk.

I grabbed a jacket from the backseat and slipped on gloves. Then, moving slowly to avoid making noise, I got out of my car. Pointless, since I was alone.

The overlook was bordered by a low steel barrier fitted with signs. I crossed to one, boot heels clicking in the stillness. According to the Burke County Tourism Development Authority, Brown Mountain could be seen directly ahead, Jonas Ridge opposite, behind my back.

I squinted into the far distance. Picked out a smoke-colored smudge riding the horizon. Not a light in sight. But I hadn't come in pursuit of a selfie with ghostly vapors. Mind kicking into scientist mode, I assessed my surroundings.

If today was typical, the overlook was often deserted. Quick exit from the highway, short walk to the guardrail, quick reentrance to the north- or southbound lane, gone. The overlook was perfect for a body dump.

After nineteen months there was little chance we'd find evidence left by that vehicle. A tire track, a paint chip, a fiber from a carpet or floor mat. For the billionth time, I wondered what on earth I hoped to accomplish.

The sound of an engine caused me to turn.

A black Range Rover was pulling to a stop beside my Mazda. An Avery County Sheriff's Department logo told me Deputy Ramsey had arrived. A dog's silhouette was visible in the backseat.

As Ramsey unbuckled his safety belt, I walked toward him. The dog rubbernecked my way, watching through the glass like a New Yorker in a taxi.

"Doctor Brennan?" My name rode a small white cloud coning from Ramsey's lips.

"Tempe. You must be Deputy Ramsey."

Yanking off a glove to extend a hand. "Zeb."

We shook. Ramsey's grip was strong, but not a testosterone killer. I liked that.

"Sorry this had to fall on you," I said.

"If you've got a dead kid from Avery, that's my turf."

"Deputy Ferris was reluctant to reengage." That was an understatement.

"So I gathered."

"I hope I haven't dragged you out here on an April Fool's errand."

"If you have, explain it to Gunner." Ramsey tipped his head in the direction of his canine companion. About whom I had doubts. Which I'd expressed on the phone the previous day.

"You're sure he's cadaver qualified?" I asked.

"Cadaver, drug, fugitive. Taught him myself."

"So you said." Trying to hide my skepticism. I've worked with a lot of cadaver dogs, canines specially trained to locate corpses. It's a distinct skill, different from sniffing out drugs or tracking live individuals, and requires a distinct training protocol. I'd never encountered a dog that was good at all three tasks. Or one coached by an amateur.

An awkward moment passed.

"Did Deputy Ferris tell you about Hazel Strike?" I asked, wondering how the description had been phrased.

"She did."

"Strike's a bit of an odd duck."

"She running late?" A hint. Ramsey wanted to move this along.

"She said eight. Can we give her a few more minutes?"

Tight nod.

Zeb Ramsey's features were pleasant enough—brown eyes, straight nose, brows that didn't meet in the middle. Until he smiled. Then the whole shifted into wonderful alignment.

Whoa-ho.

"May as well make introductions." Ramsey crossed to the cruiser and opened a rear door.

Gunner's parentage involved very large animals. Black, brown, and white coloring and a sprightly upcurl to his tail suggested a shepherd–chow mix.

My sort-of ex, Pete, has a chow. Gunner didn't alight in the manner Boyd would have chosen, body flying, paws scrabbling as they hit the ground. He hopped out with controlled elegance and, eyes never leaving Ramsey, padded up to me and sat.

I looked to Ramsey. He nodded permission. I extended a hand, palm down, to allow Gunner to check out my scent. The dog sniffed, then licked my fingers with a long purple tongue. Definitely chow swirling in the gene pool.

I was stroking Gunner's head when a battered red Corolla turned from the highway. Slamming to a stop beside my Mazda, Hazel Strike killed the engine and flew from the car, showing none of the restraint the dog had exhibited.

As Strike stormed toward us, Ramsey spread his feet and curled one end of the leash around a palm. Gunner tensed.

"Didn't know we'd have company," a scowling Strike said to me, back pointedly turned to Ramsey.

"Mrs. Strike, this is Deputy Ramsey."

"Don't see no reason for an army of cops." A tiny vein snaked the center of Strike's forehead, blue and sinuous and pumping like mad.

Unsure of the source of Strike's anger and, frankly, not caring, I ignored the comment. "The dog's name is Gunner."

More of the hard stare, then Strike started to speak. I cut her off.

"Deputy Ramsey and I will walk Gunner in a systematic pattern, using standard search procedure. If remains or evidence are found, all materials will be photographed in place, then sealed into containers following chain of custody protocol. You may come along if you walk directly behind us in terrain that's already been searched. If that's unacceptable, I will have to ask you to wait up here in your car." Firm, and not all that gentle.

"Christ almighty," Strike said to the sky, maybe swearing, maybe praying.

Feeling a bit guilty for my brusqueness. "Can you point out where you found the key chain recorder?"

"Course I can. I'm not an idiot."

I turned to Ramsey. "The remains were discovered ten yards downslope, on the Brown Mountain side." The night before, I'd reviewed the file on ME229-13. And the lousy photos provided by Opal Ferris. "I'll get my kit and meet you at the guardrail."

Ramsey reclipped Gunner's leash, and the two led the way. I followed. Strike brought up the rear.

Below the guardrail, the gradient dropped sharply. As we picked our way downhill, clutching branches of mountain laurel to keep from sliding, I could hear

Strike panting above and behind me. And feel the crosshairs of her glare on my back.

Twenty feet of fighting gravity brought us to a fairly wide ledge. Though the yellow-pink dawn had yielded to crystalline blue day, towering loblolly pines blocked practically every square inch of sky. Perpetual shadow created by the overhead branches and the steep valley sides kept the space between trunks devoid of underbrush. A thick carpet of needles covered the ground.

Slipping my pack from my shoulders, I pulled out Ferris's pics and searched them for a landmark. The others watched, Strike panting, Ramsey stoic. Or bored.

Around me, every tree looked the same. In my mind, I reviewed Ferris's verbal description. Though it wasn't stellar, from the wording I suspected we'd descended at the same end of the guardrail that she had.

"According to Ferris, the remains were found scattered over in that direction." I pointed east.

We set out, needles soft and spongy beneath our boots. We hadn't gone five yards when Strike spoke, sounding winded and sulky.

"That tree. There. That's where I picked up the key chain."

I turned, wondering at the woman's certainty. At the clues she was noting that I was not.

Behind me, Ramsey asked,"What key chain?"

I gestured that I'd fill him in later. Gunner continued snuffling the ground, still on task.

"You're sure?" I asked Strike.

"Can we skip the part where you and Johnny Law both act like I'm dumbass stupid?"

Not waiting for a directive, Strike veered toward a pine that looked identical to the others around it. I followed. So did Ramsey and Gunner.

"That's my mark." Strike pointed to a V-shaped gash in the bark, three feet up the trunk. "Made it with my knife." She dropped to one knee and brushed back needles, revealing half-buried roots worming across the ground. "Thing was right there." Indicating a recess where two gnarly tributaries V'ed together.

I looked at Ramsey. He looked at me.

"This tree's as good a starting point for our grid as any," he said.

"I suggest we keep the dog leashed first pass, then give him his head if nothing excites him."

"Let's do it."

But Gunner had his own thoughts on the matter. A sound rose from his throat, more "yo" than "hot damn." All eyes snapped his way.

The dog's head was forward and low. His eyes were fixed on a spot somewhere over Strike's shoulder.

Ramsey reached down to unhook the leash. "Go."

Gunner trotted forward, nose probing needles to his left and right. Approximately ten feet southeast of our position, he took one last sniff, exhaled loudly, and dropped to his belly at the base of a pine easily double the size of its neighbors.

"That's his alert." Ramsey was already moving.

I was right on his heels. Behind me, I heard Strike grunting as she clawed her way upright.

Drawing close, I scanned outward, following the trajectory of Gunner's snout. Saw nothing.

While Ramsey praised the dog, I ran my eyes slowly over the ground. Ran them back. Still saw zip.

False alarm?

An icy breeze lifted a few strands of my hair. Branches shifted ever so slightly. A sliver of light cut the canopy and fell on the brown shag covering the earth. From deep in the thickly meshed needles, I saw a wink of red, there then gone.

Swapping latex for woolen gloves, I inched forward and dropped to my knees by the tree. Moving gingerly, I scooped handfuls of needles and set them aside.

As with Strike's key chain pine, a plexus of roots radiated outward, dark and woody, like a primordial hand clawing the forest floor. Wedged in a hollow below one knuckle was a red and yellow mass about the size of a peach pit.

Rotten fruit? A dead rodent or bird?

I poked at the mass with a gloved finger. It felt hard.

I pulled out my Nikon, jotted info onto an evidence marker, and shot pics from several angles. Documentation complete, I returned the camera to my pack. Throughout, Ramsey and Strike watched in puzzled silence.

Gripping with a thumb and fingertip, I tried to rotate the mass right. Felt movement. Maybe. Rotated left, then right, over and over. Slowly, reluctantly, the knuckle yielded its grip and the thing slipped free.

I placed the little mass on my palm. It was semitranslucent, red and yellow on one end, brown on the other. When I flipped it, two soil-crusted knobs were visible on the underside.

I pulled a magnifier from my pack and brought the knobs into focus.

Felt my heart throw in a few extra beats.

"What is it?" Strike asked.

I was too shocked to answer.

9

"Finger bones?" Strike sounded confused. Understandable. I was confused.

"More than bones." Still studying the glossy mass on my palm. "I may see two partial fingertips."

"Inside that goo."

"Yes."

"It's pine tar."

Ramsey's comment caused me to look up.

"Pine trees ooze sap, especially along their bases. Over time, the stuff turns rock hard."

"Like amber."

"Given a few thousand years, yeah."

Of course. Pine sap would be bacteriostatic, exclude oxygen, and provide a barrier against scavenging, conditions favorable to the preservation of soft tissue. I'd once had a case in which a large node of pine sap was inadvertently collected along with human remains. Embedded in the node was a perfectly preserved mouse head. Hanging outside it was the rest of the skeleton.

Like the phalanges poking from the mass in my palm.

"So she falls here following an attack, or her body ends up here after being thrown from the overlook. One hand lands at the base of the pine." Strike gestured toward the tree. "Over time the sap oozes up, or drips down, whatever the hell it does, and encases a couple of fingers."

Strike's scenario sounded sadly realistic. But I was only half listening. As I sealed our grisly find into a Ziploc, my eyes were already scanning for more.

The sun was low when we finally quit. Didn't matter deep in our loblolly sanctuary. There was no more reangling of rays slipping through overhead branches. No lattice of shadow and light changing shape underfoot. Now only perpetual gloom.

Though we grid-walked Gunner then gave him his head, the dog alerted only two more times. Both were legit.

In the end, we found six phalanges, two metacarpals, a scaphoid, and a hamate, all weathered and chewed. Yowsa! A whopping ten out of fifty-four hand bones. We also scored a rusty screwdriver, eight aluminum cans, and a hunk of what looked like an old tent stake.

All the bones were adult and indeterminate in size. I doubted any would yield much information.

But the flesh in the pine sap was a different story. One that had me totally jazzed. Someone had died or been dumped on the mountain. One readable print could provide an ID.

If that person was in the system. Or a valid comparison sample could be obtained.

Ramsey insisted I take the remains with me. Adamantly. Made sense. I had ME229-13 at my lab. Chances were good the hand had been part of the same person.

Upon reaching terrain favored by AT&T, I phoned Larabee. As expected, he was not happy that I'd gone to Burke County. After riding out a fairly lengthy rant, I explained our discovery.

Wanting to avoid jurisdictional complications, and the ire of his boss, Larabee ordered me to wait until he'd contacted the OCME in Raleigh. His return call came ten minutes later. Though surprised that Burke County remains had originally gone to Charlotte-Mecklenburg, the state's chief ME was assigning the case directly to me.

Strike stayed till the end, then tore off with a pedal-jamming, gravel-spitting roar. Sonofabitch. Again, I'd failed to obtain the audio recorder.

All day Strike's attitude had swung between sulky and petulant. I wondered about the source of her hostility. Didn't give the question a whole lot of thought.

As I'd been dialing Larabee, a text from Mama

had pinged in. I'd read it while awaiting his callback. Nothing urgent. Just querying my health and state of mind.

I wanted to go home, take a very long, very hot shower. Eat dinner. Curl in bed and share the day's news with Birdie. Maybe Ryan.

But no one does passive-aggressive like Mama. Her subtext: I am old, have cancer, and very few visitors.

Your mother is twenty miles away, my conscience piped up.

I checked the time. Half past five. I could share a quick dinner with her and be home at the annex by nine.

The euphoria fizzled, leaving no contender but guilt.

Thus, instead of home, I was driving east, hair sweaty under a Charlotte Knights cap, clothes filthy, nails crusted with mud. Not looking forward to Daisy's appraisal.

Near Marion, I turned east off Highway 221. Heatherhill Farm came up quickly, if not flamboyantly. The sign is so tastefully understated, those needing it for guidance blow right by.

I turned onto an unmarked strip of asphalt cutting through mountain laurel higher than my head. Soon, the dense tangle gave way to more finely groomed acreage.

In the dark, Heatherhill looked like a small college

campus. Besides the main hospital there were garden-fronted structures of varying sizes. Ivy-covered chimneys, long porches, white siding, black shutters. From my many visits I knew the outbuildings included a chronic-pain center, gym, library, and computer lab. Still wasn't sure which was which.

I turned onto a tributary lane and, fifty yards down, pulled into a gravel rectangle enclosed on three sides by a white picket fence. I parked and took a flagstone path to a small brown bungalow with flower boxes below each window. A sign above the door said RIVER HOUSE.

I stood a moment, feeling a tense edge of anger. Or remorse. Or some long-denied emotion I couldn't identify. It was always like that. The moment of hesitation before the plunge.

The afternoon's breeze had turned surly and cold. Gusts whirling down the mountain snapped my collar and elbowed the bill of my cap. I looked up. The sky showed a million stars but no moon. All around me, except for wind, utter silence.

On the inside, River House looked exactly as promised on the outside. The gleaming oak floors were covered with Oushaks and Sarouks. The upholstered pieces were done in soft beiges and tans, the wooden ones stained and distressed to look old. The designer, striving for calm and serene, had achieved that and a sense of limitless cash.

After presenting ID to a smiling attendant at a Louis-the-somethingth desk, I wound through the living room, past gas-fed flames dancing in a stacked stone fireplace. Mama's suite was down a side corridor, the last on the right.

Before turning, I glanced left, into the dining room. Half a dozen diners of various ages sat at linen-draped tables centered with flower arrangements showing not the slightest hint of droop. I knew Mama wasn't among them. Daisy prefers eating solo, at the small desk by her sitting room window.

The door was open a crack. A fact that set a tiny alarm dinging deep in my brain. Normally Mama is a bugger on security and privacy. Did the breach mean apathy, thus a dark phase? Carefree jubilation? A random mishap lacking significance?

Mama was, indeed, at her desk, fork forgotten in one hand, staring through the glass at the woods beyond. Perhaps at a flickering memory from another time. Perhaps at nothing.

I studied her a moment. She'd lost weight, but otherwise looked good. Which told me zilch. Despite her myriad mental issues, or perhaps because of them, my mother is an Oscar-Tony-Emmy-class actress.

On hearing me, she turned, all bright green eyes and soft, crinkling crow's-feet. The smile faded as she took in my appearance. "Oh, my."

"Yeah." I chuckled. "Good look, eh?"

"My sweet girl. Have you run away from the circus?"

"Good one." Refusing to rise to the bait. I intended to keep the visit light and sweet. No arguments about my dress, coiffure, or marital state. No pressure on Mama to begin the chemo she was resisting with every fiber of her ninety-pound being.

"Or did you have a fight with your lovely detective?" Nonchalantly pointing the fork at me "What's the gentleman's name?"

"Andrew Ryan."

"Wait. I know." Mama's face lit up. "You've come from a crime scene." Her voice went low and breathy. My work fascinated her. "You've dug up a body."

Nope. No talk of murder or death. Or marriage proposals. Mama would make a Broadway production out of that.

"I was doing a consult in Burke County. It was no big deal." Crossing to inventory her plate. "I was close so I decided to drop by for dinner. What's on the menu?"

Mama is not easily dissuaded. Ever. "You can't share with your doddery old mother?" Spreading her arms. Which looked like twigs inside her thick Irish-knit sweater. "Sweet lord in heaven, where do I ever go? With whom would I discuss the intricacies of your professional life?"

Wind rattled the window at Daisy's back, shimmying the reflection of her upturned face. A sad image bubbled up in my mind. Mama, alone in her self-imposed exile, talking to no one but Goose and the

Heatherhill staff, doing little that didn't involve her journal or laptop.

Mama's logic was sound. She was isolated. She was also better at keeping secrets than the CIA. How could she compromise a case in which I knew neither the victim's identity nor the cause of death?

"Okay, Sherlock." Sighing theatrically. "Let me wash up."

Mama arced the fork as a conductor might flourish a baton. "The game is afoot."

I went to the bathroom and scrubbed my hands and face. Cleaned my nails. Considered my hair. Decided that situation was hopeless and retucked it under the cap. When I returned, a second plate and a chair had appeared at the desk.

Between mouthfuls of baked chicken, mashed potatoes, and minted peas, I explained ME229-13 and the day's exploits with Gunner and Ramsey. I described finding the hand bones and the glob of pine tar. I left Strike out. And the possibility that the victim could be Cora Teague.

Mama listened, rapt. Despite her faults, my mother is a very good listener. When I'd finished, there was a lengthy pause, a prompt to continue. Instead, wanting to stay on safe ground, I shared some of my newfound knowledge about Brown Mountain. Mama flapped a hand, either derisive or disinterested. When I said that was it, she began asking questions. In fact, for the next hour, my mother questioned the bejaysus out of me.

Things went well, and I stayed longer than I'd planned. Outside, the wind had decided to go all out. I scurried to my car, head down and gripping my cap, the hedges lining the flagstones tossing like ocean waves in a storm.

By the time I got home it was eleven-twenty. I removed the Ziplocs from my pack and stashed them in the fridge. After feeding an extremely unhappy cat, I stripped off my clothes and hit the shower.

Smelling of ginger-citrus body wash and lavender shampoo, I finally crawled into bed at ten past twelve. As on the previous night, I considered but decided against phoning Ryan. Too late.

Again my conscience had to have its say. The guy is a night owl. Why the reluctance?

Good question. Avoidance of the elephant in the room wearing borrowed and blue? Or did the reason go deeper than that? An unwillingness to share Cora Teague? A subliminal desire to keep separate that which was mine?

Despite my exhaustion, I lay awake a long time, stroking Birdie's head and listening for out-of-place noises. Happily, I heard none. Only the hum of feline purring and the rattle of the screen in its frame. Eventually, icy drumming on the glass. Maybe slush, maybe rain. That was my last drifting thought.

Then I was full-throttle awake, heart in my throat. Alicia Keys was singing about a girl on fire.

Good news never comes at two in the morning. My

mother had cancer. My daughter was in a war zone.

I fumbled for my mobile. Dropped it. Banged my elbow groping under the bed.

"I hope I didn't wake you, sweet pea."

"Are you sick?"

"Not at all."

"Mama, it's the middle of the night."

"I am so sorry." Whispery, excited. Insincere. "But I've discovered something I think you should know."

"You're sure you're all right?"

"I'm just fine."

"I've had a very long day. Can we talk in the morning?"

Mama sighed, a long, disappointed breath meant for me to hear. "I suppose."

"Are you feeling unwell?"

"Asked and answered."

There was a time I'd have tried harder to put her off. Not anymore. I've learned from experience that Mama determined is an irresistible force.

"Shoot." I rolled to my back, phone to one ear, fairly certain of her next words.

"After you left I got online."

Yep. There they were. I pictured her in bed, laptop resting on upraised knees, face mottled with reflected light from the screen.

"Uh-huh." I stifled a yawn.

"Are you listening?"

"I am."

I heard the comforter rustle, knew Mama was repositioning herself for a dramatic delivery.

"You will not believe what I've found."

She was right. I didn't.

10

A brief comment about Katherine Daessee Lee Brennan.

Throughout my childhood, Mama was as unpredictable as a summer afternoon at the beach. For months she'd be happy, funny, clever—a presence as vibrant as sunshine itself. Then, without warning, she'd retreat to her room. Sometimes to a faraway place. Harry and I would draw pictures at our little table, whisper in our beds at night. Where had she gone? Why? Would she come home?

Doctors with differing degrees provided varying diagnoses. Bipolar. Schizobipolar. Schizoaffective. Disorder of the moment. Take your pick. Pick your meds. Lorazepam. Lithium. Lamotrigine.

No drug ever worked for long. No treatment ever stuck. A cheerful breather, then the darkness would reclaim her. When I was a child, Mama's mood swings frightened me. As an adult I've learned to cope. To accept. My mother is as stable as a skink on a skittle.

When Mama was in her late fifties and emerging from a particularly murky plunge, I bought her a computer. I held little hope she'd find the cyberworld attractive but was desperate for something to occupy her mind. Something other than me.

I walked her through the basics—email, word processing, spreadsheets, the Internet. Explained about browsers and search engines. To my surprise, she was enthralled, took class after class at the Apple Store, then at the local community college. Eventually, as was typical, her proficiency far exceeded mine.

I wouldn't call my mother a hacker. She has no interest in stealing ATM or credit card numbers. Couldn't care less about the workings of the Pentagon or NASA. But, when determined, there's nothing she can't tease from the World Wide Web.

Mama is also an incurable insomniac.

Given that combo, I wasn't surprised she'd taken my tale of Gunner and Ramsey and run with it. But I was mildly unsettled by what she'd found.

"What was recovered?"

"The article doesn't elaborate. Out of delicacy, I suppose. I applaud such discretion. The public is given entirely too much detail—"

"What does it say?"

"It simply reports the discovery of possible human body parts." The last four words delivered with precision. "That is a direct quote."

"What paper is this?"

"*The Avery Journal-Times*. That's Avery County."

"I know that."

"There is no call to be snippy, Temperance." Very snippy.

"Sorry, Mama. I'm half asleep." Swinging my feet to the floor, I turned on the light and grabbed a pen and an old envelope from the bedside table. "When did the story appear?"

"April 29, 2012."

"Does it say where the remains were found?"

"Indeed it does." A quick breath. "The find was made off the Blue Ridge Parkway, two miles north of the junction with Route 181. That would be mile marker 310. I checked with Google Earth."

Of course she had.

"Are you aware what is at that location?" she asked.

"I am not."

"The Lost Cove Cliffs Overlook."

I hadn't a clue what she was getting at. Was struggling to unravel it when she spoke again.

"Overlook?" Delivered as though deeply meaningful.

Right. "Mama, do you know the number of overlooks in the Blue Ridge Mountains?"

A cool silence followed. I knew an answer to my rhetorical question would be winging my way before morning.

"And what does one view from this *particular* overlook?" Curt.

"More mountains?" Again, I wasn't following.

"*Brown* Mountain. Just like the Burke County overlook."

"That is an odd coincidence."

"I am having trouble seeing it as coincidence."

"Who found these body parts?"

"Hikers."

"Has anyone established that the stuff was human?"

"Stuff?" Sniff of disapproval. "Really, darling."

"Did you find any follow-up stories?"

"I did not. And I searched very thoroughly. Keep in mind this was not headline news. The original piece was very brief."

"Did the journalist provide contact information?"

Keys clicked. "Those having knowledge of the situation are asked to contact the Avery County Sheriff's Department." She read off a number. The same number that had appeared on caller ID when Zeb Ramsey phoned.

"Can you forward the link to me?"

"I can."

That night I dreamed of lights on a distant ridge.

Unsurprisingly, I woke late. A quick toilette, then I fed Birdie and headed to the MCME, anticipating Larabee's sermon with as much relish as I had Mama's fashion critique.

Driving across uptown, I pictured Larabee sitting at his desk, pumped by an early morning run, ready to leap into action at the sound of my office door. He wasn't there.

After entering the new Burke County remains into the system, which assigned them case number ME122-15, I opened a file and made notes on the circumstances surrounding their discovery. Then I took the Ziplocs to the stinky room, placed the bones on a tray, and submerged the pine tar node in a jar of acetone and set it in the sink.

When finished, I called Joe Hawkins. He agreed to meet me as soon as I'd freed whatever was congealed in the node.

A quick cup of the sludge that passes for coffee in the staff lounge, and I began photographing the ten hand bones, periodically crossing to check on progress in the sink. All morning the node remained hard as a marble.

The bones were as uninformative as I'd feared. I tried some metric analysis based on measurements of the metacarpals. They came up middle road all the way. And finger and hand bones reveal zip about race. In the end, all I could say was young healthy adult.

Like ME229-13. The hand bones were consistent in every way with the torso bones, but there was no conclusive proof both sets of remains came from the same person. Positive association could only be established with DNA. And I wasn't optimistic on that front.

Discouraged, but not surprised, I returned to my office and dialed Avery County. Ramsey was in and took my call quickly.

"So that's it?" he asked when I'd finished relaying my observations.

"You can rule out old codgers wandering off in their sleep."

"Case practically solved." Pause. "But you're saying we could have two people?"

"I think that's highly unlikely."

"What about the bits in the pine sap?"

"I'm working on it. Did you make inquiries about Cora Teague?"

"I ran the name, got nothing. No address, no phone, no SSN, no passport, no credit or tax history. There is a birth certificate, registered with the Avery County Register of Deeds in 1993."

"Don't parents apply for a social security number at the same time they apply for a birth certificate?"

"You're asking the wrong guy."

"According to Strike, after high school Teague did a brief stint as a nanny. Otherwise she never worked."

"Nannies are often paid under the table." I could hear Ramsey playing with something, maybe the phone cord. "Listen, Doc. It's a big country out there. If the kid decided to vanish, changed her name, she'll be damn near impossible to find."

I nodded.

"And Strike's right. There's no MP file."

"Did you run the parents?" I asked.

"Yeah. Nothing popped. No arrests, complaints, calls to the home."

"Where do they live?"

"Larkspur Road, off 194. Nothing out there but buzzards and pines."

I almost hung up without mentioning it. "I learned something odd last night. Could be meaningless."

Ramsey waited, still jiggling whatever he was jiggling.

"In 2012, an article appeared in *The Avery Journal-Times*." I scrolled through messages on my iPhone, found an email from Mama from 3:12 A.M. I opened it and clicked on the link. "According to the story, body parts were found off a hiking trail near the Lost Cove Cliffs Overlook."

"Human?"

"That's unclear."

Ramsey left a small skeptical pause. "When?"

"April twenty-ninth."

"Six months before I signed on."

"Probably coincidence, but that's also a viewing point for Brown Mountain."

"What are you suggesting?"

"Nothing. I'm wondering about follow-up."

"Human remains should have gone to the coroner."

"Did they?"

"I'll look into it. And I can check whether the reporter is still around."

After disconnecting, I went back to the hand bones and the node.

Five hours of soaking and poking finally got the job done. By three that afternoon, two shriveled hunks of flesh lay in the sink, slimy remnants of the node scattered around them. I inspected each with a hand lens.

And actually arm-pumped the air. Dopey, but I did.

Each hunk had a sliver of nail tagging one end, a distal phalange partially visible at the other. I took X-rays and examined each for detail.

An arrow-shaped phalange told me the larger hunk was the tip of a thumb. The other, based on size, was the tip of a first, second, or third digit. The proximal articular surfaces of both phalanges were crushed and ragged, the work of an industrious scavenger and pals.

Totally pumped, I dialed Joe Hawkins's extension. While awaiting his arrival, I got the fingerprint kit from the storage closet and dug out an inkpad and a ten-print card. No fancy scanners at the MCME. We do it the old way, by rolling and pressing.

Hawkins arrived, looking his usual cadaverous self. Tall and gaunt, with hollow cheeks and dyed black hair, the guy sent from central casting to play the mortician.

I showed Hawkins his "subject" and provided the case number. He listened, face blank. Typical Hawkins. No questions, no reactions. No mistakes. Though not exactly jolly, he's far and away the best autopsy tech in the place. Had achieved that status decades before my arrival.

While Hawkins jotted information onto the print card, I began shooting close-ups of the hand bones. For a while the only sounds in the room were the click of my shutter release and the occasional clink or tap at the sink.

Unless the fingers are desiccated or stiff with rigor, printing a corpse usually takes very little time. I was so engrossed with my photos I lost track of the clock. When I looked up, a full half hour had passed.

Hawkins was still hunched over his task. Tension in his neck and back suggested something was wrong.

"Tough going?" I asked.

No answer.

"I'm happy to help." Thinking Hawkins's hands were very large, the fingertips very small.

Still no response.

I noticed several print cards discarded on the counter. Each had two black ovals. I assumed the larger represented the thumb, the smaller the finger.

Hawkins usually gets prints on the first try. Why the problem? I had no idea his age, but knew it had to be well past sixty. Was arthritis compromising his dexterity? Was he embarrassed that I'd see?

I crossed to the counter and, casual as hell, picked up and glanced at one of the print cards.

I picked up another.

And another.

Hawkins turned from the sink, gloved hands held up and away from his body. His eyes met mine, the dark comma below each crimped in confusion.

"What the hell?" His fingers splayed in puzzlement.

I could conjure no explanation.

11

During the second and third months of gestation, when a fetus is one to three and a half inches long, tiny pads form on the fingertips. During the third and fourth months, the skin goes from thinly transparent to waxy, and the first ridges appear on the pads. By the sixth month, when the average fetus is a whopping twelve inches long, its fingerprints are formed and fixed for life.

Scientists aren't in total agreement as to how it works. One theory holds that the speedier basal layer of the epidermis is scrunched between its slower-growing counterparts in the epidermis above and the dermis below. Pressure from straining against its slower neighbors causes the skin to buckle into folds. Movement in the womb then throws in a few more twists. Whatever the process, the end result is a mind-boggling amount of variation.

Fingerprint ridging falls into one of three broad

patterns: arches, loops, or whorls. Each ridge shows further individuality in the form of endings, bifurcations, and dots.

An ending is the place at which one ridge stops and another begins. A bifurcation is the place where a ridge splits, forming a Y-shaped pattern. A dot is a segment of ridge so small it appears as, well, a dot.

There are often hundreds of these "points" of identification on one finger. The relationship between each point and the surrounding ridge detail is so complex it is believed no two patterns are exactly alike.

Bottom line: Fingerprints kick ass for individual ID.

Not so for ME122-15. The little ovals on the print cards were solid black. No ridges. No dots. Not a single arch, loop, or whorl.

"Is the skin damaged?" I asked, fearful the acetone had been corrosive.

Hawkins shook his head. "Skin's fine. Just no prints."

"How can that be?" Inane. If I didn't know, how could he?

Hawkins just gave me a long, solemn stare.

"Have you ever seen this before?"

"I've rolled fingers that make these look fresh as a pork belly, never failed to get at least one partial."

"Could the prints have been intentionally removed?"

Hawkins stripped off his gloves, toed the lever on

the biohazard pail, and tossed them in. "Anything's possible since they transplanted that face."

Having no clue to the meaning of his comment. "Should we give it one more try?"

"Waste of time." The lid clanged shut.

"I suppose there's no point submitting the cards."

"Nope."

Normally the prints would be sent to the Charlotte-Mecklenburg PD forensics lab to be scanned into AFIS, the Automated Fingerprint Identification System. Using digital-imaging technology, AFIS obtains, stores, and analyzes fingerprint data from all over the country. Originally created by the FBI, the database contains tens of millions of individual prints.

But the name is misleading. AFIS doesn't identify, it searches. Using biometric pattern recognition software, the program compares an unknown print to those in the system, and returns information on possible matches, ranking them from most to least likely. A fingerprint analyst then compares the print he or she has submitted to the "candidates" suggested by the program. A final decision is made by a human being.

But that wouldn't happen with ME122-15.

"Want these things back in the jar?" Hawkins jabbed a thumb toward the sink.

"I'll take care of it." Distracted. "Thanks."

I stood a moment, running possibilities.

Had ME122-15 removed his or her own prints?

To avoid the law? To escape a past life? Had a killer removed the prints postmortem? To mask the victim's identity?

Was obliteration even possible? Or just a Hollywood Men in Black myth? I'd seen no evidence of scarring or chemical burning. Intentional mutilation seemed unlikely.

A *pssst* sounded somewhere deep in my memory banks. Something I'd heard or read. A research article? A conversation with a colleague?

The door opened then closed, breaking my concentration. But it was the age of Google. Speculation was obsolete.

After removing samples for possible DNA testing, I sealed the fingertips in a jar of formalin, the bones in their Ziploc, and placed both in the cooler. Then I hurried to my office.

It wasn't as easy as I'd thought. But eventually I found an online publication in the *Annals of Oncology*. May 27, 2009.

A sixty-two-year-old man traveling from Singapore to the United States was detained by immigration officials after a routine fingerprint scan showed he had none. The man, identified only as Mr. S, had been undergoing treatment for head and neck cancer with a drug called capecitabine, brand name Xeloda. As a result of the therapy, Mr. S had developed a condition known as hand-foot syndrome, official name chemotherapy-induced acral erythema.

I dug deeper. Found an article in *Actas dermosifiliográficas*. May 2008. It was in Spanish and credited to nine authors. I learned the following.

Chemotherapy-induced acral erythema, also known as palmoplantar erythrodysesthesia, or hand-foot syndrome, is a reaction of the skin to a variety of cancer-treating agents. The symptoms include swelling, pain, and peeling on the palms and soles of the feet. And loss of fingerprints.

I did a few cyberloops on capecitabine. The drug was most commonly used in the treatment of head, neck, breast, stomach, and colorectal cancers.

A long shot, but a possible lead. Ramsey could contact physicians and hospitals to ask if any young adult cancer patient had suddenly stopped showing up for chemotherapy. Cora Teague was reported to have health issues. He could also run the question past her family.

I was reaching for the desk phone when it rang. It was the first in a string of calls that would trigger a case of fire-breathing heartburn.

As usual, Strike spent no time on pleasantries.

"What the hell kind of turncoat move was that?"

"I beg your pardon?"

"Sharing my intel with an outsider."

"Deputy Ramsey is hardly an outsider."

"Is he you? Is he me?"

"His department has jurisdiction." Questionable.

"He's Avery County. We were in Burke."

"You suspect the remains in my possession are those of Cora Teague," I said firmly, but not all that patiently. "Should your theory prove true, that's Ramsey's watch."

"What did you tell him about the audio?"

"I'm glad you brought that up. Given that this is now a formal investigation, I must ask that you turn the recording over to me." A reach, but close enough.

"Not a chance in hell."

"Then I shall have Deputy Ramsey request a warrant."

There was a moment of flat silence. Then, "Foolish old woman. Somehow I've misplaced the damn thing."

I have a flash-point temper. Which I know I must keep in check. Instead of blasting Strike, I remained diplomatic.

"I thought the goal of websleuthing was to solve cold cases."

"Don't mean I want to share what I got with the world."

"Law enforcement is hardly the world."

"That what you call that yahoo?"

"Deputy Ramsey is hardly a yahoo."

"I'm sure a Harvard degree hangs on his wall."

The first tiny flicker sparked in my gut.

"Mrs. Strike. Are you familiar with the term 'obstruction of justice'?" Cool.

"I'll look it up."

"Why are you calling?"

"Wanted you to know I'm going back at the family."

"That's a bad idea."

"Maybe. But it's my idea."

"Don't—"

Three sharp beeps. She'd disconnected.

I kicked out at my desk. Hard enough that I had to remove my shoe to see what damage I'd done to my toe. Hurt like hell, but nothing was broken.

I was again reaching to punch digits on the landline when my mobile rang. After checking caller ID, I took a long, deep breath, clicked over to speaker, and laid the device on the blotter.

"Good morning, Mama."

"Good morning, sweet pea. I hope you got a good night's sleep. You sounded so tired when we talked."

"I did." I hadn't, but what was the point?

"Did you speak with your deputy? What's his name?"

"Ramsey. Not yet. I plan to call him shortly."

"Have you examined your hand bones?"

"I have. They told me very little."

Mama waited a theatrical beat. Then, "There's more."

Hearing the familiar breathless note, I scanned the desktop for something to skim. "More?"

"I found another."

"Another what?"

"Lookout. For Brown Mountain."

"I would guess there are many."

"Well, you would be mistaken. No matter how deeply I dug, the same three came up again and again. And only those three."

"Really?"

"It's called Wiseman's View."

"Where is it?" Absently.

"Just south of Linville. In Avery County."

"Mm."

"Are you listening to me?"

"I am." I wasn't. I was perusing the table of contents in the latest *Journal of Forensic Sciences*.

Mama stopped talking. A test. The dead air grabbed my attention.

"What are you suggesting?"

"You must search."

"At Wiseman's View."

"Of course at Wiseman's View."

"For more bones."

"Really, Tempe. You're reputed to be excellent in your field. Must I spell everything out?"

"You're suggesting body parts might have been thrown from all three Brown Mountain overlooks."

"Hallelujah, let the light shine!"

"Mama, I—"

"What have you retrieved so far? Parts of a hand and parts of a torso?"

"Yes." I hadn't told her about the fingertips. Not sure why.

"Do they go together?"

"They could."

"But so far you have no limbs and no head."

"No." The tiny flicker was growing warmer and starting to spread.

"Correct me if I'm wrong, but a head might perhaps, just perhaps, prove useful in determining whose body parts are turning up?"

"Yes."

A sliver of a pause, then, "Will you at least discuss my theory with your deputy?"

The eagerness in her voice tore a hole in my heart. Mama had shown so little engagement lately. Her only joy seemed to come through vicarious involvement in my work. Through secondhand thrills.

Like Hazel Strike and her websleuthing pals?

"Sure, Mama," I said. "Good job."

"You'll keep me fully informed?"

"I will."

"Ciao."

"Ciao."

I blew out a breath. Debated. Was my mother's idea a harebrained notion? Or a solid investigative strategy? Run it past Larabee? Ramsey? Would either agree to another romp in the woods?

It was like Groundhog Day. Same reach to dial the landline. Same pause as my mobile rang. Sang. I'd yet to change the ringtone. Same quick check of caller ID.

Allan Fink.

Crap.

This time I didn't pick up. Or listen to the message. I knew what Allan wanted. Couldn't endure another lecture on fiscal responsibility at that moment.

My eyes dropped to the calendar blotter on the desktop. Thursday, the second of April. No sweat. Tomorrow I'd find everything Allan needed for the IRS.

The flicker was now a bonfire in my chest.

I pulled my purse from the drawer and dug out two Tums. Slapped them from my palm to my mouth. Chewed and swallowed.

Then Ramsey phoned.

"I tracked down the story," he said, no greeting. "But not the journalist. He's long gone. You were right. A group of kids from WCU stumbled across bones and called the department." He used the acronym for Western Carolina University. "Dozens of hiking trails crisscross the Lost Cove Cliffs area. Anyway, a deputy went out to collect what they had."

"What made the kids think the bones were human?"

"That was my question. You'll love this. They were anthro majors."

"What happened to the stuff?" Sorry, Mama.

"The coroner was on holiday. The sheriff back then hadn't a clue what to do with 'old bones,' as he viewed them; wasn't all that interested. The kids suggested sending them to their professor, who, it turned out, was a forensic anthropologist."

"Marlene Penny." I knew her through AAFS. Though far from brilliant, and well past seventy, she was ABFA board certified and reasonably competent.

I heard paper rustle. "Yeah, that's the one. I've got a copy of her report. Want me to read it?"

"Just the basics."

"She didn't exactly knock herself out. One page. A skeletal inventory lists a partial tibia, fibula, calcaneus, and talus." There was a beat as he dug for relevant facts. "The two tarsals were connected by dried-out tissue. The leg bones were separate."

"Any estimates as to age, sex, that sort of thing?"

"The bones were too fragmentary." Pause. "Most of each had been carried off by animals. But she thought everything came from one individual."

"And that individual was human?"

"She's definite on that."

"Where are the remains now?"

"Doesn't say."

I inhaled deeply. Exhaled. Then, "Got a few minutes?"

"Sure."

I told Ramsey about the audio recording. About websleuthing. About Hazel Strike's strange hostility toward him. Throughout, I could hear the rhythm of his breath hitting the receiver. Knew he was listening carefully.

When I'd finished, he asked, "Gunner's hand bones tell you anything?"

"They're consistent with the torso bones from Burke County."

"That's it?"

"That's it."

"And the fingertips?"

I told him about the missing prints. About chemotherapy-induced acral erythema. About the possibility that the victim had been a cancer patient undergoing treatment at a local hospital. About Cora Teague having left her nanny job, reportedly for health reasons.

Then I told him about Wiseman's View.

The line was quiet for so long I thought he'd hung up. I was about to speak when Ramsey made a suggestion. I agreed to his plan and we disconnected.

Using one hand to cradle my head, I placed the other on my fiery chest.

12

I managed to get out without a summons to Larabee's carpet. Metaphorically speaking, of course. Our offices have tile floors.

He phoned at four while I was shopping for groceries. A task I avoid until my pantry resembles a bunker in postwar Iraq. Or I'm out of cat food.

I considered ignoring his call. Decided I might as well face the inevitable.

"Where are you?" Larabee's tone was razor sharp.

"Sorry I missed you today." Cheery as Snap, Crackle, and Pop smiling up from my cart.

"Are you at the office?"

"The Harris Teeter on Providence Road. Need anything?"

Larabee ignored my offer. I could hear a lot of noise in the background. A thick hollowness suggested he was outside. "I've been at the airport all day and don't see myself breaking free anytime soon."

I froze, a can of peas halfway off the shelf. "What's up?"

"Some ass-bucket movie director backed into the tail rotor of a chopper while shooting a film."

"Decapitated?"

"That's being kind."

"He had permission to work on an active helo pad?"

"At Wilson Air Center, the part for the hoity-toity."

I'd been to Wilson, a facility for private and corporate flights. Sadly, not often enough. "Do you want me on scene?" Please say no.

"No. But I may need you tomorrow. The damage is extensive."

"I'm free all day."

"I'll do the autopsy first thing in the morning. Assuming we've finished tweezing the tarmac."

That didn't sound good. "Keep your chin up," I said.

"Down," he corrected. And was gone.

As I threw random items into my cart, the conversation replayed in my head. The upside: My trip to Burke County wasn't mentioned. The downside: Allan and the IRS were once again bumped.

Dinner that night was green chicken chili. Risky, given the state of my innards. But the recipe calls for five ingredients. My kind of cooking. Plus, I freeze the leftovers for future meals.

I ate while half watching the local news. A

perfectly coiffed anchor reported, with appropriate solemnity, the discovery of three bodies in a home in Shelby. Went sunny while announcing the approval of Presbyterian hospital as a Level II trauma center. Darkened again as she described the previous day's fatality at Wilson Air.

The screen cut to footage of the private terminal, undoubtedly shot from the far side of yellow police tape. I recognized Larabee and one of the MCME death investigators. The morgue van. The segment finished with the usual line about nondisclosure of the decedent's name pending notification of his family.

After clearing the dishes, I considered, for a heartbeat, returning to the mounds of paper spread across the dining room table. Decided instead to look more thoroughly into websleuthing. Strike's surliness on the mountain both annoyed and confused me. Wasn't the goal to clear unsolved cases?

First, I visited sites that explained websleuthing. I learned that, in one way, the pursuit is like geocaching. Participants are everywhere. The guy who fixes your muffler. The kid who bags your groceries. The old woman who sold you a latte in Rome. Or Riga. Or Rio. Anyone with a computer and curiosity can jump right in.

Then I went to the actual sites. Checked out blogs, newsgroup posts, chat room threads. The more I looped and read, the more uneasy I grew.

Many websleuths seemed straightforward, eager

in their desire to bring long-ago killers to justice, to match nameless remains with missing persons. Some were intelligent, their posts objective and on point. Wind. Vegasmom. Befound. Others, though equally earnest, were less cogent in their thinking. Or their prose. Crispie. Answerman. Despite the brainpower, or lack thereof, the majority came across as honest and resolute, committed to the free exchange of information.

I'm not a psychologist, but I also sensed a very different type of player. A type lugging a whole lot of baggage. A type bringing a mindset born of personal history, personal kinks.

Among this second group, some seemed bent on igniting discord while watching from the safety of online anonymity. Their comments and responses, often vicious, hinted at megalomania. At paranoia.

I understand the nature of Internet dialogue. There's no nuance, no tone. Just words on a screen. As with texting, messages can often be misinterpreted, leading to confusion, sometimes hurt. A portion of the heat in some debates, which was substantial, could be attributed to lack of clarity. But not all. Many posts seemed meant to goad, to incite acrimony.

It was also obvious that some were in the game not for justice but for glory. These players were cagey and guarded. Having accumulated vast files, they were loath to share their hard-won information, particularly with legitimate sites such as NamUs or the Doe

Network. A few exhibited a level of territoriality that was silverback in its ferocity.

And there was one element of the subculture that I found particularly disturbing. Websleuths could turn on each other like wolves at a carcass. Case in point: Todd Matthews.

Matthews was a veteran cybersleuth and a supporter of the Doe Network from its inception. When NamUs was born and Matthews hired on as its administrator, a cadre of former supporters viewed him as a defector and a sellout. The point is justice, they said, not a steady income.

After much mudslinging in both directions, the Doe Network accused Matthews of breach of confidentiality and failure to uphold administrative standards. In April 2011, the board voted to kick him out. He went, but not with a smile on his face.

The Doe Network wasn't alone in bickering over power and control. Cold Case Investigations, Porchlight International, CLUES—many sites had experienced their own melodramas. All the squabbling and name-calling left me feeling like I'd snooped into the texts of a gaggle of junior high divas.

At nine-thirty, I took a break. Waiting for the kettle to boil, I decided to change tack. During my earlier visit to CLUES to learn about Cora Teague, I'd discovered that Hazel Strike used the ID luckyloo. I decided to follow threads in which luckyloo had engaged.

And found a feud that made all others pale in

comparison. The barbs and accusations flying between luckyloo and someone posting as WendellC, though far from poetic, were clear in their meaning. The two couldn't stand each other.

Without knowing his actual name, I learned that WendellC was a legend among websleuthers. He'd scored many solves, but one in particular had boosted his status to superstar. I followed a link to a story chronicling the case.

In 1984, the partial skeleton of a teenage girl was found wrapped in a quilt in a farm field in Cuyahoga County, outside Cleveland, Ohio. A complete skull was recovered, allowing a facial reconstruction. In time the image, barely more than a sketch, appeared on websites across the cyberuniverse.

Over the decades, scores poked and prodded and dug, but no match to a missing person was ever found. The victim came to be known as Quilt Girl.

Now and then stories ran in the local Ohio papers. In 2004, on the twentieth anniversary of the skeleton's discovery, the case was featured on *America's Most Wanted*, along with the original facial reconstruction. Tips flooded in. None panned out.

In 2007, more than two decades after Quilt Girl turned up among the soybeans, WendellC read an article in *True Sleuth* magazine. The piece revisited the case of Annette Wyant, an eighteen-year-old freshman who'd disappeared from Oberlin College in 1979. A photo accompanied the story, along with an age-progressed image suggesting Wyant's appearance at age forty-eight.

WendellC was familiar with the facial reconstruction done on Quilt Girl. Annette Wyant's picture looked nothing like it, thus the reason no link had ever been suggested. But WendellC noted one striking fact. Oberlin College was less than forty miles from the farm where Quilt Girl had been found. He phoned the Cuyahoga County medical examiner and requested an autopsy photo showing close-ups of the skull. Reluctantly, the current ME complied.

Upon viewing the image, WendellC noted another striking fact. Annette Wyant and Quilt Girl both had a marked overbite, a feature not reflected in the facial reconstruction. He again phoned the ME, stating his belief that the skeleton was that of the missing student.

Dental records were dug from a file archived by long-departed personnel. Twenty-three years after her discovery, Quilt Girl went home to her family.

I googled, found articles on the disappearance, more recent ones on the identification. Annette Wyant was buried with little fanfare in her hometown of Plainfield, Illinois. The *Chicago Tribune* ran a small story. The Cleveland *Plain Dealer*. In both, a middle-aged woman was pictured standing graveside. Beside her was a tall, craggy man in an ill-fitting suit. A caption identified the woman as Wyant's sister, the man as Wendell Clyde of Huntersville, North Carolina.

No arrest was ever made. From experience, I guessed

Wyant's cause of death remained "undetermined."

Intrigued, I returned to the websleuthing sites.

In discussion after discussion, fellow amateurs praised WendellC's brilliance and perseverance. Congratulations poured in from around the globe.

Hazel Strike was furious and did not mince words. In post after post, luckyloo called WendellC a backstabbing snake. A pissant charlatan. A scumbucket fraud. Strike claimed she and Clyde had worked as a team. Accused him of taking credit for joint discoveries. WendellC was equally vitriolic in his responses.

I'd have found the dispute amusing were it not for the virulent tone. I lasted another half hour. Then, repulsed by the juvenile nature of the spat, I went to bed.

I spent Friday up to my elbows in brain tissue and bloody bone fragments.

The helicopter victim was a thirty-two-year-old man named Connolly Sanford. His first stint as a director would be his last. And his funeral would definitely be closed casket.

While Larabee autopsied Sanford's body, I examined what remained of his head. Which wasn't much. Other than some portions of right parietal and occipital, the largest chunk recovered was the size of an ear. Both of which I had.

ID wasn't in question, since an entire film crew

had witnessed the event. Nor was manner of death. Larabee just wanted confirmation that the cranial trauma was entirely the work of the chopper.

Larabee was still at it when I finished at three. After cleaning up and changing from scrubs, I phoned Marlene Penny at WCU to ask about the Lost Cove Cliffs bones. Got rolled to voice mail. Left a message asking that she call me.

Before leaving, I reported to Larabee that I'd found no hidden bullets, no poisoned darts, nothing to suggest any villains save the chopper blade and very bad footwork. He thanked me, looking exhausted. I wished him a good weekend, then bolted before he could remember his annoyance over the Burke County caper. Or ask how I intended to follow up.

Ramsey called while I was brushing my teeth. I confirmed that I was good to go as planned.

I thought about phoning Ryan. Talking to him always boosted my spirits. Always helped me rearrange my thoughts into more productive patterns. Almost always. At that moment I hadn't the energy to deflect talk of cohabitation. Or vows. Instead, I turned off my ringer.

My body's exhaustion quickly overwhelmed my mind's agitation. Sleep descended like a thick wool blanket.

A good thing. The next day lasted about three months.

13

Birdie, up before the alarm, persuaded me to wake by chewing my hair.

The cat feigned starvation, so we moved directly to breakfast. As he crunched Science Diet, I ate a bagel with cream cheese and downed high test strong enough to hold the spoon upright.

Satiated, Bird scouted locales for his first morning nap. I filled a thermos with the remaining coffee, then made sandwiches and snugged them into my pack, all the while marveling at the presence of salami and cheese in the fridge. I had zero recall of buying either.

As I prepped, opposing feelings vied inside me. It was Saturday. Duke was playing Carolina in the NCAA final four, and I wanted to stay home, order pizza, and watch the game. I wanted to determine the identity of ME229-13.

Back in my room, I checked the weather forecast on my mobile. Charlotte was looking at sunny skies and a max of forty-five degrees. An icon indicated two missed calls. I clicked over.

Ryan had phoned but left no message. The familiar nagging guilt knocked softly. I refused it entry.

Hazel Strike had phoned. She asked that I call her back.

Knowing it would be colder at higher elevations, I dressed in jeans, a long-sleeved tee, wool socks, and field boots. Grabbing an extra sweater, I jammed the phone into my pocket and clumped downstairs. A moment gathering outerwear and my backpack, then I set off. It was 6:45 A.M.

I drove I-85 south to Gastonia, then 321 north to Hickory and onto I-40 west. The skyscrapers of the city, then the cookie cutter homes and strip malls of the burbs, slid by in the darkness around me. I paid no attention. My thoughts were on Mama. And Ramsey. And a place high in the mountains I'd never seen.

By the time I reached Morganton, the world beyond my windshield was a Monet canvas of muted ambers and greens. Utility poles, trees, and fence posts threw long fun-house shadows across the road and the fields stretching from each shoulder.

I rode north on 181 to Jonas Ridge, then cut left and looped back southwest on NC 183. Winding through the Pisgah National Forest for the second time in a week, I passed only four other vehicles. I counted.

Eventually I spotted a sign pointing the way to Wiseman's View. I turned onto Route 1238, a forest service access road, gravel and barely wide enough for one car. I was just a few miles from the tiny community of Linville Falls.

After four miles of sharp turns and steep changes in gradient, which I can't say I enjoyed, a second sign appeared among the foliage. I turned in to a paved parking area, wondering how many automotive parts and dental restorations had rattled loose.

Surprisingly, several cars were present—a red Camry, a pickup with a crack running the windshield in the shape of Cape Cod, a silver Audi A3, a black SUV. The sheriff's department logo on the SUV told me Ramsey and Gunner had already arrived. I got out and looked around. Neither deputy nor dog was in sight.

The air was brittle with early morning chill. Not the damp Quebec cold that seizes your breath and numbs your face in seconds. But cold enough. And a biting breeze was swirling through the mountains around me.

I slipped into my jacket, then tucked the sweater, cap, and gloves into my pack. After taking my kit from the trunk, I stood a moment to listen.

And heard a symphony of tiny noises. The *tic-tic-tic* of my car's cooling engine. The steady in and out of my own breathing. The scratch of branches overhead.

I glanced up. The wind was playing hell with a thrush working hard at construction.

Wishing the bird luck, I crossed to an opening in

the trees beyond the SUV. It led to a walkway, narrow and, for the moment, paved with crumbling asphalt. The terrain plunged steeply beyond a rusty guardrail contouring its right side. Within yards, the trail cut left, hugging the mountain, and out of sight.

I pride myself on being unflappable. Mostly it's true. But, full disclosure, one thing flaps me: unprotected heights. It's not the fall I fear, it's the hard landing.

Heart beating a little too fast, I adjusted the pack's shoulder straps, tightened my grip on the kit, and stepped onto the trailhead. The mixed pine and deciduous forest was so thick it was like crossing into a trompe l'œil mural built of shadow and light. From far below came the sound of energetic water.

I advanced, boot heels scraping loud in the crisp morning air. Here and there, a slash of sunlight strobed to the asphalt and I caught glimpses of the steep drop-off to my right.

Fifty yards ahead I heard footsteps and stopped. In seconds a couple appeared walking single file toward me. She strode confidently, gaze bouncing all around. He moved cautiously, eyes straight ahead. I pressed my back to the cliff face to let them pass.

As the sound of their movement receded, I listened again. Nothing but the muted rush of water.

Another hundred yards, and the walkway ended at a rock outcropping surrounded by the same rusty guardrail. Pulpits had been constructed on two sides, oriented toward points of interest. Four people stood near the one facing west, three gathered close, one off by himself. The three had done their shopping at L.L.Bean. The loner looked like a T. rex dressed for a hike.

Ramsey was elbow-leaning the rail opposite, Gunner at his side.

"Good morning, Carolina!" I called out in a muted Robin Williams DJ voice, the bravado meant mostly to steady my own nerves.

The dog's ears shot up, then, purple tongue dangling, he trotted forward to meet me. I patted his head.

The deputy watched my approach for a few seconds, then his head swiveled back to the vista he'd been admiring. For a moment we both gazed in silence.

"We're looking east toward Linville Gorge."

"Impressive," I said.

"One of the deepest canyons in the eastern U.S. And one of the most rugged. Know why it's here?"

I shook my head.

"The Linville River starts high up on Grandfather Mountain, plunges two thousand feet in just twelve miles before leveling out in the Catawba Valley. All that pounding water carved right through the rock."

"How far are we above the river?"

"Roughly fifteen hundred feet, mostly straight down." A beat, then, "Ever hear of William and John Linville?"

"No."

"Father and son explorers. In 1766 the Cherokee took exception to their being here and scalped them both."

"Ouch."

The corners of Ramsey's mouth lifted ever so slightly. "Got their name onto a busload of landmarks."

It was true. In addition to the gorge and river, caverns, a waterfall, a wilderness area, and several towns bore the name Linville.

"Still a tough way to get press," I said.

Again, Ramsey may have grinned. Or not. He raised an arm and gestured, fingers straight, palm sideways. "Beyond the gorge is Jonas Ridge." His hand did little chops as he named a series of rock formations. "Sitting Bear, Hawksbill, Table Rock, the Chimneys. The area's a labyrinth of hiking trails."

"Good word, labyrinth," I said.

He did grin at that. Below the knit cap, drawn low to his brows, his face performed its rearranging act. Oh, boy.

"Where's Brown Mountain?"

"See that low peak in the distance, beyond the ridge?"

I nodded.

"That's her. Maybe eight miles off."

"Where does the light show take place?"

"Most tourists point their cameras there." He indicated the mountainside opposite.

"Think they're real?"

"I've seen them." At my look of surprise, "Kind of a flickering, like people waving flashlights around in the trees."

"What's your theory?"

"Some say swamp gas."

"Swamp gas never spontaneously ignites in nature."

"Agreed. It takes a specific mix of chemicals. Researchers have created it in labs. They say it happens with a pop followed by a blue-green flame."

"No slow burn."

"Nope."

The gaggle behind us moved our way and took up positions along the rail. The loner trailed the others, but again stayed apart.

"Cherokee widows?" I asked.

"So you know the local lore."

"Very little."

"Problem is the ladies are supposed to wander the sky, not the land. But the lights aren't refracted above the ridge, they're down in the trees." As though my suggestion had been serious. "And I doubt the Cherokee had lantern technology."

"Carrying torches for their dead hubbies?"

Ramsey ignored the pun. Or didn't get it. "I've done some looking. Haven't come across a single mention of such a legend in Cherokee writings. Only references I've found are in literature concerning the lights. Doesn't mean native stories don't exist. Just means I didn't find them."

"Reflections of moonshine stills?" I threw out the only other theory I knew.

"You think illegal moonshiners are going to set up ops right there among the hikers and the rock climbers, in plain view of the state's most popular overlook?"

"In the heart of the labyrinth." Jesus. Was I flirting?

Ramsey straightened.

"But cause doesn't matter. What *may* matter is that a lot of folks believe the lights are real, and that they're paranormal or mystical or what have you."

"That the mountain is haunted."

"In a sense." Ramsey's jaw tightened, relaxed. "A few believe they're the work of the devil."

It took a moment. Then the implication hit. "Are you suggesting that's the reason human body parts might have been tossed from these overlooks? Devil worship?"

"Demons? Aliens? Nymphs? Sprites? Who knows? These mountains have more than their share of loons."

I said nothing.

"Sound crazy?" Ramsey asked.

"I've heard crazier."

Down the rail, the three tourists continued pointing and jabbering. The loner had drifted closer to us. He wasn't admiring the view. He stood motionless, eyes down, as though mentally plotting his route.

Ramsey straightened. "Crazy or not, no one did any tossing from here."

"I agree. Too populated. And too hard to access."

"Let's roll."

"Where?"

"The place I'd choose to off-load a body."

Ramsey strode toward the walkway, Gunner trotting at his heels, leaving me no choice but to follow. When I reached the parking area, the canine was in back, the deputy at the wheel of the SUV. The passenger and rear doors stood wide. Subtle.

I dumped my gear in back and climbed in. After pulling from the lot, Ramsey surprised me by continuing to talk.

"What do you know about the Teagues?"

"Not much." I told him what I'd learned from Hazel Strike. John. Fatima. Five kids. No MP report on Cora, the second youngest, last seen by an anonymous poster on the websleuth site CLUES.net three and a half years earlier.

"I did some asking around." Ramsey turned onto 1238, and we began bumping and lurching south along the ridgeline. "Teagues belong to some oddball Pentecostal group. Congregation has maybe a hundred members."

"What's it called?"

"Church of Jesus Lord Holiness."

"Snake handlers?"

I referred to the holiness movement, founded by George Went Hensley back in 1910. Members handle venomous snakes, drink poison, and, if successful in hooking up with the Holy Ghost, speak in tongues.

Holiness churches are big in Appalachia, including the mountains of North Carolina.

Ramsey shrugged. "I've no idea the theology. All I know is they keep to themselves."

"If they're holiness, they wouldn't be crazy about Satan," I said.

"Don't figure they would." Sun slanted across Ramsey's face, lighting his nose and deepening the lines and creases cornering his eyes and mouth. "I swung by the Teague place."

That surprised me. "Were they cooperative?"

"I wasn't invited in for biscuits, if that's what you mean. Talked to John through the screen door."

"What was your impression?"

"Intense." He thought a moment. "Belligerent."

"Abusive?"

"Possibly."

"And the mother?"

"Never saw her."

"What did John say about Cora?"

"She left with a man. Both are sinners. Both will burn in hell. Get off my property or I'll bust your ass."

"Think he's telling the truth?"

"About busting my ass?"

"About Cora."

"The guy's big into God and not what you'd call forgiving."

Ramsey pulled to the shoulder and cut the ignition. I looked around. Saw nothing but the same mix of trees, the same unpaved road we'd been navigating for the past ten minutes.

After pocketing the keys, Ramsey draped one arm on the wheel and turned sideways toward me. "Except for one thing."

I couldn't interpret Ramsey's expression. But his voice had a hardness that hadn't been there before. I waited.

"At your suggestion, I dropped by Cannon Memorial yesterday to ask about dropout chemo patients." Ramsey referred to the Charles A. Cannon, Jr., Memorial Hospital in Linville. "Got zip. But when I floated the name Cora Teague, one doc suggested I take a look at the death of the younger brother."

"Eli died when he was twelve."

Ramsey gave me an odd look. "Right."

"Cause?"

"Acute traumatic subdural hematoma. Parents said he fell down the basement stairs."

"But this doctor had reservations?"

"He was working the ER back then. Remembers the kid. Couldn't discuss details because of confidentiality, you know the drill. But he's always felt that something was off."

"Meaning the injury didn't tally with the parents' version of events?"

Ramsey's fingers tightened on the wheel. He nodded.

I heard the voice of a terrified girl on a recording.

Sensed the dark specter of Brown Mountain outside my window.

"You're thinking zealot father. Rebellious daughter." My voice sounded hushed in the quiet interior of the SUV. "Violent death of a younger sibling."

"Could be a deadly trifecta," he said.

14

"Where are we?" I asked.

Ramsey cocked his chin toward the trees ahead and to the left. "See that gap?"

"Mm." I didn't.

"It's the head of a trail leading down into the gorge. They're all named. Pine Gap. Bynum Bluff. Babel Tower. This one's called Devil's Tail. Used to be popular with advanced hikers."

"Used to be?"

"The park service stopped maintaining it after a storm knocked out the lower portion." Ramsey's eyes met mine. "Devil's Tail's off the websites now, so only the locals know it exists."

I nodded, indicating I caught his meaning.

"Ready?"

"Bring my gear?" I asked.

"First, let's see what we see. Follow Gunner's nose."

Hearing his name, the dog rose and wagged his

tail once. Ramsey and I got out. When the rear door opened, Gunner stepped forth with that refined grace I had come to admire.

"Watch your footing," Ramsey warned.

Oh, yeah.

Ramsey's "gap" was little more than a barely perceptible thinning of the old-growth forest. With Gunner in the lead, we picked our way through pines and hardwoods on a narrow scar of soil covered with ivy and creepers. Bursts of sunlight through the bare-branch and pine-needle canopy created an almost dizzying effect. Invisible spiderwebs feathered my face, and fallen branches threatened to strafe my ankles. But not for long. Ten yards from the road, the earth dropped away.

No guardrail. No reassuring park service signs. Just open sky and weathered rock ancient as the planet.

A pump of adrenaline set my nerves humming. Maybe the sheer drop-off. Maybe the fact that Ramsey was right. The spot was deserted and easily reached. An object thrown from it might never be found.

As I held back, Ramsey and Gunner trotted straight to what looked like the end of the universe. One deep calming breath. Then, moving cautiously, I joined them and braced a boot on a half-exposed boulder at the rim of the precipice.

"It's a long way down." Ramsey spoke without looking at me.

Heart rate in the stratosphere, I arm-wrapped a

maple, planted both feet, and leaned forward. Below, I could see snatches of what remained of the Devil's Tail, descending sharply among the trees. A stretch of forest, then the trail reappeared at a shallow depression bordered by a small rocky ledge. The arrangement reminded me of the formation at the Burke County site.

But several things differed. This ledge was even more heavily wooded. On it appeared to be a crude shack. Beyond it and just below, the ground pooched out again, like a third stair step, then plunged as a naked cliff face straight into the gorge.

I looked at Ramsey. He was studying Gunner. The dog was tense. Ears back, head low, eyes fixed on the shack.

"What is that?" I asked.

"Probably an abandoned park service shed."

"It has Gunner's attention."

"It does."

"Could he catch a scent from this far away?"

"He's done it before."

"Is it possible for us to get down there?"

"The path from here to the first outcrop is in pretty good shape."

I must have looked skeptical.

"How about I check out what's tweaking Gunner," Ramsey said. "Anything suspicious, I'll report back."

"Not a chance." Sounding monumentally more confident than I felt.

"Okay, then. Let's do it."

Ramsey whistled once, short and shrill. The dog bounded to his right, vanished, and, seconds later, reappeared on the Devil's Tail. A flash of brown, then he was gone.

Ramsey took the lead. I followed, eyes glued to the ground.

The deputy's "pretty good" translated to steep and treacherous. Lurching from tree trunk to tree trunk, I picked my way downward as though traversing a minefield. Now and then a boot skidded, sending pebbles and clumps of mud cascading before me.

As I progressed, my brain logged information. The scent of pine. A faint trace of skunk. Lichens. Black lace branches overhead. A delicate chain of silver bell at my feet.

Birds cawed complicated grievances. Far below, a river carved igneous rock. At one point I heard a flurry in the underbrush followed by a truncated shriek. I paused, breaths puffing from my mouth like tiny fog clouds. I pictured a hapless rabbit or squirrel, eyes already filming, fur darkening with blood.

My mind flashed possible predators. A copperhead. A timber rattler.

Ignoring my overly gruesome imagination, I continued for what seemed another five miles. Actually, ten more yards and the gradient leveled off.

Gunner was on his belly, gaze fixed on one corner of the shed. Ramsey was beside him, jacket unzipped, elbow flexed, hand poised at his hip. Shadows marbled his face like deep purple bruises.

For one lunatic moment I felt a chill, as though some feral presence inhabited the dark stained-glass world we'd invaded.

Shake it off, Brennan.

I crossed to Ramsey. Up close I could see that the shed was barely managing to hold together. The roof was tin, each sheet rusted and pulling free from the nails meant to secure it. The walls were crude pine planks, probably homemade and quickly slapped together. Here and there a board had fallen free, or loosened at one end to drop to an unworkable angle.

Wordlessly, Ramsey pulled a Maglite from his belt and gestured me behind him.

Really? I questioned with lifted palms and brows.

"Another reason the trail's unused is the hefty black bear population."

"Right." Moving to Ramsey's back.

"I've spotted no scat. Still, it's wise to avoid surprises."

"What about Gunner?" For some reason I felt compelled to whisper.

"What about him?"

"He's okay with bears?"

"He ignores them, they return the courtesy."

Without warning, Ramsey banged the tin with his torch. Causing me to jump.

No hibernating hulk jerked awake with a snort. No enraged mama *Ursus* charged out to confront us.

"Yo!" Ramsey shouted.

Silence.

Satisfied that no one was home, Ramsey rounded the corner of the shed. With me beside him, he pushed with his free hand, and the door swung on its hinges. We both craned forward.

The shed's interior was a tangle of shadows. Where the curling tin and errant boards had created gaps, faint gray slashes crisscrossed at disparate angles.

Ramsey thumbed the switch, raised the flashlight to shoulder level, and we stepped across the threshold. The air was cold and dank. As my eyes adjusted to the darkness, my nose took in earth and damp wood and rotting vegetation.

Ramsey swept his light slowly and methodically. Particles of dust twirled and danced in the bright white beam.

Wooden shelving lined the wall directly ahead. I noted a roll of chain linking, several saws, pruning shears, a long-handled ax, a stack of park service signs, all rusty and coated with grime. On and among the tools lay the desiccated remains of generations of spiders and insects.

The beam crawled on, probing. Found a rake and shovel leaning against the north wall. A ladder at its base.

"Sure enough," Ramsey said, perhaps to me. "Park service storage."

Every angle in the place was thick with cobwebs. One corner held a crumbling bird's nest. Below it, white rivulets streaked the walls and dried twigs scattered the floor.

"Looks like no one's been in here for a while," I said.

"Looks that way."

Ramsey ran the beam across the floorboards.

"Zero evidence of trespass."

I referred to the absence of the detritus typically found in abandoned dwellings: cigarette butts, fast-food wrappers, empty cans and plastic bottles, used condoms. The reek of human feces and piss.

"None," Ramsey said.

"That strike you as odd?"

"Can't imagine the locals slogging down to pilfer old tools. Too much sweat hauling the junk back up the mountain."

"Kids looking for a place to hang out?"

"Hang out?"

"Drink beer. Smoke weed." Jesus. Was this guy clueless?

"Same answer. There are much easier places to do the do."

Do the do?

"What about outsiders?" I asked.

"The trail hasn't been posted online or in park service brochures for years."

"You and I spotted the shed from above."

"We were looking."

"You don't find it surprising that no hikers, climbers, hunters, bird-watchers, bat counters, mushroom collectors, or stargazers ever came here to squat?" A bit too sharp.

Not bothering to answer, Ramsey did another round with the torch. He was right, of course. Still, it bothered me. It's basic physics. When a space is devoid of matter and energy, something moves in to fill the vacuum. In the case of abandoned structures, that something is inevitably Homo sapiens.

An icy gust sliced through a crack and whirled in an eddy around me. I zipped my jacket to my chin and jammed my hands in my pockets, wondering if I was on the dumbest wild-goose chase in history.

Or was the chill I felt triggered by forces other than wind?

"Come on." One last sweep, then Ramsey clicked off the flash. "There's nothing here."

We were moving toward the door when we heard a bark. Just one. Loud and firm.

Ramsey paused, a sickly slash of gray turning his face cadaveric. Then, "Gunner's got a hit."

Eyes scanning three-sixty, we hurried from the shed. Gunner was no longer at its corner.

"Where are you, boy?" Ramsey called out.

The dog gave another solitary yelp, muffled by the trees. He was below us and off to the right.

We hurried to the edge and peered out into the gorge. Ramsey's right arm was again cocked and ready for action.

My eyes registered a few thousand shades of brown, here and there flashes of a trail I wouldn't have tried when decades younger and Crank-Up-the-*Enola Gay* drunk.

"There." Ramsey pointed downslope. "On the ground. Do you see that?"

I sight-lined his finger to a giant pickup-sticks jumble of trees. At first I saw nothing but a tangle of dead trunks and branches.

Then I spotted Gunner, down, snout pointed at a slash of blue.

"What is that?" Squinting and shielding my eyes.

"Gunner's question, precisely."

An image popped from some corner of my mind. Recent intake. I pushed it aside for later consideration.

"Can we get to it?" I asked.

"Follow me." Ramsey's voice had a tense edge. "Lean your weight toward the mountain and place your feet and hands as I do."

Ramsey eased off the ledge onto what remained of the trail and began inching downward, body paralleling the slope. I followed, heart going like mad.

This third step down of the Devil's Tail was like the first two on steroids. Intent on mimicking Ramsey's every handhold and breath, I didn't think about the return trip.

A lot of panting, sweating, and, on my part, cursing, and we finally maneuvered the last few feet. Gunner flicked us a one-second glance, then refocused on the scent that had tickled his olfactory lobes.

The dog was staring at a swatch of blue plastic impaled on a stub of pine branch wind-whittled to a shiv-like point. I leaned down to inspect it. Saw a segment of rim and a small round hole that had once held a handle.

"Looks like part of a bucket." Trying not to sound disappointed.

"That's not why he alerted," Ramsey said.

I straightened to look at the dog. Gunner was staring at a rock lying slightly downslope, wedged among the upended roots of a long-dead hardwood. His eyes, huge and eager, showed far too much white.

I edged closer to Gunner's find and squatted.

The thing was rocklike, but not a rock. Though solid and gray, its sides were symmetrically curved, its top and bottom flat.

I reached out and touched one flat surface. It felt rough and gritty. Using two hands, I flipped the object. Though heavy, its weight was much less than I'd expected.

Seeing the down side clarified the lack of poundage.

I stared, puzzled.

Then, slowly, an improbable possibility shaped up in my mind.

I dropped to my knees and repositioned myself for a different view.

Barely breathing, I raised my gaze to the impaled fragment of bucket.

No.

My mind rejected the notion.

Yes.

A feeling cold as a grave washed through me.

15

"It's concrete." My heart was thudding, fast and hard.

Ramsey just looked at me.

"Concrete was added to the contents of the bucket and allowed to set. The bucket was thrown from the trailhead, intended for the gorge. On the way down it hit the shed and cracked."

I looked to see if Ramsey was with me. He was.

"When the bucket landed here and impaled on the pine, already damaged, the plastic burst and the hardened concrete rolled free."

"How do you know the bucket hit the shed?" With nothing at all in his voice.

"Gunner alerted at the southeast corner. There are blue flecks embedded in the boards. I noticed them earlier, but it meant nothing until now."

Ramsey thought about that. "Why would concrete and plastic interest a cadaver dog?"

"They wouldn't." I gestured at what had been

the down side of the bucket-shaped mass. "Take a look."

Ramsey dropped to a knee beside me. For a very long moment, he studied the concrete. Then, "The center's hollowed out."

"Yes."

"In the shape of a head."

"Half a head."

"The aforementioned bucket contents."

"Yes."

"Someone put a severed head in a bucket, added concrete, then tossed the works into the gorge," he summarized tonelessly.

I nodded, though he was still looking down.

"So where's the head?"

"The concrete popped out of the bucket, somehow split down the middle. Maybe water got into a crack then froze. Whatever. Once exposed to the elements, the head began to go south. Scavengers smelled the decomp and organized a picnic."

Ramsey's brows dipped, but he voiced no disapproval of my turn of phrase. "Gunner's picking up on that."

"The concrete may retain traces of organic material. Skin, hair, blood." Brains. I left that out.

"Which could yield DNA?" Suddenly meeting my eyes.

I waggled a hand. Maybe yes, maybe no.

Ramsey's face remained impassive but I could see

the gears meshing behind his eyes. "The head left a negative impression."

"Yes. It created a mold."

"Like the ones used to make death masks."

"Similar concept."

"Using the mold you can create a three-dimensional cast of the victim's head and face." Thinking it through aloud. "A bust."

"I can try. But this is only the right half." I indicated the concrete, then the forest around us. "The left half's somewhere out there."

"Well, then." Ramsey rose to scan the mountainside. "We sure as hell need to find it."

I stood, knees protesting the imposition. Brushed dirt from my hands and jeans.

Almost smiled.

So Deputy Do-Right could cuss after all.

Without warning, something lifted the tiny hairs on my arms and neck. At first, not so much a noise as an anomaly in the air. I paused, listening.

Before I could identify what had tripped the alarm in my neurons, a force blasted me sideways onto the ground. Breath exploded from me, and my lungs knotted into spasm.

As I struggled for air that wouldn't come, sound gathered into a soft rumble that grew in volume. Added thrashing, cracking, the snapping of dry branches.

Sweet Jesus!

Something big was skidding and jumping directly toward us! Drawing my knees to my chest, I tucked my chin and threw my arms over my head.

None too soon. In seconds, a heavy mass struck the pile of dead trees at my back. Soil and bark spit upward, then showered down. I heard a whoosh, a thud, then the object continued thundering downhill.

Stomach in free fall, I stayed fetal, pulse banging in my ears.

"You okay?" Close to my ear, yet a million miles off.

I couldn't move. Couldn't breathe.

Again the voice. Anxious.

Ten wild heartbeats, then my lungs relaxed a micron.

I inhaled. Inhaled again, deeper.

The oxygen helped. The trembling in my limbs began to subside.

"Were you hit?"

Still, I didn't trust my voice to answer.

Lowering my arms, I pushed to all fours and ran a wrist over my mouth. Spit soil and muck.

"Are you hurt?"

I shook my head, mind still numbed by panic.

"You're sure?"

"Yeah."

I glanced sideways. Ramsey was up on his knees, face filigreed with shadow from the branches above. Dirt and dead flora decorated his jacket and cap.

"What the hell?" Rotating to my bum.

"I'm guessing a rock. Which is now at the bottom of the gorge."

"How?"

Before Ramsey could answer, Gunner made his entrance.

"And where were you, chicken balls?" Still rattled, I fell back on humor.

The dog cocked his head but didn't reply.

Ramsey got to his feet and extended a hand. I took it and pulled myself up. Tested my legs. Reasonably steady.

"You good to climb?" Ramsey looked genuinely concerned.

I nodded. Not sure that I was.

"Yeah?"

"Yeah." I jabbed a thumb at the bucket fragments and concrete. "What about—?"

"I've got it."

Our ascent took close to forty minutes. Very tentative. Very cautious. You can imagine. I'll skip the details. Once topside, Ramsey drove until we both had signal.

Reconnected with the wonders of wireless communication, I phoned the MCME. Took three tries. Still stoked on adrenaline, I kept fumbling the keys.

Larabee bounced me, as expected, to the chief ME in Raleigh. The directive was the same as before. Collect any small stuff and take it to Charlotte. If there's big stuff, call for a van.

While we were talking, an incoming call lit up the screen. I recognized the number. Hazel Strike. I ignored her.

Ramsey phoned his boss. Briefed him on the bucket and concrete. And the rock.

The sheriff, Kermit Firth, unlike his predecessor, was a certified criminal investigator. Firth said he'd give a courtesy heads-up to Burke County but felt his department could best handle the situation. The Avery rescue squad would search the mountain, and Avery techs would handle any evidence recovered.

Listening to Ramsey lay out the plan, I sensed a wee bit of jurisdictional rivalry. Wasn't sure, didn't care.

By the time we returned to the Devil's Tail, my stomach had settled and was voicing serious complaint. I offered to share my sandwiches and coffee. Ramsey accepted and threw in Twix bars.

We moved to the trailhead, where we could look down on the shed. Though far too much time had passed to worry about scene preservation, cop instincts die hard.

We ate in silence, eyes roving the shadowy little ledge below. The gorge. The distant mountains in their smokelike mist. Gunner stayed by Ramsey, not begging, just looking hopeful and alert.

I was jamming wrappers into my pack, idly

skimming my gaze over my surroundings, when my hand froze.

"Jesus." On a sharp intake of air.

I scrambled to my feet and crossed to the point on the promontory's edge where Ramsey and I had stood early that morning. The boulder on which I'd braced my boot was gone. In its place was a gash in the earth, dark and moist, like a fresh wound on the edge of a lip.

Deep gouges marred the walls of the gash. Freshly turned soil littered its perimeter.

Hearing Ramsey approach behind me, I stepped sideways. He studied the hole, the scoring, the fresh sprinkling of mud. When his eyes met mine they were dark with anger.

"Someone put some effort into dislodging that baby."

"Yes."

"Not likely a coincidence that we were downslope."

"No."

"That thing could have killed—"

Ramsey's thought was interrupted by the hum of engines. We both spun toward the road. The deputy signaled to his dog with a slap to the thigh. Gunner joined us and we moved into the shadow of the trees.

The hum grew louder, cut off abruptly. Doors thunked. Voices sounded.

We waited.

In minutes, six people appeared lugging a lot of

equipment. Four wore jackets identifying them as rescue squad members. Two were in civvies. With them were a German shepherd and some sort of Border collie mix. Gunner eyed the dogs with suspicion but stayed with us as we stepped out into the open.

Two of the jacketed guys weighed maybe a hundred pounds bundled. One was in his late twenties, the perpetual frat-boy type. The other was older, with buzz-cut hair and one pierced ear. The third was fair and blond and, I suspected, an accomplished blusher. The female jacket wearer had spent a lot of time at the gym. Big eyes, greasy bangs, not yet on a first-name basis with thirty.

Both crime scene techs were short and wiry and, when eventually zipped into their hooded Tyvek suits, difficult to distinguish.

There wasn't a smile in the lot. Not hard to guess the source of their displeasure. They'd been dragged from their big screens and the basketball matchup of the century.

As the squad strapped on complicated gear involving belts and ropes, I apologized for taking everyone away from the game. They were not quite surly but close.

I showed them the concrete mold and the bucket, and described the shed. Explained the body parts found at the other two overlooks, and the theory that the victim, whose name I withheld, might be a resident of Avery County.

I suggested a possible postmortem interval of three to four years, and warned that any remains would be fragmentary. No one made the mistake of asking why, after such a lengthy PMI, the hunt was so urgent it had to be today.

By two-thirty, the searchers were over the side, Ramsey and Gunner included. Turned out the deputy was AMGA certified. American Mountain Guides Association.

At Ramsey's suggestion, I stayed at the trailhead with the CSU techs and a handheld radio. Made sense. I have zero climbing skills, but am kick-ass at crime scene recovery.

We took photos of the hollow vacated by the boulder, then mixed a batch of dental stone and poured a cast of the gouges left in the mud. Maybe useful if a suspect tool was recovered, maybe not. My best guess was crowbar, but that was reaching.

While the stone dried, the techs moved down to the shed. They'd dust for prints, collect the bucket fragments, shoot video and pics. No one was optimistic.

Once I'd bagged the cast stone, I sat with my knees up and my back against a tree. In less than an hour the techs returned, dropped at a pine five yards off, and alternated between smoking and chatting in low tones while the rescue squad continued their work below.

• • •

All afternoon I listened to voices floating up from the gorge. Shouted questions and instructions, responses, most too muffled to make out the words.

I'm not very good at staying on the sidelines. I get edgy and find it hard to sit still. Especially when the action is right at my feet.

I kept rising to pace. Pointlessly testing the radio. Thinking. About taxes and the IRS. About Mama and cancer. About the actual origin of Opie Taylor's name.

Mostly, about Ryan and his impossible proposition.

I'd played the bride. Done the rings and flowers and white lace. Pete and I had spent decades together before his grand betrayal. But time heals. Eventually I'd allowed myself to love again. And then Andrew Ryan had shattered my heart anew.

Ryan had never married. Why now? Why me? Had he changed? Does anyone ever change?

I'd vowed no more vows. Was it wise to alter that pledge?

Round and round. Over and over. Like a loop in my brain.

At one point, as distraction, I clicked through photos on my iPhone, knowing it was foolish, but doing so anyway. Screw it. There was no signal. If my battery died, I could use the radio.

I looked at faces I hadn't seen in far too long. At smiles I'd once shared. At happiness I'd once enjoyed.

Mama, all done up in Gucci. My sister, Harry, with her big Texas hair and even bigger heart. My daughter, Katy, in head-to-toe army combat gear.

Ryan, arm draped around my shoulder in Montreal. A selfie. I knew his pilly green sweater so well I could smell the wool.

That photo hit me straight in the gut. Why the sudden stab of pain? The sense of loss? Or was it elation? Jesus, what was it I was feeling?

Resolved. When back in civilization I'd book a flight to Montreal. Surely I could eke out a few days. And even a short visit would make Ryan happy. Hell, it would make me happy. Unless the pressure was too great. Or the friction too stressful.

Unless. Unless. The more I thought about marriage the more I felt my head would explode.

Around four, clouds drifted in, harmless white cotton-candy wisps streaking the blue. Over the next two hours, the wisps bloated, darkened, and gathered into ominous thunderheads.

By seven the sky was spitting and night was closing in fast. The team called it quits.

The searchers had done the best they could. Found more of the bucket and a handful of cranial fragments. Gunner had made the big score—the missing half of the concrete mold.

As the rescue squad disengaged from their copious gear, the techs took photos of the paltry assemblage I'd spread out on a tarp. They clicked, I bagged and tagged. A promise of notes and additional photos; then, still aggrieved by the injustice of missing their hoops, everyone split.

Rain was falling in earnest by the time Ramsey, Gunner, and I climbed into the SUV. Not pounding, but cold and steady.

I braced myself as we lurched and rocked back up the access road toward Wiseman's View. Several minutes passed before Ramsey spoke.

"Long day."

"It was," I agreed.

"Could be a tough drive back to Charlotte."

"I'm not looking forward to it."

No response.

Exhausted, I closed my eyes. No. Better to stay awake. I opened them. Watched drops sparkle in the headlights then disappear into blackness.

After some time, Ramsey broke the silence. "Here's my thought. Tomorrow's Sunday. No one's going to look at anything before Monday."

He cut the wheel to avoid a pothole, maybe a small night creature. I turned toward him. His gaze was pointed straight at the windshield. I waited.

"There's a nice B and B not far from headquarters. How about you stay up here tonight? Tomorrow we have a good mountain breakfast, then we surprise Mama and Daddy Teague after Sunday service?"

While I was considering, my iPhone snatched a sliver of signal and beeped. I checked my voice mail. Hazel Strike really needed to talk to me. Though her voice sounded urgent, I ignored the message.

I'd left extra cat food. Could tag a neighbor for breakfast duty.

I made a call to Joe Hawkins on his private number. Apologized for phoning on Saturday evening. Explained what I wanted from him.

Taxes? Screw it.

I stayed.

16

I woke suddenly, clueless where I was. Then recall.

Turned out the "nice" B&B belonged to Ramsey's aunt, a lady in her seventies with nurturing instincts to give Clara Barton a run for her cap. And, despite snowy hair, a lime-green bathrobe, and crocodile slippers, a demeanor that suggested she was not to be crossed.

We'd arrived at eight, damp and muddy and shivering. While I showered and Ramsey washed up and changed shirts, Aunt Ruby had prepared her version of a light snack. Leftover meat loaf, ham hocks and beans, pickled beets, mac and cheese, peach cobbler and ice cream. I was unconscious before my head hit the pillow.

Now I lay a moment, listening to birdsong and watching dawn bring details of the room into focus. Rosebud wallpaper. Acres of gingham. Pine pieces so thickly lacquered they looked like plastic.

Outside, a rooster resolutely announced daybreak. Somewhere in the house a door closed. A soft squeak, then water trickled through old piping.

I turned on my pillow to check the bedside clock, a round affair topped by double bells with a tiny hammer between. Both scrolly hands were pointed straight down.

I threw back the quilt, swung my feet to the floor, and, wearing the panties and tee I'd slept in, tiptoe-hurried to an upholstered rocker I'd scooched in front of a heat vent. My jeans had dried where I'd scrubbed the knees and rear. I pulled them on, added the same bra, sweater, socks, and boots in which I'd left home twenty-four hours earlier.

The bath, two doors down a flowery hall, was mercifully empty. Pedestal sink. Black and white tile floor. Freestanding tub with a plastic curtain featuring dolphins and crabs.

On the sink were a cellophane-sealed toothbrush and a tube of Crest. I brushed, yanked my hair into a pony, and headed downstairs.

The dining room was through a parlor that stayed true to the theme upstairs. Centered in it was a long wooden table flanked by benches. Along the walls were two-tops. Ramsey was at one, already working on waffles, bacon, and scrambled eggs.

When I drew near, the deputy did that half-standing thing men do when joined by members of the opposite sex. My bum had barely hit the seat when Aunt Ruby appeared carrying a stainless-steel pot. The robe and slippers had been replaced by a floral dress, pink cardigan, and sensible shoes.

"Good morning, missy." Raising the pot.

"Thanks." I held out my mug.

"Did you have a good sleep?"

"I did."

"Pancakes or waffles?"

"I'm not really a breakfast—"

"Can't start the day without food in your belly."

"Pancakes."

"Sausage, bacon, or both?"

"Sausage."

"Coming right up."

"There's no point arguing," Ramsey said when she'd gone.

"Oh, I definitely get that."

Ramsey raised interested brows. No way was I explaining Mama at seven in the morning.

"What's the plan?" I asked.

"The early service kicks off at eight. We'll be waiting outside when it ends."

"You're sure the Teagues will attend?"

"Yes."

"Why don't we just go to their home?"

"I'm fond of surprises."

"You want to catch them off guard."

"Something like that."

Ramsey ate and I sipped for a while. I was about to

ask if he'd learned more about the church when Aunt Ruby returned bearing sufficient food to feed a small nation.

Despite myself, I downed all three pancakes, the unrequested eggs, and two of the five sausages. One pumpkin scone.

I was working on my second coffee when a couple appeared in the doorway. The man had a long gray braid snaking down his back. The woman, at least a decade his junior, was tall and slim with very short hair. Both wore boots and cargo pants, and had bandannas tied around their necks. I guessed they were hikers.

The two were talking quietly. On seeing Ramsey's uniform, their conversation slammed down in mid-word. A quick scan, then they settled at a corner table, the farthest from ours.

I glanced at Ramsey to see if he'd noticed. A subtle nod said he had.

Aunt Ruby again intercepted the question I was about to pose. She beamed at us through spotted lenses and waggled the pot.

"No more coffee, thanks," I said.

"Just a check," Ramsey said.

The wrinkled lips made a sound like air exploding from a piston. Then, to me. "Zeb tells me you're a doc up from Charlotte."

"I am."

"Says it's strictly professional."

"It is."

Ramsey pulled two tens from his wallet and placed them on the table. Aunt Ruby ignored him.

"He's a fine boy," she said.

He's pushing fifty, I thought.

"He tell you I'm the reason he left Georgia?"

"He didn't."

"Broke my hip." With her free hand, she patted the joint in question. "Zeb came to tend me. Never left."

"I'm sure you enjoy having him close."

"He's all I've got. Just wish he'd find him a new wife. Last one wasn't so hot."

My eyes flicked to Ramsey. A blush was rising from his collar and mottling his cheeks.

Not noticing her nephew's discomfort, perhaps not caring, Aunt Ruby yammered on.

"Now don't be thinking I'm a delusional old fool. I know that whole marriage mess is the reason Zeb stayed. That and the snarl left by our moron sheriff. The dead one, I mean. The new one seems a bit brighter. Well, what the hooey." Her hand flapped the air as though shooing a fly. "The turnover made for a job. So here he is."

Ramsey rose, clearly embarrassed. I followed and went to gather my belongings. At checkout, Aunt Ruby was obstinate in refusing payment for my room.

I thanked her for her generosity. Then, while Ramsey went to bring the SUV around and, I suspected, run the plate on the vehicle belonging to the hikers, Ruby and I engaged in small talk.

"Seems a bit warmer today." I figured weather was always safe.

"Spring's a-coming. Always does." Pause. "So where you off to?"

"Church." Also safe.

The rheumy eyes narrowed behind the speckled glass. "Don't reckon I'd count Zeb among the believers."

"It's business."

"His or yours?"

"Both."

"Which church?"

"Jesus Lord Holiness."

Again, the derisive pooching of air through her lips. I waited.

"You've come all the way up here to go to Mass with crazies?"

"What do you mean?"

"Those folks are barmy. Nuts. Batty as loons." The old gal didn't mince words.

"Can you elaborate?"

"I knew one of them once. Nice person until that church bunch got hold of her. Made her crazy."

"Define 'crazy.' "

"Where do I start? They reject the pope and the president. Honest to God, probably penicillin and pizza." An elevated tone suggested strong thoughts on the subject. "Parishioners are supposed to stay all hush-hush. But my friend, *former* friend, let on how they think."

Three of her words linked up in my head.

"Wait. Are you saying the group is Catholic?"

"Not sure the Vatican would lay claim to that lot. But yes, they're some sort of splinter faction. Charismatic or Pentecostal or whatever you call it. All into faith healing and prayer meetings and speaking in tongues."

I was about to probe further when Ramsey pulled up in front. Aunt Ruby walked me to the door and held it wide with one scrawny arm. I again said thanks, then hurried outside.

"You two be careful out there," she squawked at my back.

"What's that all about?" Ramsey asked as I was buckling my seat belt.

I recapped the conversation I'd just had with his aunt.

Slowly shaking his head. "She does have some pit bull tendencies."

The previous night, in the dark, Ruby's place had been nothing but a long gravel drive ending at a yellow porch light. Curious, now that I could see it, I looked around.

The B&B was a two-story, green frame with lavender trim, an old farmhouse undoubtedly treated with less whimsy in its previous life. Wrapping its front and left side was a porch overlooking a lawn now brown and soggy with postwinter melt off.

A small sign identified the home's current status

as the Cedar Creek Inn. Overnight the clouds had passed, and the rising sun was now bronzing the Cedar Creek's roof and windows.

The drive took fifteen minutes. I was glad I wasn't making it solo. Our target lay deep in a hollow, many lefts and rights off the blacktop. The entire trip, I saw not a single sign. We encountered no other vehicles.

Ramsey knew the way. And timed our arrival well.

The Church of Jesus Lord Holiness sat with its back to a mountain. A tire swing hung from the branch of an enormous oak off to its left. Picnic tables sat in four rows of three by the tree's trunk.

Roughly thirty cars and trucks waited in a paved parking area in front. Ramsey joined them and killed the engine. We both eyed the setup, assessing.

The main building was small, perhaps constructed specifically for worship, perhaps converted from some previous use. Its exterior was whitewashed, its windows plain—no fancy grillwork or stained glass.

Two steps led up to a stoop that looked as though it were scrubbed daily. A pair of double doors bore matching wrought-iron crosses. Above the doors, a simple wooden cross rose from the peak of the roof. No bells, no steeple.

An outbuilding sat twenty yards off the right rear corner of the church. Same double doors. Same whitewashed exterior. No cross. A gravel track forked from the entrance road toward its rear.

I lowered my window. From inside I could hear the muted sound of a piano being played with gusto. Warbly singing, the kind typical of small congregations.

I strained to listen. Caught a phrase or two. Latin. That tracked with Ruby's account.

Ramsey started drumming a thumb on the wheel.

"It won't be long."

My comment drew a questioning glance.

"They're singing the Agnus Dei." Lamb of God. "The Mass will end soon."

"You Catholic?"

I offered a noncommittal lift of one shoulder.

Six days a week. In my little green jumper, patrolled by Gestapo nuns. In my Sunday best, flanked by Mama and Daddy. Memories still slice through my dreams. The smoky sweet incense. The gloomy organ drone. The poorly padded wood under my bony kid knees.

Ten minutes of watching, then a priest and an altar boy emerged, both in full ecclesiastical garb. Together, robes billowing like clothes-lined laundry, they pulled wide and secured the doors to shiny metal rings embedded in the stoop.

The boy disappeared back inside, then, one by one, two by two, and in family groupings of varying sizes, the worshippers trooped out. Every male over ten wore a suit and tie, every female a hat or veil.

The priest shook hands with the men, blessed the women and children with a pat on the shoulder or head. An hour of torturous restraint, yet all the kids stayed with their parents. Not one bolted for the tire swing, a game of tag, a cartwheel, a run with arms outstretched like a plane.

The exit parade was tapering off when Ramsey's thumb went still.

The priest was speaking to a couple I guessed to be in their fifties. He was built along the lines of a bulldog. She was taller, more so with the headgear. Both were sporting black.

"Showtime," Ramsey said softly.

I unbuckled my seat belt.

"Best let me do the talking,"

"Works for me," I agreed.

Ramsey got out and began weaving through the back-pewers now arriving at their cars. Ignoring the distrustful looks and the chorus of *wheep-wheep*s around me, I hurried to keep up.

The priest was of average height and scarecrow thin. Black hair greased and combed back from his face, acne-scarred cheeks, indigo eyes. On spotting us, he abandoned the conversation to watch our approach. The Teagues turned to see what had robbed them of their pastor's attention.

Recognizing Ramsey, or his uniform, John's face went rigid. Unconsciously or not, he rolled his shoulders and spread his feet, a kid preparing for a double dare.

Still tracking us, the priest leaned in and said

something I couldn't hear. John nodded, but remained coiled.

"Sunday blessings, Deputy." The voice was deep and rich as honey on toast. "What can I do for you this fine day?"

"Good morning, sir. We'd like a few words with Mr. and Mrs. Teague." Neighborly grin, just a simple country sheriff doing his job. "Won't take but a minute, then we're on our way."

"Of course, of course." The priest smiled and arced an arm at the church behind him. The flapping vestment made me think of a giant green bird. "But at the Lord's house? On the Lord's day?"

"And you are?" Ramsey was still grinning, but far less warmly.

"Father Granger Hoke. Father G to my followers."

"Mr. and Mrs. Teague know the reason we're here."

"May I ask what that is?" Again flashing yards of priestly dentition.

Ramsey stared at John, who stared right back.

Up close, I could see that Teague was rat-faced, with an undersize jaw and florid complexion. His wife was bland and colorless, the type you'd pass on the street and later be unable to describe. Though she kept her eyes down, a twitch in one lower lid danced feathery shadows across her cheek.

Hoke's smile swung between Ramsey and the couple at his side, holding, but losing ground.

"First that meddling old hag, now you. This is harassment." John's voice was deep and gravelly. The one I'd heard on the audio? I lowered my breathing, anxious to catch every nuance.

"Hag?" Ramsey asked.

"The clown-haired one. The woman needs a good—"

"Hazel Strike?" The question was out before I could stop myself. "When did you last talk with her?"

Teague looked my way, but offered no reply.

"When girls go missing we take the situation seriously." Ramsey, getting back on point.

Hoke's lips tightened and his brows rose slightly. Surprised? Wary? His hands dropped into an inverted V in front of his genitals.

"No one's missing," Teague growled.

"You've heard from Cora?"

A beat, then, "Proverbs thirty, seventeen." Teague's pitch was low and threatening. "The eye of one who mocks his father and who despises the childbearing of his mother, let the ravens of the torrent tear it out, and let the sons of the eagles consume it."

"Now, John, we mustn't forget." Hoke placed a fatherly hand on John's shoulder. "The sweet Lord Jesus also preaches forgiveness."

"Everything all right, Father?"

Hoke and Teague turned. Ramsey and I looked past them.

A man had appeared in the open doorway. Maybe

thirty, very tall, with broad shoulders sloping from a powerful neck, and the same flushed skin and rodent features as Teague.

"Owen Lee, please join us." Again, the smile and flapping brocade.

Owen Lee stepped forward onto the stoop. Stopped. Crossed his arms and regarded us, expressionless.

"Owen Lee is John and Fatima's eldest," Hoke explained. "And a very valuable member of our parish. Every day, I thank God for Owen Lee's support."

Ramsey nodded to the younger, refocused on the elder.

"Cora?" The deputy's tone was now pure steel.

"Hebrews thirteen, four." Teague's eyes, hard on Ramsey's, burned with the fervor of a zealot. Perhaps with hatred. "Whoremongers and adulterers God will judge."

Fatima flinched, as though shocked with live current. Owen Lee stood stoic. The guy looked vaguely familiar. In the way a beef carcass looks vaguely familiar. Something about his build. Pete? Harry's second husband, the guy we called the Hulk?

"Where is your daughter, sir?"

"Run off to serve the flesh. To fornicate with a man who bears the devil's—"

"And who would that be?"

Teague slid a glance to Hoke, who nodded encouragement.

"Mason Gulley." Spit, as though the name were a bitter taste in his mouth.

"Mason is another of our parishioners," Hoke offered. "Or was, until recently."

"How recently?"

The priest gave a nervous clip of a laugh. "Dear me, Deputy. I'd have to check my—"

"Estimate."

After considering, Hoke said, "Mason helped with our renovation project. Not all of it, but toward the end. We painted, upgraded the family center, replaced the old steps. It was a parishwide effort, every hour of labor and every ounce of material donated gratis." Nodding toward Teague. "John's generosity made the new parking area possible. It was such an outpouring of God's—"

"Then he stopped attending?"

"I believe so."

"When was that?"

"2011. As I recall, the project finished up around the time school started."

Ramsey to Teague. "What makes you think Cora left with Mason Gulley?"

Teague only glared. Behind him, his son watched and listened.

Ramsey's eyes moved to the priest.

Hoke's fingers tightened on the burly shoulder inside the ratty black suit. Again, he nodded reassurance.

Teague's Adam's apple rose and fell. When he

answered, the feral edge to his voice sent ice up my spine.

"Because the Lord Jesus whispered to me that Satan himself come down from the mountain to claim their whoring souls."

17

Most autopsies follow a standard routine. After an external exam, the legendary Y incision is made. The organs are removed, weighed, and inspected. Key vessels and nerves are observed.

With the gut cavity emptied, a U-shaped cut is made across the crown of the head, from ear to ear. The scalp is pulled down over the face in front and the neck in back. The scalp's tough underside is searched for blood or bruising, the skull's outer surface for nicks or fractures.

Then a handheld surgical saw is revved up. A removable cap is created, asymmetrical to avoid slippage when the skull is reassembled and the scalp stitched back together.

The cap is detached with a tug and a slurping suck, revealing the dura mater, a thick membrane encasing the brain. The dura mater is checked for epidural hematoma—pooled blood that may have pressed on the brain and resulted in death. And for subdural hematoma on the flip side.

Though "gray matter" gets all the press, the brain's outer surface is actually white and laced with the gauzy arachnoid and pia maters. At this point the brain's fine webs and fissures are observed for evidence of subarachnoid hemorrhage, intracranial bleeding triggered by the brain banging around inside the skull, shearing delicate vessels on its surface.

Next, fingers are inserted under the open brow, the frontal lobes are hooked and lifted, and the nerves and vessels leading to the face are snipped. The tentorium cerebelli, the shelf of dura mater that protects the cerebellum and brain stem, the "reptile brain," is severed. Using a scalpel long enough to reach the base of the skull, the spinal cord is cut, and the brain is slipped free. The cerebrum, cerebellum, and medulla oblongata now lie in the pathologist's hand. Or in the skullcap, maybe a stainless-steel bowl used like a catcher's mitt.

The brain is placed in a formaldehyde solution, where, over the next two weeks, its consistency changes from Jell-O to cheese. After every inch of its complex surface is observed, it is cut with a long fillet knife, much like sausage. Slice by slice, its internal structure is studied.

But none of that would happen with the remains discovered off the Devil's Tail trail.

Since refrigeration was unnecessary, the bones,

bucket fragments, and concrete had spent the weekend locked in the Avery County property room. Ramsey had promised delivery early Monday morning. He'd also promised to look into Mason Gulley.

After leaving the Holiness church, Ramsey had dropped me at my car. Provisioned with unwanted sandwiches, cookies, and apples from Aunt Ruby, I'd made a surgical strike at Heatherhill Farm, then headed home.

At the annex I'd booked a flight to Montreal, then gone straight to bed, not glancing at the accusing paper muddle on the dining room table. In the morning, I'd again shot past it to the kitchen, then straight out the door.

For the hundredth time, I glanced at the clock. Ten-seventeen. Impatient, I phoned Ramsey. He said he was at the CMPD forensics lab, dropping off the bucket. Estimated he'd be at the MCME in half an hour.

In most jurisdictions, weekends mean paychecks, idle hours, and booze. Daddy gets hammered and clocks Mommy with the blender. Junior kills a six-pack and then himself, going ninety in a buddy's Camaro. Sis leaves a bar to score crank and ends up in a dumpster. Bottom line. Mondays are often hectic for those looking after the dead.

Today was no exception. With the MCME humming around me, I went in search of Larabee, half hoping he'd already started an autopsy. No such luck. He was on the phone, but gestured me into his office.

Larabee listened, chin propped on one palm. I updated him on Ramsey, the Teagues, including Cora and Eli, Mason Gulley, the Church of Jesus Lord Holiness, Brown Mountain, the Devil's Tail trail, the bucket, concrete, and bones. Everything but my romp with the renegade rock.

"You can't just hit the mall on weekends?"

That merited no response.

"The priest, a guy who calls himself Father G, advised Teague to cooperate."

"Holiness doesn't sound Catholic to me."

I summarized what Aunt Ruby had said, mentioned the serpent folks. Larabee knew of them, had a colleague who'd autopsied a preacher with substandard handling skills.

"I may roll a few questions past a more traditional member of the clergy." I already had one in mind.

"Troubling that the parents never reported her missing."

"Yes."

"You still think she's dead." More statement than question. Larabee is uncanny at reading me.

"I do."

"You want to cast the head," he said.

"I want to try."

"Did you obtain antemorts?"

"Ramsey said he'd get pics from the parents."

"Long shot."

"To the moon and back."

"You really think Teague is capable of killing his daughter?"

I pictured the fiery eyes. Heard the venomous voice.

"I think it's possible."

"Well, it's your lucky day. Nothing's landed that needs anthropology expertise." He swiveled his chair, typed a few keystrokes, then ran a finger across the spreadsheet that appeared on his monitor.

"Log it as case number ME135-15."

"The concrete, too?"

He thought about that. "Sure. Who knows what's trapped inside."

Larabee stood. Meeting over.

The landline was ringing when I entered my office. Ramsey was in the lobby. I told the receptionist, Mrs. Flowers, to send him back. He arrived carrying a large canvas satchel.

"What did they say at the lab?" I asked.

"They'll check for prints, trace, body fluids, the usual. Based on the background I provided, they weren't optimistic."

"Did you tell the Teagues they should provide DNA samples?"

"I did. Not a chance."

I looked at the satchel. The pull on its handles and the double sag in its belly suggested considerable weight. "Do you mind carrying that to an autopsy suite?"

"Lead on."

"You can leave your jacket here."

"Yes, ma'am."

In the stinky room, I asked Ramsey to glove and remove the two hunks of concrete. At my direction he placed them on the counter, hollow side up.

First I shot a series of photos. Then, after gloving and masking, I ran sterile cotton balls and swabs around the interior of each hollow, repeated the process again and again.

Ramsey watched, feet spread, thumbs hooking his belt.

I was sealing the specimens into plastic evidence bags when I noticed two pale filaments wrapping the cotton topping one stick. I looked more closely at the others. A few had collected similar strands.

Could we get that lucky?

Heart beating a little faster, I took the swab to a dissecting scope, flipped the light switch, and adjusted focus.

The filaments were mere microns in diameter, like fibers of silk, only more brittle. Each was gossamer pale, almost translucent.

"Damn," I muttered under my breath.

Or out loud. I heard Ramsey shift, but he said nothing.

"I thought it might be hair, but these look so fine."

Ramsey's heels clicked across the tile. Wordlessly, I

held out a mask. He took it. I stepped back. He bent and squinted into the eyepiece.

Seconds passed. Then, "What about a kid?"

"The hollow is too big to have been made by the head of a child."

"What's the shiny stuff?"

"What do you mean?"

"The cotton's glossy in spots."

"Let me see." Not so gently nudging him sideways.

Ramsey was right. Here and there the white fluff looked oily and discolored. Hair product? Lotion? Decomp? Sweat? Possibilities ping-ponged in my brain.

I took a million more swabs, labeled and sealed them. When I was certain nothing more could remain in the smallest crevice or recess, I inspected the edges along which the concrete had split.

My recall was correct. The surfaces were clean and smooth. Miraculously, there was no evidence of chipping or erosion.

Hawkins had come through in response to my request. On the counter were aerosol cans of a liquid rubber coating product and containers of silicone sealant. In the sink was an apparatus I assumed to be a vise, maybe intended for furniture repair, maybe for something entirely different. I didn't care. It was perfect.

After spraying every inch of the hollow, I applied the sealant to the broken edges. Then, using muscles I knew would later demand an accounting, I counterbalanced Ramsey as we jammed the two halves of concrete tight to each other.

And waited a full five minutes.

Then with further Maria Sharapova grunting on my part, we maneuvered the restored mold into the apparatus, bottom side up. Ramsey held it steady while I tightened the clamps.

More sealant. More tightening.

Satisfied the glue would hold, I went in search of a power drill. Found one in the back of the last storage closet I checked.

Returning to the stinky room, I donned goggles and handed a pair to Ramsey. Then I plugged in the cord and placed the drill tip where I expected the least thickness in the concrete.

My eyes rolled up to Ramsey's. His looked back from behind the big plastic lenses. He raised a thumb.

I fired up the drill. It screamed and spit dust and tiny shards into the air. The acrid smell of scorching metal and hot rock permeated the room. I held my breath, willing the concrete not to crack.

It seemed like an aeon. But in less than a minute the tip of the bit poked through to the hollow interior. I pulled the drill upward and, exerting circular outward pressure, enlarged the opening I'd created.

No spiderwebbing fissures. No radiating fault lines.

On its own, my arm shot up in a high-five gesture. To my surprise, the deputy's hand met mine. Mildly embarrassed, we both turned to removing our goggles. Then I mixed a batch of Duraplast, a fiber-reinforced plastic not unlike the material used by the Avery techs to take tool-mark impressions at the Devil's Tail.

While Ramsey watched, I inserted the spout of a plastic funnel into the opening and began to pour. The soft *glug-glug-glug* seemed to go on forever.

When the hollow was full, I set the funnel on the counter. For a moment, we both studied the pasty white liquid through the little round hole.

Was I nuts? Overreaching? Saying I had misgivings would be like saying Descartes had qualms about God.

"Did you get photos?" I broke the silence.

"Yes, ma'am. In my jacket."

"Okay. Bones first, then pics."

While Ramsey returned to the satchel, I covered the autopsy table with a plastic-backed paper sheet. As I palmed the fold lines flat, he placed a small Tupperware tub at its center.

I pried off the lid, deposited and distributed the fragments so none overlapped. All had come from an adult human skull. All were weathered and badly chewed.

Quick inventory. Six bits of parietal. Two bits of occipital, one with a squiggly remnant of lambdoid suture. Four bits of frontal, one with a portion of supraorbital rim.

The half inch of suture had edges that were smooth

and unfused. The vascular grooves on all endocranial surfaces were shallow. Age: young adult.

The curvature on the frontal suggested a brow ridge of moderate size. Which meant sex could be male or female.

There was no marker to even hint at ancestry.

"Now what?" Ramsey asked when I'd told him.

"Now you deliver the swabs to the lab." I stripped off my mask and gloves. "And we wait."

"How long?"

"This sucker's big." Gesturing at the hardening cast. "Probably overkill, but I want to give it a couple of days."

"Sorry I'll miss the unveiling."

"Could be a bust."

"Isn't that the goal?"

Not bad, Deputy. I'd missed my own pun.

Back in my office, Ramsey collected his jacket, slipped an envelope from one pocket and handed it to me.

"One's a bit outdated, the other was taken a few months before Cora 'ran off.'" Hooking air quotes around the final two words. "But I think I got the views you wanted—one from the side, one from the front. Mama and Daddy didn't offer a wide range of choices."

"Then these will have to do."

"I'm going to make some inquiries, see what I can dig up regarding the nanny job."

"Did you ask the Teagues?"

"John felt revealing the name of Cora's employer would be a breach of confidentiality."

"That's bizarre."

"It is indeed."

When Ramsey had gone, I checked the contents of the envelope. Two color prints.

I slid the photos onto my blotter and arranged them side by side. One showed a girl of twelve or thirteen with pale skin, freckles, and long blond braids. John Teague stood behind her, hand on one of her shoulders. A second man stood facing her, thumb on her forehead. He was wearing red robes and a miter—the ceremonial garb and headgear of a Catholic bishop. "Confirmation. March 19, 2006" was handwritten on back.

The other picture had been taken outside. A young woman was seated at a picnic table, arms crossed, huge green eyes grimly fixed on the lens. Her hair was drawn tightly back from her face. Long wavy strands flowed forward over her shoulders, sparking in the sun like liquid gold.

Like the filaments I'd swabbed from the concrete?

I sat staring at the time-gap versions of Cora Teague, doubts winging in my head like startled moths. Was she dead? Would I reveal her in 3-D death mask form? Would the cast even work?

The landline shrilled into my thoughts.

"I'm in autopsy room one." Larabee sounded nuclear-level amped. "Get down here. Fast."

18

Larabee was on the far side of a gurney, studying a corpse still packaged in its going-for-a-ride bag. The zipper was closed, but the contouring of the lumps told me the occupant was a good-size adult.

The man on my side of the gurney had his back to me. The silhouette looked familiar—tall, with shoulders too narrow for the waist and bum. Yet it was wrong, somehow.

As I paused, palm still pressed to the door, the man turned. And confirmed what I'd hoped had been a case of mistaken identity.

Eyeing me coolly was Erskine "Skinny" Slidell, CMPD homicide squad. And a magnum-force legend in his own narrow mind.

Slidell graced me with a nod.

"Detective." Discreetly assessing what was off about Slidell's appearance.

His face was clammy and gray. Autopsies did that

to him. Otherwise, he looked better than I'd seen him in years. Perhaps ever. I guessed he'd lost fifteen to twenty pounds. He was rocking a suede jacket, shirt with no tie, and khakis combo, and his hair was buzz-cut, Bruce Willis style.

"Come here." Larabee gestured me to him with an agitated curling of gloved fingers.

"Doc, this don't—"

"Bear with me, Detective." Larabee was clearly not up for attitude from Slidell.

As I rounded the gurney, Larabee picked up a clipboard holding an intake file.

"Sixty-one-year-old white female. Height: seventy-one and a half inches. Weight: one hundred and eighty-two pounds. Spotted by a neighbor at eight-oh-seven this morning wedged under a dock in the lower pond at the RibbonWalk Nature Preserve."

"Where's that?" Charlotte is lousy with parks. I hadn't heard of this one.

"Derita neighborhood, off Nevin Road. It's got a couple of ponds, a wetland bog, trails."

Across the gurney, Slidell cleared his throat. Loudly.

Larabee ignored the not so subtle prod. "The victim lived a few blocks away. According to the neighbor"—checking one of the sheets clipped to his board—"Franco Saltieri, she liked to walk there."

"Any history of depression?"

Larabee shrugged. Who knows?

Realizing the significance of Slidell's presence. "You're thinking murder?"

"Unless Granny opted for a midnight dip."

Larabee did not acknowledge Skinny's attempt at humor. "There's an awful lot of facial trauma."

"How long was she in the water?"

"Saltieri says he saw her around seven Saturday morning. She must have died sometime after that."

Given the cool weather and the short period of submergence, the body would have undergone little postmortem change. I wondered why I'd been summoned. Was about to ask when Larabee flipped back to the cover page and read off a name.

"Hazel Lee Cunningham Strike."

The room receded around me.

"Isn't Hazel Strike the woman who came here to see you?" I sensed Larabee's eyes on my face, narrow and watchful. "The websleuth?"

I could only nod.

"That's what I thought."

I heard a clipboard clatter against stainless steel. The buzzy rip of a zipper. The whistle of air in Slidell's nose.

"Is this Strike?"

I took a second to clear my head. Deep breath. Then I looked down.

The garish hair lay wet against the right side of Hazel Strike's face. The skin was morgue white, shadowed where the underlying bone had caved in—

the cheek, the upper rim of the orbit. The lips hung slack, revealing bruising and broken teeth.

"What's he mean, she came to see you?" Slidell demanded from the far side of the gurney.

"He means she came to see me," I said, not looking up.

At that moment Hawkins pushed through the door. Larabee gestured him in, then refocused on Slidell and me. "How about you two take this elsewhere so we can get on with the autopsy?"

I cast one last glance at Hazel Strike's face. Recalled the messages on my phone. Urgent. Pleading that I call.

Mind already packing for a guilt trip, I brushed past Slidell and headed out into the corridor. Skinny hesitated a beat, then followed.

In my office, I took up position behind my desk. Slidell sat facing me, shoulders and jaw tight, already in confrontational mode.

"When'd she come here?"

"A week ago."

"Why?"

Words and images were spinning wheelies in my mind. I tried to force them into alignment. To arrange them into some sort of meaningful pattern. Slidell granted me at least thirty seconds of patience.

"We gonna do this today, Doc?"

"Fine."

I relayed what I hoped was an accurate chronology. Strike's hobby as a websleuth and her visit to the MCME. Cora Teague. My trips to Burke County, the Lost Cove Cliffs, and Wiseman's View, the three overlooks for Brown Mountain. The printless fingertips, the fragmented skeletal remains, the Devil's Tail trail concrete with its contents now hardening in autopsy room four. Deputy Zeb Ramsey. John and Fatima Teague and the Church of Jesus Lord Holiness. The suspicious death of their youngest, Eli, at age twelve. The insistent calls from Hazel Strike the previous Saturday.

Slidell listened, taking not one single note. When I'd finished he looked at me as though I'd said Elvis was tone-deaf.

A comment was coming at me when Slidell's mobile buzzed at his belt. Without excusing himself, he got up and strode from the office. For the next ten minutes I could hear the cadence of his voice through the door. A pause. Then a new conversation. Perhaps act two of the previous one.

I'd moved on to paperwork when he finally returned.

"So the old lady called you."

"Hazel Strike was sixty-one."

Slidell gave a derisive twitch of his chin.

"She phoned several times," I said. "Left messages requesting that I call her back."

"When was this?"

"Last Saturday."

"Times?"

"One was early morning. One was afternoon, the other I'm not sure."

"Did you call her back?"

"No."

"Why not?"

"I was busy." Again a pang of guilt. What had Strike wanted? Had she been afraid for her life? Whom else might she have contacted for help?

"You've not seen her since this little skip through the woods?"

"No."

Slidell began ticking points off on his fingers. To my surprise the nails were, if not manicured, uncharacteristically clean and trimmed.

"Here's how I see it. One, Cora Teague is a big girl and free to diddle whoever she wants. Two, no one's filed an MP—"

"She *was* reported missing."

"That's not what you said."

"Her disappearance was entered on a websleuthing site called CLUES.net."

"Online." Voice triple-coated with disdain.

"Yes."

"By who?"

"Someone posting as OMG." Though tempted, I didn't correct his grammar.

Slidell's brows rose ever so slightly.

"You know. Oh my God."

Not a flicker of understanding.

"I assume OMG is cyberjargon. Like LOL. Laughing out loud. Or G2G. Got to go."

Slidell took a deep, long-suffering breath. "So you've no clue who this nutbucket is."

"No."

Slidell's knowledge of the Internet is limited to running data such as prints, weapons, or vehicle registrations, tasks he usually shunts off to subordinates. He doesn't own a computer. Fully aware of the folly, I surged on.

"I tried Twitter, found no user with a handle containing just the letters OMG. That's as far as I got before I had to move on."

"And you've no clue who this Hazel Strike is. Was."

A mental image popped. Strike sitting in the chair now occupied by Slidell, elbows on her knees, face vibrant with compassion for the forgotten dead.

"Lucky," I said.

"What?"

"She went by Lucky. You know. Like the cigarette—"

"Yeah, yeah. Poetic."

"Strike was investigating Cora Teague. She even spoke to the family. It can't be coincidence. There has to be a connection between Strike's murder—"

"Maybe murder."

"—and Teague's disappearance," I continued.

"Maybe disappearance."

"Deputy Ramsey is not too busy to exert some effort." Glacial. Read: not too pigheaded.

"This ain't Avery County. Here's how it's gonna play out here in the big city. Doc Larabee says someone offed Strike, the bastard's going down."

"What can I do?"

"Stay out of my hair."

I let a few moments pass to indicate how distasteful I found his attitude. Then, "I am not an amateur."

"You're a squint." TV cop lingo. Classic Slidell.

"I have been helpful in the past."

"We're not talking bones here. Nothing personal, but if this drops to me, I prefer to work it without interference."

Interference? I wanted to smack his surprisingly clean-shaven face.

The landline rang, saving me from the impulse. It was Larabee.

"How's it going?" I asked.

"As I suspected." I heard water pounding a sink in the background, a male voice I assumed to be Hawkins. Larabee said something to him I didn't catch. "I found significant cranial, facial, and thoracic trauma, the result of at least seventeen blows with a blunt object."

"That suggests a whole lot of rage."

"It does."

"Cause of death?"

"Massive intracranial bleeding."

"Any defense wounds?"

"None."

Slidell's eyes were riveted on me.

"Water in the lungs?"

"No. She was dead before she went into the pond. Is Slidell still there?"

"He's here."

"Tell him I'm signing Strike out as a homicide."

"I'll send him back to see you."

"And it's not even my birthday."

"Your reward for a job well done."

I hung up and relayed what Larabee had said.

As Slidell was pushing to his feet, a synapse fired in my brain.

"I did some Internet research," I said. "There's a side to websleuthing I found disturbing."

"People playing Whac-A-Mole with virtual mallets?"

The comment was inane, so I ignored it.

"For some, not all, the pursuit is ego-driven and intensely competitive."

"Whac-A-Sleuth?"

"Are you interested in this?"

Slidell sighed and chest-crossed his arms.

"Hazel Strike engaged in a lengthy and bitter dispute with a websleuth calling himself WendellC."

"What's that short for?"

"The man's name is Wendell Clyde." I described Clyde's role in identifying Quilt Girl. His resulting stardom. "Strike accused WendellC of taking credit for discoveries they'd made together."

"So?"

"The exchange was beyond nasty. Much of the language was truly vicious."

Slidell blinked, then opened his lips to blow me off.

"News reports said Clyde was living in Huntersville."

Slidell's belt vibrated again. This time he ignored the call.

"So you're saying there was bad blood between Strike and Clyde?"

"The two hated each other."

"And the guy's living right up the road."

"He was in 2007. That's when the articles ran."

"You're suggesting Clyde whacked Strike?"

"Far be it from me to interfere." Childish, but Slidell sparked that in me.

"Snotty don't suit you, Doc."

"I'm suggesting Wendell Clyde is a good place to start."

19

Before leaving the MCME, I checked the schedule at my gym. Perfect. An evening yoga session at six. Stretching and breathing to help counter the stress.

Who was I kidding? The class meant one more hour away from the square mile of paper covering my dining room table.

I got to the annex around seven-thirty, relatively relaxed. A state of mind that lasted maybe ten minutes.

The phone rang as Birdie and I were sharing a Fresh Market chicken pot pie. It was Zeb Ramsey. I clicked on.

"I put the drive time to use." Ramsey was eating something—maybe French fries. I could hear chewing punctuated by rustling. "Called in some favors on Mason Gulley, the kid the parents thought Cora ran off with."

I waited out some wet mastication.

"He wasn't easy to track, but my 'associates'"—I

could hear quote marks around the word—"managed to kick a few things loose. Gulley was born in '94, which makes him a year younger than Teague."

We each took a bite of our respective foodstuff.

"Gulley's father, Francis Gulley, left home after high school to become the next gospel wonder in Nashville. His mother, Eileen Wall, came from a speck-in-the-eye town way over on the Tennessee border. Eileen dropped out her junior year to hit the footlights on Broadway. When they met, she was bagging burgers at a Wendy's in Asheville, and he was scrounging pickup gigs as a drummer. A year after they moved in together, little Mason came along."

"Did they marry?"

"No. And neither was enamored with the concept of parenthood. They split for California, leaving the baby with Gulley's mother, Martha Regan Gulley."

"Why not Eileen's parents?"

"The father was a boozer and the mother had MS."

"Grim."

"Grimmer. Both were killed in a head-on the day after Christmas, 2000."

While listening, I watched Birdie tongue a gravy-free pea onto a small collection of peas and carrots on the floor. Couldn't help but admire his skill at triage.

"So Mason was raised by Grandma and Grandpa Gulley. Mostly Grandma. Oscar Gulley died of congestive heart failure in 2004. He was eighty-one."

"Is Martha still alive?"

"Grandma was more than a decade younger than her husband. Still lives in Avery County." Ramsey paused, but I heard no paper or dental action. "She's raising the second of Eileen's children, a girl named Susan Grace."

"Seriously?"

"In 1999, Eileen dropped Susan Grace off at age one month. Two overnights, then back to L.A. Within the year, Eileen had OD'd on heroin."

"Was she still with Francis at the time of her death?"

"They'd split."

"What happened to him?"

"By then he was calling himself Frank Danger. He got popped a couple times in L.A. Petty stuff. Loitering. Disorderly. Resisting. The last arrest was in '06 for possession of marijuana. He was ordered to rehab and given probation. After that the trail goes cold."

"Never became a rock star."

"No."

Was Mason Gulley's paternity really relevant? His parents' loser past?

"Cora Teague went to Avery County High," I said. "Was Mason Gulley a student there?"

"No."

"Where?"

"I'm on it." A beat. Then, "Apparently very few people knew this kid. My associates got some odd comments from those who had come into contact with him. A checker at the Food Lion, a pharmacist, a—"

"What does that mean, odd?"

"Folks said he was strange."

"Strange?"

"Weird."

"Weird?"

"Just repeating what was reported to me."

I thought about that while working on a hunk of chicken.

"Time to get back to sheriffing." I heard movement, probably Ramsey swiveling to cradle the handset.

"Hang on." I swallowed. "There's more."

The line went still.

"Hazel Strike was killed last night."

"The websleuth who came with us to the overlook?" Shocked.

"Yes."

"What happened?"

I told him about the autopsy. About the injuries that suggested Strike's killer was driven by rage. About her feud with Wendell Clyde. About Slidell's refusal to include me in the investigation.

When I'd finished, a thick silence hummed from the mountains to the Piedmont. I knew Ramsey was pondering the same notion I was. The improbability of coincidence.

"Have you worked with this guy before?"

"Oh, yeah."

"He solid?"

"Slidell's got the personality of an anal polyp, but he's a good detective."

"Want me to give him a call?"

"Doubt that will move Skinny. Better to do it his way." I circled back. "Both the Gulleys and the Teagues belong to Jesus Lord Holiness church. Cora and Mason could have met there."

"The priest's estimate was correct. Those questioned thought Gulley dropped from sight in 2011. That puts his disappearance around the same time as Teague's."

We both chewed on that. And on the brutal reality of Hazel Strike's death.

"Now what?" I asked.

"You game for another trip up here?"

"I am."

We made plans, then disconnected.

Birdie and I gave the tax issue our full attention. For about thirty minutes. Then I showered and we both settled in bed.

Surprisingly, I was eager to talk to Ryan. Probably Slidell—a need to vent. Perhaps a need for more. Whatever. I was tired of trying to sort my untidy emotions.

Ryan answered after two rings. "Just the person I hoped it would be."

"Glad I could make your day."

"Your calls always fill me with joy."

"Try to control your giddiness." I smiled. This felt good.

"Will do." I could hear Ryan turning down some frenzied sportscaster in the background. He was at home. "What's up?"

"I rebooked my trip."

"*C'est fantastique!* When do you arrive?"

"Next Friday. Sadly, it's just for a long weekend. I'll email the flight information."

"I'm really glad." He let that lie for a beat. "So. Any news on your case?"

I took a moment to organize my thoughts. So much had happened. I decided to start with the recent and work backward.

"Do you remember our discussion about websleuthing?"

"I do. And Lucky Strike." I heard a hum, then the sound of ice cubes dropping into a glass. "She was looking for a kid named Cora Teague."

"Strike was killed last night. Bludgeoned to death then dumped in a pond."

"Jesus Christ. Are you okay?"

"I'm fine." How to put it without overplaying my involvement? "After Strike left my office last Monday, I began looking into what she'd said."

"Does her theory have legs?" A liquid, probably Scotch, splashed onto the cubes.

I told him about the printless fingertips from Burke County. The fragmentary bones from the Lost Cove Cliffs. The concrete mold from the Devil's Tail. Brown Mountain. Zeb Ramsey. The Teagues. The Gulleys.

Granger Hoke and the Church of Jesus Lord Holiness. Wendell Clyde.

The account took half an hour. Throughout, all I heard was the clink of ice and the occasional swallow.

As he listened, Ryan went through the same mental lassoing I had. His questions came back clear and succinct.

"Why no prints?"

"I'm not sure. Could be the result of chemotherapy. Ramsey asked at local hospitals, but found no AWOL cancer patients."

"What did the WCU anthropologist say?"

"I've yet to hear back from her." Note to self. Follow-up call.

"And the Teagues refuse to give DNA?"

"They insist Cora is elsewhere and fine."

"There's no evidence of a crime so you can't force them to talk."

"Voilà."

"You've got a vic with no cause of death and no way to ID her."

"Or him. With what's been recovered, I can't determine gender or race. I've sent samples to the lab for DNA testing, to try to establish that it's just one person, maybe later to establish ID. But I'm not optimistic they'll find enough to sequence. Everything's badly chewed and weathered."

"And the younger Teague kid died under suspicious circumstances."

"So says the treating ER doc."

Ryan shifted gears.

"You're liking Wendell Clyde for the Strike murder?"

"You should see these online exchanges, Ryan. They're toxic. And the guy lives just outside Charlotte."

Or did.

"Skinny's not buying it?"

"Who knows what goes on in the far country of Slidell's mind. By the way, he's undergone some sort of transmutation."

"Meaning?"

"He's lost weight and looks"—I groped for a word—"groomed."

"He's got a girlfriend."

"Seriously?"

"He's back with Verlene."

Slidell and Verlene Wryznyk had been an item sometime in the Paleozoic. She'd dumped him, but, over the years, they'd remained friends. The previous winter Slidell had covered for his lost love when she accidentally shot her squeeze of the moment, a State Bureau of Investigation agent with a very tall ego and very loose hands.

"No way!" I was so stunned that at first I missed the implication of Ryan's comment. "Wait. How do you know that?"

"He called me a couple weeks back. Had a question about shoes."

"Shoes."

"He admires my taste."

"Skinny?"

"Can't blame him. I'm the man when it comes to footwear."

"Ryan," I said, a note of reproach in my voice.

"I'll tell you all about it when you're here."

Before I could press, Ryan looped back.

"You think Strike's death is related to the Cora Teague situation?"

"I don't know what I think."

"Did you ever get the audio recorder from her?"

"No. Hopefully Skinny will find it when he tosses her house." Another note to self. Call Slidell.

A moment of thoughtful silence, then, "Granger Hoke is a Catholic priest?"

"Jesus Lord Holiness is a breakaway group that has issues with Rome. The congregation is small but fervent. And fiercely private. John Teague is a real piece of work."

"Could the remains you recovered tie in to some form of crazy involving Brown Mountain and Satan?"

Ramsey had mentioned that same possibility. The implication for Hoke and his flock didn't need stating.

Until my father died and Gran whisked Mama, Harry, and me south to the land of Baptists and Presbyterians, my upbringing was Catholic. I was schooled by nuns peddling water-and-wine miracles, virgin birth, and resurrection. The hopelessness of unbaptized pagan babies. The evils of venial and mortal sin. The power of forehead ash, penance, and prayer.

To my young mind, life everlasting was a pretty sweet deal. But the cost of a ticket was mighty high, the odds of achievement extremely low. It seemed I was doomed before I'd begun. My birthright was wrath, greed, sloth, pride, lust, envy, and gluttony. My female body was the devil's wicked lure, meant to be veiled and used only for reproduction.

Unquestioning obedience was my only salvation. And endless ritual. Friday fish. Saturday confession. Sunday Mass.

All were called but few were chosen. The God-fearing and God-compliant. The alternative was Satan and a fiery hell.

". . . to Brennan?" Ryan's voice had gone lower, the edges softer.

"I'm here." Please don't.

"I love you."

I made a noise that could have meant anything.

"That's good to know," Ryan said.

"It's late."

A blip of a pause.

"You're dodging me, Tempe. And avoiding the issue. I'm not talking about putting off a trip to the dentist. Or coming up here. I'm talking about our lives."

"I know." Barely audible.

"Avoidance is corrosive."

"I hate long-distance discussions." Knowing as I spoke that the phone wasn't the issue. "We'll talk when I'm there."

"I do love you. And I'll wait. But not forever."

An icicle of pure crystalline pain slashed through my chest.

20

Ramsey's directions guided me to the end of a blacktop lined with cuter-than-Heidi's-bloomers log cabins, the type rented short-term by summer tourists and fall foliage devotees. All were shuttered and dark. Final approach was via a long gravel drive shooting from a cul-de-sac much too large for any purpose I could imagine for such a remote locale.

Addams Family on crack. That's what flashed through my mind as I parked.

Martha Gulley's home was a rambling two-story frame behemoth that hadn't seen paint since the Babe signed with the Red Sox. Complete with dormers, weather vane-topped tower, wraparound porch, and greenhouse, the place looked like the bastard offspring of a Gothic–Victorian tryst.

I was taking in detail when Ramsey pulled up. I got out and waited for him to join me.

"Did you know about this beauty?"

"I've been by here, but never had cause to enter." Ramsey was surveying the property, one hand shading his eyes. "Rumor has it that old Oscar was hoping to create an East Coast version of the Sarah Winchester house. Died ten years into the project."

"Is that the mansion in San Jose?"

"It is. Back in the day, Sarah lost her child then her husband, spent the rest of her life adding on to an old farmhouse. By the time she passed the place had one hundred and sixty rooms and sprawled over six acres. Story is she did it to escape the ghosts of people killed by Winchester rifles."

Ramsey certainly did like history.

"You think Fester's still got his lab in the basement?" I asked.

"Who?" Swiveling to face me.

"Never mind." History, not sitcom TV, was Ramsey's thing. "Does Grandma know we're coming?"

"She does. And she's not thrilled."

I tipped my head toward a black Chevy Tahoe parked beside the greenhouse. Which looked like it hadn't nurtured flora in many decades. "She still drive?"

Ramsey shrugged. Who knows?

We crossed a brown, rutted patch of weeds, once a lawn, and climbed to the porch. Ramsey thumbed the bell. The action triggered no muffled bonging or chiming.

Ramsey knocked on the door. Which looked

jarringly new. And cheap, maybe a Home Depot stock item.

A full minute. Then a bolt snicked, a chain rattled, and the door swung in. A whole eight inches.

Through the gap I could see a figure silhouetted against very inadequate lighting. A tall figure. Grandma Gulley's height was such that I had to lift my chin to meet her eyes. Which were green and wary behind heavy black-framed glasses designed for a man. They landed on me a nanosecond, then hopped back to Ramsey.

"Don't know what you're wanting from me, Sheriff."

"I'm just a deputy, ma'am." Self-effacing grin.

"Who's she?" Tip of the head in my direction.

"Dr. Brennan."

"Don't believe in doctors."

"Thank you for agreeing to see us, Mrs. Gulley." Friendly as apple pie at the fair. "You said late afternoon would be convenient?"

"Weren't like you give me much choice. Is this about Mason?"

"May we come in?"

A dramatic straightening of the shoulders. Then Grandma stepped back and angled the door a few inches wider. Ramsey and I slipped through and she slammed and locked it behind us.

The entrance gave directly onto a parlor that, like the house, looked frozen in time. The drapes were drawn and only one lamp was lit. In the dimness I made out an old upright piano, a corner hutch, three groupings of wooden and upholstered furniture.

A stone fireplace occupied most of the wall to our left. In front of it, a pair of ancient sofas faced off across a table made of tree trunk sections covered by a slab of glass.

At one end of the far sofa sat Granger Hoke, Roman collar a little white square in the gloom. Palm-smoothing the greasy black hair, he rose to greet us.

I trailed Grandma across the room, impressed by the size of the woman's frame. Though her neck was now scrawny and her jawline flaccid, it was clear she'd once carried substantial bulk.

"Deputy." Hoke volleyed off a wide smile and a hand. "It's so nice to see you again." The high-beam welcome swung to me. "To see both of you."

"Sir." Ramsey shook with the priest. "This is a surprise."

"Yes, yes. I hope my presence isn't an intrusion. Martha is quite nervous. She's never been interrogated by the police."

"This is hardly an interrogation."

"Of course not." Conspiratorial chuckle. Old people. "But Martha is one of my parishioners. When she called, I couldn't say no. We've prayed to Jesus to give her strength." Hoke arced an arm, the same gesture he'd employed on the church stoop. No green bird now. In lieu of vestments, he wore a simple black suit. "Shall we?"

The priest resumed his seat. Grandma settled down-sofa from him. Ramsey and I sat facing them, at separate ends of a scratchy, overstuffed horror.

"Your home is lovely," I said to put Grandma at ease.

"The Lord Jesus don't condone waste. Most of it's closed off. No sense heating unneeded space."

"How long have you lived here?"

"Is that important?"

"No, ma'am. I understand your husband worked many years constructing the house."

"A fool's venture."

Having dazzled at warm-up, I yielded the floor to Ramsey as planned. While my ears took in the conversation, my eyes roved the room.

Bronze sconces jutted from walls papered with green and beige stripes and trimmed with dark-stained baseboards and crown molding. A chandelier hung from the ceiling above us, encircled by an ornate bronze medallion.

Beyond the parlor, through double wooden doors, I could see a wallpapered hallway shooting left. Roses, not stripes. Across the hall was what appeared to be a very large kitchen. Nothing else was visible from where I sat.

Over Hoke's shoulder, the corner hutch was a shrine to all things Catholic. A large crucifix stood at center stage, thorns, stakes, and corpus carved and painted in vivid, though inaccurate, detail.

A cast of supporting players was also present, some in sculpture, others framed and under glass. Our Lady of Something, palms spread, heart pumping red. Francis of Assisi, feet hidden by bunnies and lambs. Thérèse of Lisieux, head veiled, arms laden with roses. The rest, though vaguely familiar, I couldn't ID.

Jesus stared down from a patch of stripes between the hutch and the fireplace, eyes saying he had no qualms about reading my mind. And that he smelled trouble.

The various tables and shelves held not a single personal photo. No baby in a silly hat. No kid in cap and gown. No dog asleep in a patch of sun.

I refocused on the interview. Ramsey was ignoring Hoke, directing his comments solely to Grandma. The priest was maintaining a poker face. But I could tell his mind was working and he was listening carefully.

The old woman's hair, a dull yellow-white, was pulled back and secured in a complex arrangement of braids. The hem of her dress skimmed the tops of black oxfords planted firmly and close together.

"It's a pity we haven't met prior to this, ma'am." Ramsey was still laying thick the country boy charm.

"I don't go out much."

"That's Avery County's loss."

Hoke raised a brow and feigned amusement.

"Martha is eighty-two, Deputy. Still, she never misses a Wednesday or Sunday."

"Does your granddaughter drive you? Susan Grace I believe is her name?" Affable, but letting both know he'd done his homework.

"She does."

"She still lives with you, then?"

"Is this about my grandson? If so you're wasting your time. I can tell you right up. Mason's gone and there's no two ways about it. Stole my money and run off with a woman."

"Cora Teague."

"Yes, sir."

Though her answers were firm, it was clear the old woman was terrified. All clenched fingers and jittery eyes.

"Where did Mason attend school?" Ramsey used an old interview trick. Switch topics to keep your subject off-balance.

"I homeschooled the boy."

"Why?"

"Mason's different."

"Different how?"

"Different enough so's I couldn't send him to public school."

"Meaning?"

"Unnatural."

"Do you know where Mason and Cora have gone?" Another sharp-angle turn.

"I do not. Nor do I wish to."

"He's your grandson."

"He's evil made flesh." Spit with such bile it startled me.

"Ma'am?"

"Mason's soul belongs to the devil."

"What makes you say that?"

The man-glasses whipped to Hoke. The priest dipped his chin without turning his head. The dim lighting shadowed his face, making it impossible to read his eyes.

"Mason's never looked right, never acted like a boy's supposed to act."

"What does that mean?" I couldn't help blurting.

"He carries the mark of Satan." A blue-veined hand made the sign of the cross, forehead, sternum, then shoulder to shoulder.

Because he's gay, you ignorant old bat? I felt a rush of anger, twisted and jumbled with feelings from now and from long ago. Ramsey intervened before I could fire off another question.

"Do you have a picture of your grandson?"

"I do not."

"Not one little old snapshot?" With a sweet-talking grin.

"Burned every one."

"And why is that?"

"Father G said I should."

Hoke leaned sideways and asked the old lady

in a whispery voice, "Have I permission to share a confidence, my dear?"

"Yes, Father."

"Thoughts of Mason are very disturbing for Martha. She was having nightmares, not sleeping. I thought the exercise might prove beneficial. A sort of purging."

Ramsey's eyes stayed on Grandma, but he said nothing. Another interview trick. Allow silence, hoping the interviewee will feel compelled to fill it.

We'll never know if the ploy would have worked. Before Grandma had time to succumb, wood juddered softly. We all turned.

A girl stood by one of the hall doors. She was tall, with a linebacker's build, but a softness to her body that suggested future weight issues. Thick black bangs covered the upper halves of her eyes. I guessed her age at around sixteen.

"Susan Grace." Hoke did his sunny priest bit. "How nice. Please join us."

The girl held her shoulders hunched, her arms wrapping her ribs. A frozen moment, then, "Why are they here, Grandma?"

"Do you have homework?" Ignoring her granddaughter's question.

"Are they asking about Mason?" Susan Grace's voice was deep and low, almost masculine.

"Homework."

"Will they find him?"

"Susan Grace. You know you mustn't meddle in grown-up matters."

"Does anyone even try?"

"Young lady!" Loud and sharp. "Do not allow yourself to be hostage to Satan."

Susan Grace blinked, and her bangs did a round-trip on her lashes. "I have ballet class tonight."

"I don't like you out driving alone in the dark."

"Pray to the Lord Jesus for my safe delivery." Flat.

Hoke and Grandma twitched in tandem, like puppets whose shoulder strings had been lightly jerked.

Susan Grace regarded us a very long moment, half eyes utterly devoid of expression. Then she turned and disappeared down the hall.

The atmosphere in the room was suddenly ice.

"My, my, my." Hoke's chuckle was casual, but edged with something not previously there. "Kids."

"I'm sorry, Father." Grandma kept her gaze on the gnarled old hands tightly clenched in her lap. "She knows better."

Ramsey gave me a sideways flick of a glance. His chin lifted ever so slightly. I nodded understanding, ignoring a melancholy pang. Ryan and I had used the same signal dozens of times.

The deputy and I rose. So did Hoke. Grandma stayed where she was, eyes meeting no others.

Seconds later Ramsey and I were outside in the late afternoon sun. Inexplicably, I was hearing that warning ping in my head. Not a full-throttle signal of danger, but a subliminal dispatch suggesting alertness.

"Was the kid being sarcastic?" I asked.

"A subtle zinger for Grandma? Maybe the priest?"

I raised my brows.

Ramsey raised his.

"Think something's off?" I asked.

"Maybe." Ramsey was again staring at the house.

"Can't you get a search warrant? Two. One for here and one for the Teague place?"

"Based on what?"

I was about to comment on the inconvenience of the Fourth Amendment. Stopped, realizing how much I'd sound like Slidell.

I got to Heatherhill just in time for dinner. The menu was loin of lamb, green beans with slivered almonds, parsleyed spring potatoes, pistachio mousse. The food was good on the plate, not just in print.

Not so for Mama. She was listless and ate practically nothing. I tried to draw her into conversation, got mostly shoulders for my efforts. Even those responses were lame—limp little lifts, more hitches than shrugs.

Still, Mama's hair and makeup were flawless, her cashmere jogging suit perfectly matched to her tan Coach sneakers. I vowed to buy a small gift for Goose, already gone when I'd arrived.

Mama didn't ask about my work, about the overlooks and the remains that had excited her just a few days earlier. Except for one comment on the state of my nails, she didn't criticize or critique. Mostly, she spent the time shut away in her own private world of thought.

Desperate to engage her, I introduced the topic I'd been dodging so diligently. A topic I'd yet to share with her.

"I have some news, Mama."

She gave a curious flick of one perfectly plucked brow.

"Andrew Ryan has asked me to marry him."

That got her full attention. "Your French detective?"

"French Canadian."

"How delightful. When is the wedding?"

"I haven't said yes."

"Do you love this man?" Asked after a long, scrutinizing look.

"Yes."

"Then why on earth not?"

"It's hard to explain."

"You can't keep brooding over Pete's infidelity."

"My hesitation has nothing to do with that." Deep down knowing that Pete's betrayal had yet to grant me permission to leave the building. That now and then the pain still came knocking at the door. "Ryan is complicated."

Her face didn't change, but I saw her turn inward

to roll that around. Then she took both my hands in hers and said, "Love is composed of a single soul inhabiting two bodies."

"Aristotle."

She nodded. "Do you feel such a connection with this man?"

An icy clamp took hold of my tongue. For the life of me I could think of nothing to say.

I stayed a couple of hours. We didn't mention Ryan again. When I left, she absently turned one cheek for a kiss.

Walking the path to my car, I couldn't fend off the guilt coming at me on multiple fronts. Mama was on a downswing. I'd largely neglected her of late. Discussion of possible nuptials had done nothing to cheer her.

Hazel Strike was dead, perhaps because I'd ignored her calls. Ryan was set to decamp, peeved that I'd continued to duck his proposal.

I was nowhere on Cora Teague or the Brown Mountain bones. So far my actions had generated only vague suspicions, no solid leads. No hundred-watt bulbs lighting up over my head.

I was so deeply immersed in self-reproach, at first I didn't hear movement in the darkness behind me. Subtle noises that shouldn't have been there. Suddenly, I was motionless, breath frozen, straining like some startled woodland creature.

Yes.

The airy swish of nylon. The soft crunch of gravel.

Abruptly stilled. Far off, the blurry murmur of wind slipping through some secret passage.

My mouth went dry. My heart pounded my ribs.

My car was five yards ahead. I fumbled in my shoulder bag. Another harebrained move. Why hadn't I carried the keys in my hand?

Because no bogeyman lurked at Heatherhill. But someone or something was stalking me.

Run! My mind screamed.

Instead I whipped around.

Saw a shadowy silhouette in the blackness.

21

"Who is it?"

No response.

"Who's there?"

My adrenals were pumping hard. In the dark, the guy looked huge.

Still nothing.

"I'm armed." Groping for pepper spray years past its shelf life.

Finally, a flicker of movement. An arm going up? A wink of pale skin.

"I want to talk to you." The voice was surprisingly calm.

"Stay back." Mine wasn't.

Another subtle realignment of the shadows. Then footsteps. Heavy. Determined.

It was a bad place for an encounter. Hedges lined both sides of the path. The parking lot to my rear was totally deserted. My pursuer blocked a return to River House.

The footsteps were fast closing in.

"Stop!" Inside my purse, I popped off the cap and death-gripped the can. If the spray failed, I'd kick the guy's plums into his brainpan.

The sheen of black hair. Eyes obscured by over-privileged bangs.

My finger eased off the nozzle. My pulse dropped a micron.

"Did you follow me here?"

Susan Grace nodded, a shadowy shape-change in the gloom.

"You lied to your grandmother about ballet."

"She can confess for both of us." Deep and low and neutral. And it was impossible to read the expression on her face.

"Why follow me?"

"I want to find Mason."

"I have nothing to tell you."

"Are any of you really looking for him?"

"Perhaps Cora and Mason don't want to be found."

"Cora." Bitter. "My brother would never ever leave without telling me where he was going."

"Where do *you* think he is?"

She was so close I could hear the hitch in her breathing. I waited, letting her choose her own timing.

"I have something to show you."

"Are you parked in the lot?" I jabbed a thumb over my shoulder.

"Yes."

"Okay." Hoping the kid wasn't slit-my-throat nuts. "Let's go to my car."

Two vehicles hulked dark in the otherwise empty quadrangle. I scanned for signs of a second presence, saw nothing but bushes, trees, and white picket fencing. While unlocking the Mazda, I transferred my iPhone to a jacket pocket for easier access.

I got in and slid my purse between my belly and the wheel. Susan Grace tossed a backpack to the floor, then dropped onto the passenger side. When she swung her feet in, her knees were high and pressed tight to the dash.

"Feel free to adjust the seat."

She did.

Seconds passed. A full minute. Again, I held my tongue, not wanting to press.

"My life's like living the freakin' *Song of Bernadette*." I assumed she meant the Henry King film.

"I was raised Catholic." Seeking common ground. "My father loved that movie."

"Catholic?" She laughed, a quick angry scrape. "You met my psycho grandmother and her Nazi priest. We're not just Catholic. We're über-Catholic. Supercolossal kick-ass-and-take-no-prisoners Catholic.

"We pray in Latin because English isn't pious enough. We beg forgiveness on bloody knees because God demands penance for sins we've never committed. Sins we've never thought of committing. Sins we've never even heard of."

"Are you talking about Jesus Lord Holiness?"

"Of course I am. We are the righteous. The devout. We speak in tongues to the Holy Ghost. We shun the unanointed, the unbaptized, the unvirgin, the unclean. Pretty much anyone who isn't us. And, whoa-ho! If you *are* one of us and you screw up, watch out. We have ways of punishing the wicked!"

"Susan Grace—"

"We follow rules even the pope has kicked to the curb." Whipping sideways to face me, all round eyes and trembling lips. "We're so goddamn sanctimonious, we've kicked the big guy himself to the curb!"

She laughed again, that same humorless scratch of breath.

I'd heard kids vent. Heard them curse a parent, a coach, a teacher who ousted them for wearing a Korn T-shirt to class. This was different. Susan Grace's intensity suggested a fury that was deep and powerful.

"I'm sorry." Lame, but that's what I said.

"I don't need a shoulder to cry on." Brittle. Now embarrassed by her outburst.

"What do you need?" I asked softly.

"I need someone to find my brother." After backhanding tears from her cheeks, she yanked a zipper on the backpack and pulled something free. "I heard the cop ask Grandma for a photo of Mason."

"You have one?"

"No. But I have this."

She shoved the thing toward me. I took it and turned on the overhead light. Which was lousy, but good enough to identify a Black n' Red personal planner barely holding together at the binding.

"There's a picture. Use the ribbon."

I lifted the end of the narrow red satin placeholder. It took me to the middle of the journal.

"Be careful. It's old."

In the murky light I saw what looked like an illustration from an antique medical text. Though black and white, the image had the sepia dream quality characteristic of turn-of-the-century photographs. Yet the detail was clear.

The subject, a male in his teens, was shown in four views. A full frontal head shot. A close-up of the neck. A close-up of the fingers and toes. A close-up of the mouth, upper lip curled back by a second party to reveal the dentition.

The man had wispy blond hair and dark crescents below his eyes. Blotches of pigmentation cornered his mouth and formed irregular, netlike patterns on his neck. His fingernails looked brittle and weak. His toenails cut sideways across the ends of the first digits.

But the subject's most remarkable feature was his dentition. The incisors, both upper and lower, were reduced in size and flanked by daggerlike canines.

On almost every tooth, the enamel was darkly dull in spots.

At the top right, the collection of photos was identified as "Plate LXXXIV." At the bottom left was printed: "Copyright, 1905, G. H. Fox." Centered below the collage were the words "Ectodermal-Dental Syndrome of Unknown Origin."

"Who is it?" I asked.

"When I found the pictures I showed them to Grandpa. He tossed a freaker. Said it was his older brother, Edward, who died a long time ago. Insisted I give him the page and never discuss it with Grandma. *Totally* off-limits. Like my parents." Again she swiped at her cheeks, obviously fighting a blitzkrieg of emotions. "I staged my own hissy, so eventually he let me keep it."

"Why are you showing this to me?"

"My brother looks like Edward."

Different. Unnatural. Evil made flesh.

"Do you have the rest of the book?" Careful to mask my revulsion for Grandma's medieval interpretation of Mason's peculiarities.

"No. Just this page. It's, like, a hundred years old. Someone cut it out and saved it."

"Do you know who or why?"

"Probably my grandfather. Here's what I managed to worm out of him."

A short, thoughtful pause.

"Grandpa was named for Oscar Mason, a

photographer back at the turn of the century. Medical stuff mostly, but kind of famous. Grandpa's family was living in New York then, and they were friends with Mason. Maybe neighbors. Anyway, Oscar Mason noticed something was off with Edward, and asked if he could take pictures of him. Some doctor put the pictures in a book and gave Great-Grandpa a copy as a thank-you."

An almost inaudible *ting-a-ling*. A galaxy away in my memory banks. Oscar Mason? G. H. Fox?

"Susan Grace, I have to admit, I'm lost."

The young woman sat silent. Perhaps regretting her impulse to reach out to me. Perhaps deciding on a line in the sand—what to share, what to hold back.

Apparently she decided on caution.

"You need to talk to the Brices." Voice whispery, eyes cutting left then right to take in the darkness outside our little bubble of light.

"Who are the Brices?"

"Cora Teague worked for them as a nanny."

"Go on."

"They used to be members of Jesus Lord Holiness."

"But not any longer?"

"No."

"Why did they leave the church?"

"I can't say."

"Why did they fire Cora?"

"I can't say."

"There's not much I can do with that."

Susan Grace leaned toward me, hands clenched on the edge of the center console. "Do you know about Eli?"

"Eli Teague?"

"Yes."

"What about him?"

Absolute frozen silence.

"Susan Grace?"

"Eli didn't fall down any stairs." Hushed, but ardent.

"What are you suggesting?"

More silence.

Wind nudged the car and whistled through the gaps surrounding the windows.

"Susan Grace, it's late. I'm going to have to—"

"The Brice baby died on Cora Teague's watch."

"Died how?" Something cold began congealing in my chest.

"I don't know."

"That's why Cora was fired?"

"That and other things. You need to talk to them. I think they live in Asheville now."

"Are you saying Cora killed Eli and the Brice baby?" Using mind-bending effort to keep my voice steady.

"My brother is nutso over Cora Teague. He'll do anything for her. The woman is—" In the oozy light offered by the little overhead box, I could see one lip corner hitch up. "You know what Grandma calls her? A she-devil."

"I'm confused. Are you saying Mason *might* have left with Cora?"

"Never without telling me."

"How can you be sure?"

"It's like he's possessed. He loves and hates her at the same time." It was another nonanswer.

"But you can't be certain they aren't together."

"Yes." Susan Grace's face went hard. "I can." The angles and planes shifted as she struggled toward a decision about divulging further or cutting her losses. "Mason and Cora disappeared at the same time. July 2011. That's true. But I talked to my brother almost every day after he left. And he wasn't with her."

That stunned me. "Where was he?"

"Johnson City, Tennessee."

"Why?"

"I can't tell you that."

"Where did Cora go?"

"I never found out. And I really tried."

"Tried how?"

"Mason asked me to watch for Cora. To play spy. I was a kid, it seemed like a fun game, *Mission: Impossible* or something. We were secret agents, but Mason was undercover, so I had to do the snooping and report to him."

"But you never saw her."

"Maybe once, at a convenience store. But I was in a car. We were going fast and I couldn't really see the person's face."

"How long did the game go on?"

"A month, maybe a little longer."

"You spoke by mobile?"

Susan Grace snorted. "God forbid I tread the treacherous landscape of mobile technology. Grandma would have a thrombo. Mason called me on a pay phone outside my school. We had prearranged times. It was all part of the game."

"What happened?"

"In September, he just stopped. For a couple of weeks, I'd wait by the phone. He never called again."

"How did he get to Johnson City?"

"Probably hitchhiked. When Mason put on a cap he looked pretty"—she glanced down at her hands—"normal."

"Do you know where Mason was staying?"

"A motel. That's all he'd say."

"He was living off money he stole from your grandmother."

"Mason didn't steal it. I did."

"And gave it to him."

"Yeah."

I thought about the pay phone. After four years I doubted the calls could be traced.

"Did you ever call him?" I asked.

"Mason didn't want to, but I said I'd quit the game if he didn't give me his number. I called once, but he wasn't happy. I never used it again."

"Any chance you still have it?"

She handed me a folded paper. "It really sucks. Mason has the kindest heart you could ever imagine." A hiccupy sound escaped her throat. She inhaled, as though to continue. A beat, then she let the breath out as a sigh.

I wanted to say something comforting. But my head was spinning. And the little bell had been joined by a voice. A voice warning that I could be listening to adolescent delusion.

Was that it? Or did we have it all backward?

Who was Cora Teague?

22

Maybe it was Mama's Aristotelian allusion. Maybe leftover adrenaline from my encounter with Susan Grace. Again, I felt an overwhelming desire to talk to Ryan.

While driving, I phoned him. Got voice mail. Left a message.

I also called Ramsey. He picked up. I relayed my conversation with Susan Grace.

"What's your take?"

"She's one angry kid."

"Who wouldn't be, living in that house?"

I couldn't disagree.

"So Mason has his kid sister spy on his girlfriend while he goes to ground in Johnson City."

"Susan Grace didn't put it quite like that."

"She can't say why Mason went away."

"More like she won't. And let me add. For sixteen, she's very articulate."

"And she doesn't care for Cora."

"That's an understatement."

"Did she explain why?"

"No." Eyes flashed red on the shoulder, late-to-bed deer startled by my headlights. I eased back on the gas. "She said she doesn't like how her brother sucks up to Cora. And that her grandmother would call her a she-devil."

"The old bat probably calls you a she-devil."

"I'm flattered."

"So they play Boris and Natasha for a while, then Mason drops off the grid."

"Yes."

"Where was the kid staying in Johnson City?"

"Susan Grace didn't know, but she had a phone number. I'll text it to you."

"Is she afraid something has happened to him?"

"She swears he'd never leave without giving her a heads-up."

"Unless he's putting miles between himself and a homicide."

"Unless that. Or could it be Cora?"

"Could it be Cora what?"

"Needing to boogie."

Ramsey thought about that. Then, "Brice. Don't know the name."

"Susan Grace said the family might be living in Asheville."

"So she thinks they've left Avery."

"You'll find them?"

"I'm on it." Ramsey's pet phrase.

I told him about the photo of Edward Gulley.

"Thus Grandma's homeschooling of little Mason," he said.

"I'm surprised she didn't drown him at birth."

"What's wrong with him?"

"I'm on it."

"Bold attitude."

I was approaching the outskirts of Charlotte when Ramsey called back.

"Brice, Joel and Katalin. Joel is a welder. Katalin is a baker. They have one daughter, Saffron, a second grader. They lost a child, River, in the summer of 2011. He was nine months old. Shortly after River's death they moved from Avery to Asheville."

"Did you phone them?"

"I spoke with Joel. Briefly."

"How did the baby die?"

"Sudden infant death syndrome."

"Terrific."

"What?"

"Most professionals define SIDS as the unexplained death, usually during sleep, of a seemingly healthy baby less than one year old. It's like saying 'undetermined.' You'll talk to the coroner? Get the full story?"

"If I can track him down."

"Did the death occur on Cora's watch?"

"Joel refused to discuss Cora Teague."

"Did they hook up with Cora through Jesus Lord Holiness?"

"Also not a popular topic."

"Did you ask why they fired her?"

"Wildly unpopular."

"Did you ask why they left the church?"

"Also off-limits."

"How did he respond?"

"Hung up."

"What was your sense?"

For a long moment, I heard nothing but Ramsey's breath. Then, "I sensed a whole lot not being said."

I tried to focus on my driving. But my mind kept running in loops.

What would happen when I opened the concrete mold in the morning? Had my idea worked? If so, whose face would I see? Cora Teague's?

Why had Hazel Strike phoned me on Saturday? Why was it so urgent that I call her back? Did she have news to share? Or was she alarmed and looking for help? To whom had she turned when I was unavailable? Had that person killed her?

Had Strike revisited John and Fatima Teague? Grandma Gulley? The Brices? Had one of them felt so threatened or incensed they'd traveled to Charlotte to demand she cease the harassment? Had things gotten out of hand?

Had Wendell Clyde learned of Strike's meeting with me at the MCME? Of her continuing interest in the disappearance of Cora Teague? Had Clyde confronted her? Bludgeoned her to death and dumped her body in the pond?

Susan Grace popped back into my thoughts. Twice she'd phrased questions in a way that bothered me. Once in the car, once at home.

Was it just a turn of speech? Or was she being literal?

I wondered if Ramsey had noticed. Wished I'd mentioned it to him.

The light at the intersection of Queens Road and Queens Road was red. It's Charlotte—don't ask. While waiting out the green, I hit a key on my speed dial.

Three rings, then a gruff "Slidell."

"It's Dr. Brennan."

"I know."

I'm well, dickhead. Thanks for asking.

"I'm wondering if there's been any progress on Strike."

"Ain't we all?" I could hear voices in the background, a ringing phone. Figured Slidell was in the homicide squad room.

"You're working late," I said.

"You got a specific concern?"

I told him about my conversation with Susan Grace.

"The kid thinks Cora Teague is bad news."

"She does," I said.

"Teague stole her big bro's attention. She's jealous."

"Maybe. But she posed a couple of questions in a way that bothered me."

Slidell made an indecipherable sound in his throat.

"She asked her grandmother: Does anyone even try? She asked me: Are any of you really looking?"

"And?"

"Isn't that a strange way to put it?"

"You said she's a strange kid. Look, I gotta—"

"It implies that others are searching for Mason."

"What's this got to do with Strike?" Impatient.

"Maybe Strike's hunt for Cora Teague led her to Mason. And maybe she wasn't the only one looking."

"You talking about this rival websleuth, Wendell Clyde?"

"You have a better idea?" Sharp. Slidell's skepticism was making me surly. And I was tired.

"Yeah. I'm thinking it's time I head out for some 'cue."

Easy.

"Strike told me she was going back up to Avery. She probably visited John and Fatima Teague, Grandma Gulley, maybe the Brices. Could be she angered or frightened someone."

Slidell started to speak. I pressed on.

"Or maybe Wendell Clyde learned of Strike's trip, lost it, and took her off the board."

Long pause. Then, "Remind me—when did she call you?"

"Strike called me three times on Saturday. I'm

guessing she was up in Avery at the same time I was."

"But you never talked to her."

"No."

Slidell responded with a stretch of silence. A long one.

"I tossed Strike's crib today. Shit bucket out in Derita."

"Derita is a perfectly fine middle-class neighborhood."

"Yeah. All kids and poodles and Granny's paint-by-number on the walls."

I rolled my eyes. Which, given my fatigue, did not feel good.

"But Strike wasn't into decorating. Couple bedrooms, kitchen, bath, living-dining combo, all painted piss yellow. The only art in the place was a calendar taped to the refrigerator door. Had an ad for birdseed down in one corner."

I wondered what high culture adorned Slidell's walls.

"Any sign of a break-in?" I asked.

"No."

"Did it appear Strike was killed there?"

"No blood, no overturned furniture, broken glass, rifled drawers."

"No sign of a struggle."

"Or someone cleaned up."

"You requested CSU?"

"Never thought of that."

Take a breath.

"Do you know if they found a key chain containing a voice-activated audio recorder?"

I heard springs squeak, assumed Slidell was reaching for the list of items recovered by the techs.

"Nothing like that on the log. Why?"

"Strike had one when she first visited me. Said she'd found it at the Burke County overlook where the initial remains were discovered in 2013."

"What was on it?"

I described the three voices.

"Jesus leaping Christ. You didn't make her give it up?"

"I had no warrant to compel her to do so." Curt.

I heard a voice, then the line went hollow as Slidell pressed the receiver to his chest. I was turning in at the annex when he reengaged.

"So the house yielded nothing of interest?" Wanting to wrap up and get inside.

"I didn't say that. One bedroom was ass to armpit with cartons full of file folders. We're talking an episode straight out of *Hoarders*."

"Websleuthing cases?"

"I got some guys going through 'em."

"Is Cora Teague in there?"

"I got some guys going through 'em."

"What about a computer?"

"No cell. No computer."

"Did you check her car?"

"I don't know how I'd muddle through without you."

"She had to have a laptop. She spent a lot of time on—"

"The weird wide web. I get it. The house has wi-fi."

I killed the engine. Out my windows, the lawns and gardens of Sharon Hall looked as dark and deserted as the grounds of Heatherhill.

"Did you locate Wendell Clyde?" I asked.

"Yeah. The toad still lives in Huntersville. First thing tomorrow, I haul his ass to the bag to discuss his recent accomplishments."

"Do you want me—"

"I can handle it."

We both set a land speed record disconnecting.

It was almost eleven. Though exhausted, I knew the subliminal *ting-a-ling* would be ruthless in denying me sleep.

After appeasing Birdie, I texted Mason's Johnson City phone number to Ramsey, then got online and started searching. There wasn't a lot. But what I found explained why the wee synapse had fired.

Oscar Mason was a pioneer in the field of medical photography and radiography and, for over forty years, head of the photography section at New York's Bellevue Hospital. Throughout his career he provided hundreds of illustrations for works published by physicians associated with the hospital and its medical college. Mason retired in 1906, died in 1921.

Okay. That tracked. Edward Gulley would have been among his later subjects.

Mason served as president of the American Institute, Photographic Section, and held office in the American Microscopical Society.

Impressive. But why had I heard of the guy?

I read on.

Bingo.

In 1866 a morgue was constructed at Bellevue, modeled after the much larger showpiece for the dead in Paris. Beginning the following year, Mason's duties included photographing deceased unknowns. Photo and corpse were numbered correspondingly, and the bodies were displayed for up to seventy-two hours on stone tables behind a wall made of iron and glass. Unclaimed UIDs were eventually buried at the Hart Island City Cemetery.

Thus the mental *bong!* Back at the gray dawn of history, I'd learned of Mason through a grad course on the evolution of coroner systems. We'd viewed examples of his work, read an annual report in which he pleaded for a facility to allow him to photograph cadavers indoors.

I followed more links. Found a factoid that caught my eye.

"Oscar Mason's most notable photos appeared in the great dermatology atlases written by George Henry Fox."

The World Wide Web is a spectacularly wondrous creation. It took little searching to find Fox's *Photographic Atlas of the Diseases of the Skin*. The entire four volumes, published between 1900 and 1905 and now public domain, had been digitized, colorized, and uploaded.

I scanned image after image. The table of contents. Found no mention of an "ectodermal-dental syndrome of unknown origin." No plate showing Edward Gulley with his shadowed eyes, spotted skin, wonky nails, and mangled dentition. But the style was unmistakable. Grandpa Gulley's page had come from a Fox publication.

Though unnecessary, I pulled up the picture I'd taken with my iPhone before parting with Susan Grace. As Uncle Edward stared at me glumly, I compiled a list of his oddities.

This round took longer. But my diligence paid off. By 2:00 A.M. I had a diagnosis for Mason and Edward Gulley.

I dropped into bed, saddened, but also elated. And confused.

Sleep came hard and fast.

But the subconscious is also a wondrous creation.

An hour later I was wide awake. This time the synapse was clamorous.

I knew whose face I'd be viewing the next morning in stone.

23

A breeze was working to stir things up, but with the soft nonchalance characteristic of spring. Sunlight through the magnolias was throwing shifting patterns across the patio bricks.

The early morning beauty was wasted on me. Two hours had passed since I'd phoned Hawkins. I was on fire to get to the lab.

When I arrived, Mrs. Flowers was busy at her gatekeeper post. Flicking her a quick wave, I hurried to change into scrubs.

The concrete was as I'd left it. Except for the layer of chemical remover now coating the silicone sealant.

Not even stopping for coffee, I rang downstairs. Hawkins arrived in minutes. After gloving, he spent an eternity removing the white gook with a small plastic scraper. Finally, the sealant was gone and the cracks were visible.

While I steadied the concrete, which probably accomplished little, Hawkins loosened the clamps. Together, we muscled the mold out of the vise and onto the counter.

"Ready?" he asked.

I nodded.

Simultaneously, we eased up on the pressure. The concrete split along its original cracks. I held my breath as we both tugged backward.

The two sides parted. The liquid rubber coating had done its job. The mold slid easily from the dental stone filling its interior. As we wiggled the detached halves free, I stabilized the cast, then lowered it onto the counter.

The product of our work lay facedown. The head appeared to be reasonably well formed, though dented where air had bubbled or where the concrete had been damaged. Impressions of hair feathered its outer surface.

Using two hands, and again barely breathing, I carefully rolled the cast, then upended it onto the flat base formed by the top surface of the dental stone.

I've seen photos of famous death masks, a few originals. John Dillinger. Dante. Napoleon. Mary, Queen of Scots. Each gruesome effigy had captured, in a cold, macabre way, the spirit of the person no longer among the living.

Each viewing had triggered goose bumps like those now puckering my flesh.

Hawkins and I were standing shoulder to shoulder, staring, when Larabee pushed through the door.

"Do we have liftoff?" Seeing the bust, his grin morphed to an O. "Holy bleeding lizards." Larabee joined us and planted his hands on his hips. "I'll be damned."

"Yeah," I said softly.

The detail far exceeded my wildest hopes. Except for some minor distortion in the eyelids, it was like looking at a face recumbent in sleep. Long slender nose. Prominent cheekbones. Jaw that would have benefited from a less obtuse angle.

"Is it Cora Teague?" Larabee asked.

"No."

"Any idea who?" Surprised.

"Mason Gulley."

"Who the flip is Mason Gulley?"

"Do you have a few minutes?"

"Sure." Looking at his watch. Mind undoubtedly on a body on a table down the hall.

"I'll meet you in your office. I want to collect my phone and some printouts."

While Hawkins cleaned up the stinky room, I briefed Larabee on everything that had happened since I'd seen him on Monday. Then I showed him my iPhone image of the G. H. Fox plate.

He studied the screen, brows V'ed low over his nose. "The facial looks like a shot from one of those old-timey photo booths."

"It's a page from a historic medical text. The pictures were taken by a Bellevue Hospital photographer named Oscar Mason."

I showed him photocopies of images I'd downloaded from the Internet. He viewed them, then turned back to the phone.

"Who's the subject?"

I told him about Edward Gulley. And Mason. And Susan Grace.

"I'll admit, there's a resemblance to your cast. But how can you be certain it's this kid Gulley?" Clearly dubious.

"Ever hear of Naegeli-Franceschetti-Jadassohn syndrome?"

"Refresh me."

"NFJ syndrome is a genetic condition, inherited as an autosomal dominant."

"So if a parent has it, each child has a fifty percent chance of inheriting."

"Yes. People with NFJ syndrome sweat very little or not at all, so hot weather and intense physical activity are not well tolerated. An affected individual may have dark spots on the abdomen, chest, or neck. Sometimes around the mouth and eyes. The discolorations are lattice-like in patterning, and tend to appear between the ages of one and five. They may fade during the teen years or persist for life."

"I see the abnormal pigmentation." Larabee, still

eyeing Edward Gulley. "Reticulate." Referring to their netlike appearance.

"Other symptoms include thickening of the skin on the palms of the hands and soles of the feet, brittle fingernails, and, less frequently, nails that are poorly aligned on the big toes."

"Check all of those boxes."

"Dental anomalies are common, including missing teeth, yellowed and spotted enamel, early cavities, and early tooth loss."

"I see all of that. But to conclude that—"

"Another defect associated with NFJ syndrome is absence of fingerprints."

The brows V'ed up. "Oh."

"The thumb and fingertip from the Burke County overlook had no prints."

"What's the population incidence of NFJ syndrome?"

"It's estimated to be one in two to four million."

"Pretty good odds."

"Yes."

"So it's likely Mason Gulley's head was in that bucket."

"Yes. The fine blond hair from the swabs. Witness statements that Mason was odd. Grandma Gulley's assertion that he was unnatural. The death mask resemblance to the photos of Edward Gulley. The lack of prints on the pine tar fingertips, assuming they're his. It all points to NFJ. Thus, to Mason."

"So *all* the other remains found so far are his?"

I raised both palms. "All the bones are consistent in terms of age and body size. There are no duplications. I can't say they're all from the same person. I can't say they aren't."

"Will a maternal Gulley relative provide a DNA sample?"

"Not a chance with Grandma. Susan Grace is a minor."

Larabee considered. "So it's still possible parts of Cora Teague were also recovered."

"Or someone else."

"I'm sensing you don't think so."

"I don't think so."

"You know it's not enough."

"I know."

"We won't be giving an NOK notification."

"No."

Larabee drummed reflective fingers on the arm of his chair. "It's pretty clear Gulley was murdered."

"His head was in a bucket."

"Any thoughts on that?"

I shared Susan Grace's comments on Cora Teague, the fatal "fall" of her brother Eli, the SIDS death of the Brice baby. Then asked, "Who was the ME up there back then?"

"Avery County has a coroner," Larabee said.

"Great." Unlike medical examiners—doctors in most, though not all, cases in North Carolina—

coroners could be anything from a mechanic to a mortician.

"Not sure who the wise voters had in office in 2008 or 2011. Let me look into it."

"What's up with Strike?" I asked as Larabee jotted a note.

"Haven't heard word one from Slidell."

"He planned to interview Wendell Clyde this morning."

"The battle of the websleuths." Larabee gave a tight shake of his head.

"The Internet exchanges between Strike and Clyde were vicious."

"Shall we make Skinny's day?" Leaning forward to punch keys on his phone. Two rings, then, "Slidell."

"Tim Larabee here."

"Can't talk, Doc. I'm at a scene." Racket carried through the speaker. A slammed door. The distant wail of a siren. Agitated voices.

"How about a quick update on Hazel Strike?"

"That soap opera just took a new twist." We waited as Slidell barked an order at someone. "I'm in a condo off Carmel Road, looking at a whole lot of brains on a wall. Selma Barbeau, seventy-two, Caucasian female, widowed, living alone. Some bastard rearranged her face with the Brooklyn Smasher she kept by her bed for protection."

Larabee's eyes met mine. "Barbeau was murdered with a baseball bat?"

"Eeyuh."

"You think it's the same guy who killed Hazel Strike?"

"Naw, Doc. Widow ladies get bludgeoned on my beat all the time."

I scribbled a name and raised the paper for Larabee.

"Have you interviewed Wendell Clyde yet?" he asked.

"Clyde's cooling his heels downtown. Not looking good as our doer anymore, but a little sweat'll improve his attitude."

I congratulated myself for not commenting on Slidell's contradictory imagery.

Back in my office, I was about to hit speed dial on my iPhone when the thing vibrated in my hand. Unidentified caller. Not sure why, but I answered.

"Hi, Mom. This has to be very brief."

"Oh, God. Katy! I'm so happy to hear your voice." She sounded a million miles off. I pictured her in a call center, an M16 slung over one shoulder, a line of soldiers waiting at her back.

"How are you? Is everything okay? Do you need anything? I can send a package." So fast I was almost babbling.

"I'm good."

"How's Afghanistan?"

"Perfect today, better tomorrow."

"Funny. Is it still cold?"

"We hit eighty degrees yesterday."

"You're sure you don't need anything?"

"Mom, I'm good. My unit is moving out. I just wanted to call and say hi."

"Moving out?" Calm.

"No big deal. But it may be hard to phone for a while."

"A while?" Absolutely calm.

"Not long. Anything new on the home front?"

I'd told Mama. It seemed only fair to tell Katy. And prudent. "Andrew Ryan has asked me to marry him." I didn't add that he'd done it months ago.

A splinter of a pause, almost unnoticeable. Then, "And?"

"I haven't given him an answer."

"Why?"

"I'm not sure."

"Do you love the guy?"

"Yes."

"So why are you stalling?"

"I wouldn't call it stalling."

"What would you call it?"

"Thinking."

"Are you still skittish because Dad burned you?"

"No." Yes.

"It was a dick move, but that doesn't mean Ryan will cheat."

"No."

"So what's the problem?"

"I'm not sure."

"Go for it."

"That was quick."

"Someone has to be. Does Grandma know?"

"Yes."

"What did she say?"

"Go for it."

"Gotta love Daisy."

"Mmm. Have you talked to your dad?"

"I'm going to call him now. So I should go. Love you!"

"Love you, too, sweetheart. Stay safe."

"Always."

She disconnected.

I took a moment to come down. Then, feeling a mix of elation and alarm, which I carefully hid, I phoned Ramsey.

Like Slidell's, Ramsey's voice came riding a tumult of sound. He was also mopping up after violent death. His encounter involved a Buick, a Bronco, and a bottle of Jack D.

Over the intermittent sputtering of his radio, I told him about Mason Gulley. And about Slidell's new theory concerning Hazel Strike. Ramsey must have picked up on something in my voice.

"You're not buying that Strike's murder is unrelated to what's gone on up here? To her investigation into Cora Teague?"

"No." A sudden thought struck me. "I think Strike was in Avery County last Saturday. When we were together in Burke, she had issues with you. Do you suppose she could have sent that boulder our way?"

"Why?"

"To distract us? Because we pissed her off? Because she was crazy?"

"Or could Wendell Clyde be our guy? Maybe thinking Strike was down there with us?"

Always questions. Never answers.

"Any success with the impressions?" I was referring to the hollow vacated by the rock.

"Tool mark guys are saying crowbar."

"Any particular kind?"

"No."

Great. That narrowed the possibilities to roughly ten zillion.

"The Devil's Tail bucket definitely contained Mason Gulley's head," I said, as much to organize my own thoughts as to continue briefing Ramsey. "And I'm sure the Burke County thumb and fingertip were his. That suggests that the original torso bones from Burke are also Mason's. Which leaves only the Lost Cove Cliffs material."

"You hear back from the WCU prof on that?"

"No."

We both waited out a loud burst of static. Ramsey must have turned down the volume, because the crackling grew more muted.

"So someone cut this kid up and tossed his body parts from at least two, maybe three overlooks."

"Looks that way," I said.

"Who?"

"I'm not liking what I'm hearing about Cora Teague. Dead sibling. Dead baby. The she-devil ref."

"Killer, not vic." Ramsey's tone suggested he'd been dipping his toe in the same murky waters.

"Maybe we've been going at it all wrong."

I heard him inhale deeply. Exhale. "What do you propose?"

"I'll try again to contact the anthropologist who did the analysis on the Lost Cove Cliffs remains. I'll also phone our DNA folks to see if they've had any luck sequencing anything. I'd sure as hell like to know if we're looking at a single victim."

"And on my end?"

"How about we meet in Asheville first thing tomorrow?" I said. "Have a chat with the Brices." A return to the mountains was the last thing I wanted right then. Though, mercifully, Asheville was a quicker drive from Charlotte than the trek to Avery County.

"Roger that."

A second, then Ramsey read off an address. I wrote it down.

"In the meantime, I'll see what I can dig up on the Brice baby's death. The more info we have, the better we can press them."

"And maybe look into Cora Teague's health issues," I suggested.

"You know how that will go."

I did. Cora was a minor. No one would reveal squat about her medical history.

"Be clever," I said.

"Deputy Devious. Going ten-eight."

Dead air.

I wasn't sure the meaning of Ramsey's code. But I liked the guy more with each interaction.

I phoned the DNA section. Was told the person running the samples, a tech I didn't know named Irene Trent, was out to lunch. I requested a callback.

The conversation reminded me I'd eaten nothing since a bagel at seven that morning. The clock now said two-fifteen.

Quick trip to the staff lounge. I zapped a frozen burrito. While downing it with a Diet Coke, I tried Ryan. Again got voice mail.

For a second I saw Ryan's face, softly shadowed in the yellow porch light. In my mind I heard his stumbling proposal. We hadn't spoken in days. Why wasn't he returning my calls?

A pinprick of fear. Had I waited too long? Had he changed his mind about wanting me to come to Montreal? About wanting me at all?

I spent the next hour photographing the bust of Mason Gulley. Different angles. Different lighting effects. In some shots the resemblance to Uncle Edward was freaky. In the black and whites, Mason looked eerily alive.

Observing the wretched stone face, I again felt

revulsion for Martha Gulley. How could a woman revile a child for a genetic lapse that occurred at his conception? Condemn her own grandson?

Trent finally phoned back at four. She didn't laugh when I asked how the DNA testing was coming, but she came right to the edge. Fair enough. I'd submitted the samples only one week earlier. Her opinion, when pushed: The bone was shit. Don't bet the farm on a testable sample.

As we were disconnecting, I remembered the swabs I'd taken from the hollow inside the concrete. Asked to be transferred to trace.

Got voice mail. Left a message.

I was on a roll.

Next I tried Marlene Penny at WCU. Was shocked when she picked up. Disappointed with what she could tell me.

The bones, found by her students in 2012, represented portions of a lower leg and foot. Due to extensive surface abrasion and fragmentation, she'd been unable to determine gender, race, height, age, cause of death. The remains had been sent to the University of North Texas for DNA testing. All attempts at amplification had failed. The bones were now in a box in her lab.

"Shall I scan and send you copies of my photographs?"

"Sure. Thanks. Eventually, I'll need the bones."

I provided my email address and we disconnected.

I was sitting, dulled by frustration, when my mobile

started buzz-skipping across the blotter. I tipped my head to read the caller ID.

Great.

One steadying breath. I clicked on. "Hey." Perky as a cherry topping a sundae.

"Oh, Tempe." Breathless. "Are you just too unbearably busy to talk?"

"Never too busy for you, Mama. What's up?"

"I was *so* afraid to tell you. I was petrified what you'd think. What you'd say." So tremulous her words were taking little hops. "That's why I was unforgivably distracted during your visit. Then you told me your news. Well, I was—"

"What is it? What's wrong?"

"Oh, sweetheart."

"Tell me!" Heart racing.

She did.

In long, swoopy superlatives and giddy little gasps.

24

Mama's words buzzed like an electrical short in my head. As I walked to the car. Drove home. Prepared cheeseburgers and ate them with Birdie.

I didn't want to reflect on what Mama's euphoria could mean. Didn't know in reality what I thought of her tale.

My mother, gray-haired and dying of cancer, was madly in love.

I didn't fly to the phone or fire off a text or an email. Frankly, I wasn't sure where to reach out. Her Heatherhill doctor, Luna Finch? Goose? Harry?

Somewhere in her giddy outpouring, Mama had mentioned my sister. I decided to start there.

Harry didn't answer her cell. A chirpy voice asked me to "Leave a short message like this one!" I did. With a far less bubbly air.

Baby Sister called as I was brushing my teeth.

"Have you talked to Mama?" I asked, still swishing and spitting.

"Now, Tempe, don't you take that snippy tone. She's happy."

"She's crazy."

"Well aren't we Judge Judy."

"You're right. That was insensitive. But Mama is hardly what you'd call a stable personality."

"She says she's taking her pills."

"Mama always says she's taking her pills."

"She's under the eye of a boatload of doctors."

"That will do it." Our mother was a master at sleight of hand. Had, over the years, evaded medication in the most creative of ways.

"Goose knows all Mama's tricks." Defensive.

"Right. So who is this geriatric gigolo?"

"Clayton Sinitch. And he's not all that old."

"Please say the guy's not thirty-five."

"The guy's not thirty-five."

"Harry!"

"He's sixty-three."

"What does he do?"

"Owns a dry-cleaning shop."

"Well hallelujah! Mama can get her pants pressed at a discount."

"And all her pleats starched."

I caught the purry innuendo. Wanted absolutely nothing to do with the image.

"Where is Sinitch from?"

"Arkansas."

"How did she meet him?"

"He's recharging his batteries at Heatherhill."

"How long has she known him?"

"That's not important."

I waited.

"I don't keep her calendar, Tempe. I don't know. Maybe a couple of weeks."

"Harry." Oh so controlled. "She's out-of-her-Guccis swept away with the guy."

"Maybe a bit of romance will do her good."

"Or maybe it's a con and the asshole's going to break her heart."

"She's agreed to the chemo."

"What?" Mama hadn't told me that.

"She's agreed—"

"Because of Sinitch?"

"He vowed he'd love her when she's bald as a coot."

"What else do you know about him?" Rolling my eyes. Immediately feeling guilt for having done it.

"He buys her flowers and chocolates. They hold hands. They take meals together in the dining room. He scolds her for putting salt on her food."

"Really?"

"I gather they're also spending quality time in her suite."

"Harry!"

I wasn't believing this. Was confused over what to feel. Mama's apathy on my last visit wasn't due to an impending downward spiral. She was either preoccupied daydreaming about Sinitch or focused on hiding the guy's existence from me.

"Don't let on I told you about the chemo," Harry said.

"Why not?"

"Apparently she doesn't want you to know. Now promise."

"Harry, this is—"

"I mean it. Not a word."

"What's a coot?" Defeated.

"I think it's some kinda bird."

I said good night and we disconnected.

No way I was up to phoning Ryan.

A 2014 National Geographic publication on the world's best cities described Asheville, North Carolina, as "a mecca of awesome mountain scenery, bohemian art, and high southern cuisine." The little burg has repeatedly snagged the top spot on surveys ranking towns as to livability. More than once, it has been voted the most desirable place to live in America.

Asheville is artists and street musicians and microbreweries. The nineteenth-century Downton-Abbey-eat-your-heart-out Vanderbilt house. The University of North Carolina–Asheville.

But, like Avery to the northeast, Buncombe County is a schizoid mélange of the civilized and the backward. Outside the prize jewel, there are no tourists. No antiques shops, Christmas boutiques, or vegan bistros. Out past the ski slopes and nature outfitters, gun cabinets are kept stocked and the Ten Commandments rule with an iron fist.

This time Ramsey arrived first. He was waiting at one of a half dozen cement tables outside Double D's, a red double-decker bus turned coffee shop on Biltmore Avenue in Asheville's small downtown.

"Costa Rican drip." He slid a mug my way. "Hope it's still hot."

"Thanks." The cream was frothed and configured into a meaningfully artful design whose symbolism was lost on me. The coffee was tepid but tasty.

"Good drive?"

"Yeah."

"Ladies first?"

"I have little to report. Still waiting on DNA from the bones, trace from the concrete." A lobotomy on Slidell.

"Good work." Ramsey pulled the obligatory spiral from his jacket and thumbed a few pages. "Joel Brice is thirty-four, a sculptor, part of Asheville's large, I don't know, hippie community I guess you could call it. Crystals. Sandals. Hummus and yogurt."

"I thought he was a welder."

"He works in metal. Katalin is thirty-six, bakes organic breads to sell to area restaurants. Neither has an arrest record. Their daughter Saffron is seven."

"Where does Saffron attend school?" Not sure why I asked.

"She's homeschooled."

"Like Mason Gulley."

"And a lot of kids. The Brices are Unitarian now, but for several years belonged to Jesus Lord Holiness."

"Until River's death."

"Yes."

"That's quite a philosophical leap from über-Catholic to Unitarian."

"Perhaps they're spiritual seekers."

As usual, Ramsey's expression was impenetrable. Was he mocking me? Them?

"The Brices live a few clicks north of here." Repocketing the spiral. "We can ask them all about it."

Ramsey knocked back the dregs of his coffee. Came away with a milky mustache. I pointed to his upper lip. He wiped it with his napkin and stood.

We left my car and took the SUV. No Gunner. I kind of missed him.

The neighborhood was one of mature trees, sagging overhead wires, and modest homes, some newer, most probably built in the twenties and thirties. The Brices' house was one-story, with green siding and a fully roofed porch that kept the front door and windows in perpetual shade. Curtains draping a double dormer window suggested an attic bedroom.

The house, like its neighbors, sat on a small ridge above street level. The porch was accessed by narrow steps rising from the sidewalk through bushes that were probably pretty in summer.

Ramsey and I had a routine by now. As he rang, we stood to either side of a door whose small glass window was divided by scallopy mullions. Reminded me of a Gothic cathedral in miniature.

A dog took great interest in the sound of the bell. A big dog. Or a small one with truly impressive vocals.

In seconds the door swung open, releasing the sweet, doughy smell of baking bread. A girl regarded us, relaxed but curious. Cujo, not so relaxed, but at least he didn't charge out the door.

"Who is it? A female voice came from somewhere beyond the girl's back.

"A policeman." The girl's dark hair was center-parted and braided. Her eyes, deeply green, looked out from a pale, heart-shaped face.

"Hold Dozer, Saffron baby." Footsteps hurried toward us.

The girl placed a hand on Dozer's head. The dog stopped growling, but continued eyeing us with open suspicion. Composed of a big chunk of mastiff, the beast easily outdid me in poundage. And drool.

The woman appeared holding both arms up and away from her body. They were white with flour and her face was red with exertion. Her smile, at first friendly, wavered on seeing the deputy's uniform.

"Katalin Brice?"

"Yes. And you are?" Eyes moving between Ramsey and me.

"Deputy Zeb Ramsey." Displaying his badge. "This is Dr. Brennan." Glossing over my qualifications. "We'd like to speak with you briefly."

"About?"

"May we come in?" Directed more at Dozer than his mistress.

Katalin Brice looked past us to the street. In the morning sun, her short curly hair sparked like copper, her eyes like the sapphires in a brooch I'd inherited from Gran. Totally sans makeup, she was stunning.

Perhaps reassured by the Avery County logo on the SUV, Katalin stepped back. "Dozer, go to your bed."

Radiating disapproval, the dog withdrew.

"I'm baking and mustn't let the dough sit. Do you mind if we talk while I work?"

"Of course," Ramsey said.

Katalin and Saffron led us to the back of the house, through living and dining rooms that were worn but spotless. The hardwood floors looked original, the paint fresh.

The furnishings, sparse and eclectic—papasan chairs, string beads hanging in a doorway, a framed poster of Gandhi—reminded me of my grad school apartment. A plaque on one wall read: "Someday, after we have mastered the winds, the waves, the tides and gravity, we shall harness for good the energies of love."

Every horizontal surface held a metal objet d'art. Most were abstract, all swooping curves and jutting appendages. A few appeared to be animals, though the species were none I'd ever encountered.

The kitchen was surprisingly large. At its center was a heavy pine table flanked by benches. Beside the stove was an enormous oval cushion now occupied by Dozer.

The table held a stainless-steel bowl, a rolling pin, and a lump of dough large enough to sink a beluga. Six bread pans waited in a line on the counter.

"Please." Winging an elbow outward, using the inside of the other to brush errant curls from her forehead. "I'm sorry about the mess."

Ramsey and I dragged a bench from under the table and settled, one at each end. Saffron slid a book down the one opposite and sat. Dozer watched, eyes rolling with the action, head never leaving his mat.

"Teilhard de Chardin." I began my always-engaging warm-up.

At first Katalin looked confused. Then her smile broadened. "You noticed the plaque in the dining room. Do you know him?"

"We are not human beings having a spiritual experience. We are spiritual beings having a human experience." The only quote I could dredge up by the French priest-philosopher.

"Yes. That's one of my favorites."

While Katalin kneaded, Ramsey began. At the

mention of River, the rolling and punching increased in intensity.

"We are so very sorry for your loss," I jumped in. "I can't imagine the pain of losing an infant."

"It was nature's will."

"SIDS."

"Yes."

"Can you elaborate?" As gently as I could.

"River died in his sleep. What is there to say?"

Noting movement across the table, I stole a glance at Saffron. Her body was tense, her eyes fixed on her mother's face.

"Was a physician involved?"

"The baby was dead, so the coroner was called. No need for a doctor."

"Do you know who that coroner was?"

"No." Knuckle-punching the dough. To Ramsey, "You're the one who phoned. You talked to Joel."

"Yes," he said.

"Joel is at his studio. He won't be happy that you're here."

"We won't stay long." A beat, then, "You and your husband were members of the Jesus Lord Holiness church at the time, is that correct?"

"We attended briefly."

"Why that church?"

"Joel and I believe there is more to existence than worldly concerns."

"Why did you leave?"

She paused. Again used the inside of her elbow to brush hair from her face.

"We thought spiritual fulfillment might best come from ancient ritual, from people seeking personal engagement with forces existing on a higher plane." Back to the bread. "We tried Jesus Lord Holiness. It wasn't for us. Now we belong to the Unitarian church. Its principles align more closely with our current worldview."

"And that would be?"

She answered slowly, prefacing each sentence with a series of jabs to the dough.

"We believe that all humans are welcome at the table of God's love and fellowship. That the divisions that separate us are artificial, that all souls are one. We don't focus on an afterlife, strict doctrine, or a written creed. We express our faith through acts of justice and compassion."

I wasn't sure if she was summarizing Unitarian beliefs or those of Joel and herself. But it sounded more reasonable than hellfire and speaking in tongues.

"What can you tell me about Granger Hoke?" Ramsey asked.

"Father G." Katalin lifted, then dropped the dough. "No comment."

"Did you know Mason Gulley?"

"Only to say hello."

"Your impression?"

"He was a sad young man."

"Cora Teague was your nanny?"

Across the table, Saffron's little shoulders hiked up sharply.

Katalin reached out to her daughter. "It's okay, baby."

"Do you remember Cora?" I asked the child gently.

Saffron whipped to face her mother, eyes wide with alarm. "Why are they asking about Cora?"

"She's missing," I said gently. "Deputy Ramsey and I are trying to find her."

"Will she come to our house, Mommy?" So shrill Dozer shot to his feet.

"No, sweetheart."

"Which one, Mommy?" Saucer eyes probing her mother's. "Which one?"

"Come here."

Saffron flew from the bench and fired around the table.

Katalin hugged then released her daughter, leaving two white handprints on the girl's back. Cupping the small chin, she said, "I want you to take Dozer out into the yard. Can you do that for me?"

A solemn nod, then the child skittered off, the dog on her heels.

"That was a very strong reaction," I said.

"Saffron feels things deeply."

"Still."

"She doesn't like Cora Teague."

"Do you know why?" Skimming a glance at Ramsey.

"When Saffron was three she broke her wrist falling from her tricycle. Cora was with her at the time. I suspect she unconsciously associates the pain with the person."

"Has she talked about the incident?"

"We try to focus on happy things."

"How did Cora explain the accident?"

"Explanations." Something flickered in Katalin's eyes, there in the blue, then gone. "It doesn't matter if the water is cold or warm if you're going to have to wade through it anyway."

"Also Teilhard de Chardin?"

She nodded.

"Was he the reason you tried Catholicism?"

"Perhaps." She pointed an elbow at the empty bread pans. "I'm sorry. I have deliveries due by noon."

Ramsey and I followed her to the front door. We were on the porch when her words made us pause.

"There was a pillow in the crib." I turned. Katalin was looking not at us but at something off in the distance. Perhaps off in time.

"With River," I guessed.

She nodded.

"I never put a pillow in his crib." Almost a whisper.

"Did you tell someone?" I asked.

The deep indigo eyes swung to me, so filled with pain the connection felt like a blow. "Father G."

"What did he say?"

"Beware of sinners bearing false witness."

25

Ramsey's cell buzzed as we were descending the steps. He checked the screen, then tossed me the keys.

I unlocked the SUV and got in. While he stood outside and talked, I scrolled through email on my iPhone. Trying not to appear curious, but covertly watching.

Ramsey's body language was, for him, animated. Shifted weight. A hip-planted hand. A cocked chin. I wondered if the call was business or personal. Either way, it was not going well.

For the first time I considered the deputy's private life. Aunt Ruby had said her nephew needed a girlfriend. That he'd come from Georgia and that his marriage had ended badly. He had a dog. Beyond those few details, I knew nothing.

One email was from Larabee. As I opened and read it, Ramsey clipped the cell to his belt and strode toward the car. He wasn't smiling.

"Sorry." He started the engine but didn't shift into drive.

"Just got word from my chief," I said. "The Avery County coroner who would have handled both the Eli Teague and River Brice deaths was a guy named Fenton Ogilvie. He died in 2012."

"Right. He'd just passed when I joined the department. A retired ambulance driver." Ramsey gave a small shake of his head. "They found him at the bottom of an elevator shaft. Apparently Ogilvie was quite a character."

"Meaning?"

"No point in speaking ill of the dead. But the guy seems to be remembered for two accomplishments. Keeping himself perpetually drunk, and cultivating one colossally cirrhotic liver."

"And the elevator thing."

"And that." A few thumb-taps to the wheel. "Your comment about Cora Teague's absenteeism got me thinking. I pulled the date from Eli's death certificate, then called Avery High. Cora was out for six weeks after the kid died."

"The death of a sibling would be traumatic."

"Six weeks?"

"That is a lot."

"I also got the name of Cora's doctor."

"The school kept it on file?"

"Terrence O'Tool. His office is in Newland. If you're up for it, we can swing by there now."

"Damn right I'm up for it." Inwardly groaning. Newland meant back to Avery, a good hour and a quarter longer return to Charlotte.

I followed Ramsey. Whose driving shaved at least fifteen minutes off the trip. And my life.

We were almost to Newland when he surprised me by pulling to the shoulder. I followed suit and he walked back to my car. I lowered the window and he leaned down, one arm on the roof. To anyone passing it looked like I was getting a ticket. From a very careless cop.

"Check it out." Ramsey tipped his head toward a large log cabin on the opposite side of the road. The front porch featured a pair of picnic tables, a life-size carved wooden bear, a plastic trash can, a rectangular tank that probably held bait during fishing season.

The cabin's single window was covered with flyers curling from the inside of the glass. Above the door was a neon sign saying J.T.'S FILL UP AND FIX UP.

In front were two gas pumps. In back was a low, windowless structure made of corrugated tin. Running along its foundation was a paved area divided into rectangles by chain-link fencing.

I looked a question at Ramsey.

"John Teague's entrepreneurial genius. Guidebooks, gum, and gas for passing motorists. Plaster, paint, and plywood for do-it-yourself locals."

"What's in back?"

"John's kid trains dogs."

"Owen Lee."

"Yeah."

"People send their pets to live in that dump?"

"I doubt these pooches are pets."

"Still."

"As I understand it, Owen Lee operated out of his home until the missus took issue with the barking and poop. Four summers back he built the eyesore you're looking at and moved the operation here. He must have customers, because he's still training dogs."

I was about to ask a follow-up when the man in question rounded the building leading a German shepherd the size of a panzer. He paused on seeing us, face blank.

Ramsey flicked a wave. Ignoring the greeting, Owen Lee unlocked a gate and walked the dog inside an enclosure.

Ramsey slapped the roof of my car, then returned to his SUV. On the road again.

Newland, until its incorporation, was known as the Old Fields of Toe, named not for a digit but for the town's location at the headwaters of the Toe River.

Today Newland's main claim to fame is that it's the highest county seat east of the Mississippi. There's not much there—the courthouse and library, a few shops, the Shady Lawn Lodge, the Mason Jar Cafe. Out in the boonies, mile upon mile of Christmas tree farms.

Ramsey drove past the Avery County Courthouse and his departmental headquarters. After passing a feed store, a True Value hardware, and a pharmacy, he made a jigsaw pattern of turns, then pulled onto a patch of gravel fronting a two-story duplex that was brick on one side, frame on the other. Below the brick were broad picture windows stenciled with the name of a realtor.

The frame half was painted white and had an angled roof sloping down from left to right. Upstairs were two windows, both hung with closed blinds. Downstairs was another window, also covered on the inside, and two concrete steps leading to an aluminum door. A very small plaque identified the structure as the O'Tool Professional Building.

"Lofty," I said.

"There are two of them in there. O'Tool, Cora Teague's doctor, and a dentist."

Ramsey and I got out and entered. It was like stepping into a time warp.

The waiting area contained several cracked vinyl chairs and laminate tables laden with ancient magazines. A coatrack. A toy box. A dusty plastic plant. The art consisted of posters warning about unwanted medical and dental conditions. Shingles and gingivitis seemed to be big.

A woman occupied one chair. Her sleeping baby looked patient. She did not. An elderly man occupied another, eyes glued to a dated copy of *Field & Stream*.

A staircase rose steeply on the left. A single door

opened off the back wall. Between them was a reception counter staffed by a woman who had to be in her eighties. She had blue-white hair permed into tight little curls, bifocals, and a pink scrub top dotted with little blue bunnies.

The woman looked up at the sound of our entrance. Tracked our approach with an expression equal parts welcome and confusion. A white rectangle above her left pocket said MAE FOSTER, R.N.

"Deputy." Foster's smile revealed badly yellowed teeth.

"Ma'am." Ramsey grinned and nodded. "We'd like to speak with Dr. O'Tool."

"Do you have an appointment?"

"No." The tone made it clear that we did not need one.

"One moment, please."

Foster left her post to disappear through the door, closing it carefully and quietly behind her. As we waited, I sensed interested eyes on our backs.

The door opened shortly, and Foster gestured us into the inner sanctum. I heard the woman with the baby cluck in annoyance.

"Please." Foster herded us into an office. "Dr. O'Tool is seeing a patient but will be with you soon."

Most of the office was taken up by a large wooden desk. Behind it was a Herman Miller Aeron chair that looked like it had taken a wrong turn from NASA. Behind that, a credenza pressed up to the wall.

Opposite the desk were two upholstered chairs. Ramsey and I each took one. Wordlessly, we looked around.

Bookcases were filled with journals and texts. The desktop was stacked with medical files, some thin, some thick as telephone books. On the credenza were a few framed photos, a glass trophy, and a small gold cross. I looked to see if Ramsey had noticed the latter. He had.

Above the credenza, a single framed diploma declared Terrence Patrick O'Tool a graduate of the Quillen College of Medicine, East Tennessee State University, class of 1963. I was doing the math on his age when the good doctor came hurrying in.

Before Ramsey and I could get to our feet, O'Tool circled the desk, dropped into the whiz-bang chair, and swiveled to face us. His hair was white and so sparse I could see right through to his scalp. His skin was saggy below his eyes, shiny on his forehead, chin, and cheeks, as though stretched too tightly over the bones.

Though a starchy lab coat hid his frame, I could tell O'Tool was small and lean. And obviously spry.

"I don't know you, Deputy." Implying this was an uncommon occurrence.

"Zeb Ramsey. I'm relatively new, sir. Dr. Brennan is from Charlotte."

"Welcome." A long way from warm. Or curious. A fellow professional, yet not a single question about my background or area of expertise. "My nurse tells me this is urgent."

"We won't take up much of your time."

"Saying that just did."

Scratch the opening act. Ramsey got right to the point. John and Fatima Teague, Jesus Lord Holiness church, Cora's disappearance, the theory that she left with Mason Gulley. As Ramsey talked, O'Tool kept nodding his head.

"Until she disappeared, Cora was your patient. Is that correct, sir?"

"Have Mr. or Mrs. Teague given you written permission allowing me to discuss their daughter's medical history?"

"No."

"If I did treat Cora, and I'm not confirming that I did, you know I'm bound by patient–doctor privilege."

"Did?"

"Excuse me?"

"You used the past tense."

"Did I?"

"I can get a warrant."

"Perhaps you can."

A beat, then Ramsey tried again. "Suppose I tell you that Cora and Mason may have come to harm."

"Do you know that for a fact?"

"It's a strong possibility."

When O'Tool said nothing, Ramsey hit him with a zinger.

"Is it possible Cora Teague could be hurting others?"

The doctor's eyes, unblinking, revealed nothing. I couldn't tell if he was being cagey, or was simply obtuse.

"Cora's brother Eli died at age twelve," Ramsey continued.

"I knew Eli."

"Any thoughts on the incident?"

"The death of a child is always tragic." O'Tool's face remained passive and utterly composed.

"Like River Brice."

"Yes. I heard about the baby."

"Did you know the coroner Fenton Ogilvie?"

"I did. Safe using the past tense there."

"Ogilvie signed both the children's deaths as accidental. Was he competent?"

"Fenton was poorly toward the end of his life."

"Meaning he was an alcoholic."

"Is that a question?"

"The Brices fired Cora because of health issues. What were they?"

"Really, Detective."

"Let me lay down some facts, Doctor." Ramsey's voice had gone steely. "River Brice died on Cora Teague's watch. Saffron Brice broke her arm while in Cora Teague's care. Saffron is distressed on hearing her former nanny's name."

"I'm sure the child—"

"The ER physician who treated Eli Teague had reservations concerning the explanation of events surrounding his death."

"Did he share those reservations with Ogilvie?"

"He noted them in the chart."

Blank stare.

"Cora missed six weeks of school following Eli's death. Where was she during that time?"

Nothing.

"Cora may be dead or she may be out there. And she may be dangerous. Dr. Brennan and I need to know what's wrong with her."

There was a long flatline of silence. When I was certain O'Tool would dismiss us, he spoke in a very low voice.

"Cora's issues were primarily behavioral."

"What does that mean?"

"I was treating her for epilepsy."

O'Tool's comment was moronic. "Epilepsy isn't a behavioral issue," I blurted. "Epilepsy results from abnormal electrical activity in the brain."

"Yes." Frosty. "It does."

"Are you trained in neurology?"

"I am a GP."

"Did you refer Cora to a specialist?" I was growing more outraged with every word that came out of his mouth.

"Cora was having seizures. An EEG showed an epileptic focus in her right temporal lobe. It did not require a specialist to diagnose TLE, temporal lobe epilepsy."

"Did you prescribe an AED?" I referred to antiepilepsy drugs. Of which there are dozens.

"For a while the child took Depakote. It did not help. If anything, the medication made her episodes worse. Ultimately, her parents chose to discontinue use of all pharmaceuticals. To treat the condition in their own way."

"Treat it how?" Ramsey asked.

"Cora was on a regime to ensure that she ate regularly and got enough sleep every night. John and Fatima were working hard to keep her stress levels low, and to ensure that she used no drugs or alcohol."

"Are you for real?" This was sounding straight out of the dark ages.

"Cora had"—O'Tool stopped to correct himself—"has good periods and bad periods. During the bad periods, when she has fits, her parents keep her at home."

Fits?

"When did you last see her?" Sensing my growing indignation, Ramsey retook the reins.

"The summer of 2011. Her puppy had died. She was very upset and blamed herself."

"What happened to the dog?" I demanded, feeling the now familiar cold tickle.

O'Tool's eyes leveled on mine, filled with thought, perhaps with no thought at all. "It fell from Cora's upstairs bedroom window. I've often wondered how the animal managed to climb onto the sill."

I was about to ask another question when someone knocked on the door. "Dr. O'Tool?"

"Yes, Mae."

"Mrs. Ockelstein is growing impatient."

"Show her into room two and take her weight and blood pressure." Turning to us. "I have patients."

We were dismissed.

Back in the SUV, I shared my apprehension concerning Cora Teague.

"Eli, the baby, the puppy." I realized I was speaking too loudly, tried to tone it down. "Maybe Mason Gulley."

"You think Cora killed them?"

"She's the common link."

"Could epilepsy make her violent?"

"Unlikely. But an epileptic should be taking antiseizure medication."

"You question O'Tool's handling of Cora's condition?"

"That knucklehead couldn't handle a hangnail without a manual. And I'm sure he wasn't being fully honest with us."

"You think he was lying?"

"Maybe. Or at least holding back."

"Why?"

I raised my hands in a frustrated "who knows?" gesture.

"So what are you suggesting?"

"I don't know. But every path leads back to Cora."

While I was driving, names and faces whirled in my brain like flakes in a snow globe. Terrence O'Tool. Fenton Ogilvie. Grandma, Susan Grace, and Mason Gulley. John, Fatima, Eli, and Cora Teague. Joel, Katalin, Saffron, and River Brice. Father G and Jesus Lord Holiness church.

Again and again one name swirled to the surface.

Twenty miles down the road the thought scissored in. A wild jolt of realization.

I pulled to the shoulder and dialed my cell. And floated the name Granger Hoke.

26

While awaiting a callback, I diverted to Heatherhill.

As before, I arrived during supper. To my surprise, Mama's suite was empty.

Recalling Harry's words, I doubled back to the dining room. Through the wide arched doorway I spotted Mama at a table for two. Her dinner companion, I assumed Clayton Sinitch, was short and so bald the overheads reflected off his scalp. Round specs, plaid shirt, cardigan, bow tie. I wondered if his look was intentionally retro or just old-guy dorky.

Mama was wearing pearls and a pale gray sweater. Her face was pink with pleasure, perhaps with the wine sparkling red in a goblet by her plate.

As I watched, Sinitch reached out and placed a hand on hers. Mama dipped her chin and glanced up through lowered lashes, a flirtatious mademoiselle.

Something surged in my chest and knocked against my ribs. Anxiety? Love?

Envy?

Unexpected tears burned the backs of my lids.

Behind me, a clock chimed softly. Feeling like a voyeur, I quietly withdrew.

The return call came twenty minutes later as I was clicking my seat belt after a quick stop at a KFC. I checked the screen, then answered.

"Thank you for calling me back so quickly." Setting the bag on the console and the phone on the dash.

"Quiet night in the rectory."

Aren't they all? I wondered.

"How is your mother?"

"You know Daisy." He did. Father James Morris, Mama's confessor the on-and-off times she viewed herself as Catholic, still served as pastor of St. Patrick's in Charlotte. Rector, actually, though I wasn't totally clear on the distinction. I knew his status was higher than a priest, lower than a bishop.

"I will take that to mean she is well."

"I'm driving, Father. So I've got you on speaker."

"Conversation won't be a distraction for you?"

"I'm eager to hear what you've learned."

"Sadly, not much. Because of the hour, all I could do was check the *Official Catholic Directory*. It's a publication for clergy that, among other things, lists all parishes and priests."

"You found him?" The car was a smell-bubble of fried chicken. As we spoke, I dug and scored a drumstick.

"Yes and no. Granger Hoke isn't currently listed, so I worked my way back through old annual editions. Nothing is ever discarded around here. It took a while, but my perseverance paid off. Granger Hoke was born in St. Paul in 1954."

"I thought the entire population of Minnesota was Lutheran."

Morris ignored the quip. Humor had never been his strong suit. Growing up, Harry and I had called him Rigor. Even Gran had joined in the joke at times.

"No, not at all. Minnesota has many Catholic parishes."

"Garrison Keillor?" I hinted. "Never mind."

"Hoke was ordained in 1979 after training at Mundelein."

"Near Chicago."

"Yes. It's part of the University of St. Mary of the Lake. Hoke ministered in the Midwest for almost fifteen years—Indiana, Iowa, Illinois—smaller, non-urban parishes from what I can tell. Eventually he was relocated to Watauga County in North Carolina."

"Then what?"

"After that he disappears."

"What does that mean?"

"I don't wish to speculate. I'll research further in the morning." Morris's voice sounded tighter. I wondered if there was something he wasn't telling me.

"Thanks, Father. I'm very anxious to learn more."

As I drove through the darkness, my brain ran

an unrelenting quiz-show barrage of questions. Where was Hoke after moving east? Had he left the priesthood? Was he off doing missionary work? Was he too ill to work? Had he been relieved of priestly duties?

Questions. More questions. No answers. But my focus had shifted to Hoke.

Overnight, spring took control in Charlotte. No more compromise. Winter, be gone.

As I crossed the patio, the air felt velvety soft on my skin. A million crocuses poked yellow and white from the wet black earth in my garden. The Bradford pear was thick with newborn leaves and blossoms resembling tiny pink embryos.

My moods are strongly influenced by weather. Despite frustration over the Brown Mountain bones, worry for Mama, agony over Ryan, and an early ambush call from Allan Fink the tax tyrant, I felt invigorated. Capable of solving every unanswered riddle. Or maybe it was the coffee.

My optimism was about as long-lived as a virtual particle. Angled in a space in the lot outside the MCME was a familiar Ford Taurus. The car's exterior gleamed shiny white, as though recently washed and waxed. While passing, I glanced through a side window. The interior was neat, the backseat empty except for a blue canvas athletic bag.

Shocked at the automotive tidiness, I hurried inside,

hoping Slidell had come with news about Hazel Strike. When I pushed through the door, Mrs. Flowers waved me over with a birdlike flick of her wrist.

"Detective Slidell is in your office." Breathless. "I hope that's okay."

That was the instant my buoyancy began to erode.

"He's not here for Dr. Larabee?" I asked.

"No, no. He wants to see you. He was quite insistent, and I didn't know—"

"It's fine." It wasn't. "How long has he been here?"

"Just a few minutes."

Hardly breaking stride, I hurried toward the back.

A wall of cologne met me at my office door. Purchased at a drugstore and applied with gusto.

"Morning, Doc." Slidell didn't stand, didn't even straighten in his chair.

"Good morning, Detective."

I sat, slid my purse into a drawer, laced my fingers on the desktop, and waited.

"Your guy's out."

"My guy." Not following.

"Wendell Clyde."

"You ran him?"

"All over the map."

"Does he have a criminal record?"

"Couple drunk and disorderlies, twenty years back. Nothing recent."

"What do you mean he's out?"

"He's a dick and a half, but he ain't the doer."

"On Strike."

"No. On JFK. I'm working some grassy knoll angles in my spare time."

I bit back a retort and raised my eyebrows.

"First off, did you know Clyde's about nine foot eleven?"

"Is that relevant?"

"It is when you're wrestling the baboon into a backseat. I nearly—"

"The average baboon weighs fifty pounds." Juvenile. And slightly inaccurate. But I wasn't discussing species variation with Skinny.

Slidell pulled a paper from his jacket and tossed it onto the blotter. I unfolded it and studied the image, probably taken with a phone and printed on a computer.

The subject was seated in one of the small interview rooms at the Law Enforcement Center. I recognized the faux wood table and gray metal chair, the mauve patchwork carpeting and off-tone upper wall.

Slidell hadn't exaggerated. But Wendell Clyde wasn't just tall. He looked like an Easter Island head with arms and legs. His deep-set orbits were hooded by slashing brows and separated by a jack-o'-lantern nose.

"You interviewed Clyde?"

"No. I read his mind. Which ain't impressive."

"Your point?"

"Some guys you get the feeling there's more than meets the eye? This prick, what meets the eye's more than he's got."

"Meaning?"

"Low on charm, high on T." Slidell's shorthand for testosterone.

"Clyde was aggressive?"

"He had his moment."

"Until you snapped him with a wet towel."

"Something like that."

"What's his story?"

"He's an honest plasterer, searches for dead people as a hobby."

"What did he say about Hazel Strike?"

"He didn't send the lady birthday cards."

"Was he willing to take a polygraph?"

"Eager as a beagle on bacon. But it don't matter. Clyde alibis out."

"No shit?"

"No shit."

"Tell me." Deflated. The mood collapse was now total.

"Clyde claims he was at the Selwyn Avenue Pub from seven P.M. Saturday until one A.M. Sunday. Says a lot of people saw him there."

"That doesn't clear him. He could have—"

"You want to talk or listen?"

My molars clamped tight.

"He claims he was being interviewed for a piece

on websleuthing. A blogger from Dubuque named Dennis Aslanian."

Slidell paused, maybe daring me to interrupt. I didn't.

"From the pub, Clyde went with Aslanian to a couple more bars, eventually to the guy's room at a Motel 6 by the coliseum. The star-crossed lovers stayed together until Aslanian left Charlotte early Monday morning."

Slidell was right. If Hazel Strike died on Sunday, and Aslanian backed Clyde's story, Clyde couldn't have killed her.

"You've talked to Aslanian?"

"There's an idea."

I took a deep breath. Got a noseful of Stetson or Brut.

"I've left messages with Aslanian advising a timely reply. Today, I'll swing by the Motel 6, the pub when it opens, float Clyde's mug."

"Where is he now?"

"Had to cut him loose."

"Do you still believe there's a serial killer targeting elderly women in Charlotte?"

"I do."

"So Clyde's not topping your list."

"Not even close."

"Why are you telling me, not Larabee?"

Slidell didn't move or say anything for a long moment. Then, "Brief me on this Brown Mountain thing."

"I don't know that Brown Mountain is really a factor."

"Yeah yeah yeah." He actually snapped his fingers.

I told him about the remains, including the printless fingertips and the head in the bucket, about Mason Gulley and his NFJ syndrome, about Granger Hoke and the Jesus Lord Holiness church, about Cora Teague and the innocent dead that seemed to litter her path, about the alcoholic coroner, Fenton Ogilvie, about Terrence O'Tool and his inept diagnosis.

When finished, I stared at Slidell. He stared back at me. A full minute passed.

Sometimes Skinny surprises me. He did so now.

"You think it ain't epilepsy? That maybe this kid's crazy?"

"'Crazy' is not a medical term."

"That maybe she's goofy as a guppy and killed her brother, the baby, and the pooch? That maybe someone's covering for her?" The bags under Slidell's eyes twitched as another theory darted into his brain. "Or maybe someone snuffed her?"

"Who?"

"You said the father's a hot wire."

"He's tightly wrapped. But kill his own daughter?"

"Maybe some kind of honor thing. Or maybe one of Hoke's wingnut Jesus freaks did it."

"Why?"

"Murder draws eyes. Maybe they saw the kid as a threat to their nasty little secrets."

"Maybe they killed Mason Gulley." On impulse, I swiveled my chair, grabbed Ramsey's envelope, and slapped a photo onto the blotter. "That's Cora Teague. Somehow I don't see a teenage girl dismembering a body and distributing pieces from assorted overlooks. Also, the voice recorder isn't consistent with the girl as killer." Slidell was voicing the same suspicions I'd been refusing to accept.

Slidell eyed the snapshot, opened his mouth, closed it. Another long moment passed before he tried again.

"Hazel Strike was the one first poked a stick down the hole?"

"She was," I said.

"She went to Avery?"

"Yes. She searched an overlook and I know that she talked to Cora's parents. And that she called Cora's school and the hospital where Eli died. I think she was up there again the Saturday she phoned me." The day before she was killed.

"She was."

"Seriously?"

"I checked Strike's cellphone records. Jesus Christ, you'd think I was asking for a tap on Obama's private line."

"And?"

"She hardly uses the thing, but they got a couple pings early that morning. Towers put her on I-40, probably heading for Avery. After that the thing's either shut off or the battery dies."

"Have you found the phone?"

"No."

"Any progress on her laptop?"

"I got a message from IT asking for a callback. Why is it those geeks always sound like they just swallowed a gerbil?"

Taking the question as rhetorical, I offered no theory.

Again, Slidell's lips parted. I'll never know what he intended to say. When the landline shrilled, he inhaled deeply and dropped his eyes to his hands.

The call was coming from the CMPD crime lab.

It was the start of a cascade that would end with horrific results.

27

Early in the twentieth century a French investigator named Edmond Locard observed that when two objects come into contact there is always some exchange of material. Ditto two people. I touch you. You touch me. We share bits of ourselves. The notion became known as Locard's exchange principle.

Seems obvious in the age of *CSI* and *Bones*, but back then the idea was madly cutting-edge. Today the concept keeps thousands employed in forensics labs around the globe. Hair, fur, fibers, fabric, rope, feathers, soil, glass, biological or chemical substances, whatever. Trace evidence experts identify and compare materials hoping to tie a suspect to a victim or to a crime scene. And the process can be quite high-tech.

Which is why the analyst, a newbie named Bebe Denver, was droning on.

Across from me, Slidell took out a Swiss Army

knife and began mining a surprisingly unclogged thumbnail. It was like rubbernecking a traffic wreck—I had no desire to watch but couldn't help myself.

". . . elemental analysis using atomic absorption, or with a scanning electron microscope equipped with an energy-dispersive spectroscope. Using the gas chromatograph or the mass spec one can separate out chemical components. Are you with me, Dr. Brennan?"

I didn't want to be rude, or to dampen her enthusiasm, but it wasn't my first trace rodeo. I just wanted the bottom line before Slidell left blood spatter all over my office.

"Sounds like you were very thorough," I said.

"Yes."

"Could we stick to the results for now? Later, if I have questions, discuss the process?"

"Of course. I'll put everything in my report. Every single detail."

Hot damn. A dissertation on elemental analysis. Life doesn't get better than that.

"Perfect," I said.

"The concrete itself is a mixture of portland and a number of other cements. I identified hydrated lime, shale—"

"The basics?"

"Right. It appears to be a blend of cements, sand, and gravel—a concrete designed to set quickly."

"Like Quikrete."

"Exactly."

"Available at any Home Depot."

"Yes." A little dispirited.

Slidell stayed focused on his nails. But I knew he was listening.

"And the material I swabbed from the interior surface?"

"That's interesting." Keys clicked. "The substance contained triacylglycerols, triglycerides or fats, and small quantities of free fatty acids, glycerol, phosphatides, pigments, sterols—"

"So what is it?"

"Olive oil."

Denver took my nonresponse as confusion.

"Triacylglycerols are normally composed of a mixture of three fatty acids. The oleic-oleic-oleic triacylglycerol is most prevalent in olive oil, followed by palmitic-oleic-oleic, then oleic-oleic-linoleic, then palmitic-oleic-linoleic, then stearic-oleic-oleic, and so on."

"Olive oil." Thinking aloud.

"Olive oil contains more oleic acid and less linoleic and linolenic acids than other vegetable oils." Again, mistaking my comment as a request for elaboration.

"You're sure?"

"I also found microscopic bits of olive."

I was chewing on that as Denver surged forward.

"The other substance was more challenging. I found a small concentration on just one swab, barely enough to analyze." More keys. "Acid resin, gum, boswellic acids, 4-0 methyl glucuronic acid, incensole acetate, phellandrene—"

"Translation?"

"I'm not certain. The boswellic acid is interesting."

Something unimaginable winged from under Slidell's nail onto my blotter. I plucked a tissue, gathered the gunk, and dropped it into the waste. Slidell trolled on.

"Boswellic acid comes from plant resin. In African and Indian traditional medicine it's used to alleviate inflammation. Studies are looking into its usefulness in the treatment of autoimmune diseases like rheumatoid arthritis and Crohn's. Also certain cancers—leukemia, brain, breast."

"Where does one get boswellic acid?"

"Online, a pharmacy, a health food store. It's readily available."

Like Quikrete.

"Thanks, Bebe." Hiding my disappointment poorly. "I appreciate your diligence."

After disconnecting, I shared Denver's report with Slidell.

"So why's the stuff in a bucket of concrete with Mason Gulley's head?"

I pictured Edward Gulley, with his unfortunate hair, nails, skin, and teeth.

"Maybe Mason mixed boswellic acid with olive oil and put it on his hair or scalp." I knew the suggestion was lame as I made it. "Or applied it to his skin or cuticles."

"Stylin'." Refocusing on the manicure.

"Could you give that a rest?"

"What?" Slidell's eyes rolled up.

I gestured toward the grooming routine. "It's distracting."

Sighing theatrically, Slidell folded and repocketed the knife.

"Where's your buddy Ramsey on the Gulley thing?"

"*Deputy* Ramsey is pursuing a number of leads."

Slidell snorted, then de-de-de'ed the opening riff from "Dueling Banjos."

"You of all people should understand he hasn't the luxury of concentrating on just one case."

"Well oh my God in a tutu. Ex-*cyooz*-ay moi."

A dozen neurons fired at once. Images exploded.

Hazel Strike in the chair now overflowing with Skinny. Conversation threads in a websleuthing chat room. A page in an outdated medical text. Susan Grace Gulley in the dark in my car.

Awareness exploded in my forebrain.

I snatched up the phone and dialed Ramsey. Launched in without preamble.

"Oscar Gulley was named for the photographer Oscar Mason, right?"

"You're talking about Grandpa." Ramsey, confused but trying to loop in.

"Yes. Susan Grace said her grandfather was

named for Oscar Mason. Suppose she meant both her grandfather *and* her brother were named Oscar Mason Gulley. Gramps went by Oscar, Mason went by—well you get it, right?"

"Yes." Drawn out. Indicating he didn't.

"OMG. The person who posted on CLUES about Cora Teague's disappearance. The websleuthing site." I knew I was talking way too fast. "I took the username to mean Oh My God. But what if it's initials, not cyberjargon?"

Slidell was watching me, left eyebrow cocked.

"Oscar Mason Gulley," Ramsey said.

"Yes."

"I'll be darned. What made you think of that?"

"I'm with Detective Slidell. He made a ballet reference." Putting it kindly. "That made me think of Susan Grace, because she lied to her grandmother in order to follow me, and the photos of Oscar's brother, Edward, and Hazel Strike's account of CLUES, and my own research. Bang. Suddenly it all came together."

"The brain as supercollider."

"Yes." Uncertain the accuracy of the analogy.

"Want me to call Grandma?"

"Better to go to the courthouse and pull the birth certificate."

"I'm on it."

When we'd disconnected, I started to explain to Slidell.

"I got ears."

"Should I ask Susan Grace about the olive oil concoction?"

"And say what? Hey, Sis, did Big Bro put goop on his hair? Larabee's not confirming ID, so, far as the family knows, the kid's still kicking."

Slidell was right. Such an odd question would arouse suspicion.

Before Slidell left, I got online, logged in to CLUES, and double-checked the dates of OMG's postings. The first occurred in August 2011, roughly a month after Cora Teague dropped from sight. The last was in September, approximately one month later.

Slidell was halfway through the door when Ramsey phoned back. I put him on speaker.

"You're dead-on. Mason's birth certificate lists his full name as Oscar Mason Gulley. Grandma filed it. Neither parent had bothered."

"Slidell and I checked dates," I said. "OMG's posts tally with Susan Grace's story about Mason going to Johnson City. The posts end around the time he stopped contacting her."

"Okay," Ramsey said. "Say it's true. OMG is Mason Gulley. What does it mean?"

Not one of us could put forth a reasonable guess.

When Slidell left I sat a moment arguing with myself, weighing obligation to a nameless victim against personal commitment. Then, moving at sloth speed, I dialed and canceled my flight to Montreal.

Dreading the upcoming discussion, I called Ryan. Got voice mail. Guilt-ridden at feeling I'd escaped a bullet, I sent a lengthy email explaining my decision. Ryan would understand. Or he would not.

But did *I*? Was I relieved over dodging an unpleasant phone conversation? Or over avoiding the trip?

I found Larabee in his office, briefed him, as I'd promised Slidell I would. No anthropology case had come in, so I told him I'd be heading home to work on my taxes.

Larabee's look expressed what he thought of my procrastination. He'd probably filed in January.

I really did plan to stick with it. And did. Until four-fifteen, when Father Morris phoned.

"I have information for you." In a somber news-caster voice that sent a frisson of a tingle up my spine.

"Great." I reached for a pen.

"I think it best if we speak face-to-face."

"Sure." Looking at the paper piled around me in not-so-neat stacks. At the half-full carton. Half-empty? "Shall I come to the rectory?"

"Yes. Perhaps in an hour?"

"I'll see you then."

I disconnected and looked at Birdie, who was looking at me. I could swear the cat shrugged.

St. Patrick parish is in Dilworth, a neighborhood one circle outside of uptown. Though modest as such structures go, the church is actually a cathedral, the mother ship for the Diocese of Charlotte. Neo-Gothic in style, it has the usual limestone and stucco exterior, domed nave, bell tower, and stained glass. High above the front doors stands a statue of the good saint holding his staff.

St. Pat's was forty years old when renovations began in 1979, a face-lift that continued on and off for three decades. New marble altar, pipe organ, and bell. Spiffy copper roof, shiny hardwood floors, Celtic cross on the lawn. Perched on her hill, the old gal is now nipped and tucked and looking damn fine.

While visiting me a few years back, an out-of-town friend queried the high number of colleges in Charlotte. Not understanding the Queen City's love affair with religion, she'd misinterpreted the town's abundant and expansive religious complexes for institutions of higher learning.

St. Pat's is no exception. With its main church, parish family life center, gardens, lawns, parking lots, convent, and rectory, the grounds resemble a small university campus.

Ten minutes after leaving the annex, I parked where Morris had directed and climbed the steps to the rectory. A thumb to the bell produced a soft lyrical bonging. I was about to give it another go when the door opened.

"Tempe. Please excuse my casual appearance." Morris was wearing a most unpriestly combo of jeans, plaid shirt, and green wool vest. "I've completed my pastoral duties for the day."

"You look very stylish." Jesus, was that appropriate? Crap. Jesus as an expletive? Double crap. Decades since I'd last donned my little uniform, priests and nuns still made me nervous.

Morris smiled. "Shall we go into the study?"

The foyer had a tapestry on one wall, a woman chastely cloaked from head to toe, bathed in heavenly light. A red Persian on the floor, a carved wooden chair in one corner, an elaborately banistered staircase on the right. The study was a short way down a very wide hall. Portraits of somber clerics hung on both sides at perfectly spaced intervals.

The study was wood-paneled and lined floor to ceiling with shelves on three walls. Another Persian underfoot, this one in tones of green.

A cement-manteled fireplace was centered on the fourth wall. Before it were two Queen Anne chairs and a small table. Above it was a jarringly colorful painting. To one side was a small glass-fronted secretary.

Morris led me to the fireplace grouping. I sat. He didn't.

"Can I offer you something? Perhaps tea?"

"Tea would be great," I said.

I half expected him to ring a tiny bell to summon a shuffling nun with a dowager's hump and mummy-wrinkled face. Instead, he hurried from the room.

I ran my usual mental inventory.

The painting was a landscape. Maybe. Lots of oranges and blues and what I thought could be a horizon.

A desk took up the far end of the room, mahogany with clean, sleek lines. Facing it were two uninviting wooden chairs. A ploy to keep whiny or cantankerous supplicants moving along with their tales?

The shelves were filled with books, journals, and the occasional decorative piece. Through the glass secretary doors I could see framed snapshots, a silver tray holding a small flask of yellow liquid and remnants of what appeared to be dried palm frond. Mother-of-pearl opera glasses. A brass candlestick.

Morris returned with a tin of tea bags, two napkins, two spoons, and two mugs of steaming water.

"Hope you don't mind instant."

"My usual poison." Jesus!

I chose peppermint. He went for chamomile. As we removed the wrappers and began dipping, he started in.

"No one wants to talk about Granger Hoke."

Though my pulse kicked up a notch, I never broke stride with my bag.

"I hope you can keep what I tell you confidential." Setting his mug on the table, his dripping bag on the napkin.

"I will try my best. But—"

Morris held up a hand. "I understand that may not be possible if Hoke is involved in something criminal.

It's just that the church has received a great deal of bad press in recent years."

"Father," I said, but stopped there, unsure of what to say. His reference needed no explanation.

"Don't misunderstand me, Tempe. What was done to these children is vile and disgusting. And sinful. Any priest who engaged in such behavior must be punished to the full extent of the law."

"But you feel the situation has been misrepresented by the media?" I didn't like where this was going.

"Much of the coverage has been fair and justified. Some has not. All I am saying is that another scandal would be devastating to the church."

Morris dropped the hand and lifted his mug. Didn't drink.

"A few rogue priests do not define who we are. Deep in my soul I believe the clergy is made up of moral and honorable men. Men who love God and their fellow human beings and want to make a difference in this world."

Morris looked past me for a moment. But I saw his face reflected in the secretary glass. In his eyes I saw pain, perhaps fear.

My mouth went dry. I braced myself, certain Morris was about to tell me Granger Hoke had sexually molested children.

I could not have been more wrong.

28

Morris turned back to me, face tired and sad.

"In 1998, Granger Hoke was defrocked for performing unauthorized exorcisms."

"Exorcisms." Not sure if the feeling washing through me was relief or shock.

"Yes."

"As in driving out demons?"

"I suppose you could put it that way."

"How would you put it?"

"As defined in the catechism of the Catholic Church, an exorcism is the public and authoritative demand, in the name of Jesus Christ, that a person, place, or object be protected against the power of the Evil One, and withdrawn from his dominion."

"Satan."

"He is real, in some form."

"This isn't the fifteenth century, Father."

"No. It's not." Patient smile. "But evil still exists in

this world and exorcisms are still performed. In fact, the Vatican reviewed the process and revised the rite in 1999, though use of the traditional Latin form is still permitted."

"Performed under what circumstances?" I'd seen *The Exorcist, The Rite,* but that was Hollywood. I was having trouble wrapping my mind around the concept of Lucifer in America in the age of Silicon Valley and Twitter.

Morris sipped his tea before answering, perhaps compiling a list in his head.

"Indicators of demonic possession include supernatural abilities and strength, speaking in foreign or ancient languages not known to the subject, knowledge of hidden or remote things to which the subject cannot be privy on his or her own, aversion to holy objects, profuse blasphemy, sacrilege."

I could only stare.

"The underlying assumption is that the subject retains his or her own free will, but the devil has taken control of his or her physical body. The ritual involves prayers, invocations, and blessings that—"

"Who can perform an exorcism?"

"Technically, anyone."

"Technically?"

"Yes. But the church recognizes the dangers inherent in exorcisms conducted by untrained individuals. And the potential for charlatanism. So only an ordained priest is permitted to perform the rite. And only with the express permission of his bishop. Don't misunderstand me, Tempe. Exorcisms occur extremely rarely, and only following careful medical and psychiatric evaluation."

"Granger Hoke is an ordained priest."

"Was."

"Fine. What was the problem?"

Morris raised the mug to his lips, lowered it without drinking.

"At one time, the function of exorcist was part of the ordination of priests. In hierarchy, the office fell somewhere above deacon and below full priest. Few seminaries now train exorcists, and today any ordained priest may perform the rite. But only those appointed by the bishop or archbishop are allowed to do so with the blessing of the church."

"Official exorcists."

"Yes."

"How many are there?"

"Typically, one per diocese or archdiocese."

"And Hoke wasn't one of those sanctioned." I could see where this was going.

"No."

"Yet he kept doing it."

"Though reprimanded and told to desist. But unauthorized exorcism wasn't the only issue. Hoke was eventually relocated from the Midwest to North Carolina. In the mid-nineties, while pastor of a small parish in Watauga County, he began deviating from traditional Catholic teachings, shifting toward a more fundamentalist, Pentecostal doctrine."

Morris nodded to himself and looked down at his mug.

"Did you know that exorcisms are performed by charismatic, Pentecostal, and many other brands of Christianity? I read recently that, by conservative estimates, there are at least five or six hundred evangelical exorcism ministries in existence today, quite possibly far more."

"Hoke put a hellfire spin on his preaching?"

"He did."

"And it got him booted."

"Defrocked. After that he vanished for a while, eventually reappeared in Avery County and established the Jesus Lord Holiness church. Though ordered not to do so, he calls himself a priest, wears a cassock and collar, says Mass, administers the sacraments, and preaches his own distorted version of Catholicism."

"Which features a starring role for Satan."

"Yes."

Somewhere beyond the quiet of the study, a door closed.

"Are exorcisms legal?"

"As long as the subject agrees of his or her own free will."

"So the church has no way to stop a rogue like Hoke."

"Sadly, no."

"Anything else?"

A second slipped by. When Morris answered, his voice had the same guarded tone I'd heard on the phone. "No."

In that brief hesitation I knew he was lying. Or at least holding back.

"Thank you, Father." I stood.

Morris walked me to the door. Said "God be with you." Offered a blessing. I took a pass.

"Remember what I've said about honor among priests, Tempe. I believe in it. And I believe in the church."

I didn't respond, knowing my voice would betray my suspicion about his forthrightness. I started down the steps.

"Tempe."

I turned.

"Be careful."

I left him, bathed in lamplight, framed by the needlework woman in her halo and robes.

Back home, I hit the fridge, made myself a ham and salami sandwich, and popped a Diet Coke. My mind was snapping with a horrifying new solution to the puzzle. But there were still gaps.

Nerves humming, I booted my Mac, eager to dig up everything I could on Granger Hoke. To snug into place the last missing pieces.

And found zip.

But I learned volumes about exorcism.

Hours later, I slumped back in my chair. The room had darkened around me. The cold cuts and bread felt solid as a rock in my gut.

I knew the victims. The probable cause of death. The meaning of the trace.

Inexplicably, I felt an overpowering desire to talk to Ryan. More than a desire. A need.

I lit a lamp and relocated to the couch. Dialed.

Ryan answered sounding, well, nothing. When motivated, the man is a master at disguise.

"Hey," I said.

"Hey," he said.

"Did you get my email?"

"Yeah." Too flat.

"You do understand why I had to cancel?"

"It's a mean business we're in." There was a nuance I couldn't read low in his voice.

"Are you working something?" To avoid treading dangerous ground.

"Homicide. Farmer found facedown in his barn outside Saint-Amable. Jean-Guy Lessard."

"Is it going well?"

"Not for the asshole I've got in the box."

"What's the story?" Barely interested. Wanting to get on with my own.

"Lessard feels sorry for the neighbor kid, hires him for odd jobs as an excuse to toss money his way." I heard the flare of a match, a soft fizz, an expulsion of air. "Tuesday, Lessard goes into town, so the kid decides to check out the safe. Lessard returns early, surprises him. The kid panics, puts three slugs in his chest."

"No good deed goes unpunished?"

"You've got it."

"It's a solve, Ryan. You did your job."

"Pop the bubbly." No masking now. Ryan sounded raw-edged and spent. "The poor schmuck leaves behind a wife, three kids, and a crappy ten acres."

"I'm sorry."

"Sorry doesn't help. You at home?"

"I am. You?"

"Yeah." Ryan took another deep pull on his cigarette.

"I had it all wrong," I said.

A moment. Then, "The Teague thing?"

"Yes."

"You don't think the kid's dead?"

"I do think she's dead. And Mason Gulley."

"I'm listening."

I told him about my conversations with Susan Grace Gulley and Katalin Brice. About Mason Gulley's head in the concrete. About Denver's trace evidence report.

"What the hell's boswellic acid?"

"A substance extracted from the resin of trees in the family Burseraceae. Most of it comes from the Arabian Peninsula, Somalia, India."

"For what?"

"It's an ingredient in a wide range of health and aromatherapy products. And a component in frankincense."

"Wise men bearing gifts."

"I think it was the three kings, but yes." Birdie hopped onto the couch. I paused to allow him to curl beside me. Perhaps for melodrama. "Frankincense and olive oil are commonly used in the performance of exorcisms."

"Exorcisms?"

"Yes."

"Like vomit and levitation and rotating heads?"

"That's movie bullshit."

"What's your point?"

"Millions of people still believe in evil spirits."

A fractional pause. "You talking about Hoke and his holiness nut brigade?"

I provided a condensed version of what I'd learned from Morris. The unauthorized exorcisms. The shift toward a hellfire theology. The defrocking.

"Wait. Back up. What are you saying?"

"Mason's grandmother referred to him as unnatural. Cora's father called her a whore. Both are missing. The trace suggests Mason was exorcised."

"Let me get this straight. You're suggesting the priest killed Cora Teague, dismembered her, and tossed her body parts from overlooks surrounding Brown Mountain?"

"Ex-priest. And I'm not saying it was Hoke."

"Who?"

"I don't know."

"And this unknown perp killed Mason Gulley following or during an exorcism, cut off his head, stashed it in concrete, then tossed his body parts from the same overlooks?" Ryan's skepticism was thick as pea soup.

"Could you be a little more condescending?"

"Convince me."

"Think about it. His own grandmother said he was evil made flesh."

"What was her beef?"

"She thought he didn't look or act like a boy should. Maybe it wasn't just the NJF syndrome. Maybe Mason was gay."

"Then why run off with Cora Teague?" That tone again.

"I'm just thinking out loud here, Ryan."

"And Teague?"

"Ramsey and I talked to Cora's physician, a buffoon who hasn't updated his skills since the Bronze Age. He was treating Cora for epilepsy."

"You're suggesting Gulley was killed because of bad nails and bad teeth, and Teague was killed because she had seizures?"

"If she even had them. I think Cora's issues were psychiatric."

"Go on."

I told him about River Brice, Eli Teague, and the puppy.

"Whoa. You're saying the kid was homicidal?"

"I'm saying a lot of crap went down around her."

I waited out another cigarette moment. Smoking meant Ryan was stressed. I was sorely regretting my impulse to share.

"Here's my take. You have no positive ID on any of the Brown Mountain remains. No DNA. I'm guessing Larabee's not signing off on Gulley based on a hunk of cement and oddball fingertips."

"No."

"You have no known victim, no primary scene, no weapon, no motive, no witnesses, no legit suspect. You don't know for sure if Cora Teague is dead. Or even missing. Her mental state is mere speculation."

My face felt like hot tin. Ryan was right. It was all conjecture.

I said nothing.

Ryan took another deep drag, then asked, "How does Hazel Strike fit in?"

"I'm not sure. Strike phoned me three times on Saturday. Maybe she'd uncovered something and told the wrong person."

Because I'd ignored her. Again the guilt.

"Hoke?" Ryan said.

"I never said the killer was Hoke!" So sharp Birdie scrambled to his feet.

"*Tabernac*. Don't bite my head off."

"Sorry."

"Have you rolled this past Slidell? He hasn't mentioned it."

"When did you talk to Slidell?"

"Couple times."

"Why?"

"I wanted his take on something. Does that bother you?"

It bothered the hell out of me.

"Let's talk about something else," I said.

I heard the sound of Ryan's phone switching ears. "How's the weather down there?"

"The trees are in flower. It's spring."

"It's snowing here." On a very long breath. "The river is still frozen."

"Try to stay warm."

"I lit a fire."

The melancholy in Ryan's voice sent a million images flaring in my head. His face, which I knew by heart, down to the scar on his brow from a biker's bottle. The tiny flecks of teal in the too-blue eyes.

I saw in detail the place he was sitting. Where I'd sat so many times. The stone hearth. The snowy river spreading out beyond the wide wall of glass. The leather couch, scratched by Birdie's claws in an embarrassing rollover.

The guilt and anger morphed into a sudden aching. A hollowness, like a void calling out to be filled.

"Fly down for a visit," I said softly.

"I'd like that."

"Soon?"

A beat. Then Ryan sighed. "I didn't mean to give pushback."

"Just playing devil's advocate?"

"Clever pun."

"It's what I do."

I smiled. Wondered if Ryan was smiling a thousand miles to the north.

The moment, if it was one, ended quickly.

"Lay out your scenario for Slidell. See what he thinks."

"Does Skinny think?"

"He's a good cop."

I fell asleep wondering at Ryan's newborn appreciation of Skinny Slidell.

29

I woke feeling edgy and out of sorts, as though my skin was no longer large enough for my body. Small wonder, given the stalled progress on the investigation. And the sterling state of my personal life.

It was raining like hell, which ruled out a jog. And I was too bummed to suit up and drive to the gym.

After a bagel and coffee, dressed in baggy sweats and bunny slippers, I settled at the dining room table, determined to stay put until I'd eyeballed every goddamn receipt in the box. At least I'd get Allan Fink off my back.

By four I'd pretty much decided that rolling the dice on a tax audit was preferable to the paperwork hell in which I was stuck. I was deciphering an illegible bill from a restaurant I'd never heard of when a sharp knock rattled the back door. Delighted to escape, I headed to the kitchen.

And froze before clearing the swinging door.

Through the window I could see a figure standing on the back stoop. Tall. Male. Wearing jeans and a weathered brown leather jacket.

A knot twisted my stomach. I was still feeling off, actually worse than earlier due to the added joy of eyestrain. The last thing I needed was rancor or confrontation.

But something else was peeking around the foreboding that had ballooned in my chest. Something that fluttered softly, like a butterfly on a leaf.

I crossed to open the door. "Surprise, surprise!" A bit too cheery.

Ryan drew a bouquet from behind his back and held it out. "Supermarket special. Best my driver could do."

"Thank you." I took the flowers. "They're lovely."

"You're lovely."

"Right."

For as long as I've known Ryan, he has possessed an uncanny knack for showing up when I look my worst. Self-conscious about the sweats, ratty hair, and absence of makeup, I stepped back.

Ryan entered the kitchen. We kissed. I gestured at the table. He removed his jacket and sat. I noted that he carried only a very small duffel.

"I can't believe you're here," I said.

"Yeah. Took the dawn flight. Better than having to connect."

He looked tired. I wondered where he'd been since landing at mid-morning.

"Would you like a beer? Something else?"

Ryan shook his head.

"Quite the covert op," I said. "You never let on when we talked last night."

"I didn't know last night. Hope you're okay with impulse."

"Of course." Actually, I was far from okay. Though happy he'd made the effort, I felt, what? Ambushed? Pressured? Definitely pressured.

Moving with fabricated composure, I got a vase from the pantry. Turned on the tap. Filled the vase with water.

"I thought it might help if we talked face-to-face." Ryan spoke to my back.

I started to toss out a flippant remark. My usual reaction to anxiety. Instead, I unwrapped the flowers.

Ryan went straight for the kill.

"I wrote you a letter, Tempe. An old-fashioned, pen-and-ink communiqué meant to wing its way to you via stamps, aviation, and human sweat."

I continued disentangling and arranging blossoms.

"I tore it up. They were just words on paper. And hardly expressive."

"Don't undersell yourself, Ryan. You're an excellent writer."

I heard him catch his breath as though to speak. A beat, then he let it out and the chair creaked softly.

I turned to face him.

Ryan looked at me, the astonishing blue eyes full on mine. "I'm sorry, Tempe. I'm sorry for everything. For trying to make you into what I want you to be. For being less than what you want me to be. For loving things and places that keep us apart. For leaving you that first time. For running away when Lily died."

"Ryan—" My heart was going hard and a little fast.

"I love you, Tempe. I came here to tell you that. Just that. And to promise that I will never hurt you again."

I opened my lips to respond. Could find no words. Seconds ticked by on Gran's mantel clock.

"Nothing to say?" Ryan's tone held not the slightest note of impatience.

"I'm waiting for the part that begins with 'but.'"

"There is no but. I love you."

"Does this mean you'll stay for supper?" Regretted as soon as the quip was out.

Ryan's head dropped, then hung a moment. When it came up he regarded me with a look of obstinate imperturbability. And more. Compassion. Kindness. Remorse?

"I know Pete hurt you. I'm not Pete. I know I hurt you. I can't change that. But *I* am changed."

I started to respond. He raised a hand to stop me.

"I know you have obligations. Katy. Your mother. Your job. Responsibilities that tie you here as firmly as I'm tied to Quebec. But we can make it work."

I swallowed, not trusting myself to speak.

"I will never betray you, Tempe."

I felt as though liquid nitrogen had been injected into my bloodstream. I'd heard that promise before. That exact statement.

Ryan must have read the look on my face. He rose and gathered his duffel.

"Wait," I said softly.

He did. But clashing emotions were scrambling my wiring. Seconds passed. A full minute. No sound left my lips.

"It's okay, Tempe."

"No. It's not. You're right. I've been paralyzed by indecision. It's childish and self-indulgent and unfair to you."

"I understand."

"Do you? Because I don't." Suddenly words poured forth, racing like water carving a mountain gorge. "I know that I love you. That I'm happiest when I'm with you. Not because you buy me flowers or make me laugh. Or share my love of Giacometti or *The Hitchhikers Guide to the Galaxy*. I don't simply love you. I genuinely like you. I admire and respect you. And, in most situations, you respect me."

"Most?" Puzzled.

I flashed on the times I'd been in a tough spot and Ryan had ridden in all guns blazing. Literally. "Your impulse to save the day on my behalf scares the hell out of me, Ryan. It makes me wonder if you really believe in me as a capable person."

"You mean intervening when some scumbag is about to shoot you?"

"That's one example." Defensive.

"I don't want you hurt."

"And I don't want me hurt. But your overprotectiveness implies that I can't take care of myself. That I can't handle difficult situations on my own. I love you, Ryan. But I need my autonomy. I need to know I can rely on *myself*."

"That's it? No more cop-to-the-rescue routine?"

"That's just part of it." Jesus! What was the rest? I took a moment. Then, "If Katy ever comes to harm I know I'll reach out to those I love. To Mama, Harry, maybe to you." I could feel my cheeks flaming, but there was no turning back. "When Lily died, you chucked me away like last week's garbage."

Ryan started to interrupt. I barreled on.

"I don't need you in my life, Ryan. I learned to live without you once. Twice. I didn't like it, but I survived." Quick shallow breath. "I don't need protection. I don't need a bodyguard. I need someone who will be there, both physically and emotionally. When life is good, and when life gets rough."

"And you doubt my ability to fill that role?" Flat.

"I don't know what I think, Ryan." Stepping back and staring down at the furry cottontails on my feet.

A very long, very leaden silence slammed between us. No one moved. The clock ticked.

After what seemed a lifetime, I looked up. The sadness on Ryan's face nearly broke my heart.

"Will you spend the night?" I asked, barely above a whisper.

Something skittered across the troubled blue irises, vanished before I could read the meaning. Two more ticks from Gran's timepiece. Three. Four. Then Ryan's lips hitched up in an unexpected grin.

"I've delivered my stirring and persuasive communiqué. You've responded with equal eloquence." Delivered with a lightness that was obviously forced. "I think now it's best that I leave."

"That's not how I want it."

"Nor I." His eyebrows did a few Groucho hops.

"Then—"

Ryan crossed to me and kissed my cheek. Tucked an errant strand of hair behind my ear. "You need to be by yourself."

"Where will you go?" I asked.

"Home."

I nodded, tears threatening hard.

Christ on a flagpole! Don't cry! Don't you dare cry!

Cupping my chin in his palm, Ryan tipped my face up so my eyes met his. "We are different in many ways, Tempe. But our differences complement each other. Together we were better, stronger. More than just the sum of you and me. I truly believe that."

I ached to wrap my arms around him and press my cheek to his chest. But there was a rigidity to his shoulders now, a tautness to his mouth that froze me in place.

Behind me, footsteps crossed the floor. Inside my head, words crashed like cymbals. *By yourself.* And Ryan's chosen tense. *We were. We were.*

The door opened and closed softly.

I stood paralyzed, mind spinning, fire burning beneath my breastbone.

Certain I'd driven away a true shot at happiness.

Uncertain why.

30

Saturday night.
Gonna keep on dancing to the rock and roll.

After a good cry, then supper, I decided that serenity would come only via resolution of the Cora Teague situation. I also decided that, like me, Slidell probably had no social life. If he did, screw it.

I went to the study and phoned him as Ryan had suggested. Skinny listened, interrupted with a minimum of tasteless commentary.

When I'd finished, "Yeah, well, just one problem, Doc. Exorcists aim to kick Satan's ass. They don't aim to kill."

"No, they don't aim to kill. But the rites can and do turn deadly."

I put Slidell on speaker and used the notes from my online research, editing as I read aloud.

"In 1995, a twenty-five-year-old Korean woman from

Emeryville, California, turned to Jean Park at his self-created Jesus-Amen Ministries. The woman couldn't sleep and meds didn't help, so Park decided she was possessed by demons. During the six-hour exorcism, the woman was struck as many as one hundred times, causing multiple rib fractures and internal injuries. After she died, members of the congregation sat with her body for five days because Park told them she'd wake and be cured."

I heard a female voice in the background.

"Hold on," Slidell said.

The phone went muffled. Slidell returned moments later. "Look, I just wanna—"

I continued, abridging even further.

"1997, the Bronx, a five-year-old girl was tied down and forced to drink a cocktail of ammonia, vinegar, pepper, and olive oil. Her mouth was taped shut. When she died, her grandmother and mother wrapped the body in plastic and left it outside with the trash. Their proof of demons? The child had thrown tantrums.

"1998, Sayville, New York. A seventeen-year-old girl was suffocated with a plastic bag because her mother was trying to destroy a demon inside her.

"2008, Henderson, Texas. A thirteen-month-old girl was bitten more than twenty times and hammered to death. Mama and her boyfriend felt the baby was possessed by a demon."

"That ain't the same. Those cases are just whackass parents—"

"Fighting demons in the name of God." I barreled on. "2011, Floyd, Virginia. A man and his fellow church members felt his two-year-old daughter was possessed by evil spirits. The kid was found dead on a bed surrounded by Bibles. Her injuries included fractured ribs, abrasions, lung contusions, and hemorrhage. Cause of death was manual asphyxiation.

"2014, Germantown, Maryland. A mother, acting with a female accomplice, stabbed her four kids, killing two, convinced that evil spirits were moving back and forth through the children's bodies. The women identified themselves as members of a group called Demon Assassins."

"Sounds like some kinda death metal band."

"Those are just a few examples." I was surprised Slidell knew the genre. "There are dozens of news stories about the dangers of exorcism. Whole websites dedicated to the subject."

"But you're talking amateurs, right? Priests get training so things don't go off the rails."

"Let me share some facts, Detective. During an exorcism, the 'possessed'"—the air quotes were pointless; Slidell couldn't see me—"person is often restrained. Tied up. Strapped down. Straitjacketed. Many exorcists, priests or otherwise, see the rite not as a prayer but as a confrontation."

"So the padre does some hocus-pocus and commands the demon to haul ass. The church tells him how to do it."

"The priest is *supposed* to follow procedures approved by the Vatican. But guess what? Many ad-lib. And think about this. The exorcism, once begun, must be completed no matter how long it takes. Hours, days, weeks—"

"No play no pay?"

"—because if the exorcist quits, the demon then pursues him."

"Yeah, that's a motivator. But what's this got to do with Strike?"

"It's got to do with Cora Teague. Teague was epileptic. I think she died in the course of an exorcism. Ditto for Mason Gulley, who had a genetic condition that affected his appearance."

Again, the female voice, now more insistent.

"I'm coming!" Slidell barked, I assumed to Verlene, not bothering to cover the handset.

"Remember the key chain audio?" I pressed on.

"The one you failed to seize."

"Three voices. Two men and a girl. Maybe Cora secretly recorded her own exorcism."

"Why?"

"To blackmail those responsible? To slip to the press? Because she was scared shitless the assholes would kill her? Does it matter?"

"Just for the sake of argument. Who's on that tape with her?"

I'd asked myself the same question. "Maybe Hoke and her father, or another member of the congregation. Maybe a specialist brought in from outside."

"You make these yaks sound like the AMA."

"There actually are professional organizations. The American Association of Exorcists. The International Catholic Association of Exorcists. The International Association of Exorcists. Which, by the way, was recognized by the Vatican in 2014."

"Don't misconstrue this to mean I'm agreeing with you. But, even if you're right, Teague and Gulley ain't my cases."

Misconstrue. High oratory for Skinny.

"Strike was investigating Teague." I spoke with exaggerated patience. "Strike had the key chain. Strike went to Avery. Strike was murdered. Her death has to be connected."

Slidell thought about that. Or at least refrained from comment for a while. Then, "There was nothing on Teague in any of Strike's cartons."

"What about Mason Gulley?" I asked.

"Nada."

"What's in the files?"

"Shit on Strike's citizen sleuth operation. I got guys cross-checking names."

"How long—"

"More breaking news. Wendell Clyde's alibi is solid."

"He was with the blogger all weekend."

"Aslanian. Yeah. I'm sure they'll be announcing

their nuptials any minute. Look, there's a function I gotta go to."

"Will you run Granger Hoke? See what pops?"

"That pleasure should drop to Deputy Dick."

"I'm certain there was something in Hoke's history Father Morris was hiding."

"Deputy."

"Okay." Blasé as hell. "But it will be embarrassing."

"What the sweet Christ are you talking about now?"

"Ramsey beating you out on a collar for Strike."

I heard the beep of Slidell hanging up.

I glared at my mobile, as if it, not Skinny, was the source of my irritation. Or maybe it was. Seemed all I'd done for days was talk on the phone. Mostly to people questioning my ability to reason.

And then there was Ryan. Nope. No thinking about Ryan until the case is resolved. Until. No. Leave it. Focus on the case.

I needed action. Involvement. Yet there was nothing I could do.

Frustrated, I phoned Ramsey and told him everything that had happened since last we'd spoken. Clear. Succinct. No conjecture. No grabbing-at-puzzle-pieces speculation. His response shocked me.

"I've been doing my own research. Hoke killed a kid."

"Holy shit."

"In a way. The death occurred during an exorcism."

"What happened?" I was too stoked to acknowledge Ramsey's joke.

"Full details were never released."

"Of course not."

"The incident took place in Elkhart, Indiana, in 1993. Hoke was solo priest at a small Catholic parish called Church of the Holy Comforter."

I bit back a comment on the irony of the name.

"During a Wednesday night prayer circle a mother volunteered her nine-year-old daughter for exorcism. The rite was performed two days later in the family home. The mother held the child's arms while Hoke sat on her back."

"Restricting her lungs and causing suffocation." The anger was so bitter I could taste it in my throat.

"Yes."

"To expel a demon living inside her."

"Yes." I heard Ramsey swallow. "Later it came out that the girl was autistic."

"Sonofabitch." My skin tingled freezing hot as I leaned back in my chair. So this was what the good Father didn't want to tell me. "Was Hoke charged?"

"No. Following an inquiry, the death was ruled accidental."

Screw facts. I unfurled my theory about Hoke and his bullshit church.

"Look, Doc. The guy is several exits past weird, but accusing him of murder is pretty far out there."

"Hoke suffocated a nine-year-old girl," I snapped.

Humming silence. I could practically hear Ramsey clicking through the same faults in my thinking that Ryan had pointed out.

His next revelation surprised me almost as much as his first.

"We may have Strike's laptop."

"Are you serious?"

"A vagrant found an old Gateway while dumpster-diving behind Dunn's Deli in Banner Elk."

"Have you told Slidell?"

"I was about to call you, then him."

"Where's the thing been for five days?"

"The fine citizen held on to it, thinking he might make a few bucks. But the battery's dead and he had no way to charge it. Failing to find a buyer, he decided to try for a reward by turning it in. He called us about two hours ago. The thing just landed here at headquarters."

"What makes you think it belonged to Strike?"

"The initials HLCS are on the cover."

Hazel Lee Cunningham Strike. The now familiar flicker of guilt went through me.

"Can you boot it?"

"We're searching for a charger."

"Skinny's out with his girlfriend. Call. Make him look important."

Of course I couldn't sleep. A nonstop PowerPoint played in my head. Images. Recorded voices, two bullying, one frightened.

At two I gave up and went downstairs. It was becoming a pattern.

After making tea, I sat at the dining room table. Stared at the hated box, which stared back.

Ignoring the accusatory ruckus of unsorted receipts, I drew a tablet and pen toward me. Based on Ryan's comments, I headed columns. "Victims." "Cause of death." "Place of death." "Time of death." "Motives." "Suspects." "Weapons."

I eyeballed the empty lists. Got the same result as with the box stare-down.

I tore off and crumpled the sheet. Began a diagram. Nodes with names and notes. Lines connecting the nodes.

Cora Teague—Graduates high school, goes to work for Brice family. River dies, returns home, disappears.

Eli Teague—Dies at age twelve, ER doctor suspicious.

John Teague—Owns convenience store–gas station op. Religious zealot, pugnacious.

Fatima Teague—Housewife, submissive.

Owen Lee Teague—Failed at real estate, dog trainer.

Realizing I knew little about Fatima or Owen Lee, nothing about the other Teague siblings, I began a list of questions on a separate sheet.

Mason Gulley—NJF, disappears same time as Cora Teague. Johnson City, TN(?) Posts as OMG (?) about Cora Teague on CLUES.net, turns up dead at Brown Mountain overlooks.

Grandma Gulley—Catholic, judgmental. Big.

Susan Grace Gulley—Slips me information about Mason, spies on Cora during Mason's stay in Johnson City, TN. Detests Cora. Angry, rebellious. Big.

I added questions below the one concerning the Teagues. Where did Mason stay in Johnson City? Why? Why wouldn't Susan Grace divulge the reason Mason went to Tennessee?

Hazel Strike—Websleuth, finds CLUES.net post about Cora Teague, finds my NamUs post, finds recorder at Burke County overlook, confronts me with theory UID ME229-13 is MP Cora Teague. Murdered.

More questions. Why did Strike go on hiatus from websleuthing? Where was she murdered? By whom? How did her body end up in the pond?

Granger Hoke—Defrocked priest, Jesus Lord Holiness church, deviant brand of Catholicism, exorcist, accidental death of child during rite.

Joel, Katalin, River, and Saffron Brice—Disillusioned Jesus Lord Holiness members. Saffron, broken arm. River, SIDS.

Terrence O'Tool—GP, epilepsy, inadequate treatment, gold cross, uncooperative.

Fenton Ogilvie—Coroner, alcoholic, died in elevator fall.

I studied the jumble of lines and nodes. Felt my head begin to go up in smoke.

Tearing off a blank page, I created a new list labeled "Human Remains."

1. Fragmentary leg and foot bones found at Lost Cove Cliffs Overlook. Sent to Marlene Penny at WCU.
2. Partial torso found at Burke County overlook. Sent to me. ME229-13.
3. Fragmentary bone and printless fingertips (Mason Gulley / NJF?) found on return trip to Burke County overlook with Strike and Ramsey. ME122-15.
4. Fragmentary bone and concrete mold (Mason Gulley?) found with Ramsey at the Devil's Tail trail near Wiseman's View overlook. ME135-15.

I reread the four entries. Threw down my pen in frustration. My unanswered questions far outnumbered my facts. The exercise had been as useful as a slap on the butt.

One more try. "Dates."

1993: Cora Teague is born.

1996: Eli Teague is born.

2008: Eli Teague dies.

2011, Spring: Cora Teague graduates high school and goes to work for Brice family. River dies. Cora is sent home.

2011, July: Cora Teague and Mason Gulley disappear. (Gulley goes to Johnson City, TN?).

2011, August: OMG (Mason Gulley?) posts on CLUES.net about Cora Teague.

2011, September: OMG's posts stop.

My hand froze. I closed my eyes and conjured an image. A conversation with a green-vestment-clad man on a windy day.

A high-voltage impulse fired in my brain.

I knew when and where Mason Gulley was killed.

31

I was awake until four. Fortunately it was Sunday, so I could sleep late. Tell that to my stoked-with-a-breakthrough brain.

I waited until eight to start dialing. Ramsey's voice mail stated that he'd be out of contact until Monday. I left a message, then tried his landline at the sheriff's department. Was told the same thing. Left the same message.

Slidell. Message.

Nine o'clock came and went with no call back from either. Ten.

I was working through the loathsome box, reading the same receipts over and over, putting them in piles, picking them up and putting them in different piles, when my cell finally warbled an incoming call.

I grabbed it.

"You were seen in the hall of the mountain king."

"Sorry?" I kicked into nuance analysis mode, not

sure if my mother was being cryptic or irrational.

"You were spotted at Heatherhill Thursday night."

"Oh."

"Were you secretly plotting with the wizards and shamans who oversee my well-being?"

"Mama, are you taking your meds?"

"Of course I'm taking my meds. Why is it if I wax the least bit lyrical you always ask about pills?"

"Sorry." Resolving to phone Dr. Luna or Goose.

"Why didn't you come to see me, sweetheart?"

"You weren't in your suite." True. "I figured you were with Dr. Luna or having a treatment." Not so much. "I didn't want to interrupt."

"Such a long trip to not interrupt."

"I was up in Avery County anyway."

I braced for a broadside of questions about the Brown Mountain remains. Didn't come.

"Would you mind tackling that hideous drive again?"

"What do you need?"

"Time with my daughters."

"You've called Harry?" Pulse kicking up at her use of the plural. At the implication of a dual offspring request.

"I have."

"Are you unwell?"

"Really, Tempe. I love you. But you are so tediously predictable."

I waited.

"I could not be better." High melodrama sigh.

"Harry is coming to North Carolina?" I asked.

"Your sister is always so supportive."

What the hell did that mean?

"Can you explain what this is about?"

"Must a desire to see my little girls be about something?"

"No." Yes.

"I really must go now. Lunch is at noon. Then I have a massage. I will see you soon?"

"Of course."

"It's Grieg."

"What?" Totally lost.

"'In the Hall of the Mountain King' is by the Norwegian composer Edvard Grieg."

With that she was gone.

I pitched the phone to the table. Which drew a stern look from Birdie.

Did Mama's summons have to do with her cancer? The chemo? I couldn't ask about that. Harry had sworn me to secrecy. Or was it about Clayton Sinitch? Mama was often recklessly impulsive. Was she about to make a potentially disastrous decision?

Snatching up the mobile, I hit a speed-dial button. Got Harry's annoying little message. Left the same few words I'd left twice earlier. Call me. It's urgent.

I glared at the box. At the mountain range of paper spread out before me.

My eyes landed on the tablet and drifted down my

list of questions. One by one, I considered. Came up with zilch.

Then: Why wouldn't Susan Grace divulge the reason Mason went to Tennessee?

As of last night, I was certain I knew when and where Mason had died.

I saw Susan Grace in the gloom of her grandmother's parlor. Recalled the old woman's admonition. *Do not allow yourself to be hostage to Satan.*

I saw Susan Grace's face shadowed in my car. The trembling lips, the dinner-plate eyes half hidden by bangs. Had I misread the girl? Had her intensity been born of fear, not fury?

Cora Teague. Mason Gulley.

Suddenly the air in the room bit cold at my skin.

There is evil in the world. Evil that demands compliance with unyielding dogma. Evil that believes in dark forces.

In that instant I understood.

Susan Grace feared defiance would be interpreted as demons in need of purging.

And purging could kill.

What the hell! I thought. What the bloody hell!

Decision. I would go visit Mama. Heatherhill would put me closer to Avery when Ramsey called back. Or Slidell.

No farther without backup. Just Heatherhill.

• • •

While winding through Charlotte, I called Harry again. Though Mama had contacted her, Baby Sister had not booked a flight east. For once we agreed. Our mother is unsurpassed at genteel manipulation.

Once on I-40, I retried Slidell.

"What the freakin' hell is so urgent you gotta bust my chops the first weekend I'm off in over a month?"

"It's Hoke."

"What? Am I listening to one of those messages beamed over and over for space aliens? You already said that."

"I'm convinced Cora Teague and Mason Gulley died during botched exorcisms."

"Earth here. Anyone out there? Anyone out there? Anyone out there?"

"Will you listen to me?"

"Tell it to Ramsey."

"He's unavailable."

"Me too."

"It all comes back to Hoke. To his church."

"I'm working Strike. She ain't an MP. She's an actual stiff in the morgue with a tag on her toe. The morgue on my patch."

"Strike is connected."

"Maybe I'll call NASA. Ask how to make my own audio so's I can keep looping a message saying back off."

I launched my grenade straight at his solar plexus.

"Mason Gulley died at Hoke's church. Or his body was dismembered there."

"How do you know that?"

"Ramsey and I went to Jesus Lord Holiness to talk to John and Fatima Teague. Hoke was present."

"It's his church."

"We asked about Cora and Mason."

"And Daddy said he won't be walking his slut kid down the aisle. We getting to something new here?"

My fingers tightened on the wheel.

Easy.

"Mason died with olive oil and incense in his hair. Those are materials used in the rite of exorcism."

"That don't mean—"

"The Gulleys are Jesus Lord Holiness members. Mason stopped attending around the time a parish renovation project was wrapping up." I pictured shiny brass rings embedded in a pristine stoop. "Those renovations involved the pouring of cement to replace old stairs. The project ended in September of 2011."

Surprisingly, Slidell didn't interrupt.

"Mason and Cora disappeared in July of 2011. In August, Mason started posting on CLUES.net as OMG. Those posts stopped in September."

"Wasn't that when he was in Johnson City?"

"I think Mason returned from Tennessee and something bad went down at the church. There was an exorcism, he died. There were bags of cement lying around, power saws . . ."

I let the gruesome thought hang.

"And Strike?"

"She probably found out and confronted Hoke. Strike was up in Avery on Saturday, the day before her body was found."

Slidell did the throat thing.

"Surely it's enough to get a warrant," I said.

"So far it's all speculation. A judge will want more."

"Like what?" Too charged.

"Call me crazy, but, evidence?"

"Human remains? A death mask screaming Mason Gulley? The olive oil and incense? Fingertips without prints? Two missing kids? A priest who strangled a nine-year-old girl?" Waaay too charged.

"Where's Ramsey?"

"I don't know. But consider this. Susan Grace lied to her grandmother to contact me. She revealed things Hoke and his bunch probably don't want known. If they find out, she could face the same fate as Cora and Mason."

"I'm on my way to the gym."

"The gym?" A word I couldn't imagine in Skinny's vocabulary.

"You got something against working out?" I heard soft scraping, probably Slidell's hand rubbing his face. "Write down what you told me. Anything else you can think of. Send it. In the meantime, don't do nothing stupid."

I pulled off at a gas station and quick-thumbed

an email to Skinny as requested. Sent it with a cc to Ramsey. Then I clicked the icon for Google Earth and typed in an address I thought to be close to the location I wanted to view. Got coordinates. Using those, I estimated other coordinates, finally found what I needed.

I spent a few minutes zooming in and out, checking the landscape. After hitting the ladies', I bought a Diet Coke and filled my tank. Then I got back on the road.

I blew right past Heatherhill and straight on to Avery.

I pulled in and killed the engine. Mine was the only vehicle in the lot.

Through the dusty lens of my windshield, the scene looked like a landscape titled *First Hint of Spring*. Tentative shoots were now greening the winter-brown grass. Delicate vines were sending threadlike feelers up the hardwood trunks. High above, the pines were enjoying good chemistry with an indifferent breeze.

The buildings stood out white against the green-on-blue curves of the mountains behind. I saw no one outside. No movement through the cracks between and below the big front doors. No sign of a human presence.

I realized I wasn't breathing.

Exhaling, I checked my iPhone for signal. Maybe, just maybe, one flickering bar.

I sent texts to Slidell and Ramsey. The former would

be livid. The latter, who knew? Screw it. Skinny was too stubborn to listen, Ramsey too busy. Anyway, I wasn't crashing the Manson family at the Barker Ranch. This was, though creepy, a church. Worst-case scenario, someone would show up, be pissed, and order me to leave.

As I dropped the phone into my shoulder bag, a red light flashed in a far corner of my mind. A gaggle of neurons called out. *Someone hacked up a kid and put his head in concrete. Here!*

I was running on less than three hours of sleep. I was exhausted. But I had to know.

Pulling my nerves together, I opened the car door and strained to listen. Heard the staccato whine of a frustrated insect. The trickle of water not far off. Otherwise, it was still. Traffic still, voice still, bird still, wind still.

I wanted to stay behind the wheel and drive away. Instead, I got out, popped the trunk, and thumbed open the clasps on my scene recovery kit. I dug out two vials, took one tablet from each, placed both in an empty spray bottle, added the remains of my drinking water, and shook. The mixture went into my purse, along with a small flash and a UV penlight. I lowered the trunk cover and, after skimming my surroundings, started toward the church.

The nearer I got, the more the temperature seemed to drop. Which was ridiculous. The sun, though a hair closer to the ridgeline, was as bright as when I'd arrived.

I stopped at the foot of the steps. Then, heart thudding like hoofbeats, I climbed and put my ear to the door.

My nose registered sunbaked wood, dust, polyurethane sealer. My ears registered absolute silence. I tried the handle. Of course it was locked.

While crossing the lawn, I'd noted two north-side windows. I rounded the corner. Both were too high for a view of the church's interior. And shuttered. I moved to the back of the building.

And came face-to-face with the muzzle of a Browning semiautomatic shotgun.

32

I froze. The best thing to do when looking down the barrel of a twenty-gauge.

Hoke was by a stand of fir five feet beyond the back wall of the church. He was wearing a black shirt, black pants, and a white clerical collar. Spiky shadows dappled his face and shoe-polish hair.

Though I couldn't see Hoke's expression, there was no mistaking his mood. He was coiled, elbows winging, shotgun pointed straight at my chest.

"Father Hoke," I said.

"Father G. Raise your hands."

I did.

"You're trespassing."

"Isn't everyone welcome in the Lord's house?"

"You've no business here."

"Deputy Ramsey will be arriving shortly." I couldn't tell what impact my bluff had. If any. "We'd like to talk to you."

"Again you would disrupt our Sabbath?"

"I'm sorry for that."

"Your business couldn't wait one day?"

"Deputy Ramsey and I were concerned. Are concerned. We won't let it drop."

Hoke's grip tightened on the gun.

"There's no need for firepower." Fighting to quell the adrenaline roaring through me.

"I don't want to hurt you. I'm a man of God."

"Nothing says God like a loaded Browning."

"You blaspheme."

"The gun's not loaded?"

Hoke stepped forward out of the shadows, barrel still level on my sternum. "What do you want?"

"We know about Cora Teague." Confrontational. But the best my sleep-deprived-adrenaline-pumped brain could provide.

"You know nothing."

"Inform me."

"Leave it alone. You will only cause pain."

"Like the pain you caused Cora?"

No response.

"And Mason Gulley?"

"You have it all wrong."

"I also know about the little girl in Elkhart."

"You've done your homework."

"I have. I learned that you are no longer a priest. That the church rejects your fire-and-brimstone brand of Catholicism. Your demons and—"

"Satan exists."

"So does Lady Gaga."

"Do you find this amusing?"

"Definitely not."

"Your attitude reflects everything wrong with modern society."

"What's wrong with modern society?"

"This country has spiraled into total cultural desolation."

"Are we back to rocker chicks?" I knew goading him was dangerous, couldn't help myself. Blame it on a combo of fear and fatigue.

"You mock. But Satan is at work in the world."

"Headquartered on Brown Mountain?"

"Again, you make fun."

"Most people view the devil as allegory."

"A by-product of mankind's free will." Hoke snorted, a bristly little explosion of air. "Satan is real. And he will not stop until he has delivered mankind unto damnation."

"By setting up shop in kids like Cora and Mason."

"The climate has never been more favorable for Satan and his minions."

"Why is that?"

"Today's young people are being raised in a time when criticism is out of fashion. Can't be too hard on their fragile little egos. Morality is off the curriculum. Can't be prejudiced or politically incorrect. Youth are forced to swim through a daily sea of pornography and greed, to function in an atmosphere ruled by what's in it for me."

"Your critique is a bit harsh." I felt vibration in my purse. Ramsey? Slidell? I couldn't risk lowering my arms to dig for my phone.

"We were a nation built on a Christian God. People went to Mass. Listened to the clergy."

"Not all Christians are Catholic." Stalling. Looking for that moment.

"Methodist. Baptist. Catholic. Denomination doesn't matter. Worship is out of style. No one cares about the Bible, the sacraments, the Ten Commandments."

"Millions of Americans still attend church."

Hoke wasn't listening. He was rolling up his sleeves for a sermon he'd undoubtedly delivered ad nauseam.

"Even mother church has watered down her mainstream teachings. Today's clergy mustn't emphasize hell or purgatory. Mustn't encourage confession. Talk of sin is a downer. We mustn't induce guilt trips. Angels? Forget it. Far too mystical."

"What does this have to do with Cora and Mason?"

"People are floundering. With no moral code, the vulnerable haven't the capacity to resist. The weak are fertile ground for Satan."

"Targets for demonic possession."

"Exactly." Said with such vehemence, I flinched. "And once possessed, there is no remedy."

"That's where you come in."

"The victims of Satan have nowhere to turn."

"The church supports the concept of exorcism. The Vatican just held a conference on the topic. Some two hundred nuns and priests attended. The pope praised the work of the International Association of Exorcists." The few tidbits I could recall from my online searches.

"The Holy Father is isolated in the Vatican, surrounded by cardinals. He is no longer effective." Hoke's eyes flicked to the church building, came back to me, flaring with anger, maybe fear. "Out here, in the trenches, most priests and bishops don't listen. They think exorcism makes the church look foolish and anachronistic. They are wrong. The devil is *real*. Demonic forces are *real*. The Bible says so in passage after passage. Ephesians six, eleven: 'Put on the whole armor of God, that ye may be able to stand against the wiles of the devil.'"

Again my cell vibrated. I was picking up signal, though sporadic. Good. I could be located.

I spoke to cover the sound. "The church says an exorcism should be performed only after extensive medical and psychiatric evaluation."

"Psychiatrists. With their fancy jargon and therapy and bottles of pills." Again the nasty expulsion of air. "A lot of good psychiatry did the woman who drowned her five kids. Or the teen who shot up a school full of children. Or the man who killed boys and buried them under his house."

"What qualifies you to distinguish between psychosis and possession?"

"The Holy Spirit gives me the power of divination."

"And what if you and the HS guess wrong? What if your subject is actually epileptic? You throw water at her and wave a crucifix in her face?" I knew I should tamp it down. But I was viciously tired and making poor decisions. "Do you consider what harm you might be causing?"

"I can sense when someone is afflicted with a demon."

"Even if you can, the church requires that an exorcism be performed by a properly trained priest."

"Deep down my fellow clergy are skeptics."

"All of them?"

"The devil is God's oldest enemy, and no fool. When the exorcist doesn't believe, the Evil One wins."

"And you believe."

"With my whole being."

"So you armor up and go at Satan freelance."

"My authority comes from God, not Rome. Luke ten, seventeen to nineteen: 'And the seventy returned again with joy, saying, Lord, even the devils are subject to us through thy name. And He said to them, I beheld Satan as lightning fall from heaven. Behold, I give unto you power to tread on serpents and scorpions, and over all the power of the enemy; and nothing shall by any means hurt you.' "

Hoke's eyes were shiny with something I couldn't identify. Piety? Madness? I had to get away.

I cocked my head ever so slightly, pretending that I'd heard a car but was trying to mask it.

Hoke fell for the ploy. His gaze slid from mine, went over my shoulder toward the road.

Make a run for it? Grab the gun? Kick Hoke in the nuts?

A nanosecond's hesitation. Then the moment was gone.

When Hoke looked back, the glint in his eyes chilled me.

"Why have you come here?" he hissed.

"You exorcised Cora. Things got too rough. Or perhaps she had a seizure."

"I'm not who you think I am."

"I know you're not a killer. Cora's death was an accident. Like the child in Indiana."

From where I stood, I could see Hoke's breathing get faster.

"Did Mason find out? Did he confront you?"

My voice was rising. I forced it to stay even.

"Or was Mason also a victim of one of your little parties?"

Even Hoke's bones seemed to stiffen. Still he said nothing.

"We found him, you know. Off the overlooks. What the animals left, that is. His bones. His head in the bucket of concrete."

Hoke licked his lips, a fast flick of pink.

"What did you do with Cora? Did you dismember her too?"

"I loved Cora. It should never have happened."

I hadn't spotted that coming.

"What should never have happened?"

"Such a beautiful child until the devil laid claim."

"The devil." Not attempting to hide my disgust.

"You didn't see her. The bulging eyes, the wicked smiles, the twisted limbs—"

"The devil had sweet fuck-all to do with it. Cora Teague was epileptic. Where did you dispose of her body?"

Hoke's Adam's apple was now running an elevator service. He said nothing.

"Did Cora also end up ransom for the Brown Mountain Devil?"

"No, no. We don't worship Satan. We battle him. We offer ourselves as hostages to those he torments."

"We? Who helped you?"

"You must stop."

"That won't happen. Deputy Ramsey knows I'm here. He'll arrive any minute, and he'll have a warrant. Ever experience a crime scene search?"

Hoke only glared. In the pale afternoon sun his acne-scarred flesh looked like a grainy close-up beamed from the moon.

"Let me draw you a picture. A police team will pull up in a big black truck. They'll go over this place with tape and tweezers and powders and sprays." My voice was spiraling again. "They'll dig up your lawn, shoot video and stills, confiscate your records. They'll find every dirty little secret you have shoved up your pulpit or stashed in your underwear drawer."

I took a deep breath. Fought to recover my grip.

Several seconds of absolute stillness hummed between us.

Hoke looked down at the gun in his hands, blinked, as though surprised to see it there. Then he looked back at me. "I wish you had left us alone."

A beat, then the barrel jerked toward the rear door of the church.

"Inside," he ordered, voice sharp as razor wire.

I knew that being cornered would limit my options. That it might mean death.

"No," I said.

"Now!"

I held my ground.

Hoke's finger slid forward into the trigger guard.

33

I walked as slowly as I dared without provoking Hoke. He followed up the steps, right on my heels.

"Open the door."

My mind ricocheted for words that might turn the situation around. Finding none, I obeyed.

The hinges squeaked softly.

The muzzle of the Browning nudged my left shoulder blade.

I stepped across the threshold. Inhaled a cocktail that transported me through time and place. Candle wax. Wood polish. Incense. Smoke.

The only illumination came from cracks outlining the shuttered windows, two on each side, one in back, to the right of the door we'd entered. The oozing sunlight formed slivers of white, rectangular at the bottom, arched at the top.

As my eyes struggled to adjust to the gloom, something clicked behind me. A chandelier kicked to life, bringing the room into focus.

The nave, which wasn't large, took up the entire building. A row of wooden pews ran down each side, angled to allow room for a center aisle. There were maybe twenty in all.

Up front, six feet beyond us, was a lectern, centered and facing the pews. Beyond it was the altar, a simple wooden table draped with a white linen cloth. Empty now.

A piano occupied the corner to our far right. On the wall above it was a board for posting hymn selections. The last sung were 304, 27, 41, and 7.

Every surface was wood, no plaster. The walls were painted cream. The ceiling and floor were stained the same dark walnut as the pews.

"Look around."

I turned, arms still held high. Hoke was standing with his feet spread, his Browning pointed at me.

"I don't understand."

"You accuse me of murder. Look around. Satisfy yourself."

"I never used the word 'murder.' "

"This is God's house. I would not defile it."

"I prefer to leave the search to—"

"Look around." Sharp. "I have nothing to hide."

Hoke's eyes fixed on mine with an intensity that sent the hairs on my neck standing tall. I held his gaze and didn't move. He made a tight circle in the air with the muzzle, indicating, I assumed, the space in which we stood.

"May I lower my hands?"

"I'm watching you."

I explored the room, feeling crosshairs on my back. There was little to search. No closet, restroom, cellar, or lobby. No drawers or cabinets. Nothing under the altar, on the lectern, inside the piano; only sheet music in the bench. The place was immaculate.

But almost four years had passed. Plenty of time for scrubbing and purging. Still, knowing Hoke's stance on God, I doubted he'd chosen the church for his dirty work.

I looked at my captor. "I have luminol in my purse. May I use it?"

"What's it for?"

"Indicating the presence of blood."

Hoke nodded, once, reluctant, and tightened his grip on the gun.

Moving slowly, I reached into my bag and withdrew the plastic bottle. Sprayed around the altar, near the piano, at a couple of pews. Nothing lit up. No surprise. I was sure this wasn't the place. Was going through the motions more for Hoke's reaction than as an actual test.

While returning the bottle to my bag, I tried for a peek at my mobile. It was lying facedown. No way I could see if I even had signal. No way I could tap in my code and a speed-dial selection without drawing attention.

I turned and looked a question at Hoke. A challenge?

"Now we go to the family center." He repeated the jabbing thing with the shotgun.

"How do I know you won't shoot me?"

"You don't."

Hoke killed the light and closed the door behind him as we single-filed out. Our steps sounded loud in the stillness, one set of footfalls echoing the other.

I smelled danger, hot and coppery as fresh blood. But the Browning allowed me no options.

The sunlight was slanted now, angling golden across the sea-green tips of the newborn grass. Trees were casting long shadows inward from the western edge of the clearing.

As we drew close I could see that the family center, though larger, was similar in layout to the church. Front and back entrances, but accessed from ground level, no stairs or stoop. Arched windows high up on the sides and in the rear.

The only thing different was a wing shooting off the eastern side at the back. It had two windows, small and square, not arched, not shuttered, and a separate entrance.

I looked, but saw no evidence of a basement or crawl space. No ground-level window or cellar door. No high foundation. I guessed the building sat on a concrete slab.

As at the church, each front door bore a heavy iron cross. I was veering that way when the Browning's muzzle again kissed my spine.

"We go in the back."

I diverted to the gravel laneway. Boots crunched close behind me. A short walk took us past a black Chevy Tahoe and brought us to the door at the rear of the building.

My mind began to short-circuit. I was totally alone with a man with a serious God complex and a loaded shotgun. Coming here had been ridiculously, insanely stupid on so many levels. What to do?

"It's unlocked." Right at my ear.

I turned the knob and the door swung in. We entered. As before, Hoke lit the overheads. Here they were tube fluorescents.

We'd stepped directly into a large kitchen. Double-sided fridge, eight-burner stove, deep farm sink. Lots of counter space with cabinets above and below. Everything standard-issue white, probably purchased at the local Best Buy or Sears.

No vase of fake flowers. No bowl of plastic fruit. Not a single touch of whimsy brightened the room.

There were two doors on the left, both closed. Hoke sidestepped to them, eyes hard on me. Gun never dropping an inch, he quick-turned the knobs then backhanded each.

"Go on. Spray your chemicals."

One of the doors opened onto a pantry. Lots of flour, oatmeal, and pancake mix. No saws or axes. Nothing glowed.

The other door led into an arrangement I assumed

was the rectory. A tiny living room, bedroom, and bath were lined up shotgun style, one giving onto the next.

I could hear Hoke's breathing as I edged past him. Fast and hot. Like mine, his adrenaline was pumping hard.

The living room was crammed with a desk, bookshelves, a small table, and a single chair. An oval braided rug covered the floor. In one corner, a padded kneeler faced a framed portrait of a very Scandinavian-looking Jesus.

My palms went slick when I saw the photo lying on the kneeler's armrest. A school portrait. The girl stared into the lens, unsmiling, eyes hidden by defiantly thick black bangs.

Easy. Wait for your opening.

In the bedroom were a twin bed, a dresser, and a wardrobe. Predictably, the wardrobe housed pants, shirts, and jackets, all black, and a rainbow assortment of brocade vestments.

A calendar hung to the right of the door, the saint of the month a woman deeply involved with farm animals. Only two hand-scribbled reminders. I read them discreetly. Last Wednesday's entry said *Rx*. Today's said *SG*.

Susan Grace Gulley.

I felt my scalp prickle hot.

Breathe. Steady.

The bath was maybe six by six, barely room for a shower, sink, and commode. I pulled out the luminol and sprayed. Nothing lit up blue. I didn't bother with the other two rooms.

Back in the kitchen, I walked to the sink and pumped the luminol again and again. No reaction. I shifted clockwise, spraying at random spots. Got zero fluorescence.

Hoke watched, face rigid as Mount Rushmore.

Past the kitchen, male and female lavatories faced off across a narrow hall. Each had two commode stalls and a vanity sink with storage below. The shelves held soap, Clorox disinfecting cleaner, rolls of Charmin, and bundled paper towels.

The luminol produced not so much as a flicker.

The remainder of the building was taken up by what appeared to be a multipurpose room. Long collapsible tables were stacked against one wall, legs flat to their tops, awaiting the next fish fry or bazaar. Two rolling carts held the associated chairs.

At the far end of the room, a dozen folding chairs were arranged in a loose circle. Beyond them, in a corner, was an old-fashioned playpen, the kind I'd used for Katy but hadn't seen in years. Its interior was filled with an assortment of toys and dolls. Beside it, shelving held children's art supplies—paints and brushes, colored paper, glue, small scissors upended in a china mug.

Three wheeled coatracks lined the wall opposite the playpen, each with a collection of empty hangers. Otherwise, the room was empty.

As I sprayed and probed, I wondered. Was Hoke delusionally self-confident about the effectiveness of his cleanup, or woefully unaware of the sensitivity of luminol?

The windows were dimming when I finally admitted to myself a third and more likely possibility. I was wrong. No body was dismembered here or in the church. And my Google Earth check had shown no other structures on the property.

Still. In my gut I was certain Hoke was involved in the deaths of Cora and Mason.

Now what?

I had to talk my way out. Or fight.

"I apologize," I said quietly. "I was mistaken."

Several heartbeats passed.

"I'm going now," I said.

"You bring a deputy to disgrace me before my parishioners." Low and dangerous. "Now you return and accuse me of murdering children."

"Step aside."

Hoke didn't move.

"Why are you praying for Susan Grace Gulley?" I demanded, hoping a quick thrust might unnerve him.

Hoke's whole body tensed, but he said nothing.

"Did she sass her grandmother? Did the *devil* make her do it?" Shaking my hands in faux trepidation. "Will you also kill her?"

Hoke's jaw clenched and his dark eyes burned into mine. His grip tightened on the gun. In that instant I knew. He had no intention of letting me leave.

Panic fired through my blood like a hit of speed. Hoke's face blurred as I felt the fast, powerful rush.

In one lightning move I lunged, twisted, and kicked out with all my strength. My boot connected with the blue-black steel of the barrel.

Lulled by my earlier compliance, Hoke was taken by surprise. The Browning flew from his grasp and winged toward the playpen. A two-palm shove to the chest sent him pinwheeling backward. As I bolted for the door, I heard the sharp crack of bone against wood.

I pounded down the gravel lane, terrified Hoke was in pursuit. Terrified my spine would be severed by a load of twenty-gauge buck.

Legs and arms pumping, I raced across the lawn, grass and dead leaves flying up under my boots. The world was amber now. Time felt slowed, my movements sluggish, as though I were running through syrup.

I watched my car grow larger.

Ten yards. Five. And then I was there.

Lungs heaving, heart pounding, I yanked open the door, threw myself in, and turned the key. The engine roared to life. I shifted into drive, whipped the wheel, and spun a one-eighty. Pedal mashed to the floor, I shot onto the road. Though fishtailing like mad, I didn't slow until I reached the blacktop. Then, I goosed it to eighty.

I pulled in at the first business I spotted, a hole-in-the-wall diner with blue neon letters on the roof saying CONNIE & PHIL'S.

Holy crap! Holy crap! Holy bloody freakin' crap!

I stared at the diner, allowing my heartbeat to settle. A placard in the window announced fresh trout and homemade treats. Promised generous portions. Encouraged passersby to Phil up on good old mountain food.

I pulled out my phone. One call had come from Ramsey. He'd left no message. The other was from Ryan. Ditto.

I hit callback on Ramsey. He picked up right away. Background noise, voices and a slamming door, suggested he was inside.

I described my encounter with Hoke, explained my theory about the concrete pointing to Holiness church. The luminol. The Browning. My conclusion that I was wrong about that being the place Mason's body was dismembered. "It didn't go down there," I said.

"Hoke allowed you to walk away?"

"After an encouraging boot to the nuts." Not exactly true.

"It was unwise to go there alone."

"It was."

"I'll have someone pick him up."

"I *was* trespassing."

"That doesn't give him the right to threaten with a firearm."

"I thought it did."

Ramsey ignored that. "You still see Hoke as good for Cora and Mason." Statement, not question.

"Yes. He's demented. And he may now have his sights on Susan Grace Gulley." I told him about the photo on the kneeler and the note on the calendar. "That means it may be tonight. You need to track her down."

"Will do."

"Where the hell have you been, anyway?"

Following a reproachful pause. "Busting a meth lab. After hauling the parents to lockup, I drove their seven-year-old daughter to a group home in Crossnore. They think with a lot of therapy the kid may take her thumb out of her mouth and speak one day."

"Sorry." Feeling like a total shit.

Ramsey's next words took me by surprise.

"I tracked the Johnson City phone number Susan Grace gave you. Mason was staying at a rent-by-the-week motel not far from the Bristol Motor Speedway. Room with a microwave, mini-fridge, remote—all the comforts. He checked in mid-July, checked out mid-August."

"They still had the register?"

"No. I found a maid who remembered him. Apparently Mason was easy to remember. She said he was no beauty but a nice kid, that he rarely came out of his room."

"Did she know why he was there? Where he went

when he left?"

"She recalled two things. He'd seen a voice-activated recording device on TV and asked where to buy one. The day before leaving he'd told her he was heading home."

"He came back to Avery." Trying to make sense of it. "He slipped Cora the recorder. Hoke learned about it, went apeshit, they both ended up below Brown Mountain."

"Let's not jump to conclusions."

"Got a better theory?"

Ramsey had no answer to that.

"Mason wasn't dismembered at Jesus Lord Holiness, probably didn't die there." I'd been thinking about this through the whole wild dash, as much as my frazzled nerves would allow. "When things went south in Indiana, Hoke wasn't at his church. He was performing the exorcism at the child's home. You need to get warrants to search the Gulley and Teague properties."

"Maybe so."

"Maybe?" Crank it down. "Where are you now?"

"At my desk. We got a charger for Strike's laptop, but can't crack her password. Suggestions?"

I stared at Connie and Phil's sign. Got no inspiration. Then, "Try luckyloo."

"Spelled how?"

"One word, two o's."

Keys clicked. Then, "Son of a gun. I'm in."

"Check her email accounts."

More keys. Then, "There aren't any."

"Seriously? What about documents?"

"Zip."

"Anything on the desktop?"

"Nothing. It's weird."

"Strike was paranoid and not exactly generation Z. She probably stored all her case material as hard copy in the cartons, used the PC only for online searches. Check her browser history."

"How?"

I explained. Waited out a whole lot of clicking. Finally, "There isn't much. The list only goes back a couple of days."

"She probably cleared it frequently, thinking that might increase Net security. Or decrease unwanted ads."

"Does it?"

"Only if you wear a tinfoil hat."

"What?"

"Never mind. What did she look at?"

Ramsey read off some names.

That's when I made my next miscalculation.

34

"Medscape.com. EverydayHealth.com. HealthyPlace.com. Psychiatry.org. *The Journal of Clinical Psychiatry*, the *Journal of*—"

"What topics?"

Like the odors in the church, some terms arrowed straight out of my childhood. Schizophrenia. Schizoaffective disorder. Bipolar disorder. Others were new. Depersonalization disorder. Dissociative identity disorder. Borderline personality disorder.

"Jesus, Ramsey. There's your doer, your motive. Strike figured out Hoke was nuts, confronted him, he took her out."

"At the church?"

"If so it was outside. The luminol picked up zero blood. More likely he killed her in Charlotte."

"How did he find her?"

"Really? A goldfish with a smart phone could do that."

"How did he know about the pond?"

"Hell-o? Google Earth?"

"Does Hoke have a computer? Does he even have a phone?"

I had to admit, I'd seen neither in the "rectory."

"Maybe he showed up at her house," I tossed out. "Maybe he called to set up a meet. I don't know. What I do know is you need to get those warrants. Hoke's a lunatic. He killed Cora and Mason and may now be gunning for Susan Grace."

Ramsey exhaled, short and quick. "Okay. In the meantime, stay put. Go into the diner. Eat fish."

"Definitely," I said. "And call Slidell."

After disconnecting I sat in the car watching the sky fade to pewter behind Connie and Phil's bright blue neon. The confrontation with Hoke combined with fatigue and frustration had heartburn scorching my chest. I swallowed. Leaned my head against the seat back.

It wasn't the church. Then where? What others were involved?

What had Strike learned? How had that knowledge threatened Hoke?

My lids turned to lead, my thoughts to slowly churning sludge. Five minutes. I'd rest five minutes. If I drifted off, Ramsey's call would wake me.

Strike.

Trout.

Strike trout. Strike out.

Lucky Strike.

Out.

Out to see Hoke.

Hoke.

Holiness.

Holy.

Holy Hoke.

Hokeypokey. You put your heeeaaad in.

Head in a bucket.

Mason Gulley.

Cora Teague.

Cora's Treats.

Connie's treats.

Generous portions.

John's generosity.

Phil up on Connie's treats.

Fill up.

Fix up.

Connie. Treat.

Concrete.

My eyes flew open. My hands came up so fast my knuckles cracked against the wheel. The horizon was pink, the last light of dusk bleeding from the sky. I was unsure how long I'd slept, but dead certain of the meaning of the subliminal toggling.

I cranked the engine and fired out of the lot.

Minutes later I was parked off a two-lane, ten yards from J.T.'s Fill Up and Fix Up, about where Ramsey had pointed the place out. John Teague's gas station–

convenience–hardware store. "Fix up" meant buckets and saws, maybe concrete. Everything needed for the perfect dismemberment.

Sunday night. Business was booming. A couple of Harleys sat out front. An old pickup with a fractured windshield. A VW with a billion miles under its fan belt.

As I had earlier, I keyed in a quick text. Then I got out, scurried down the shoulder, and angled past the gas pumps to the front door. Light filtered through the flyers stuck to the window. Now and then I saw a flash of movement through the gaps in between.

I held my breath. Heard voices, all male. Yanking a cap from my bag, I tucked my hair out of sight and entered.

The interior was L-shaped, with the convenience store directly inside the door and a second room shooting off to the right. Straight ahead, behind a counter register, was a kid who looked at best fifteen. Tall and skinny, blotchy skin, snarl of black hair in need of a trim.

Three rows of shelving carved the main room into a pattern of two center aisles and a narrow perimeter passage. The shelves offered the usual candy, gum, and zero-food-value crap. Coolers lined the walls. Through the glass I could see milk, juices, soft drinks, and beer.

The bikers, one looking like an accountant playing weekend badass, the other a Billy Gibbons wannabe, were paying Snarly Hair for Bud and smokes. Badass said something I didn't catch. Snarly Hair unhooked one of two keys hanging from the wall behind the counter and, disinterested, handed it to him. As Badass headed my way, I cut into the room to my right.

Same arrangement of shelving and aisles. But no Doritos here. The merchandise ran from pliers and hammers to stakes and trowels. Bins offered a mind-boggling array of hinges, fasteners, screws, and nails.

Every sense on high alert, I moved toward the rear. Taller shelves held larger items—mailboxes, bird feeders, garden hoses, chain saws. Hoes and spades leaned against the back wall beside ladders arranged by height.

My pulse picked up when I saw them. Bags of Quikrete stacked to waist level.

My id toggled home another data byte.

Ramsey said the dog business had been relocated to the store four summers back. The kennel was constructed at that time. The kennel had concrete runs. If I read Ramsey correctly that meant the summer of 2011. When Cora and Mason disappeared.

Sweet Jesus. It had taken place here. Susan Grace might be here.

The heartburn sent a tendril of fire curling up my throat. I swallowed.

Behind me, the outer door opened. I heard boots thunk across the next room, a key strike against glass.

"Let's roll," Badass said to his pal.

Double thunks, the door slammed, and the hogs roared to life. As the sound of their engines receded, the door opened and closed again. More footfalls, this time firm but muted.

I crept to the point where junk food met hardware and peeped around the corner. Snarly Hair was retuning the men's room key to its hook.

A man occupied the space just vacated by the two bikers. All of it. His back was to me, his features hidden from view. He wore jeans, a gray sweatshirt, rubber-soled hiking boots.

Something about the guy triggered a humming deep in my brainpan, like angry wasps on the far side of a window.

Granger Hoke? John Teague?

The man reached backward, palm down, toward a butt pocket. His elbow winged up and his massive shoulders rotated, bringing his face into partial profile.

The wasps exploded in a collision of stored images. Realization. I was looking at John's son Owen Lee Teague. The man I'd seen at Holiness church. The hiker I'd seen at Wiseman's View.

"Hose down the runs first thing tomorrow." Owen Lee flipped a key ring onto the counter. Metal, maybe silver, in the shape of an eagle. "Don't go inside."

"I never go inside." Dull.

"Smart." Finger-pistol point. "Those dogs'll rip your face off. Give me what's in the drawer."

Snarly Hair opened the register and handed over the day's take.

"Closing time, just lock up and go. You need me, I'll be at home." Owen Lee knuckle-rapped the counter, two quick, hard pops. "Have a blessed evening." Snatching a bag of peanuts from its pin, he strode from the store.

Time to bolt. Yet, I didn't. I wanted more than buckets and saws and bags of Quikrete. I wanted proof that would nail Hoke and his lunatic pals. And I wanted to be sure Susan Grace was safe. But I had no plan. No idea what to do.

Then opportunity smacked me in the frontal.

A man stumbled through the door, eyes swimmy with the glow of too much booze. "Your goddamn pump don't work."

Snarly Hair looked up, blank. Either his poker face was superb, or he wasn't the sharpest bee buzzing in the hive.

"Yo! You gonna fix this clusterfuck?"

"Did you swipe your card?"

"Yeah, you dumbshit. I swiped my card."

"Try again."

"The problem ain't my card."

"What do you want me to do?"

"Fill my goddamn tank."

Snarly Hair looked as annoyed as possible without changing expression. Then he slouched from his post and followed the drunk outside.

It wasn't a plan. I just acted.

Heart pumping slow and hard, I shot to the counter and scooped the eagle key ring into my purse. Then I crossed to the door and peeked out.

Snarly Hair was putting gas into a Porsche Panamera, eyes on the pump. The Porsche's owner was struggling to maneuver his AmEx card into his wallet while simultaneously staying upright.

I slipped from the store and around the corner into shadow.

Cupping the screen with both hands, I checked my iPhone. No calls. I clicked on the little green box with the white speech bubble. Saw that my texts hadn't been delivered.

I hit resend. The little whoop sounded like a scream in the ocean-deep stillness.

It was full dark now. The kennel looked like a grave chiseled from the woods beyond. Moving gingerly, I angled wide, far to one end, to where I could see both the front and the back.

Kneeling behind a tree, I studied my target. Saw only one door, in the rear, out of sight of the store and the road.

I had my cellphone in my purse. I could have tried again to reach out. I didn't. All I could see was the forlorn face of Mason Gulley. The photo of Susan Grace on Hoke's kneeler. All I could hear was my own blood pounding in my ears.

I moved quickly, bloodstream charged with enough

adrenaline to float a destroyer. I was halfway to the kennel when I heard the first rip-your-face-off snarl.

Run! my fight-or-flight centers screamed.

I dropped to a squat and froze.

The dog barked several more times, loud and aggressive. Others joined in. Then they all went quiet.

They're locked up! Move!

I crouch-ran the last few yards, paused at the back of the kennel to listen. Either I was quiet enough or Fang and his buddies were letting it slide. For now.

I was debating my next move when air whooshed behind me. I whipped around, every nerve in my body electrified. A hawk was riding an updraft a few yards away, wings spread, a black double comma against the night sky.

I swallowed to return my heart to my chest. Tucked my chin.

Frowned. My boots were oddly easy to see given the twilight.

I glanced along the base of the building. To my left, low down, a dim pattern of radiance was spreading out across the ground. I inched toward it, feeling my way along the corrugated tin.

The light was coming from the top half of a semisubterranean window. The glass was covered on the outside by grime, on the inside by blackout drapes. I watched a moment. Saw no movement in the hairline gap where they met.

Why would a kennel need a basement? Why

curtain a cellar window? Why leave a light burning?

Good questions. Ones that should have brought me to a halt. Spurred me to seek backup. Instead, I continued toward the door.

Eyes cutting every direction at once, I dug through my purse until I found the silver eagle. With shaky fingers, I brailled for the lock and inserted a key. No go. I tried another. Same result.

The last key slid in and turned with a click. I twisted the knob. The door opened. I stepped into total blackness.

The air was cool and damp, the aroma a blend of earthy and man-made. Mold. Cold concrete. Shit and piss. Processed meat and grain.

The dogs heard me, or maybe picked up on the pheromones triggered by my fear. A frenzy of barking and snarling erupted to my right. Claws scrabbled. Bodies slammed chain linking.

I dug again, found my mini Maglite. Arm flexed, flash by my ear, I started left, toward a spot I estimated to be above the cellar window.

I crept past stacks of what must have been inventory for the store. Buckets, hoes, shovels, boxed power tools. Then my beam landed on a crude wooden staircase. Dogs bellowing at my back, I started down.

Eight treads brought me to a small open space with a concrete floor. My tiny blue-white oval slid over a water heater and a breaker panel, then landed on a door.

Deep breath. I stepped forward and turned the knob. Locked. I set the Maglite on the fuse box and began with the keys. Bingo. *Numero uno.*

Blood drumming like rain on tin, I pushed open the door.

The room was large enough to accommodate a single bed, a nightstand, a dresser, and a heavy oak chair. Through a doorless opening directly opposite I could see into a tiny bath. A crucifix hung on one wall. A space heater glowed red on the floor in one corner.

The nightstand was outfitted with a single lamp, its low-wattage bulb struggling but not quite up to the task. The chair was outfitted with leather-belt ligatures on the armrests and front legs.

A young woman sat cross-legged on the bed, arms pressing her thighs to her chest. Her face was down, her forehead tight to her knees. A slice of white ran across her scalp, a jagged part separating her hair into two blond braids.

The woman spoke without looking up. Maybe to me.

"Why is this happening?" Muffled. Familiar.

I was confused. Then the woman raised huge green eyes to mine.

The world contracted into a pinpoint of time and space. Nothing existed beyond the face and the chair with its hideous belts.

Impossible.

I didn't know if I was breathing or not. If my heart

was beating. If my hand, still flat to the door, was attached to my body.

"Are you here to help him?"

The timorous question hit my ears like a train roaring through a tunnel. The ugly truth slammed home. The fear dissolved, leaving nothing but a cold ball of rage in my gut.

When I answered, my voice sounded disembodied. Far away, as though coming from someone else.

"No, Cora. I'm here to help you."

35

It took several more seconds for my mind to fully assimilate. To rearrange the puzzle pieces I'd so carefully joined.

Cora Teague was alive. Captive. The victim of zealots.

"Go away."

"I'm here to help you, Cora," I repeated myself.

"It's bad."

"No."

"I'm bad."

"That isn't true."

"You'll make them come." The soft little voice pierced me like a blade to the gut. It was the terrified girl on the key chain recorder.

"I'm going to take you away from this place," I said.

Nothing.

"Is Susan Grace here?"

"Who?"

"Susan Grace Gulley, Mason's sister."

"Oh, no. Oh, no." Almost a moan.

"Are you alone?"

"I'm always alone. I have to be alone."

"We're going now."

"Going where?" An edge of panic. "Home?"

"Not if you don't want to go there."

"What's that noise?" Cora crushed her legs more tightly to her chest.

I listened. From above came the renewed din of canine fury. Only then did it register that the dogs had briefly fallen silent.

"It's all right."

"You shouldn't be here." She blinked, and a tear trickled down her cheek. "You scare me."

I realized I was braced, knees flexed, weight on the balls of my feet. Acknowledging that my posture might seem threatening, I straightened and stepped into the room.

"Cora. Listen to me."

"I'm afraid."

"Where are your shoes?" Calm, masking the turmoil churning inside me.

Cora didn't answer.

"Do you have a jacket? A sweater?"

Her eyes flicked to the dresser, back to me, wide with alarm. And something else. An emotion so intense I felt chilled to the core.

"I'll get it," I said.

"No! No!"

I stepped to the bed and placed a hand on her shoulder. She recoiled as though burned with a poker.

"Father G will never hurt you again," I said gently.

"Oh, God." Again her forehead dropped to her knees. "They're coming."

"No one is coming." Knowing my words were untrue. Hoke would be anxious. Snarly Hair would hear the dogs. Or discover Owen Lee's key chain missing.

"I can't ever leave." Almost inaudible.

"Don't be frightened."

"They come when I'm frightened. I'm frightened when they come." Spoken with a singsong lilt, as though chanting or praying.

I crossed to the dresser. Jammed the flash into my waistband and opened a drawer. Socks and undies. I bent to open another.

"Stop!"

My heart catapulted into my throat.

I whirled, expecting to see a Browning pointed at my chest.

There was no one in the doorway. No one in the room but Cora and me.

"Cora?"

The only response was the sound of agitated breathing. Cora had withdrawn so far into the corner I could no longer see her feet.

"Go away!" So loud it seemed to come from nowhere and everywhere.

Dear God! I hadn't checked the bath!

On reflex, I slammed my back to the wall and slid to the doorway. Blood pounding in my ears, I yanked out my flash and aimed the beam into the dark little space. Saw nothing but a toilet, sink, and makeshift shower.

"Be gone!" At my back.

I whipped my head around, shoulders still flat to the wall.

The wretched lighting was transforming Cora's body into a grotesque tableau of angles and shadows. Her chin was up and twisted sideways so hard the ligaments in her neck stretched taut as boards. Her fingers, tight on the quilt, looked like bone without flesh.

Sweet Jesus! Was she having a seizure? I scanned the area to make sure there was nothing she could hurt herself with. There wasn't. I was heading into the bath when another shrieked command froze me in place.

"Leave!"

Impossible! An adrenaline-induced audio hallucination. Yet there was no mistaking. It was the third voice on the recording. And it was coming from the corner.

Mind struggling to make sense, I inched toward the bed.

"Takarodj el!" Spit with such force it practically blew my cap off.

Not wanting to see, unable to look away, I aimed the Maglite at Cora. The beam lit her pale oval face, lips stretched in a rigor sneer, eyes shining with something dark and menacing. A sensation deep inside me lurched and staggered.

Easy!

I assessed. Cora's body was tense, but not in spasm.

More data bytes toggled. My last conversation with Ramsey. Depersonalization disorder. Dissociative personality disorder. Panicky questions from Saffron Brice. Which one, Mommy? Which one?

Saffron wasn't asking which home Cora might visit. She was asking which Cora.

In that instant I realized the magnitude of my error.

"We are going." Shrugging out of my jacket. "Now."

"You will die," bellowed the girl in a deep bass. It was eerie to hear a man's voice coming from such a delicate mouth.

"I'm not leaving without you, Cora."

"I'm not Cora."

I had no idea how to deal with depersonalization or dissociation. Or whatever the sweet fuck this was. Confront? Cajole? Commend?

"Who are you?" I asked.

"Elizabeth."

"Go away, Elizabeth. I want to talk to Cora."

"No one tells me what to do."

"Go away and let me see Cora."

"I act as I please."

"Do you kill as you please?" Knowing priests view exorcism as battle, my adrenaline-pumped brain chose confrontation.

The leering grin lifted on one side.

"You killed Mason."

"No loss. Meddlesome Mason."

"Why?"

"He convinced the little cow to tell the world."

"To record what was happening to her."

"She's pathetic. I protect her."

"You dismembered Mason's body and tossed it on the mountain."

"Others do my bidding. I have the power."

"You have only what Cora allows you."

"Demon power."

"Only a coward kills children."

At that, Cora's head began to corkscrew wildly. Her braids flew and saliva winged across her cheeks in silvery streams.

"Cora's brother Eli. River Brice."

The contortions grew more violent. Fearing injury, I shoved a pillow behind her head and quickly hopped back.

Several seconds of wild movement, then Cora's chin leveled and the emerald eyes bore into mine. In them I saw pure malevolence. Spawned not by some dark presence in her soul. Spawned by a catastrophe in her brain.

Yet Cora believed the demon inside her was real. I had to get her away from this place. Away from Hoke's destructive psychopathology.

"I don't believe in demons," I pressed on.

Cora hawked spit and hurled it in my direction. Missed.

"Not even a good imitation."

Cora's pupils rolled back, leaving a glistening white crescent low in each orbit.

"You are a caricature." My palms were sweaty, my mouth dry. I swallowed. "A bad performance of what Father G expects you to be."

Cora's fingers hyperextended, then contracted into claws on the quilt.

"Let me talk to Cora."

"Eriggy el!"

"Cora."

"Cora is weak."

"You don't exist. Cora created you."

"The cow is too stupid to create anything."

"Come away with me." Confrontation wasn't working. I tried coaxing. "You can explain who you are."

"Elizabeth Báthory."

"There's no need to shout, Elizabeth Báthory." I knew the name. From where? My memory cells were far too wired to help. "We'll go where it's warmer."

"Hagyjàl békén!"

As I turned to snatch my jacket from the floor, I saw the comforter shift. Still, I was a heartbeat too late. Cora was off the bed and on me before I could react.

Twisting my right arm high behind my back, she

shoved me forward and down. My cap flew and my forehead slammed the concrete. Pain exploded in my skull.

I saw black. Then a million tiny points of light.

My nose and mouth were mashed shut. My teeth were cutting the insides of my lips. I couldn't speak, couldn't breathe. I tasted blood.

As I struggled for air and coherence, a knee smashed down on my spine. Lungs burning, I struck out and back with both feet and my one free elbow. Though I'm strong, I was no match for Cora.

"Halj meg!"

I strained my neck in a frenzied attempt to lift my head. To free my air passages. Failed. Cora had me pinned.

It seemed like hours. In reality, it was probably less than a minute. I finally managed to shift one shoulder enough to rotate my chin. My cheek landed in blood pooling on the concrete. My blood. I feared I would retch.

"Cora." I gasped.

Her body tensed. Then her fingers grabbed and twisted my hair. She yanked my head up, then smashed it down hard.

"Elizabeth."

I felt her weight shift, then Cora's breath hot and moist on my ear.

"Slut."

"You're hurting me."

"Filthy bitch!"

"No. No more."

"Whore!"

She jerked my head high. My neck vertebrae screamed. A flat-palm shove and my left temple slammed the concrete. She mashed down on my right temple with more force than I would have thought possible from someone her size. Something crunched in my jaw.

The tiny white lights winked.

Then the blackness won out.

I woke to a scene that made no sense.

Cora was in the big oak chair, one wrist and one ankle strapped to the wood. Hoke lay crumpled on the floor, eyes closed, a crucifix jutting at a deadly angle from beneath his Roman collar.

The memories after that are shredded images spliced together with yawning gaps in between. The incomplete puzzle as hellish multisensory nightmare.

I remember the dogs braying in fury. Hoke's blood snaking the concrete to mingle with mine. Cora, wild-eyed, clawing at the leather-belt ligatures.

I recall an agitated male voice drifting down from above. Fragments of a one-sided conversation. ". . . done it again." "No!" "I'll hide her and I'll cover for her when she's hostage to the serpent. But . . ." "No . . ." ". . . Lord God commands thou shalt not kill."

I retain the image of a man standing over me, all

bone and muscle and dangerous scowl. The smell of his rubber-soled hiking boots.

I know I asked about Susan Grace.

I know I tried to rise but couldn't.

In my mind I hear the boom of a door slamming tin. Feet pounding down stairs. Men's voices shouting.

I see Ramsey holding a gun two-handed on Owen Lee Teague. Slidell's face close to mine.

I feel fingers probing my hair. Soft fabric wiping my face. Hands lifting my body.

The rest of that night is a huge blank containing very few pieces. A fuzzy wool blanket tickling my chin. A wobbly ride with stars overhead and straps on my chest and thighs. Flashing red lights. The back of an ambulance. A wailing siren.

Thinking.

Thinking what?

Thinking nothing at all.

36

I never again saw any of those from Avery County. Grandma and Susan Grace Gulley. Granger Hoke. Cora and her hideous family.

Except for Strike, we all came through it. Even Hoke, though he'll never audition for the Vatican choir. He lost a lot of blood and took a nick to the vocals, but Cora's thrust with the crucifix missed all major vessels. When released, Father G would be swapping his hospital gown for a jailhouse jumpsuit.

Susan Grace was never in danger. That night she'd again lied to her grandmother in order to snatch a fragment of normalcy. A deputy found her drinking wine coolers in the woods with high school friends. Hoke said the notation on his calendar was a reminder to put sealant on his gutters.

I still marvel at the dramatic entrance choreographed by Slidell and Ramsey. At Slidell's timing in nailing the truth.

Skinny had spent hours viewing security tapes covering the weekend Hazel Strike died. Footage from establishments near Strike's home and the RibbonWalk Nature Preserve, where her body was found.

At 4:00 P.M., while I was legging it away from Hoke's Browning, Slidell's diligence paid off. Strike's red Corolla appeared on camera at a gas station a quarter mile from the preserve. Riding in her passenger seat was Cora Teague.

From my texts Slidell knew I'd gone to Jesus Lord Holiness, then on to Teague's store. Smelling danger, he'd contacted Ramsey, then burned rubber up to Avery.

I suffered a concussion and a hairline fracture of my right zygoma. No big deal, but I was compelled to stay two days at Cannon Memorial so night-shift nurses could shine lights in my eyes. When finally reconnected with my clothes, I filled my prescriptions and headed back to Charlotte.

Zeb Ramsey called while I was still on meds and too loopy to talk. I phoned him back a few days later. Thanked him for saving my ass. In more polite language.

Oddly, the call seemed to continue well past its shelf life. Just before disconnecting, I learned why. Ramsey surprised me by asking me out. Dinner sometime, you know the drill. Awkward. Or was it? I wasn't sure what to think.

Turns out Ramsey's full name is Zebulon. Apparently, I asked while under the influence of pain. Or painkillers.

Slidell made himself scarce once he learned that all I had was a head thump, unsightly skin loss, and a broken cheek. Partly busy with paperwork and interrogations. Partly furious with me for going all cowboy. His phrase. Couldn't blame him. Rushing off on my own was a bonehead move.

It took two weeks, but, working both ends, Slidell and Ramsey managed to patch together the story. Most of it came from Owen Lee and Fatima Teague, some from Cora's out-of-state sisters, Veronica and Marie. Some from medical personnel treating Cora.

According to Fatima, Cora had her first "fit" at age fourteen, a few months before Eli died. She recalled that after her son's death her daughter became increasingly temperamental and started "taking on airs." As the older sisters moved away from the home, Cora's moodiness intensified. For a while John allowed her to see a doctor, but, in Daddy's enlightened view, medication made her worse.

Veronica stated that Cora was frequently anxious and afraid of ridiculously harmless things. Frogs. Coat hangers. A tree behind their house. Marie said Cora was often depressed, had trouble sleeping and a lousy memory.

The professional assessment, based on intense and ongoing psychiatric evaluation, beat the hell out of devils and demons. I had no doubt the diagnosis would stand.

I was lugging my sixth box to the curb when a familiar Taurus pulled into my drive. I straightened and waited for Slidell to lower his window.

"Riveting look." Taking in my head scarf and dingy denim. "But Rosie already got the part."

"I'm cleaning out the attic."

"Converting to a nursery?"

"An office."

"Face looks good."

It didn't. "Thanks."

Slidell chin-cocked my haphazardly stacked trash. "You know those douchebags on the trucks won't take big stuff."

"I bribe them."

"I'm a cop. Don't tell me that." Gruff, but with a level of civility that let me know he was no longer angry. "When are you leaving?"

"The eight-twenty flight tonight. Renovations start on the attic on Monday."

"You got a minute?"

"Sure. Come on in."

We settled at the kitchen table. Slidell declined a beer in favor of unsweetened iced tea. While delivering his drink, I did a discreet appraisal. Though a long way from buff, Skinny had definitely lost more weight. Workouts? Stress? The lovely Verlene?

"I gotta admit. I can't get my head around the arse end of this shrinky gobbledygook."

"Shrinky gobbledygook?" As usual, I anticipated the need of an interpreter for the conversation.

"The kid killed three, maybe four people, yet she's at some candy-ass hospital whining about her problems."

"Cora has been deemed mentally incompetent."

That drew a head wag and a whistly snort.

"She's unable to understand the charges against her or to aid in her own defense."

"She's nuts, I get that, but—"

"She has dissociative identity disorder. DID."

"That's what I mean." In his "pointing finger" voice. "You sound just like the shrinks. So, what? They saying she's schizophrenic?"

"No. Schizophrenia is a mental illness involving chronic or recurrent psychosis. People hear or see things that aren't there, think or believe things that have no basis in reality."

"Yeah, yeah. The kid don't have hallucinations or delusions. That's what they been spinning. How about you explain what it is she *does* have?"

"Multiple personalities."

"I thought that was just cheesy Hollywood movie crap."

"It's real. Dissociative identity disorder used to be called multiple personality disorder. It's a condition in which a person's identity fragments into two or more different ones. Each identity exists independently of the others, and each identity is distinct in specific ways. Tone of voice, vocabulary, mannerisms, posture, handedness—all the things we think of as making up a personality."

"How many identities we talking?"

"A person with DID can have as few as two or three, or as many as a hundred or more. Statistically, the average is fifteen." I'd spent hours researching the subject. "The usual age of onset is early childhood, so new identities can accumulate throughout life."

"Who runs the show?"

"Psychiatrists call the main personality the host. That identity acts as a sort of gatekeeper. The others are called alters, and the transitions are called switches. Switching can take seconds to minutes to days. Alters can be imaginary people, animals, historic or fictional figures, and can vary by age, race, or gender."

"So a guy can have a chick alter and a chick can have a guy?"

"Yes."

"That why the kid sounded like a goddamn drill sergeant down in that basement?"

"Exactly. And on the audio recording. The voice we thought was a second man was actually Cora speaking as Elizabeth."

"Jesus bouncing Christ. This is too fucked up."

"Dissociation is a coping mechanism—the person simply disconnects from situations that are too violent, traumatic, or painful to assimilate with the conscious self. The condition is thought to result from prolonged childhood trauma."

"So, what? The bastards beat her? Or raped her?"

"The abuse doesn't have to be physical. Or sexual. It can be psychological. In Cora's case, the severe isolation imposed because of her epilepsy combined with extreme religious fanaticism."

Slidell watched a droplet break free and roll down his glass, swiped the track, then licked his thumb. "This shrink I been talking to thinks maybe Cora didn't kill Eli, or maybe didn't kill him on purpose. Either way, he thinks Eli's death jump-started her flipping out or fragmenting or whatever the hell you call it."

"Then the older sisters started leaving home." I picked up the narrative. "Eventually Cora went to work for the Brices. She'd never been on her own before, had hardly met anyone outside the family or church, had never even seen TV. She couldn't handle the freedom, the responsibility. She was completely overwhelmed. She or an alter killed River Brice."

"I've been talking to Owen Lee. Hoke some. Their stories track with that."

"John?"

"The arrogant prick keeps hand-jobbing the idea that the kid is controlled by Satan."

"What do Hoke and Owen Lee say?"

"Cora offed the baby because she was possessed by a demon."

"So their treatment was to lock her in their spanking-new kennel and shake crucifixes at her." I'd meant to keep my voice neutral, but a note of bitterness now crept in. The thought of Cora in that place still sickened me. "Mason loved her. He guessed they had her, but didn't know where they'd taken her."

"Scared shitless of being next on the hymn list, he split for Johnson City. When Susan Grace mentioned seeing Cora, he figured it out, bought the recorder, came back to Avery and slipped the thing to her."

"Mason probably planned to expose Hoke by giving the audio to the cops or the media. Maybe to a legit priest." I'd thought this through. Over and over.

"You think Cora made the tape on purpose?" Slidell asked.

"We may never know. The device was voice-activated." I took a sip of tea. "Have you learned how Mason got to her?"

"According to Owen Lee, he had a key." At my surprised look. "During the church renovation they'd send him on supply runs to the store and the kennel."

Birdie strolled in, paused to consider, decided to join us. We watched him work maneuvers around Slidell's ankle, both picturing the scene when Mason returned to Cora's little cell. Slidell spelled it out.

"So the kid goes back to collect the recorder. Cora snaps, kills and dismembers him. When Owen Lee shows up she's covered with blood and Mason's head's in a bucket. He calls Daddy. Daddy says deal with it. And pray."

"So Owen Lee chucks the body parts from the overlooks. Did he choose the locations because of Brown Mountain?"

Slidell shook his head. "No voodoo there. He knew them from hiking."

"The DNA results came back yesterday," I said. "It was Mason's hair caught in the concrete. The olive oil and incense must have transferred to him from Cora."

"The fingertips in the pine tar?"

"Also Mason."

A beat as we both thought about that.

"And it was the same scenario for Hazel Strike." Lucky. I swallowed. "Strike drives Cora to Charlotte. Cora dissociates and kills her. Owen Lee shows up, dumps Strike's body in the pond, then hauls little sister back up to Avery."

"That's Owen Lee's version, though he denies Cora killed anyone."

"Who did?"

"The Evil One."

"Right." I didn't bother hiding my revulsion.

"Lucifer or no, Owen Lee admits that, as a precaution, he smashed Strike's phone and threw it over a guardrail, later pitched her computer into the dumpster in Banner Elk."

"What about the recorder?"

"He claims he never saw it. I'm guessing Strike

stashed the thing somewhere to keep you from getting it."

"It wasn't in her house?"

Slidell shook his head. "Good chance we'll never find it."

"Where do you think the murder went down?"

"My money's on the park. That's where Owen Lee says he found Cora. And CSU pulled a metal hiking stick out of the pond. When we tossed Strike's house we found a couple like it in the garage. I'm guessing she kept one in her car. I've got a team back out there now."

"Do you know how Cora hooked up with Strike?"

"Fatima came through on that one. She says Strike showed up at their house that Saturday. John threw her out, later found Cora missing. Seems they had a set of padded and locked rooms where they kept the kid when Hoke wasn't waging his holy war against her demons."

"Somehow Cora got out and persuaded Strike to take her away," I said.

"When John discovered her gone he called Owen Lee. Owen Lee hotfooted it down to Charlotte."

"How did he know where to go?"

"Strike left contact info in case anyone experienced a change of heart about talking to her."

"Including a home address?"

"What the dame lacked in caution she made up for in zeal."

"It was Owen Lee who sent the rock over the edge at the Devil's Tail trail."

"Yeah. He overheard you and Ramsey at Wiseman's View, panicked, and followed you. Says he just wanted to scare you off. Owen Lee ain't the brightest stripe on the flag."

"No," I agreed. "He's not."

"Here's what I don't get. How does a timid little mouse like Cora wig out and turn into a stone-cold murderer?"

"Some people with dissociative disorders have a tendency toward self-sabotage. Others turn the violence outward. But remember, in a way Owen Lee is right. It wasn't Cora doing the killing. It was her alter. And I think you've put your finger on it. I'm not a psychiatrist, but I suspect Elizabeth Báthory emerged because of Cora's sense of powerlessness."

"And this chick makes her kill?"

"Not exactly. When under sufficient stress, Cora becomes Elizabeth. It is Elizabeth who is doing the killing."

"Who the hell is she?"

"The bloody countess."

"That clears it up."

"Elizabeth Báthory has been branded the most prolific female serial killer in history. She was tried for torturing and murdering hundreds of girls."

"When was this?"

"The sixteenth century. In Hungary."

"Helluva way to get her rocks off."

"Legend has it she liked to bathe in the blood of virgins to retain her youth."

"Great role model."

"Cora's subconscious saw Báthory as powerful."

"This kid wasn't allowed TV or the Internet. Her books were screened, and, except for school and church, she wasn't allowed outta the house. How'd she learn about this countess?"

"Katalin Brice is Hungarian. Cora probably found history books in their home."

"So no speaking in tongues."

I shook my head. "Nope. She was speaking Hungarian."

"Well, she sure as hell was speaking in blood."

I offered no comment.

A few seconds, then, "Looks like the countess ain't alone in there."

"Oh?"

"The shrink's using hypnosis. Thinks he's made another acquaintance."

"It's not uncommon that other personalities become known during treatment. Who's the new one?"

"He don't want to go into detail."

Slidell and I both took a tea moment. Then he asked, voice edged with something I couldn't define, "How common is this dissociating shit?"

"DID sufferers tend to have other issues as well—depression, anxiety, substance abuse, borderline personality disorder—so it's hard to diagnose. But the condition is rare. I've read stats that put the incidence at one one-hundredth of a percent to one percent within the general population."

Slidell blew a long breath through his nose. "I don't know. Sounds like defense lawyer mumbo jumbo to me."

"You remember Herschel Walker?" Knowing Slidell was a football fan.

"Course I do. Walker won the Heisman in '82."

"Hang on." I went to the study, returned, and slid a book across the table. "You read, right?"

"Hilarious. What is this?"

"*Breaking Free.*"

"I can see that."

"Walker is the author. In the book he talks about having DID."

"Are you shitting me?"

I just looked at him. Then shifted gears. "So what will happen to Hoke and the Teagues?"

"Accessory after the fact, obstructing, improper disposal of a human body." Slidell's mouth pursed up in disgust. "And these assholes ain't counting on Jesus for deliverance. They're already lawyered up."

"If one day Cora is declared competent, could the DA possibly bring charges? Except for Owen Lee, there are no witnesses, no forensics or physical evidence."

"We got the video of the kid in Strike's car. Maybe her prints. But unless she confesses, or Hoke or a family member agrees to testify, being competent to stand trial don't mean she was competent at the time of the murders. And which of her personalities would you put on trial? The shrinks'll say she couldn't tell right from wrong or adhere to the right. Blah, blah, blah."

We both knew the chances of prosecution were slim to none. Then Slidell stunned me. With a compliment.

"You know, Doc, when speaking in bones, you're pretty good. Maybe you'll come up with something."

With that Slidell pushed to his feet. I walked him to the door. And he was gone.

37

April twenty-seven. Ten forty-two A.M.

Sun pounded through the floor-to-ceiling glass, warming eggshell walls and blond oak floors. Flames danced in a rectangular pit stretching low across a long marble hearth. At our backs, countertops and cabinets gleamed brilliant white and our images reflected off flawless stainless steel.

I loved the place. The place terrified me.

I crossed the dining room to look down on the city twelve stories below. Behind me, a realtor continued the hard sell.

Centreville was busy with the usual Monday morning shoppers, appointment keepers, dog walkers, and stroller-pushing nannies and moms. I leaned forward to peer out past the terrace.

To the east, students hurried in both directions through the gates at McGill. To the west, the Musée des beaux-arts, boutiques, galleries, shops, and residential buildings lined curbs heading toward Westmount, Notre-Dame-de-Grâce, and the West Island beyond.

The last of the mountainous winter drifts had melted, leaving streets and sidewalks iridescent with oily runoff. Here and there, chimneys exhaled thin streams of breath, pale and vaporous against the spectacularly blue sky.

Not yet, but soon the rituals of spring would begin. Jackets and boots would be exchanged for bare limbs and sandals. Tables would appear outside restaurants and pubs. Students would toss Frisbees, picnic, and lounge on newly greened campus lawns.

". . . Carrera is one of the most beautiful of all marbles. So soft and warm. And versatile. Don't you agree, Dr. Brennan?"

I turned back to reengage. The realtor, Claire or Cher, was beaming at me through tiny gold-rimmed readers perched on her nose. The woman's rigidly disciplined gray pageboy made me think of Shakespeare. Odd, but there you have it.

"And that freestanding tub? *Mon dieu!* This condo, it is truly a gem."

"An expensive one," I said.

"But the location is *très magnifique*!" Claire/Cher had an annoying habit of sucking on her teeth between overly enthusiastic outbursts. She did that now.

"Unfortunately, it's out of our price range."

From behind Claire/Cher came a narrow, squinty-eyed look. I kept my face blank.

"*Oui*, but you are a couple of such *élégance*. I had to show it to you."

"He's a cop. I'm a scientist."

"We could move further down market." Delivered as though suggesting we eat from a dumpster. "But I must warn you. This property will not be available for long."

"*Merci*." Scooping my jacket and purse from the marvelous stone. "You've been very helpful. Detective Ryan and I will discuss it."

Her stilettos clicked loud and annoyed as she followed us into the corridor, then the elevator. Outside, we went our separate ways, she toward her Beamer, Ryan and I toward rue Crescent and Hurley's Irish Pub, three blocks south.

It was early and we had our choice of tables. Wanting quiet, we opted for a two-top in the snug. A waitress appeared as we were removing our jackets. Siobhan.

Siobhan asked our pleasure. Ryan ordered a Moosehead and the Guinness beef stew. I went for fish and chips and a Diet Coke. We knew every selection. Didn't need menus.

"So," I said.

"So," Ryan said.

"It's way over budget," I said. "Don't forget, I'll still have expenses for my place in Charlotte. And we'll be spending mongo bucks on airline tickets."

"And lingerie."

The comment merited no reply.

"It's a great location," Ryan said.

"Thanks, Cher."

"Chantal."

"What?"

"Her name is Chantal."

"It should be Shylock."

"Shylock was a moneylender, not a realtor."

"She probably has a sideline."

"So harsh, *madame*."

Siobhan arrived with our drinks, allowing me time to structure a counterproposal.

"Maybe we should rent," I said. "At least until we know how the new arrangement will work out."

I was still reeling from Ryan's news. He and Slidell retired and in partnership as PIs, one working each side of the border. That was the reason for all their phone conversations. An underlying agenda in Ryan's stealth strike visit to Charlotte.

"We said in for a penny, in for a pound." Ryan smiled, and the starburst crinkles at his eyes deepened.

"Penny? That place would put us into competition with the national debt."

"Which nation?"

"Either," I said.

"Our condos here will both fetch tidy sums."

They would. The thought of selling mine knotted my gut. I said nothing.

Siobhan arrived with our food. For several moments

we focused on napkins, utensils, and seasoning. Ryan picked up the thread.

"Besides, what's money? You'll be royalty one day. The Sultana of Starch and Steam."

I rolled my eyes at Ryan's reference to Mama's upcoming nuptials. Turned out Clayton Sinitch owned not a solo operation but a chain of laundry and dry-cleaning stores. In addition, he'd invented a chemical process that earned him zillions annually. Harry had done some digging. Everyone who knew the guy said he was solid, a kind and generous widower who missed being married.

Generous, indeed. The rock on Mama's finger was the size of a bagel.

At Daisy's insistence, the happy couple was postponing the wedding until Katy rotated back Stateside. In the meantime, she and Goose were planning a bash that would, according to Harry, make Kate and William's little shindig look cheap.

I'd yet to fully admit it to myself, but it was Mama who'd inspired me to take a chance on Ryan. Her exuberance. Her trust. Her belief that love never comes too late in life. Hell, her Aristotelian wisdom about one soul inhabiting two bodies.

"Maybe we should follow Daisy's lead." Ryan spoke through a mouthful of stew.

"What lead?" Taking a cue from Birdie, I refrained from comment on proper dining etiquette.

"You do. I do."

"You'll do."

"Funny."

"I try."

"I'm serious."

"Ryan, we agreed that living together is a good first step. By the way, renovations for your office start at the annex this morning."

"May I hang my Habs poster over my desk?"

"Is it autographed?"

"Yvan Cournoyer."

"That must be worth something."

"It is to me. You can hang a picture of Dale Earnhardt in our bedroom here."

"I just might," I said. "Can we step out of *House Hunters* mode for a bit?"

"*Mais, oui, ma chère*." Lately Ryan was agreeing to whatever I wanted. "Your face looks much improved."

"God bless concealer."

Ryan scarfed a chip from my plate. "Are you feeling better about Cora and Strike? About the whole Brown Mountain mess?"

"I don't know. The investigation was so confusing. First Cora looked like a victim. Then she looked like a vicious killer. In the end she turned out to be both."

"But a victim of a very different sort. Of ignorance and religious fanaticism."

"Still, it's all so very sad. Cora should have spent her summers playing tennis and slapping on suntan lotion, her weekends drinking cheap wine with her

BFFs. Giggling at a teacher's bad hair, crying over boys, laughing over boys, whispering in the dark about first kisses. Instead, because of Hoke's delusional freak show, she spent her days under the watchful eyes of Daddy and Jesus, her nights terrified that her body was a safe house for Satan."

Ryan reached out and ran a thumb across my cheek. "True believers can be the most dangerous of all," he said softly.

Our eyes locked, blue on hazel. Inexplicably, I felt the old flicker of unease, there sharp and fast as a pinprick, then gone. I banished the uncertainty and took Ryan's hand.

"Yes," I agreed. "They can."

"Hoke and the Teagues will do time," he said. "The Brices are healing. Cora is receiving the care she needs. It's the best of all possible worlds."

"Thank you, Candide."

"You should be pleased."

"I am." I was. So why the confusion?

I took a sip of Coke. A poke at the muddle of emotions churning inside me.

"In a way, I'm most sorry for Grandma Gulley. The old woman lost her husband, her son, and her grandson. Hoke, her trusted adviser on all things godly, is heading to the slammer. I hope she can see reason and mend her relationship with Susan Grace."

"The kid's plucky."

"Plucky?"

"Susan Grace will be fine."

We ate without speaking for a while, each of us lost in our own private thoughts. I broke the silence with a question that had been troubling me.

"So who had the most irrational take on reality? Cora with her alter egos? Or Hoke and the Teagues with their belief in demonic forces?"

"Don't forget Sarah Winchester with her unwinnable battle against guilt."

"Salvation through construction." I'd forgotten telling Ryan about the outlandish mansion in San Jose.

"Dissociation. Exorcism. Delusions of architecture. They're all mechanisms to deal with a world that is too overwhelming."

"Not bad, Ryan."

"But, since you ask, Ramsey's parents get my vote."

I floated a brow.

"Who names a kid Zebulon?"

I bunched and tossed my napkin. Ryan batted the incoming down with one hand. "Here's one that's been bothering me," he said. "What does create the lights on Brown Mountain?"

I raised both brows and palms in a "Who knows?" gesture.

"Still an unsolved mystery," he said.

"It is," I agreed.

Then Ryan's face went solemn. Reaching across the table, he took my hand in his.

"I'm so sorry I wasn't there for you, Tempe. It must

have been terrifying in that kennel. Cora. Hoke. Owen Lee. The dogs."

"Slidell and Ramsey did just fine."

"It should have been me."

"No, Ryan. It's much better that it wasn't you rushing in to save me."

"I like to rush in to save you."

"I'm serious. I think—" I stopped. What did I think? "The possibility of imbalance was part of my hesitation in committing to"—I sought the perfect word, settled—"a relationship."

"To us."

"Yes. To us. I guess I botched my explanation the day you came to Charlotte."

"Your meaning was clear."

"I have to be my own person, Ryan. To fight my own battles, win or lose. I can't play damsel in distress to your Galahad."

"Message received, then and now. Just remember the next time you get a flat tire."

My eye roll was epic.

"So. What about it?" Ryan did one of his famous fast segues. "Can we afford Shylock's condo?"

I looked into the astoundingly blue eyes. Into the face that I'd loved for so many years.

"What the hell." I smiled. "A fat tax refund is coming my way."

I raised a palm. A beaming Ryan high-fived it.

When I think back about Hazel "Lucky" Strike—

nights when I can't sleep, days when I catch a glimpse of outrageously dyed carrot hair—there is one bright spot that I recall. Until then, I hadn't shared that detail with Ryan.

"Slidell found a folder in Strike's house containing a funeral plan."

"Her own?"

"She was getting on in years and had no family." And was painfully aware of the fate of the unmourned dead. The last didn't need saying.

Ryan waited.

"Skinny told me he dropped by the cemetery."

"Without you?"

"He claimed I was still busy licking my wounds."

"That was a very kind gesture."

"He thought turnout would be low." Saying it hit me with a new wave of melancholy. "He was wrong. By Skinny's count there were roughly fifty people there."

"Fellow websleuths?"

I nodded. "Wendell Clyde bought her a headstone."

"Seriously?"

"Engraved under Strike's name were the words 'Lucky to have known you.'"

Acknowledgments

Most view writing as a solitary pursuit. Not so. I get a whole lot of help from a whole lot of people. Thus, as usual, I owe a huge debt of gratitude to those who contributed to *Speaking in Bones*.

I want to thank Avery County Sheriff Kevin Frye for welcoming inquiries on the workings of his office. Dr. Bruce Goldberger gave advice on trace element analysis. Dr. William Rodriguez answered bone questions beyond my ken. Judy Jasper provided input on the Hungarian culture and language.

I appreciate the continued support of Chancellor Philip L. Dubois of the University of North Carolina at Charlotte.

I offer deepest thanks to my agent, Jennifer Rudolph-Walsh, and to my endlessly patient and skillful editors, Jennifer Hershey and Susan Sandon.

I also want to acknowledge all those who work so very hard on my behalf. At home in the United States,

Gina Centrello, Libby McGuire, Kim Hovey, Scott Shannon, Susan Corcoran, Cindy Murray, Kristin Fassler, Cynthia Lasky, and Anne Speyer. On the other side of the pond, Aslan Byrne, Glenn O'Neill, Georgina Hawtrey Woore, and Jen Doyle. North of the forty-ninth, Kevin Hanson and Amy Cormier. At William Morris Endeavor Entertainment, Caitlin Moore, Maggie Shapiro, Tracy Fisher, Cathryn Summerhayes, and Raffaella De Angelis.

I appreciate Paul Reichs's unpaid editorial input. And Melissa Fish's tireless attention to every problem I throw her way.

As always, I send a great big hug to all my readers. It is heartwarming that you are so loyal to Tempe. I love that you find me at my signings and appearances, visit my website (kathyreichs.com), like me on Facebook (@kathyreichsbooks), and follow me on Twitter (@kathyreichs), Pinterest (@kathyreichs), and Instagram (@kathyreichs). You guys are what it's all about!

If I failed to thank someone I should have, I apologize. And owe you a beer. If the book contains errors, they are my fault.

ALSO AVAILABLE IN ARROW

Bones Are Forever

Kathy Reichs

A newborn baby is found wedged in a vanity cabinet in a rundown apartment near Montreal.

Dr Temperance Brennan, forensic anthropologist to the province of Quebec, is brought in to investigate. While there, she discovers the mummified remains of two more babies within the same room.

Shocked and distressed, Tempe must use all her skills and inner strength to focus on the facts. But when the autopsies reveal that the children died of unnatural causes, the hunt for the mother – a young woman with a seedy past and at least three aliases – is on.

The trail leads Tempe to Yellowknife, a cold, desolate diamond-mining town on the edge of the Arctic Circle, where her quest for the truth only throws up more questions, more secrets, and more dead bodies.

Taking risks and working alone, Tempe refuses to give up until she has discovered why the babies died. But in such a hostile environment, can she avoid being the next victim?

"Reichs' real-life expertise gives her novels an authenticity that most other crime novelists would kill for" *Daily Express*

ALSO AVAILABLE IN ARROW

Flash and Bones

Kathy Reichs

FLASH! Illuminated by lightning, a lifeless human hand reaches from a barrel of asphalt beside the Charlotte racetrack.

Forensic anthropologist Dr Tempe Brennan must find answers before thousands arrive for the year's big race. But before she can carry out a proper examination, the FBI mysteriously confiscate and destroy the body.

It's a dead end.

Until a young engineer alerts Tempe to the disappearance of a couple twelve years earlier - and a deadly conspiracy unravels.

ALSO AVAILABLE IN ARROW

Spider Bones

Kathy Reichs

Dr Temperance Brennan spends her working life amongst the decomposed, the mutilated, and the skeletal. So the two-days-dead body she is called to examine holds little to surprise her. Until she discovers that the man is John Lowery, an ex-soldier who was apparently killed in Vietnam in 1968. So who is buried in Lowery's grave?

The case takes Tempe to an organisation dedicated to bringing home the bodies of unidentified soldiers where she must examine the remains of anyone who may have had a connection to the drowned man. It's a harrowing task, but it pays off when she finds Lowery's dog tags amongst the bones of a long-dead soldier.

As Tempe unravels the tangled threads of the soldiers' lives and deaths, she realises there are some who would rather the past stayed buried. And when she proves difficult to frighten, they turn their attention to the one person she would give her life to protect . . .

ALSO AVAILABLE IN ARROW

206 Bones

Kathy Reichs

"You have an enemy, Dr Brennan. It is in your interest to learn who placed the call . . ."

A routine case turns sinister when Dr Temperance Brennan is accused of mishandling the autopsy of a missing heiress. Someone has made an incriminating accusation that she missed or concealed crucial evidence. Before Tempe can get to the one man with information, he turns up dead.

The heiress isn't the only elderly female to have appeared on Tempe's gurney recently. Back in Montreal, three more women have died, their bodies brutally discarded. Tempe is convinced there's a link between their deaths and that of the heiress. But what – or who – connects them?

Tempe struggles with the clues, but nothing adds up. Has she made grave errors or is some unknown foe sabotaging her? It soon becomes frighteningly clear. It's not simply Tempe's career at risk. Her life is at stake too.

arrow books